Martin
WALKER

The Coldest Case

The Dordogne Mysteries

QUERCUS

First published in Great Britain in 2021 by Quercus
This paperback edition published in 2022 by

QUERCUS

Quercus Editions Ltd
Carmelite House
50 Victoria Embankment
London EC4Y 0DZ

An Hachette UK company

A CIP catalogue record for this book is available
from the British Library

PB ISBN 978 1 78747 776 6
EB ISBN 978 1 78747 778 0

10 9 8 7 6 5 4 3 2 1

Typeset by CC Book Production
Printed and bound in Great Britain by Clays Ltd, Elcograf S.p.A.

MIX
Paper from
responsible sources
FSC® C104740

Papers used by Quercus are from well-managed forests and other responsible sources.

'Walker weaves an exciting story against
a backdrop of bucolic bliss'
Daily Mail

'Thoroughly agreeable from start to finish'
Irish Independent

'This book is pure escapism . . . it's a delight to dip
into his sun-baked world'
Observer

'It's *Midsomer Murders* meets *MasterChef* flavoured
with espionage, dog breeding and veganism'
Sun

'A much-loved fiction character whose community
activities and social life, and passion for cooking,
play an integral role in the series' popularity'
Choice

'Walker's richly descriptive and captivating story
enables readers to share quality time with Bruno's
warm and sociable milieu'
Lancashire Post

Martin Walker is a prize-winning journalist and historian who has worked for the *Guardian*, the *New York Times*, the *Washington Post* and the *New Yorker*. He is the author of several acclaimed works of non-fiction, including *The Cold War: A History*, and *The President They Deserve: The Rise, Falls and Comebacks of Bill Clinton*. He is best known, though, for his internationally bestselling Dordogne Mysteries. Martin and his wife, Julia Watson, have two grown daughters. They spend their time between the Dordogne and Washington, DC.

Also by Martin Walker

THE DORDOGNE MYSTERIES

Death in the Dordogne
(previously published as *Bruno, Chief of Police*)

The Dark Vineyard

Black Diamond

The Crowded Grave

The Devil's Cave

The Resistance Man

Death Undercover
(previously published as *Children of War*)

The Dying Season

Fatal Pursuit

The Templars' Last Secret

A Taste for Vengeance

The Body in the Castle Well

A Shooting at Chateau Rock

To the volunteer firefighters, the pompiers of the Périgord

1

The three skulls transfixed him. The first, the original that had been unearthed after seventy thousand years, was not quite complete. Beside it stood a reconstruction, an exact copy but artificially filled in with the missing parts of the jaw and cranium. Behind them, glowing eerily in the museum's carefully crafted lighting, was an artist's attempt at reconstructing the face that had once covered the skull. Maybe it was a trick of the light that made it seem larger than the others. Reluctantly, Bruno Courrèges shifted his gaze back to the original, whose caption said it was the closest to a perfect Neanderthal skull ever found. It came from the rock shelter of La Ferrassie, a place he passed each day as he drove from his home to his office at the Mairie of St Denis, where for the past decade or more he had carried out his duties as the local chief of police in the Périgord region of France.

The region boasted an extraordinary wealth of prehistoric remains, from painted caves to carvings from the tusks of mammoths, and Bruno had become an enthusiast who had now visited all the known caves and was a regular visitor to the museum of prehistory in Les Eyzies, close to his home and where he now stood. The reconstructed face set him thinking.

It made him recall the curious obsession of his friend Jean-Jacques, known to the region's police as J-J, with another and more recent skull. Bruno knew this skull well since its enlarged photograph had for three decades accompanied J-J's rise to become the chief of detectives for the department of the Dordogne. For as long as Bruno had known him, and for years before that, the photograph had gone with J-J to every office he had occupied. These days, it was fixed to the back of J-J's door, where he could see the skull from his place at the imposing desk that was standard issue for such a senior official. His visitors couldn't miss it as they left his room. His fellow cops often speculated why J-J submitted himself willingly to this constant reminder of his first big case, the one he had failed to solve as a young detective some three decades earlier.

J-J claimed not to remember why he had called the skull 'Oscar' but every policeman in south-western France knew the story. A truffle hunter out with his dog in the woods near St Denis had found a tree downed by a storm. The fallen trunk had blocked a small stream tumbling down the slope and forced it into a new channel. The rushing water had then eroded a bank and exposed something that had attracted the hunter's dog: a human foot, partly decomposed and partly nibbled by woodland creatures. The hunter had called Joe, Bruno's predecessor as the municipal policeman in St Denis. Joe had visited the site and in turn had informed the Police Nationale in Périgueux and they had sent J-J, their newest young detective, to investigate.

Determined to make his name with this unexpected case, J-J had rushed to the scene, established a security cordon, demanded spades and a local photographer from the Mairie and help from the local gendarmes. With their support he had carefully unearthed the remains of a healthy young male with long blond hair, perfect teeth and dressed in a T-shirt which still bore the faded logo of some forgotten rock band. The body's own bacteria and the insect life and soil microbes had done their work in the year or so since the death, as estimated by the medical examiner. Too little flesh remained for any cause of death to be evident. The fact that the corpse had been deliberately hidden persuaded J-J that the man had been murdered.

To the horror of the watching gendarmes, J-J had donned medical gloves and carefully removed the remaining earth that still covered much of the body. He'd then commandeered a steel sheet about two metres long and a metre wide, along with a forklift truck from a nearby builders' depot and had them both manhandled up through the woods. He had then slid the steel sheet into the ground a few centimetres beneath the deliquescent remains and inserted the prongs of the forklift to raise and remove the body. Using four staves of wood beneath this steel plate, he'd ordered eight gendarmes to carry it like some heavy military stretcher, down to the flat land adjoining the campsite below. It was then taken by truck to the morgue in Périgueux for a forensic autopsy.

Meanwhile, J-J had spent an hour foraging for any sign of a bullet in the soil beneath where the body had been discovered. Nothing useful had been found, even when the gendarmes with metal detectors and volunteers from the local hunting club had made a careful fingertip search of the vicinity. They had found the sites of two small fires, remnants of charred wood ringed with stones, and some disturbed soil which, on examination, turned out to be a latrine. The burial site was but a short walk through the woods from a popular commercial campsite. It seemed to have been a regular place for what the French called *le camping sauvage*, where people squatted on a temporary and unofficial campsite in the woods without paying the fees required for a formal campground.

In those days before DNA had transformed the forensic profession, J-J had challenged himself to discover how the man had been killed. In the morgue, when the remaining flesh and organs had been painstakingly removed in the hope of finding a bullet or perhaps some evidence of poisoning, J-J had peered at every rib in search of a scratch that could have been made by a knife. Finally, in desperation, he persuaded the investigating magistrate assigned to the case to let him try one last, desperate measure. He'd used his own money to buy a large metal pot, removed the body's head and went to the kitchens in police headquarters to demand the use of a mobile cooking stove. He moved it into the courtyard and proceeded to boil the head until all the flesh had fallen away.

This took some time and the aroma at first intrigued and then horrified the other policemen in the building, along with those members of the public with businesses close by and the two local news reporters who had a small office near the entrance. The stench itself was unforgettable but at least its reach was confined at first to a limited area around the police building. Soon, however, local shopkeepers began to complain and then the Mayor and the Prefect arrived to demand an explanation, each of them wearing masks that had been soaked in some mentholated liquid. By the time they arrived, the local radio reporter had already broadcast the news that the local police were cooking a corpse.

When the policemen began to grumble, J-J had been summoned to the Commissioner's office, where he showed his letter of authorization to boil the skull. It had been signed by the magistrate who had by then departed on a long-planned weekend trip to visit his parents in Brittany and in those days before mobile phones, there was no immediate way to reach him. The Commissioner then announced that he had some urgent business at the Bergerac police station, almost an hour away, that required his personal attention. The Mayor and Prefect found themselves met by the Deputy Commissioner, who had been told of the magistrate's authorization and pleaded to his visitors that there was nothing he could do. His youngest detective was leaving no stone unturned in his pursuit of a murder case.

'You might at least have insisted that this unpleasant procedure take place in some remote location rather than in the centre of the city,' the Mayor had said, the force of his protest somewhat diminished by his mask, which made the Deputy Commissioner ask for every statement to be repeated. Finally, he led the two distinguished visitors, one representing the city of Périgueux and the other the Republic of France, to the small courtyard where they found J-J, oblivious to the stench, stirring the pot amidst clouds of pungent steam.

The Mayor strode forward and turned off the bottle of gas beneath the mobile stove. At the same moment, J-J had hauled the now fleshless skull from the pot with a pair of heavy tongs and waved it at his visitors in a manner that made them back away nervously. He then announced, his face beaming with pride, 'It worked. See for yourselves, *messieurs*. He was bludgeoned to death! We couldn't see that from the decomposed flesh.'

The Mayor, Prefect and Deputy Commissioner each looked at the tell-tale cracks between the eye and ear sockets of the gleaming white skull as the two local news reporters entered the courtyard, notebooks at the ready.

'We are looking for a left-handed killer, gentlemen,' J-J went on, who had become a policeman after a boyhood devotion to the detective skills of Sherlock Holmes. 'You will see the wound is on the right side of the victim's head, and from the shape of the cracks it was evidently delviered from in front.'

'Could this not have been established more simply, perhaps by an X-ray of the skull?' asked the Prefect.

'Indeed, sir,' replied the Deputy Commissioner. 'But you will doubtless recall that you refused to endorse our proposed budget for modernizing our police laboratory and installing an X-ray facility.'

J-J, intent only on the skull and the clues it offered, did not notice the reporters scribbling in their notebooks. The Mayor, who had an eye for such things, and who vaguely recalled having told the local hospital to refuse police requests to use their X-ray machine on the grounds that the public health came first, was already regretting his decision to demand an explanation from the police. Regretting even more his suggestion that the Prefect should accompany him, he said, 'Well, the cooking is now over, the smell will soon disperse and the vital clue has been found. It only remains to congratulate the police on their ingenuity in difficult circumstances and perhaps we might adjourn, my dear Deputy Commissioner, to the open air, and leave this enterprising young detective to his duties.'

It was the event that made J-J's reputation with the press, the public and above all with his colleagues in the police. Even the Commissioner forgave him when the Prefect reconsidered his earlier verdict and approved the budget for a state-of-the-art facility, including an X-ray machine, for the new police scientific laboratory. But this was little compensation for J-J, who then embarked on a long and fruitless attempt to identify his corpse, even though the Mayor had persuaded the local hospital to let him use the X-ray machine to document an unusual double break in the body's left leg, made some years before death. J-J had been confident that medical records would eventually enable him to confirm the name of the most celebrated *corpus delicti* in the history of the Périgord police.

There had been no local report of a missing young male with fair hair and no such missing person reported in France in the twelve months that the medical examiner estimated had been the maximum time since death. J-J went through Interpol to ask other European countries whether they had any candidates on their lists of missing persons, and even tried the United States, Canada, Australia and New Zealand, all without success. As the Berlin Wall came down and relationships improved with the police of Russia and Eastern Europe, J-J widened his search. Through French embassies, he made contact with the medical associations and the health ministries across Europe, seeking a doctor who might recall treating the unusual leg break. He turned his attention to the T-shirt on the body and tracked down the Austrian rock band that had enjoyed a brief success and sold several thousand T-shirts in Germany and Switzerland on the strength of it. Months passed and then years, but J-J's labours, to which he devoted much of his spare time, were all in vain.

He had a body, or at least a skeleton. He had a murder and had identified the murder weapon as a collapsible spade, produced in large numbers by the US army and widely available at army surplus and camping stores around the world. What he did not have was an identity, only the photograph of Oscar's skull that covered the back of his office door as a *memento mori* of the case he'd never solved.

And so Bruno, studying the artist's reconstruction of a Neanderthal face from the original skull, had the first glimmerings of an idea. The face did not look primitive. It was almost entirely human but with elements of our primate ancestors, with the same heavy jaw and prominent bone ridges above the eyes. The reconstruction seemed more real because the artist had also produced not simply a face, but the whole body from the ancient skeleton of La Ferrassie. The man was sitting, a thick and brawny arm outstretched as he made some point to a small child sitting rapt with attention before him. The child's face had also been reconstructed from another Neanderthal skull and the scene was to Bruno's eyes wholly convincing.

He paused at the next display case, startled at the sight of a young woman with a defiant or perhaps proud pose of her head. She was clad in furs with beads around her neck, her eyes looking sidelong at some scene that made her gaze watchful, even suspicious. She had a high forehead, full lips and prominent cheekbones. She had been reconstructed from a partial skeleton found at the Abri Pataud rock shelter in Les Eyzies, just along the main street from this national museum of prehistory. The skeleton of the body, a young woman of roughly eighteen years, had been discovered with the skeleton of a newborn child; her skull had been found four metres away, protected by some stones that appeared to have been deliberately placed. She was a Cro-Magnon, or early modern human, who had lived some twenty thousand years ago, nearly twenty thousand years after her people had replaced the Neanderthals.

Bruno shook his head in awe rather than in disbelief at the sight of this woman whose face had moved him. There was a lively intelligence in her features and a self-reliance in her stance that made him realize with a start of surprise that this was a woman who attracted him. He could imagine seeing her in a crowd on the street outside or gazing out from the window of a passing train or even sitting at another table in some outdoor café. He let the fantasy run on, imagining sharing glances with her across the crowded café, perhaps arranging to meet. This was a woman that stirred thoughts of might-have-beens; a woman with whom he could even imagine, across the millennia, falling in love.

The next face he recognized, but not her adornment. The reconstructed head wore a skull cap of dozens of tiny shells, carefully pierced and then sewn together. He had seen it before at the famous rock shelter of Cap Blanc, just a few kilometres up the road towards Sarlat, where prehistoric people had crafted a massive bas-relief of horses, deer and bison. They were so lifelike that they might almost be emerging from the rock into which they had been carved.

In 1911, archaeologists had found an almost complete human skeleton buried beneath the hooves of the central horse of the sculpture, the bones protected by rocks at the feet and more rocks balanced above the head. It was presumed at first to be male, but then the local landowner sold it to the Field Museum in Chicago for the equivalent in francs of one thousand dollars in 1926. Henry Field, who collected the skeleton in New York and wrapped it in cotton wool to be taken back to Chicago, noted at once that the pelvic girdle was female and arranged such a blaze of publicity that on the first day it was shown to the public, more than twenty thousand people crowded into the museum to see the first prehistoric skeleton ever displayed in the United States.

Five years later, by which time it had been seen by more than a million visitors, the skull was withdrawn from exhibition to be fully reconstructed. A detailed examination found it to be a young woman of around twenty years, 5ft 1in tall, and that she had lived between thirteen and fifteen thousand years earlier. She had been buried with an ivory point, perhaps a harpoon or spear head, about three inches long, on or perhaps inside her abdomen. This led to speculation that this weapon might have been the cause of her death, a suggestion of long-ago murder that was astutely promoted by Henry Field to bring in more visitors to his museum. He also suggested that the location of her burial suggested that she might have been one of the sculptors of the unique equine frieze.

The reconstruction of this woman's face had delighted Bruno since he had first seen it at Cap Blanc, not only because she was lovely in a strikingly modern way with huge eyes, a graceful neck and high cheekbones, but because of the skull cap of shells that she wore. It made her look like some café society beauty of the 1920s. Bruno could almost imagine her dancing the Charleston.

'What do you think of the exhibition, Bruno? You've been studying it long enough.' The speaker was Clothilde Daumier, a short, red-haired powerhouse of a woman who was one of the museum's curators and a leading expert on the prehistory of the region. She and her German archaeologist husband, Horst Morgenstern, were good friends and Bruno had been one of the witnesses at their recent wedding. As she spoke, she came forward and they embraced.

'It's wonderful,' Bruno replied. 'Thank you for inviting me to this preview. I'm overwhelmed with the skill of these reconstructions.'

'In that case, you can tell the artist yourself,' Clothilde said, steering him towards an attractive, grey-haired woman who moved gracefully as she advanced to shake Bruno's hand. 'Elisabeth Daynès, meet Bruno Courrèges, our chief of police and a good friend who has a great interest in archaeology. He even found a modern corpse in one of our ancient graves.'

'Clothilde's archaeologists found it,' Bruno said, smiling. 'I just helped find out who it was. But please, let me tell you how moved I am by your work, bringing these people back to life in this way. You are a great artist, *madame*.'

'You're very kind, Monsieur Bruno,' Elisabeth replied. Her voice was soft and well-modulated, with just a hint of an accent of the Midi. 'I always enjoy meeting Clothilde's friends. How did you realize the body you found was not some prehistoric skeleton?'

'Because he was wearing a Swatch. And Clothilde informed me that they had only been made since 1983. Tell me, have you ever worked with the police in trying to reconstruct the faces of unidentified skeletons?'

'A little, but only informally. It's a considerable investment in time and effort to do such a reconstruction and since so much of our work is seen by the courts as inspired guesswork, the police are understandably reluctant to finance such projects.'

'I find it hard to understand why the courts are so reluctant when I see your work here, *madame*,' Bruno said.

'Please, call me Elisabeth,' she said, as Clothilde steered them towards a reception area where they were handed glasses of wine and Clothilde excused herself to welcome some other guests to the preview. 'I understand the courts' point of view. If you study the verbal descriptions that people give of strangers, they usually describe the hair, its style and colour, the colour of the eyes, and whether the face is fleshy or lean. But those are three elements that we cannot discern from the skull itself. What we can do is use the contours of the individual skull, which vary much more than you might think, to reconstruct each of the forty-three muscles in the human face. So in terms of form and structure, I think we can go a long way to reconstruct the features. But the hair, the eyes, the depth of flesh – that's almost impossible.'

'So the muscular structure of a face varies with the small differences in the shape of each individual skull?'

'Exactly,' she said, nodding with enthusiasm. 'We use a laser measurement system to map the precise shape of each skull down to fractions of a millimetre and put that into a computer which creates a three-dimensional model. Then we use a high-precision 3D printer to give us the head. After that we use the laser again to compare this printed skull with a cast we make of the original skull to check that they are absolutely identical. Developing and perfecting that system took a year of work but now it's almost automatic.'

'Why bother with the computer-printed version when you have a cast of the original skull?'

'Because we can do so much of the work on recreating the musculature on the computer where it's easy to make adjustments,' she replied. 'And with the computer, we can share images of our progress with colleagues all over the world. When we reconstructed the face of Tutankhamun, we could stay in constant touch with the *National Geographic* people in Washington and the Cairo museum.'

'And if you knew the hair colour and that the body was that of a young man in his twenties, athletic and probably without much body fat, could you reconstruct something fairly accurate?'

'Absolutely, Monsieur Bruno. Should I assume that you have a particular skeleton in mind and that you're hoping to enlist my help? I'm afraid my schedule is already impossibly full – perhaps Clothilde has told you of our project to recreate the entire family of hominids from the earliest times: Australopithecus, Homos habilis, ergaster, floresiensis and of course, Neanderthals and Homo sapiens. That takes all my time.'

'I understand. But perhaps you have some young associate or student with such skills?'

'Most of what I learned in this area came from Jean-Noel

Vignal, whom I met when he was at the Forensic Institute in Paris. Perhaps you might consult him. But tell me about this body.'

Briefly, Bruno recounted the story of J-J and Oscar, and she suddenly interrupted him.

'But those dates, you say 1988 or 1989, that is when I was here in the Périgord,' she said excitedly. 'I was working at Le Thot, the park that's attached to the Lascaux cave. They asked me to reconstruct a mammoth and a group of human hunters. That was part of my earliest work in this field. I'd been working in the theatre on costumes and then on masks for the national theatre in Lille and I really became interested in ancient humans when I was making models for the prehistory museum at Tautavel in the Pyrenees. So I have a personal connection to this region at the time this young man died. Give me your card and I'll talk to some colleagues and see what might be done. Now I'd better circulate but thank you for your interest and your kind words.'

They exchanged business cards and she scribbled a personal mobile phone number onto the one she gave him.

'*Au revoir*, Elisabeth, and thank you for your exhibition and also for your help.'

2

Bruno put his idea to the back of his mind until he heard from Elisabeth that she had a possible candidate, a young student at a design school in Paris who was looking for a project she could submit to complete her diploma. Her name was Virginie. Her mother was Spanish and her father French and she had been raised in Madrid and Toulon. She had spent the previous summer vacation on an internship in Elisabeth's studio.

'Virginie is good. She knows my techniques and her work is meticulous,' Elisabeth said. 'I'll keep an eye on her progress with you and if this works out I'll probably offer her a job in my studio when she graduates. She can continue to live on her student grant but she may need help with rent unless you can find her a place in a student hostel. And she'll need a workshop. By the way, don't be alarmed by the tattoos and the piercings! She's good.'

'Ha! It takes more than a few piercings to shock St Denis. She sounds excellent, Elisabeth, thank you. I'll discuss this with J-J and get back to you.'

As soon as he'd cut the call, Bruno contacted J-J to invite him to dinner, but warned him they'd be visiting the Les Eyzies museum first.

'By the way,' he asked J-J, 'do you still have access to Oscar's skull?'

'It occupies pride of place in our evidence room here. Why?'

'I'll tell you later. And do you still have that budget for cold cases?'

'Certainly. It's part of the training budget. We assign new candidates to unsolved cases to see how they shape up. What are you up to, Bruno?'

'I'll let you know over dinner, J-J. But I think you'll like the idea.'

Bruno prepared a simple meal before he left to meet J-J at the museum. They'd begin with some smoked salmon he'd been curing for the past three days. The marinade was made of peppercorns, dill, salt, pepper, crushed juniper berries and lemon zest, with a shot glass of *eau de vie* drizzled over the mixture before it went into the fridge. The sauce to accompany the gravlax was made of Dijon mustard, cider vinegar, honey and sunflower oil. He had cooked a casserole of venison in advance and had made an apple pie that he would serve cold with ice cream.

Knowing that Fabiola, the local doctor, was on duty at the medical centre that evening, he invited her partner Gilles, a journalist, suspecting he would be intrigued by the prospect of reopening an investigation into Oscar's death. He also invited the Mayor of St Denis, whose political skills might come in useful if J-J met some official resistance to reviving his old obsession with Oscar. They met at the museum shortly before it closed, each relieved to be in an air-conditioned space and escape from the brutal July heatwave that had gripped south-west France for the past week. Clothilde showed them around Elisabeth Daynès's exhibition while Bruno explained what he'd learned from his talk with her.

'Normally, a project like this would cost a fortune, but Elisabeth has a young student who's keen to reconstruct Oscar's face from his skull as part of her diploma,' Bruno explained. 'I'm assured she's very good.'

'You're proposing that we could get something close enough to Oscar's real face that we could use it to identify him?' J-J asked. 'But how do we go about making sure enough people see it?'

'Publicity,' said Gilles. 'This is a great story and it's very visual, just made for TV and social media. You have the skull and the reconstructed face and a long-ago murder. I'm sure my old editor at *Paris Match* would want a two-page spread on that, and so would *Sud-Ouest* and TV news magazines. It's just the kind of quirky, off-beat story they love to wrap up a news bulletin.' Gilles leaned back, made a mock-solemn face and adopted the half sonorous, half-folksy diction of a newsreader. 'And now, from Périgord, how the archaeologists are helping police investigate a thirty-year-old murder that has never been solved.'

'I see what you're getting at, but I'm not sure I can persuade the powers that be to give me a budget for this,' J-J objected, but his eyes were bright as he kept looking at the reconstructed faces of the women in the display case. 'Still, I'd certainly like to give it a try. Nobody could deny that these faces are amazingly lifelike.'

'You don't need a budget,' said the Mayor. 'It seems to me that the artist will be working for free, or for not much more than pocket money. I'll have a word with the Mayor of Périgueux and I'm sure we can get her a place in a student hostel. You'll have plenty of room for her to work in that police science lab of yours, J-J. And since the original murder took place in St Denis, I imagine we can find some modest funds in our tourism promotion budget if required, so long as we can eventually put the reconstruction of the face on display for the tourists. Gilles is right, this is something that will catch the public imagination.'

They took a last look around the exhibition, pausing once more before the exhibition case that depicted the life-sized reconstruction of the Neanderthal man with the child and beside it another display of a young Cro-Magnon man, spear in hand and poised to throw it.

'It's a funny thing about these men with their straggling beards,' said J-J. 'It makes them look less modern somehow than the women.'

'Yes, I see what you mean, but imagine trying to shave with a piece of flint,' Bruno replied.

'You're both missing something,' said Gilles, a note of excitement in his voice. 'Look at the Neanderthal man with that animal fur draped loosely around him. And then look at the Cro-Magnon guy with his spear from tens of thousands of years later. His furs have been deliberately fashioned into trousers and a jacket. I'd never thought of it before but the Cro-Magnons must have invented the needle, which gave them the technology of sewing. It meant they could wear garments that were much better suited to surviving cold spells and ice ages. Maybe that's how they flourished while the Neanderthals died out.'

Later, in Bruno's living room over their aperitifs, protected from the heat outside by the thick stone walls, the Mayor turned to J-J and asked if he'd ever thought of using the DNA from Oscar's skull to help identify him.

J-J shook his head. 'It was all too new at the time, very expensive and not too reliable.

'It wasn't until 1985 that a British scientist called Alec Jeffreys first established that everyone's DNA is unique, J-J explained. The police were still studying the science behind it but a defence lawyer was quick to take advantage and the following year the lawyer used DNA in a British court in a case of two girls raped and murdered to show that his client was innocent, even though he'd already been convicted. DNA was then able to establish the real culprit. That made news and the following year it was first used in another rape case in Florida. France took some time to start using the technology, proposing to keep a national DNA database as late as 1996. It began with sex offenders but its use was not extended to those convicted of serious crimes until after the 9/11 terrorist attacks in the United States.

'Even today, we only have some five million people in our national database,' J-J told them. 'The British and the Americans each have over twenty million. But it was French police scientists who showed its limitations. There was a case of a woman's DNA connected to several murders in Austria, Germany and France, and French detectives established that the DNA came from a woman working in the factory that produced the cotton swabs used to collect the DNA from swabbing inside the mouths of suspects. The killer was finally caught – and turned out to be a man. But there's no doubt that DNA has revolutionized police work.'

That seemed a natural point to pause and Bruno invited them to the table, brought out the smoked salmon and asked how Oscar's DNA might be useful today.

'I've been thinking about that,' said J-J. 'I'll start by running it against the national database which is a long shot but it's getting better. Then I'll ask for a Europe-wide search through Interpol. I can work on that tomorrow. Our own lab can take a sample of the skull and get the DNA.'

'Isn't Jacqueline supposed to be back soon?' Gilles asked the Mayor, referring to the half-French, half-American historian who spent one term per year teaching at the Sorbonne, another at Columbia in New York and the rest of her year in St Denis. She now rented out her renovated farmhouse nearby and lived with the Mayor, an arrangement so mutually agreeable that it seemed to have subtracted several years from each of them.

'She'll be back on Friday in time for the weekend,' the Mayor said. 'She stayed on for some conference in Washington at the Cold War research centre that relates to her next book, something about a horde of Stasi documents from the former East Germany. She emailed me to say that Jack Crimson is also attending the conference. Apparently he's on some British committee that determines which official documents are to be declassified.'

'So Jack will be back here as well?' Bruno asked. He was fond of the former British diplomat and intelligence official whose daughter Miranda helped Bruno's former lover and still close friend, Pamela, run a nearby horse-riding school. They had recently started offering cooking courses to fill Pamela's gîtes in the winter months when tourists were scarce. Bruno and other friends had been roped in to help demonstrate the local cuisine.

'No, Jacqueline told me that Jack is going back to London for a few days for some committee meeting, probably relating to the conference in Washington,' the Mayor said. 'He'll be back later next week.'

The conversation drifted off to sport and then through politics over the venison until interrupted by Bruno's phone. He didn't recognize the number of the caller but thought he'd better answer and was surprised to hear the voice of his cousin Alain, the one who had gone into the air force and the relative to whom he was closest.

'Bad news, Bruno,' he began. 'It's about Mum. She's had a stroke and been taken to hospital in Bergerac, the one on Avenue Calmette. It happened sometime last night but I just heard about it from my big sister. I'll get some compassionate leave and head there tomorrow. I'm told she can recognize people but she can't talk.'

'Sorry to hear it,' said Bruno. 'What time do you expect to be there?'

'I'll have to sort out the paperwork at the base for my leave tomorrow morning and then I'll drive up. Should be there at about four and I'll stay with Annette for a day or two. Should I expect to see you?'

'I'll get there as soon as I can after four,' Bruno said. 'Maybe we can have a drink together afterwards and catch up. It's been too long.'

'Right, see you then.'

The call left Bruno feeling pensive about his aunt and his childhood in the overcrowded tenement in a grim public housing project where all six children shared a bedroom, even the eldest, Annette. Bruno only ever saw her and the other siblings when he paid a duty call to his aunt on her birthday and at Christmas, each time taking her a bottle of his home-made *vin de noix*. Annette and the eldest brother, Bernard, lived in Bergerac, in public housing. The other three siblings had all moved away and Bruno had lost touch, except for Alain. Annette worked in the kitchen of the Bergerac retirement home in which her mother had been living and Bernard had been unemployed for years, claiming disability allowance for a bad back which did not seem to stop him taking part-time jobs as a painter and decorator, working off the books and only for cash.

Alain was a senior warrant officer at the air defence control training centre at the Mont-de-Marsan airbase south of Bordeaux, better known as the home of two fighter squadrons equipped with Rafale interceptors, France's most advanced warplane. The youngest of five children, Alain was just a year or so older than Bruno and they had grown up together when Bruno, aged six, had been taken in by his aunt from the church orphanage. It had not been a happy home and Bruno had long suspected that the main reason for his welcome was the more generous welfare payment his aunt received as a *famille nombreuse* at a time when the French state was trying to increase the population. The food, he recalled, had been better at the orphanage.

'You look like you've had some grim news,' the Mayor said as Bruno returned to the table with the apple pie and ice cream. His friends nodded sympathetically when he explained the news of his aunt's stroke.

'I don't recall any of your family coming to St Denis to visit,' the Mayor went on, as Bruno served them.

'My aunt came for a weekend in the early days and it was plain she didn't like it, being woken by the cockerel, the silence for much of the time and the lack of town noises,' Bruno said, half-smiling and feeling a mixture of affection and regret. 'She was never a reader and she couldn't get over the fact that I had no TV,' he went on. 'She thought the Dordogne valley was pretty and liked the castles but refused to visit any caves, thought they'd give her claustrophobia.'

'What about your cousins?'

'We've mostly lost touch. The youngest, Alain, is roughly my age, and we always got on well. He came for a weekend when I was playing in one of those old-timers' rugby games against the youth team and he liked it a lot. He's thinking of settling near here when he gets out of the air force in a couple of years.'

'There's a programme I worked for when I was in the Senate, to let long-service veterans spend their last year training to be teachers,' the Mayor said. 'That might suit him. And we're always short of teachers in rural areas, particularly men.'

'I'll mention it when I see him at the hospital,' said Bruno. 'But I know he's been thinking of setting himself up in business. He learned to be a radar tech and electrician and now teaches air defence systems so he's good with computers.'

'Is he married?' asked Gilles.

'Not yet. Like me, he can't find the right woman.'

'You find them all right, Bruno,' said Gilles, grinning. 'You just don't seem to be able to get them to the altar. It must run in the family.'

3

Bruno was anticipating a depressing visit when he arrived at the hospital the next day. His ancient Land Rover had no air con so he had driven the forty minutes from St Denis with all the windows open, the radio giving news of forest fires in Provence. The car park seemed to radiate heat from the relentless sun and he was sweating freely by the time he reached the hospital doors.

Although looking forward to seeing Alain again, he felt oppressed by memories of his childhood. He had been the charity kid, expected to be grateful for his status as the least regarded relation in his aunt's overcrowded home. There had been some happy moments. In childhood, there were impromptu games of soccer in the street, a birthday party with a special cake, and his growing friendship with Alain. They served to remind him of the wretched times, the way Bernard the bully, seven years older, would cuff him with casual regularity and sneer at Bruno's dead mother as a whore.

In the hospital, he found his aunt in a small ward of eight people, all elderly. The place smelled of disinfectant and cleaning fluids with an underlying hint of urine. She was the only one with a visitor, Alain. Bruno kissed his aunt on both cheeks, gave her the flowers he'd brought and received a grunt of acknowledgment in return. He embraced Alain, found a spare chair, sat down on the other side of the bed and announced that he was pleased to see his aunt looking better than he'd expected. She grunted again, waving the fingers of one hand in frustration at being unable to speak. Her face seemed to have been divided into two halves, one normal and the other melting like so much candle wax. The left side of her mouth and her left eye were drooping and the skin seemed to sag with them.

Bruno wondered how sad he truly felt. He knew he had little real affection for his aunt, a woman he usually remembered as tired or angry, always ready to swat one of her brood of kids with a soup ladle or hairbrush or whatever came to hand. He could not recall ever being hugged by her but he knew he was supposed to feel grateful that she'd taken him in from the orphanage.

With an effort, Bruno thrust away these thoughts and he and Alain exchanged small talk, trying at first to include her with news of the family, her care in the hospital and the kindness of the nurses. Being unable to join in seemed to upset her so they sat quietly, each of them holding a hand. Bruno had her left hand and it was cold and seemed almost lifeless. Soon she drifted off to sleep and snored quietly.

'It's good to see you, Bruno, despite this sad occasion. It's been far too long,' Alain said. 'And thanks for coming.'

'Good to see you, too,' Bruno replied. 'You're not looking bad for a man of your advanced years.'

'Just eighteen months older and wiser than you, Bruno.'

Bruno laughed, genuinely pleased to see his cousin. Even

though Alain liked soccer while Bruno was a devoted rugby man, Bruno still knew they had a lot in common. They looked roughly the same age. Each of them had kept his hair and looked trim and fit. Alain's hair was fair while Bruno's was dark and Bruno was four or five centimetres taller. Alain had a heavier, almost stocky build but Bruno thought there was a family resemblance in their features.

'Are you still getting out into civilian life in, what is it – two or three years?' Bruno asked.

'Less than two years to go. That's still the plan, even though it'll mean I have to start buying my own clothes,' Alain said. 'But it looks like it'll be a very different life because I might not be leaving alone.'

'You've met someone?' Bruno asked eagerly.

'A tech sergeant at the base, her name's Rosalie Lamartine,' Alain said, his eyes lighting up as he spoke of her. 'She'll have done twenty years when my twenty-five are up so she'll get a decent pension. It's a bit difficult with the rules against fraternizing with people of different ranks but we've spent some weekends together and had a wonderful two-week vacation in Senegal just before Christmas. That's when we each knew this was it.'

'I'm really happy for you, Alain. That's great news. I'd better start saving for a wedding present.' Bruno punched his cousin lightly on the arm and they both laughed. 'Are you planning to marry once you're out?'

Alain nodded. 'Maybe before, if Rosalie gets the promotion she expects. Then we'd be the same rank and we could get hitched and qualify for married quarters. She's young enough to have kids, which is something we both want. She's terrific, good-natured and funny, I think you'll like her.'

He took out his mobile phone, punched the keys and proudly showed Bruno his favourite photos of his new love. Tanned a little more pinkish-red than brown and dressed in a light blue bikini that barely covered her ample figure, she was smiling at the camera while holding up a fat slice of watermelon. Bruno noted the dark hair and laughing brown eyes, good cheekbones and generous mouth and nodded in approval. She was an attractive woman.

'You're a lucky man,' said Bruno. 'She's glorious. *Le bon Dieu* has sent you a real gift.'

'Yes, she's wonderful, and the troops like her.' Alain's eyes were glowing as he studied the photo. 'And here she is in uniform. She carries her rank easily.'

He called up another photo of the same woman in standard camouflage dress, her eyes fixed on the assault rifle she was stripping. Her hair was piled up beneath her beret, showing off her neck. In another photo, still in uniform, she was chatting with some soldiers with an expression that was firm but not unfriendly.

'Bring her to St Denis for a weekend so I can get to know her,' Bruno said. 'You can have the honeymoon suite, a whole top floor to yourselves, and I'll keep my basset hound from coming up to roust you out at dawn. I'm afraid I can't answer for the cockerel.'

Alain laughed. 'It can't be worse than a bugle calling reveille. And I'll look forward to seeing your place again and trying your cooking. I've told her a lot about you and we saw a couple of articles in *Sud Ouest* about some cases you solved. Rosalie was impressed but said she was happy she'd got the handsome cousin.'

Bruno grinned. 'Are you still thinking of setting up as an electrician when you're out?'

'Maybe, I'm not sure. Rosalie is interested in a new programme, training to be a teacher during your last year in the military, while staying on full pay.' Bruno recalled the Mayor mentioning this. 'So we could be back to civilian life in just over a year. She's thinking of going to a vocational school which is also something I could do. That would mean two salaries plus two pensions. We've thought of settling somewhere near Bergerac, maybe in the wine country around Pomport.'

'It sounds like you have it all worked out,' said Bruno, feeling just a hint of envy. Still, Alain's good fortune meant there was hope for Bruno yet.

'How about you?' Alain asked. 'Any woman in your life or are you still carrying a torch for the policewoman in Paris? Isabelle, is that the one?'

'I see her from time to time and I still feel like a besotted teenager whenever I'm with her but we both know there's no hope of settling down. She's devoted to her career.'

'Maybe one of the bridesmaids will catch your eye at our wedding. I'll count on you to carry the ring and to make a speech.'

Bruno was trying to think of a suitable reply when a student nurse approached them and said the specialist was free to see them. She directed them to an office down the corridor.

'Are you the next of kin?' asked the middle-aged woman

behind the desk. A stethoscope hung around her neck and there were shadows under her eyes. She looked close to exhaustion but she'd straightened up and smiled when they entered.

'I'm her son and this is my cousin, her nephew,' Alain said. 'But we're more like brothers, really.'

Bruno felt himself almost absurdly pleased to hear Alain's words. He'd never thought of himself in that way. They could have been brothers: he and Alain were similar types, Alain in the air force and Bruno in the army and then the police. They were both men whose chaotic childhoods had steered them towards the structure and routine of military life. He was still glancing sideways at Alain when the doctor began to speak.

'My name is Dumourriez and I'm the specialist who's been treating your mother since she was admitted yesterday morning. I'm afraid I have bad news. We gave your mother a scan this morning and the results are not at all encouraging. She's had two heavy strokes and there are signs of serious brain damage. I'm sorry but don't expect her to be capable of rational speech again. Her heart is in very bad shape and she wasn't in good health to begin with. I don't think we'll be able to do much more than to make your mother comfortable for the time she has left.'

She paused and picked up a file from her desk and opened it to a page that Bruno recognized as a printout of a scan.

'Your mother certainly won't be able to return to the retirement home where she was living, they aren't equipped to care for her. We can't keep her here so she'll have to go either to a geriatric ward or, if her condition continues to decline as I expect, then she should go into a hospice.'

'You think she's dying?' Alain asked, but his tone made it clear it wasn't a question. He seemed resigned to it.

'We're all dying, I'm afraid,' the doctor said with a shrug and a clearing of the throat that might have been a resigned laugh had she not been so visibly tired.

'But I'm sure she grunted when she recognized me and she squeezed my hand when I sat beside her,' said Bruno.

'That was probably an automatic reaction. Please don't get your hopes up. And she's getting on for eighty. That's a pretty good age and it's clear she didn't have an easy life. I wish I had better news for you.'

The doctor rose to signal that the meeting was over. She ran a hand through her greying hair, pushing it back from her face. Bruno wondered how many such conversations she had gone through that day, that week. She handed Alain a sheet of paper.

'Here's a list of the local hospices,' she said. 'I've marked the two that have a vacancy. I recommend the first one if you can get her in. Under the new rules, we've already had to inform the retirement home that your mother won't be going back there so you'll need to clear out her belongings.'

'What new rules?' Bruno asked. He kept his voice neutral but there was something in his tone that made the doctor look at him properly for the first time. Under the red jacket that Bruno donned when he wanted to appear civilian, the doctor took in his uniform shirt and the police pouches at his belt.

'Gendarme?'

'Municipal, from St Denis,' Bruno replied, lifting the left side of the jacket to show the police badge attached to the chest pocket of his shirt.

'The Conseil Générale of this *département* brought in the new rule last year,' the doctor explained. 'Here in the Dordogne we have one of the oldest populations in France; one in seven is aged seventy-five or older. That means an unusual degree of pressure on retirement homes, geriatric wards, hospices – and on people like me. For you, *monsieur*, it means significantly less crime, since most crimes are committed by younger people.'

'Not for white-collar crimes, *madame*,' Bruno replied. 'But I think we understand the extraordinary pressures you're under. Thank you for what you did for my aunt,' he went on. 'When do you expect to move her to a hospice?'

'Tomorrow, two days at most. I'll keep her under observation, see if there's any reason for hope, but I have to say I doubt it.' She glanced at the file open before her on the desk then looked up again to address Alain. 'We have contact details for your sister, Annette, but you might give me your mobile phone and email, just to keep you informed. Please could you jot them down here.' She pushed the file towards him.

4

Bruno's aunt never regained full consciousness and died a few days after she was moved to the hospice. The funeral was a quiet affair, just Bruno, Alain, Bernard and Annette, and half a dozen of her friends and former neighbours. Some more residents from the retirement home turned up for the brief buffet lunch that was held after the cremation. Her other two children had sent wreaths, pleading that they were unable to get time off for the funeral. Nobody except Bruno seemed much surprised by this.

'I haven't had time yet to go through her things,' said Annette when only the family remained. 'Not that there was much after she came to the retirement home. There was a photo album, some clothes I'll give to Action Catholique, a couple of cushions she'd embroidered and a few photos in frames, her own wedding and mine, along with pictures of you and Alain in your uniforms. Not a lot to show for eighty years.'

Bruno smiled ruefully at the thought. He had half-hoped that there might be something of his mother's in his aunt's belongings. On his visits to her, he had pored over the battered photo album, trying in vain to find at least a picture of the young woman who had given birth to him, and left him as a newborn baby at a church door and then disappeared. His aunt had refused to discuss her sister, saying she was long dead, and Bruno had to move on and learn to live without the woman who had abandoned him. Sometimes there was a wistful tone in his aunt's voice when she said this. Bruno thought that in her way, and when she had the occasional moment to herself, she missed her little sister.

The death of this last connection to someone who had known his mother made Bruno pensive as he drove back to St Denis. He'd always resisted the idea of tracking her down. Occasionally he had fleeting thoughts about her and about his unknown father. He'd have liked to know what she looked like, and what strange fate had driven her to abandon him before a week was out. But he knew the search would probably leave him more frustrated than when he started.

As he slowed down to enter Ste Alvère, the vibration of the phone at his waist pulled Bruno's thoughts back to the present. He glanced at the screen, saw it was J-J and pulled over to the side of the road to take the call.

'You are not going to believe this, Bruno, but we have a new lead on Oscar,' J-J began, sounding more than excited. He went on to explain that France had some special forces troops in Mali, helping the local army deal with a group of jihadists there. All active-service military personnel had their DNA on file, like the police, but for security reasons special forces had their DNA hidden along with their identities. One of the soldiers had been killed in action recently and his DNA was put back onto the database.

'Don't tell me,' said Bruno. 'This special forces guy was Oscar's son or his nephew. Or something.'

'Right first time. He was Sergeant-Chef Louis Castignac, born in Bordeaux, and he was Oscar's son. We're checking on the next of kin he listed with the army so we may be able to find his mother and any other family. And more good news. Virginie has arrived from Paris. She has a room in the student hostel and she's already started work in the lab on Oscar's skull.'

Bruno sat staring through his windscreen, hardly aware of the half-ruined medieval tower that dominated the view. *Sergeant-chef* had been his own military rank and, like Louis Castignac, Bruno had served in France's former colonies in West Africa. Perhaps it was the funeral and seeing the family that gave him a sudden sense of kinship with Louis and made him think of the relatives who would be mourning the dead soldier. Now in the midst of their grief they were going to be caught up in a murder inquiry from long ago. J-J would be relentless in trying to solve the case that had frustrated him for thirty years. He recalled someone saying that history was a cruel goddess who drove her chariot over heaps of dead. Justice could be cruel, too, in her own way.

Bruno took a deep breath and drove home to change out of the blue suit and black tie he'd worn for the funeral. He then headed for Hubert de Montignac's wine *cave* in St Denis to buy a bottle for that evening's dinner party. The event had been arranged by Pamela and Miranda to welcome home Jack Crimson and also Jacqueline, who was coming with the Mayor. The usual gang would also be there: Gilles and Fabiola along with Bruno's friends: the Baron and Florence, the science teacher at the local *collège*.

As always on Monday evenings, Florence's twin infants would be coming and sleeping over with their playmates, Miranda's two children. Bruno smiled to himself, thinking with pleasure of the moments when all four kids thundered down the stairs, fresh and sweet-smelling from their bathtime, racing out to the stables to find the dogs and say goodnight to the horses.

Which wine should he take? The local wine store offered so much choice, with giant vats at one end selling wine in bulk for less than two euros a litre from a device that always reminded Bruno of a petrol pump. At the other end were the expensive bottles of Château Petrus, Cheval Blanc, Le Pin, Lafite and Latour that cost hundreds or even thousands of euros each. In between were separate stands for Bordeaux, for Burgundy, for sparkling and dessert wines. There was another stand for the wines of Bergerac and along one wall, an array of what Hubert boasted was the widest selection of single malt Scotch whiskies outside Scotland. There were more shelves for bottles of vintage cognac and Armagnac, a small library of books on wine, displays of glasses and decanters and a selection of local delicacies from foie gras and rillettes to fruit cordials.

Hubert, the owner of this and a small chain of other such wine *caves* in the region, with two more in Paris, was more than just an old friend. He was also one of Bruno's business partners, a fellow director of the town vineyard. Hubert knew that Bruno seldom spent more than ten euros on a bottle but Bruno said this was a special occasion and on Hubert's advice paid twenty euros for a bottle of Château Belingard's cuvée Ortus from 2016.

'You should decant it a good hour before serving,' said Hubert over a friendly glass of white wine from the town vineyard, and Bruno swore that he'd do so.

He drove on to Pamela's riding school where his basset hound, Balzac, recognized the sound of his elderly Land Rover. The young dog stopped his play with Pamela's two sheepdogs, Beau and Bella, to give a long welcoming howl and race to greet his master. Bruno crouched down as his dog galloped towards him, his long ears flapping like a pair of furry wings and his tongue hanging out like some fat pink necktie. Bruno laughed at the sight, spread his arms wide and braced himself to receive thirty kilos of flying basset.

'I've only been gone since this morning,' Bruno protested as Balzac lathered his neck and jaw. Then Beau and Bella came up, rather more sedately, and Bruno set off past the chicken coop he'd helped to build and went to the stables to visit his horse, Hector. Bruno stroked his glossy neck and gave him a carrot he'd plucked from his garden and washed before leaving. All the ponies were gone, which meant Miranda was probably still out with the schoolgirls. Bruno could hear the sound of Pamela's voice from the paddock, encouraging the novices to sit up straight and relax their hands as they trotted their horses around the circular fence.

He waved to Pamela and leaned on the fence to observe the riders, checking his watch. He was a little early. He, Pamela and Fabiola had arranged to give the horses their evening ride in good time before dinner. Pamela called out that Jack was in the office so Bruno strolled across, greeted the Englishman and put the bottle of Ortus on the desk before embracing him.

'Good to see you, Bruno, and you, Balzac,' Crimson said, bending to fondle the dog's long ears. 'I missed you both when I was away. It's such a pleasure to have dogs in my life again, and it's wonderful for the grandchildren. Growing up with dogs and horses is a great thing for the young.'

'We humans have been domesticating dogs around here for thousands of years so we've all sort of grown up together,' said Bruno. 'How was your trip to Washington?'

'The politicians over there are almost as weird as ours in England,' Crimson replied with a bitter laugh. 'I suppose every country has the right to go completely crazy once in a while and it's now the turn of us Anglo-Saxons. It's good to be back in the Périgord and I'll look forward to trying that bottle of Ortus. *Hortus deorum quo ortus es* – if I remember my Latin that's "risen from the gardens of the gods".'

'How was the conference?'

'Interesting but somewhat frustrating. It's thirty years since the Berlin Wall came down but our American friends are still sitting on a treasure trove of Stasi intelligence files that scholars think should be more widely shared. Our friend Jacqueline was particularly outspoken, as you might imagine, but without success.'

'I thought you British and the Americans had always shared intelligence under that famous special relationship you talk about,' Bruno said.

'We share a great deal, along with the Canadians and Australians, but not everything. And this stuff is still quite sensitive.

The Americans say, quite rightly, that they distributed a great deal of this archive – it's called the Rosenholz dossier – to the relevant NATO partners. Along with the Germans, Dutch and Scandinavians we've been allowed to examine anything that the CIA says concerns us.'

'But not the French?' Bruno asked.

'No, not the French, nor the Italians and Spaniards. It's partly fear of leaks but as you may know there's an old feud between the CIA and French intelligence that goes back to De Gaulle's time. Did you ever hear of a man called Philippe de Vosjoli, the only French intelligence man who ever defected to the United States?'

Startled, Bruno raised his eyebrows and shook his head at the same time. This was news to him and the very thought of a French official 'defecting' to a NATO ally was extraordinary.

'It's all ancient history, back in the sixties, long before you were born, and it was all tied up with the Cuban missile crisis. De Vosjoli was the French intelligence liaison man at their Washington embassy with good contacts in Cuba and he got some of the intelligence that alerted the Americans to the missiles the Russians were installing. The Americans trusted him, and when de Vosjoli refused to obey orders to start spying on American nuclear technology, he was recalled to Paris. Fearing arrest or worse, he refused to go and the Americans gave him asylum,' Jack said, reaching into a cupboard and bringing out a bottle of Bowmore and a couple of glasses.

He poured them each two fingers, added a splash of still mineral water and handed one to Bruno, saying, 'Cheers.' The two men chinked glasses and sipped appreciatively.

'This Rosenholz dossier was the master list of all Stasi intelligence agents. Truckloads of files of index cards were burned after the Berlin Wall fell but Erich Mielke, the minister in charge of the Stasi, ordered microfilm copies made and kept them in his office. He sent one set of copies to the KGB liaison centre in Karlshorst and a year later, after the Berlin Wall came down, a defecting Soviet filing clerk sold them to the CIA in Warsaw, allegedly for sixty-five thousand dollars – probably the best deal the Americans made since they bought Manhattan island. There's a lot of disinformation about this. Another theory says some very senior Stasi officials bought themselves immunity with the files.'

'And these were the lists of all the foreign spies the Stasi had recruited? All over the world?'

'That's right, but even more than that. Some two hundred and eighty thousand files in all, mostly East Germans. Something like fifty thousand West Germans were in the files but only about a thousand of them were serious agents. We investigated just over a hundred British citizens who were named in the files and nobody was ever prosecuted. Most of them were peace and anti-nuclear campaigners, well-meaning idealists whom the Stasi thought might be useful. Some of the stuff was clearly invented or exaggerated, probably so that the real Stasi agents could inflate their claims for expenses. The Stasi's selection control was pitiful, always after quantity rather than quality. But some of the people recruited in Germany and Scandinavia and at NATO were very important indeed.'

'And France?' Bruno enquired, finishing his glass of Scotch and shaking his head when Jack offered a refill.

'Who knows? The CIA isn't telling. Back in 2003 they claim they gave the Germans the full archive – nearly four hundred compact disks. But some parts of it were deliberately not given to the Germans, for example the British material. The Germans have been nagging us for them but we took the view that releasing all this unattributed and sometimes invented stuff about idealistic – if naive – British citizens forty years ago would do more harm than good. Most of those people in the peace movement just wanted a dialogue across the Iron Curtain and to outlaw nuclear weapons.'

'But if these files contain names of significant Stasi people in France, it must be in all our interests to expose them,' Bruno began and then paused before continuing more slowly. 'Is distribution not a political decision that an elected president should make rather than an intelligence agency? And what if the Americans know of these Frenchmen, some of them in important positions – they could blackmail them into spying for the Americans. What then?'

'You can't have it both ways, Bruno. You can't expect the Americans to share secret material with their allies one minute and then accuse them of blackmailing Frenchmen to spy on France the next. I see your point but even if the Americans gave the stuff to Paris, would we ever know if they'd given everything, or held the best stuff back? We don't know that they've given us everything about Stasi operations in Britain. In fact, some of my old colleagues strongly suspect that there's some stuff about Stasi operations with the IRA and gun-running via Libya that may be missing, probably to protect Irish-Americans who were involved.'

A car door slammed in the small parking lot outside and through the window Bruno saw Fabiola and Gilles, already in their riding gear.

'Time to ride the horses,' he said. 'Thanks for the drink, and the very illuminating conversation. See you at dinner. And do me a favour and decant the Ortus.'

'I will indeed, and I've brought a bottle of David Fourtout's red, as served at the Georges Cinq hotel in Paris,' said Jack. 'People tell me it's the finest wine made in the Bergerac. And I've got a couple of bottles of Château Lestevenie *brut* chilling in the fridge and I'm sure you'd agree that's among the best of our sparkling wines.'

'Are we not fortunate that we have so many splendid wines that can compete for that title?' Bruno said, grinning. 'Yes, it may be the best of our white sparkling wines, but what about that lovely rosé *brut* from your friends at Château Feely?'

'We must do a comparative tasting,' Jack replied. 'Enjoy your ride and make sure you're back in time for the roast lamb. Jacqueline asked Miranda for it specially and I made the mint sauce – an English delicacy.'

'Some French gourmets would suggest that's a contradiction in terms,' Bruno said, laughing as he left. 'But don't tell Pamela or Miranda that I said so.'

5

'We'll only take our four horses out this evening, the other ones have been working all day,' Pamela was saying to Fabiola and Gilles when Bruno entered the stable. He embraced each of them in turn and Pamela hugged him just a moment or so too long for mere friendship and gave him a roguish glance before turning to put the bridle onto Primrose's head. It had been some weeks since Pamela had last invited him to her bed and Bruno had assumed that their liaison – he could hardly call it an affair – had reached its end. But now he wondered – perhaps as Pamela had intended that he should.

'I thought we should head up the ridge for a gallop, blow all the cobwebs away and work up an appetite for dinner,' Pamela announced briskly as they saddled up, a plan which Bruno welcomed.

Although the heatwave continued, it was a perfect summer's evening for a ride, a soft breeze helping the heat to fade from the day. Their shadows were beginning to lengthen as they trotted through the paddock and then walked the horses up the long slope to the ridge, the two sheepdogs loping on ahead. Balzac was loping along beside Hector who was pulling at the reins in his eagerness to run. Bruno saw Fabiola had the same

43

problem, tightening the reins on the Andalusian she rode. Gilles brought up the rear. As always, he was riding the elderly mare, Victoria, although he was more and more comfortable on horseback and would soon be ready for a younger and less sedate horse.

Pamela paused when she reached the ridge and the others gathered alongside, all looking down at the valley and across to the hill of Limeuil, where the Dordogne and Vézère rivers came together on their way down to Bordeaux and the sea. It was a view of which Bruno never tired, enjoying the way that the houses and red roofs of St Denis clambered up the hill to his right. They were matched perfectly by the way Limeuil's houses did the same on the left, with the small chateau of la Vitrolle with its apple orchard and vineyards between them.

'Are we all ready?' asked Pamela, and nudged Primrose with her heels and loosened the reins to let her run.

Beneath Bruno, Hector needed no urging and leaped forward after her, drawing alongside while still accelerating and then forging ahead. The Andalusian was at Bruno's stirrup, and the echo of Balzac's bay of joy at the prospect of a run was ringing in his ears. The two sheepdogs were silent, running easily at Pamela's far side until the horses steadily drew ahead and Bruno felt his eyes narrow against the wind. It was exhilarating to be part of this racing unit of horse and man, moving in such perfect harmony as they sped along the two kilometres of the ridge.

It seemed to end too soon as the belt of woodland approached and Hector, by now three lengths clear of the others, began to slow of his own accord. He knew this ridge and its boundaries as well as Bruno and slowed to a halt at the gap in the trees towards the bridle trail that led down to the village of Bigaroque. Bruno smiled inwardly as he prepared himself for Pamela's inevitable teasing. Every time they came this way she liked to remind him that the history of the district was almost as much British as French. Pamela claimed that the village had been named by the English in the Middle Ages when they had controlled south-western France. Bigaroque, she argued, had been called Big Rock from the rocky outcrop that dominated the bend in the river that led to Le Buisson. Bruno even thought it might be true.

They dismounted to walk their horses across the bridge, and then cantered through the valley, flanked by fields of maize planted too close together. Bruno tightened his lips at the thought of the quantities of fertilizer and underground water required by this form of intensive farming. It was one of the aspects of how Brussels ran Europe's agriculture that infuriated him. He counted himself as a good European but there was a monstrous gap between the rhetoric of Brussels about the need to alleviate climate change, and the harsh reality of their policies on the ground. But soon after they dismounted again to cross the bridge at Limeuil, they were passing, on the far side of the river, the vineyards that were run by the town of St Denis. Here his mood eased at the knowledge that these grapes were now being farmed organically. They took the railway crossing that led to St Chamassy and then the trail back to Pamela's riding school, which gave them one last brief gallop before it came into view.

At the stables, they removed the bridles and saddles and rubbed down their horses before filling their water troughs and mangers, the dogs waiting by their own food bowls until they were fed. Pamela and Fabiola went indoors to shower and Gilles and Bruno stripped to the waist and sluiced themselves in the stable sink. They each kept towels and clean sweatshirts in the stables. With their hair still wet, they patted their horses goodnight and led the dogs to the main house. Gilles paused at Fabiola's car to take from a coolbox a bottle of red wine from the vineyard of Court-les-Mûts, their special cuvée called *des Pieds et des Mains* whose grapes were trodden by human feet in the traditional way. Bruno nodded his approval and then his phone vibrated. He saw it came from Claire at the kennels and answered at once.

'Bonjour, Bruno,' she said. 'Carla is getting ready to go into labour sometime tonight. I think your Balzac will be a daddy by tomorrow morning.'

'That's wonderful news,' he said, laughing with joy as he spoke. 'Is there anything I can do? Would you like me to come up to help?'

'No, it's me she'll want alongside and it's not her first litter. I checked with the stethoscope and all the pups are doing well. I think I heard nine little heartbeats. I imagine she'll have them in the small hours so I'll send you an email rather than wake you up.'

'When can we come and see them?'

'You can come anytime but I'd rather keep Balzac away for the first couple of weeks because Carla will get nervous. Some sires can be tricky. I'm sure Balzac will be well behaved but I want to keep Carla calm. And don't worry, you still get first pick of the litter, and from the heartbeats she'll have enough pups for you to have two.'

'Just so long as they're all right, and Carla, too, although you know I still prefer to think of her as Diane de Poitiers.'

'How could I forget?' she laughed. 'Do you use her pedigree name because you're a bit of a snob or do you have a thing for royal mistresses?'

Bruno laughed in return, more in delight at the coming of Balzac's pups than at Claire's teasing. 'It's the royal connection, of course, nothing but the best for Balzac. And you know I'm not as much of a fan of Carla Bruni's music as you are. Thanks for the news, my regards to Carla-Diane and call me any time if you need anything.'

Bruno instantly called Isabelle, his old flame, whose gift to him Balzac had been, and who had accompanied him to the mating earlier in the summer.

'Bruno, good to hear from you but I'm in a meeting . . .'

'It's just to say that Diane de Poitiers is going into labour. Balzac will be a father by the morning. I'll hang up.'

He just heard a whoop of joy and the words 'That's wonderful' as he closed his phone, wondering what the others at her doubtless high-level security meeting would make of that. Knowing Isabelle, she'd probably share the news with them anyway. He paused a moment before going into the house to join his friends. He'd always thought that one pup should go to Florence's children. They adored Balzac and on her teacher's salary there was no way that Florence would be able to afford a basset hound and he couldn't think of a better home. But a second pup was more complicated.

He could probably get a thousand or fifteen hundred euros for a pedigree pup but he had no intention of doing that. He did, however, feel an obligation to the Mayor, who had given him his first basset, Gigi, from one of his own litters. The Mayor had never replaced Gigi's mother when she died and Bruno knew from his affection for Balzac that he missed having a dog in his life. It would also mean that Balzac would be in the same town as his two puppies. But since the Mayor had not found a new dog, did that mean that at his age he didn't really want one? His friend the Baron had said as much after the death of his own dog, a gigantic *dogue de Bordeaux*. Bruno felt sure that if the offer were made, the Mayor would feel bound to accept it, but he'd hate to feel that it was an imposition on the man he'd come to think of almost as a father. Perhaps he could try raising the matter in a roundabout way. And Yveline of the gendarmes had said she'd be keen to have a female pup. He'd have to think about this before announcing the news to all his friends. He pocketed his phone and went into the house.

He was greeted first by the scent of roasting lamb and then by two small children arriving like little bullets to clamber at his legs. They were Dora and Daniel, Florence's children, keen to tell him of their latest exploits in Pamela's swimming pool, where Bruno had taught them how to swim earlier that summer. Then he was besieged by Miranda's two boys, who were now old enough to play rugby with the *minimes* and wanted to know when the pre-season practice would begin.

Disentangling himself, but with Dora on one arm and Daniel on the other, Bruno kissed Florence, Jacqueline and Miranda. He was then embraced by the Baron who took one of the children so that Jack Crimson could hand Bruno a glass of white wine and lead him to the big dining room where the table, already laid and with a row of candles waiting to be lit, was set for ten. He saw four open bottles of wine: his Ortus, Jack's red from Les Verdots, Gilles's foot-trodden wine and one of the Mayor's favourite Pécharmant from Château de Tiregand. Then there was one mystery bottle wrapped in a black sock. This was doubtless from the Baron, one of the blind tastings he sometimes offered to test his friends. A smaller table stood at the far end with places for the four children.

'*Mon Dieu*, this is splendid,' said Bruno. 'A fine homecoming for our two globetrotters. It could almost be Christmas.'

'And here's a gift for you, Bruno,' Jacqueline said, embracing him. She gave Bruno a wrapped parcel, about the size of a book, but it felt soft and pliable.

'We got American sweeties, like bootlaces,' said Dora.

'Only they taste of strawberries,' added Daniel, glancing at his mother before adding to Jacqueline, 'It was very kind of you to think of us.'

'Aren't you going to open it, Bruno?' asked Dora.

Bruno did, and unwrapped the parcel to find a chef's toque. It was white, pleated, nearly a foot tall and embroidered with the words 'Top Chef'. He immediately put it on over his still-wet hair and embraced Jacqueline again.

'Now I have something to live up to,' he said. 'Thank you very much, Jacqueline, but I don't think I'll be able to match Miranda's roast lamb, and a little bird told me that Grandpa Jack has made a secret sauce, just for all of us, to go with the Baron's secret bottle.'

'Florence, Pamela, Miranda and I got aprons that look like the American flag,' announced Fabiola. Gilles said he'd been given a T-shirt bearing the unmistakable face of the American president, which he found to be very ironic, suitable only for wearing in bed. Fabiola instantly vetoed that idea, unless Gilles was prepared to sleep alone. Crimson and the Baron had each been given the same T-shirt, which made Bruno feel all the more grateful for the chef's toque.

'We're starting with a chilled soup of vegetables from the garden before we have the lamb we got from Sylvestre,' Miranda announced, steering them to their seats. 'I told him you'd be one of the guests, Bruno, and he said he knew what you liked.'

Bruno nodded courteously but his heart sank a little. Sylvestre was a friend of his with a sheep farm. He knew that Bruno liked a hogget, a young sheep between one and two years old with rather more of the taste of mutton than the ones born in the spring. He was far from sure that all his friends shared his fondness for the dish, but then a new-born lamb could hardly feed ten adults and four hungry children. Bruno also knew that the English tended to prefer their meat rather less pink than the French. Well, the wine would make up for it, he thought, eyeing the row of bottles with pleasure. The Baron's mystery bottle was in the classic shape of a Bordeaux so he could rule out a Burgundy or some wine from the Rhône valley.

At least they had clear glasses. Bruno had an embarrassing memory of an evening of wine-tasting with Hubert, along with some other friends who thought they knew about wines. Hubert had served the wine in another room and brought them in already poured into black glasses. Without the customary visual clue, most of those present – including a *sommelier* from a well-regarded restaurant – had had no idea whether they were drinking white or red. It had been a lesson in humility that Bruno would not forget, even though he'd been sure he'd recognized a Chablis in the first glass. It had turned out to be a Sancerre, so at least he'd got the colour right.

The soup was excellent, red and yellow peppers with cucumber and skinned tomatoes, served with a generous scoop of *aillou*, a blend of crème fraîche and fromage blanc with garlic and parsley. Had it been his soup, Bruno might have been tempted to add a little fresh mint but then he recalled that Jack was making a mint sauce.

'*Alors, mes amis*,' said the Baron, rising to take up the covered bottle to pour half a glass for each of the adults. 'In this moment between the soup and the lamb, let's try to identify this mystery wine. And I'll give you a clue. It comes from within a hundred kilometres of where we sit, so you can rule out the Médoc, the Loire and Languedoc-Roussillon.'

They all swirled, held their glasses against the light of a candle and then sniffed. Bruno, knowing that his taste buds were still sensing the garlic in the soup, drank some water first before sipping. He wondered if the Baron was testing them with one of the smaller appellations, a Buzet or even a Duras. It certainly wasn't a Cahors. The taste was familiar, if not a Bergerac then close to it, possibly one of the new small classified regions such as the old *bastide* of Domme, further up the Dordogne valley.

The Baron went around the table. Jack thought it was a Montravel, at the western end of the Bergerac region. Gilles thought it came from further south, a Saussignac or a Duras. The Mayor was still thinking and Bruno admitted he was guessing but he thought it was a *vin de pays* from the Périgord, somewhere nearby but he was sure it wasn't from the town vineyard. He suggested it could be a wine from Domme. Finally the Mayor put down his glass and said he thought it was a Buzet.

'You're all wrong but Bruno came closest,' the Baron said. 'It's from the Domaine de la Voie Blanche, just this side of St Cyprien, so it is indeed a *vin de pays* of our own Périgord, stored in terracotta amphorae just as they did in Roman times. I bought a couple of cases and brought one along tonight, so I'll leave the other eleven bottles here for future festivities in the hope that you all enjoy it as much as I do. Now drink up and let's attack the other bottles.'

Miranda brought in the shoulder and leg of lamb on a giant platter, surrounded by whole heads of garlic, followed by Pamela bringing a large bowl of roast potatoes. The scent of the rosemary, on a bed of which the lamb had been roasted, filled the room. Jack excused himself, left the room briefly and returned with a gravy boat which he announced with pride contained his traditional English mint sauce. When the Baron asked how it was made, Jack replied that he crushed finely chopped mint leaves into a spoonful of sugar and a little oil until it had turned into a rough paste then thinned it out with vinegar. The Baron's eyes widened. Gilles and the Mayor exchanged glances. *Mon Dieu*, thought Bruno, the things I do for international understanding.

Meanwhile, Jack had wrapped a napkin around his hand, used it to seize the bone at the end of the leg, and began to carve the thick end of the shoulder that was still attached. He was using one of Pamela's Japanese knives and the slices of lamb fell away like butter. Miranda began serving the more cooked slices to her father and Pamela and to her own and her children's plates, evidently understanding that the French preferred their meat somewhat pinker.

Bruno's own portion was perfect, obviously very slowly cooked at a low temperature, and the roasted heads of garlic squeezed out their delicious tender flesh when he pressed them lightly with his knife. He took a sip of the cuvée Ortus he had brought and thought it the perfect accompaniment. Seeing the others enjoying it, despite his fear that it might be too much like mutton for their taste , Bruno raised his glass to Miranda to tell her that her lamb was an Anglo-French triumph. The others raised their own glasses to toast her, the children following suit with their own glasses of mineral water.

'My friends at school say they are allowed a little taste of wine in their water, Mummy,' said Miranda's eldest son, Mark. 'May we try that?'

She glanced at her father who gave a discreet nod and she agreed. Bruno carefully poured a teaspoon of wine into the boy's glass, turning it a pale pink and telling him that this was an important moment and the other children would be allowed their own taste of wine when they were older. That seemed to satisfy them, although Bruno was sure that Mark's younger brother would manage to sneak a sip when the grown-ups weren't looking.

'I think this may be the moment to introduce you all to my secret sauce,' said Jack, raising the gravy boat of his mint concoction. Bruno gamely accepted it and used a spoon to put a small helping of a thin green sauce onto the side of his plate.

He dipped a morsel of lamb into it and tried it, dreading what the mint and vinegar would do to his enjoyment of the bottle of Tiregand that Gilles had started to pour.

In fact, the mint and the sharpness of the vinegar went quite well with the lamb, but the sugar seemed to Bruno a bizarre and unnecessary addition. Still, in the interest of friendship he tried another portion, and this time he was accustomed to the sweetness of the sugar that had at first surprised him, and began to see that this could work. Perhaps if he tried a little honey instead of the sugar ... Suddenly he was aware of a conversation down the table, a female voice in full and vehement flow.

'I think it's shameful, a deliberate denial of history,' declared Jacqueline. 'The British have long had a thirty-year rule before the release of government papers, why not the Americans? France is now a full member of NATO, so what possible reason could they have for withholding the Rosenholz dossier? It's been more than thirty years.'

'Secret papers aren't released in Britain after thirty years, only routine ones, and they have to be cleared by a committee of historians and officials,' Crimson replied. 'And you know perfectly well, Jacqueline, that France is even more cautious about releasing state papers than the British or Americans.'

'I know that, Jack, and you're right,' she replied. 'But I don't see why serious historians in democratic countries have to work in the dark just to protect the reputations of antiquated politicians for rotten decisions they took in secret when they were in power.'

'What secret decisions are you talking about?' asked Gilles, in a voice that silenced the other conversations around the table and reminded Bruno that Gilles still wrote for *Paris Match* from time to time. 'Is this to do with that Cold War conference in Washington you attended?'

Jack laid down his knife and fork, looked up at the ceiling and said, almost with a groan, 'Now we have the media involved.'

'About time, too!' said Jacqueline, tapping the table for emphasis. 'I think I should write an op-ed for *Le Monde* about it.' She looked around the table almost fiercely before going on. 'The Americans have been sitting on a vast trove of Stasi documents, listing all the East German agents around the world, and they've shared the German sections with the Germans and the British sections with the British. But France is still deemed too untrustworthy for the CIA to let us know how badly we may have been penetrated by East German intelligence.'

'I see your point but it's all a long time ago,' said the Mayor.

'In historical terms, and in terms of official careers, it is uncomfortably short,' Jacqueline replied. 'Imagine young French students, recruited when they were in their twenties at Sciences-Po or some other springboard into government. They would now be in their fifties, in senior positions with another decade or so in office. Imagine the damage they could do.'

'But the Stasi has been extinct for thirty years,' said Fabiola. 'Who would these officials be working for now?'

'The Stasi shared everything with the KGB,' Jacqueline replied, more calmly this time. 'Moscow would be in a position to force those people to work for them. And so would the Americans, so long as we in France don't have the documentation to expose them.'

'Sounds like a hell of a good story,' said Gilles. 'And I see why you might want to run this in *Le Monde* but you'd get a far bigger audience if we ran this in *Paris Match*.'

As silence fell, Bruno filled everyone's glasses with the bottle from David Fourtout, modestly titled *Le Vin*. He asked the Baron what he thought of it, hoping that the conversation would drift off into new directions. Florence, who was sitting like Miranda at the end of the table closest to their children, came in with a question.

'Why don't the Americans trust France?'

Jacqueline looked at Crimson, Bruno looked at the Mayor, Pamela looked at Gilles and finally the Baron spoke.

'As a life-long Gaullist, I always appreciated his insistence on an independent foreign policy that put French interests first,' he said. 'De Gaulle did so during World War Two, and after it, and this sometimes rubbed up our British and American friends the wrong way. Bruno, what's that story about Lyndon Johnson's reaction when he was told that de Gaulle was pulling out of NATO and insisted that all American troops leave French soil?'

'Johnson told his Secretary of State Dean Rusk to ask de Gaulle if that included the Americans in the Normandy cemeteries who died to liberate France.' Bruno paused a moment and looked around the table. 'Much as I admire de Gaulle, I have to say I feel a little ashamed each time I think of that question.'

6

Bruno awoke just before six when his cockerel announced the new day, and since he'd drifted off to sleep thinking of Balzac's pups, he jumped out of bed to check his emails. Just before the news headlines sent automatically from *Sud Ouest* and the radio news from *France Inter* in his inbox, there was mail from Claire Mornier at the kennels, timed at three in the morning.

Félicitations à Papa Balzac. Nine beautiful pups born well; five little Dianes de Poitiers and four Balzacs.

Bruno laughed, jumped up, then bent down to caress his dog and tell him what a wonderful father he'd be and with so many offspring to his name. He swigged some orange juice from the fridge, donned his tracksuit and running shoes and led Balzac out onto the familiar trail through the woods. The birds were far too happy with their new day to interrupt their singing for a lonely runner, and the harmonious range of their various songs reinforced Bruno's sudden conviction that the world was full of little miracles and that he couldn't wait to see its latest gift.

Twenty minutes later, back at home, he turned on the radio

and emailed Claire to thank her for the news, and ask whether it would be convenient for him to come and see the puppies at around eleven. He jumped into the shower, shaved, put a fresh egg on to boil and made coffee before he dressed in his summer uniform. Back in the kitchen, he refilled Balzac's water bowl, sliced the remains of yesterday's baguette and put the pieces into the toaster. Then he went outside to feed his chickens, collect six fresh eggs and replenish their water.

His egg, coffee and toasted baguette ready, he shared the latter with Balzac and began to plan his day. He could be at his desk in St Denis before seven thirty, deal with the mail and paperwork, and escort the mothers and toddlers across the road to the *maternelle* school just before eight. He'd have plenty of time to patrol the town and show his face at the Mairie before leaving for the kennels at around ten, first dropping off Balzac at the riding school. He found a used carton for the six fresh eggs and grabbed a jar of his home-made pâté. He also took a sack of his own recipe dog biscuits, all this intended as gifts for Claire. He set off for town in his ancient Land Rover: it wouldn't be right to use his official police van for a personal trip to the kennels.

During the short drive into town he thought about the Mayor and how to offer him one of Balzac's pups without making him feel he should pay for what Bruno intended as a gift. Best to be as straightforward as possible, he thought. He parked in the main square since it was not a market day and went to his office. Shortly before eight, with Balzac on his leash, he set off for the *maternelle* nursery school, pausing only to greet his acquaintances as they opened their shops or hurried to work.

St Denis was a town that rose early. Balzac tolerated being petted by the toddlers once they and their mothers had safely crossed the road.

He and Balzac made their usual circuit of the town, past the retirement home, the church and the cemetery, turning at the Gendarmerie to head up to the old main street before turning back onto the Rue de Paris and back to the main square. The Mayor was standing at the front desk, chatting with his secretary and Roberte from the social service team while waiting for his fancy coffee machine to finish his morning brew.

'*Bonjour*, Bruno, and you, Balzac,' he said, and turned to tell his secretary to make another cup for Bruno. 'A word, if you please.' He steered Bruno into his office, closed the door and said, 'I'm a bit worried about this CIA dossier business. My instincts tell me this might not be the best time for Jacqueline to start making a fuss about it, least of all in *Le Monde*. What do you think?'

'It might ruffle some feathers, both among our own security people and across the Atlantic,' said Bruno, 'but that doesn't mean it shouldn't be aired. Our secret state sometimes seems to forget they work for a democracy. Against that, I can't say I like the idea of some witch-hunt for old Stasi spies in the current political climate with fake news and the superheated rhetoric of social media. I remember what Jack Crimson said about those well-meaning British peace activists who were listed as agents in those Stasi files. I assume the French counter-espionage people have been aware of this prospect for a while and tried to deal with it.'

'That's my feeling, or at least part of it. I'm also concerned about Jacqueline putting herself into a very public controversy with all the social media trolling that's likely to follow.'

'That has to be her decision,' said Bruno. 'I'm confident she'll think it through and we both know she takes your own views seriously.'

The secretary tapped at the door with the toe of her shoe, and came in with a tray of coffee. A wave of her freshly applied perfume drowned the delicious smell of coffee as she swayed past him, fluttering her eyelashes. He sighed inwardly, thanked her with a cool smile and held the door open for her to leave. Her flirtatious ways would never change!

'There's something I wanted to tell you,' Bruno said after she left. 'Good news. Balzac's puppies were born in the small hours of this morning, five females and four males. After your kindness in giving me Gigi when I first came to St Denis, I'd like you to have one and I'm sure Balzac would agree.'

The Mayor put down his coffee cup and beamed first at Bruno, then at Balzac, and said, 'That's wonderful news. I'm very happy for him and for you, and I'm touched by your offer. But I don't think I want to go through the serious business of training a puppy at my age. These days I like to sleep in rather longer than basset hounds. I remember chatting to the Baron about it after he lost his dog and he said puppies were best raised on a working farm or in a house with children. I rather agree.'

'I get some pups instead of a stud fee and I thought I'd give one to Florence's children. I was saving the other for you.'

'Thank you, but no. And I don't think Jacqueline is nearly as much of a dog lover as you and me. In fact, she's thinking of getting a cat. But I'm sure you'll find a good home for the second hound. It's a grand idea to offer one to Florence's kids but I'd raise it with her first. She might well think she has enough on her plate. And the children feel they have a part-share in Balzac already.'

'I hadn't thought of that,' Bruno admitted. 'You're right. I'd better check with her first. I thought I might drive up to the kennels later today and take a first look at the puppies.'

'Give them all my warmest good wishes and make sure you don't let one of them pee on your hand. That means he or she owns you. But you might want to join me tomorrow at noon in Périgueux. The Prefect has called an informal conference over this heatwave, whether we should impose controls on water, special measures for old people, setting up cooling rooms in retirement homes and so on. They're worried about another disaster like the *canicule*.'

A surge of extreme heat in 2003 had led to many deaths, mainly among the elderly and infirm. The rivers had been unusually low and the water tables so sparse that fire engines had to come in relays to pump cooling water from their hoses onto the nuclear power stations. Successive governments had since been acutely aware of the dangers, and noticeably more sensitive to warnings of climate change. A recent spate of forest fires in southern France had sharpened the swelling sense of alarm. The government had made much of the purchase of four new specialist fire-fighting aircraft.

Bruno agreed to accompany the Mayor and suggested that if they had time, they could call in on Virginie, Elisabeth's student who had started work at the police lab in Périgueux.

After checking that he had an email from Claire confirming that he'd be welcome, but this was not the time for Balzac to meet his pups, Bruno dropped off Balzac at the riding school and set out for the kennels.

En route he put in his earphones and called up on his phone the app of English lessons that Pamela had given him. He was at the third level now, which meant that Jack and Jill were no longer navigating the London Underground or watching the changing of the guard at Buckingham Palace. They were now at an industrial museum in a place called Telford and admiring the first iron bridge. It was mildly interesting and he felt slightly virtuous at improving his imperfect command of the language. Mouthing the English words, he drove out through Rouffignac and Thenon, past the magnificent chateau of Hautefort and up the familiar road to the kennels. It had taken barely an hour.

He paused before pulling into the main courtyard, admiring the familiar spread, the old barns converted into kennels and the paddock filled with the big Malinois dogs that Claire raised for the military. They were bounding around the score or so of basset hounds who had cleverly developed their own game of running in between the legs of the Malinois to make them trip over. He could imagine Balzac enjoying that. As he parked, Claire came out to greet him.

'*Bonjour*, Bruno,' she said, embracing him. 'It's good to see you, and the puppies are enchanting. How's the new father?'

He laughed. 'Blissfully ignorant of his new status.' He handed her the gifts. 'I'm sure his pups are too young for my dog biscuits but Diane de Poitiers and the other dogs may enjoy them.'

'They certainly scoffed down the last lot you brought,' she said. 'I even tried one myself and enjoyed it. Let's go see the new family.'

She led him to the familiar converted pigsty, which he had known as the mating chamber and was now a maternity ward. Before going inside she turned, looking serious.

'Stay back well behind me, kneel down so you don't intimidate her and stay silent until I say it's all right,' she said firmly. He nodded.

'Of course.'

'Even then, speak very softly. Don't touch her and please don't move towards the puppies. In the unlikely event that one of them pulls back from the teats and crawls towards you, stay absolutely still and let them explore you a little but please don't react and don't stroke them. She's very protective just now and she might reject one that has your unfamiliar smell. It was an easy birth, no complications, but still, she's exhausted and with a pup on almost every teat she has enough to deal with without you. OK?'

'Absolutely,' he said. 'May I take some photos on my phone?'

'Not if you have automatic flash. I already took some for you when she was sleeping. I'll take some more over the next few days and forward them to you. And if I tell you to leave, please do so quietly and without abrupt movements.'

She opened the door and Bruno saw the red light from the infra-red lamp and heater. He was surprised to see it being used in summer. A strong scent of dog and milk and something indefinable reached him, not at all unpleasant and faintly reminiscent of truffles. He rather liked it. Claire slipped in, pulled the door to and he waited for a few moments before she opened it again and gestured him in.

Bruno did as he was told, moved slowly, crouching, and staying by the door, letting his eyes grow accustomed to the red light. The scent was even stronger now. As he peered forward he saw what seemed to be a crawling, heaving mass of legs and heads and squirming bodies. It reminded him of some kind of hive, a complex but single organism. The image stayed with him until he was able to pick out the individual puppies. They seemed to be the usual mixture of black, brown and white in various individual patterns, and there were two who were pale brown and white. Even in the red light, the pads of their feet were as pink as their mother's teats and he smiled at the memory of Balzac as a pup, the soft underflesh of his paws this same pink before they hardened and became dark. The fullness of Diane's teats was striking and the pups were piled on top of one another to reach them. Each of the pups seemed to be affixed to a teat, except for one very small one who was nuzzling at its mother's lowered head. He felt a touch of awe as he watched, aware that as a male he was privileged to be present at this most intimately female of moments.

One, a black, brown and white pup on the upper tier of teats, seemed to lose his grip and fall off, tumbling over its siblings below and then rolling a little on the bed of hay. The mother nuzzled the pup, using her nose to push the tiny creature back up the pile to a vacant teat. But the pup seemed curious. Bruno couldn't even see if its eyes had opened yet but it raised its head a little and moved it from side to side, as if sniffing curiously at this new world before going back to feed.

He tried to count them in the constantly shifting pattern of fur and legs and pale pink tummies, but it was impossible. He assumed Claire had counted as each pup was born and he was impressed that she had already determined the sex of each one. To his untrained eyes and in the dim red light, there was no visible difference between them.

The mother was now trying to push the tiny brown and white one towards a teat, and the bigger puppy, who'd seemed curious just now, was crawling over her hind legs as though heading towards Claire. Gently, its mother pushed it back and helped it clamber over a row of siblings to find an empty teat on the second level. Bruno could have stayed watching for hours, deciding it was far more interesting and affecting than any television.

'I'm thinking of giving one of them to two young children I know,' he whispered. 'They are twins, a boy and a girl, nearly four years old and the children of a good friend back in St Denis. They adore Balzac and I think they'd love a basset of their own. When might I be welcome to bring them to see the puppies?'

'It's difficult to restrain children so not before three weeks. I'll be keeping them here for another month after that until they're weaned,' she replied. 'Grown-ups can come and take a look at the puppies after about a week or so.'

'I liked the curious one who kept moving around,' Bruno said once they were back outside in the open air. 'And the little brown and white one who was nuzzling at its mother's nose. The others all seemed glued to their milk.'

'The first one is the pick of the litter, so he's yours by right,' Claire said. 'The little one is the runt, and she's also yours since there are nine. If you want a third pup you'd have to buy it, and don't forget the vet fees, the vaccinations, the pedigree registrations and so on. When you add it all up that usually costs between three and four hundred euros for each puppy.'

Bruno nodded, saying he understood. He'd never thought of a third puppy being part of the deal.

'I have five of the litter sold already from pre-orders, at fifteen hundred each, and I'll have no trouble selling the other two,' Claire went on. 'Bear in mind that I'd like to book Balzac in for servicing my other bitches, say two or three times a year. All the pups are perfect. Balzac gets a large litter and his own pedigree is very grand, so you can expect lots more pups to give away or sell in future.'

'*Mon Dieu*, I could almost make a living out of this,' Bruno exclaimed, surprised that his dog was so commercially valuable. 'I had no idea.'

'I've already had two enquiries from other kennels whether Balzac would be available to service their dams,' Claire went on. 'You could let him out for service every month or two, for which you can charge three hundred euros a time. Or you could take a pup or two pups from each litter to sell. You see how the money soon mounts up, if that's what you want. Your Balzac is a little gold mine. Bassets are starting to become very fashionable since they're so good with children and they look so special.'

'I'd have to consider that,' said Bruno. 'I'd want to know something about the homes the pups would be going to. I mean, Balzac is my friend as well as my dog. I don't like to think of him as some sort of rent-a-sperm, fertilizing all-comers for cash.'

'They wouldn't be all-comers,' Claire laughed. 'Pedigree ladies only, preferably named after royal mistresses. I don't think you realize just how special Balzac's pedigree really is. I believe you were told when you first got him that Balzac comes from the old royal pack at Cheverny. That means we can trace his ancestry back for more than three centuries. In human terms, he's a duke or a count or something, maybe even a pretender to the throne.'

Her eyes twinkled as she said this and they both laughed at the absurdity of it.

'That's what breeding is all about,' she said. 'So it's like a fairy tale, you're the commoner, the poor but honest woodsman, secretly raising and nurturing the heir to the throne. Meanwhile, wicked and jealous aristocrats seek to hunt him down. You could even write an opera about it.'

'The mind reels,' said Bruno. 'Maybe he has an evil stepmother with two ugly daughters, each determined to catch him.'

'That's Cinderella,' she replied, grinning in return. 'Or maybe it's the tale of the prince who is raised among the common people and learns to love them while moving secretly among them, avoiding the greedy nobles. And then he seizes the moment to mount the throne and chooses to marry the poor but honest country girl who helped protect him through many dangers.'

'And they all lived happily ever after,' said Bruno, smiling a little wistfully. 'Do children today still get told those old stories? Tales in which goodness and loyalty are eventually rewarded and wickedness punished? I fear they don't hear them when they're little and I wish they still did.'

'Were you told them?' she asked, quietly.

'Yes, I was, by the nuns in our orphanage,' he said, enthused by the memory. 'There was always a Bible story but then a fairy tale, all of us children in our little cots, our eyes wide, rapt with attention, while a nun read to us all aloud. I haven't thought of that for years.'

He felt a prickling in his eyes, as though he was about to shed a tear. So he took a deep breath, then blew his nose and looked away at the bassets and Malinois romping in the pasture.

'You're an unusual man, Bruno,' she said. 'Sometimes it's hard to think of you as a policeman. Isabelle is a lucky woman.'

If only she saw it like that, he thought ruefully.

On the return journey, J-J called. Bruno pulled in to answer and was struck by the excitement in J-J's voice.

'We've had a breakthrough. That special forces guy who was killed in Mali, Louis Castignac – Oscar's Son. We've traced the next of kin he listed through army records. It's his younger sister, named Sabine. And would you believe she's a cop, so her DNA is also on file. She's a gendarme based in Metz, near the German border, born just over a year after Louis. And from Louis's birth date, we know Oscar was still alive as late as July, 1989.'

'So Sabine would have to be Louis's half-sister, with the same mother but a different father,' Bruno said.

'Right, but so what?' asked J-J. 'She's still the official next of kin.'

'J-J, wait a second. Does this Sabine know he was only her half-brother? I mean, she's already mourning his death. This news may shock her all over again.'

'*Merde*,' J-J replied. 'You're right. And the answer is that I don't know. We'll cross that bridge when we come to it. The gendarme general here has arranged for her to be temporarily assigned to us. She'll get here early tomorrow afternoon so I'll want you here for a conference some time around two.'

'That's fine. I have to be in town for a Prefect's meeting at noon,' Bruno said.

'Sabine Castignac is twenty-eight, born in Bordeaux. She's been in the gendarmes for six years, just been promoted to sergeant and she's passed the exam for officer training school. So she'll be able to deal with it professionally.'

Mon Dieu, Bruno thought to himself. J-J was never the sensitive type but this was a bit cold-blooded, even for him. He would have to find a way to steer J-J towards handling this young female colleague with considerably more care.

'Congratulations, J-J, you must be pleased. It looks like all your years of work on Oscar are finally coming good,' Bruno began. 'But what do we know about Sabine's family? It's the mother we need to talk to – she's the one who knew your Oscar and got pregnant by him so she should be able to give us his real name. And there must be family photos. We'll need all that, and the date of their wedding.'

'And does Sabine know what this is all about?' Bruno asked. 'Might it make sense to bring in another woman to support her through this? I could ask Yveline. She's wise and she's smart and I suspect Sabine is going to need all the help she can get. And now that Sergeant Jules has bought a house there's a spare lodging at the St Denis gendarmerie where Sabine could stay while your investigation proceeds. She could be a real asset if we handle this right.'

'Good thinking, Bruno. You ask Yveline and I'll see you in my office at two tomorrow.'

J-J ended the call and Bruno sat for a long moment, thinking of the drama of a long-gone murder investigation that was about to engulf Sabine's family while they were still mourning the death of their son and brother in Mali. J-J would leave no stone unturned and no family privacy protected in his determination to resolve the case that had nagged at him throughout his career. Worse still, Bruno suspected that the investigation was unlikely to come up with any clear answers about a murder that had taken place thirty years ago. Oscar had never been reported missing by family and friends so there were no relatives still grieving and seeking closure for their loss. Witnesses were likely to be dead or forgetful and leads would be thin. J-J's obsession could tear a family apart for a very dubious outcome.

7

Virginie, the student recommended by Elisabeth Daynès to reconstruct the face from Oscar's skull, had been at work for a few days when Bruno and the Mayor called in to visit her at the police lab in Périgueux. It had been Bruno's idea to visit Virginie before the Prefect's meeting. Having spent time with Claire at the kennels the previous day, Bruno was struck by the contrast between the two women. Claire so relaxed and full of confidence in her skills, while Virginie – admittedly much younger – seemed quite intense and less sure of herself.

'Are you settling in all right?' Bruno asked her, after introducing himself and the Mayor, and pointedly not looking at the metal ring Virginie wore in one nostril and the studs in her eyebrows and lower lip. 'Is there anything that you need?'

'Everything is fine, thank you, and Madame Daynès told me to say that she sends you her special regards,' she said. 'I'm really grateful to have this opportunity and everybody here has been very kind and helpful. I even have my own room at the student hostel, which is more than I had in Paris.'

Virginie was wearing a white lab coat that was far too large for her, almost reaching her fluorescent orange running shoes. The rolled-up sleeves revealed a complex geometric tattoo above

71

one wrist. Her pink-dyed hair was rolled up into a tight bun revealing pretty ears that rose into a slight point, almost like an elf. She wore no make-up but her clear skin didn't need it. Her eyes were splendid, huge and dark. Bruno knew that she was in her early twenties but she looked no more than sixteen. He suspected her waif-like appeal might attract a parade of curious and admiring policemen inventing reasons to visit the lab. He'd better have a word with J-J about it.

'Where's Oscar?' the Mayor asked. Virginie looked blank.

'The skull,' Bruno explained. 'That's what J-J – I mean Chief Detective Jalipeau – has always called him.'

'I see. I was told to call him Exhibit A,' she said, and gestured to a corner. 'He's over there on a rotating stand in that thing that looks like a microwave. It's a laser linked to a computer, making an exact image in three dimensions from which the 3D printer is building the copies I'll work on. It also means that Madame Daynès will be able to monitor what I'm doing in real time.'

'Copies?' Bruno asked. 'Why do you need more than one?'

'To try alternative eye colours, different noses, different hairstyles and body mass index.' She sounded impatient, almost bridling at someone who seemed to question her skill. He gave a friendly nod to encourage her and she relaxed a little.

'It's only the cost of the extra plastic,' she said. 'Six or seven euros each for an identical skull. That's how I was trained to work.'

'J-J told me the dead man's hair was quite long and blond, not shoulder-length. You should check that with him.'

'What's your schedule here?' the Mayor asked. 'I mean, how long do you think it should take?'

Virginie lifted her chin and gave them both a determined look. 'I'll work as long as I can every day, six days a week. I know it's urgent. But look at that,' she gestured to a large poster on the wall, a detailed illustration of the human facial muscles. It looked fiendishly complicated.

'I'll have to recreate each muscle, precisely calibrated to the shape of the skull beneath. I was already told that this was needed as soon as possible so I'll work as fast as I can without sacrificing accuracy.'

'Good for you, and your priorities are the right ones,' the Mayor said, nodding his approval and trying to put her at ease. 'But we can't let you come to the Périgord without enjoying the sights and the food.'

'I'll be happy to pick you up and take you down to our area on some convenient Sunday,' Bruno said. 'You need some time off. I could pick you up here on a Saturday and get you back here in the lab on Monday morning. We can put you up at a local house with people we know. After seeing the exhibition at the museum, I know several who'll be fascinated by your work.

'That reminds me,' he added, handing her a brown paper bag. 'There's some of my home-made pâté de foie gras in there and a jar of my onion confit to go with it, a home-made *saucisson* and a local cheese made by a friend of mine. Just so you know how good the local food can be.'

She blushed prettily and gave them a lovely smile which almost made up for the tattoo. 'Thank you, that's kind of you. I should say the food's not bad at the student hostel here, much better than the one in Paris. Even the police canteen does a great salad buffet. And their coffee is free.'

'I'm delighted to hear it,' the Mayor said. 'Here's my card with my office and mobile numbers and my email. Just let me know if there's anything I can do to help.'

'And don't forget to tell me when you'll be free to visit us in St Denis,' Bruno chimed in. 'We can take you to the museum in Les Eyzies to see Elisabeth's exhibition that puts all of her – and your – work into context.'

The two men climbed the stairs from the lab and Bruno took them on the short cut through the busy police canteen where dozens of cops – traffic, uniformed and plain-clothes – were tucking into their *steak-frites*. One or two friends from rugby or previous cases nodded and waved in recognition as Bruno strolled through, but one large cop in uniform, whom Bruno did not know, called out loudly and with an unpleasant sneer in his voice, 'Watch it, boys, it's the country copper. How are the sheep-shaggers down there in the Périgord Noir?'

This was not the time to take offence, Bruno thought.

'They're leaving all the ewes very contented,' he replied amiably. He walked on through a ripple of laughter and then turned at the door, raised his hand in a wave and declared, 'I just hope you big city guys can say the same about your own partners.'

'Do the city cops always tease you like that?' the Mayor asked, as they left the building.

'Quite often, but it's something you get used to,' Bruno said. 'Male-dominated societies like the cops and the military tend to be clannish, always ready to challenge outsiders. There's usually no harm in it but that guy was trying to be offensive. I think I'd better keep an eye on him in the future.'

He and the Mayor headed up the road to the Préfecture,

wishing they had taken the car as the sauna-like heat rose from the paving stones. The Mayor observed that it was markedly warmer than in St Denis and began discoursing on cities as 'heat sinks', a lecture that took them to the Préfecture for a predictably disappointing meeting. The Prefect, as representative of the French government, had summoned a selection of local officials to ensure that he could claim they'd been consulted and that he had support for the unpopular measure of imposing water restrictions. These would ban the watering by hose of all private and municipal gardens, outlaw the refilling of private swimming pools and the use of car wash centres. Local fire brigades would make their own preparations to tackle forest fires.

Sitting beside Bruno, the Mayor of St Denis asked if the much greater use of water for crops would continue unrestrained. Yes, of course, the Prefect replied. Agriculture was a state priority. So that would naturally include orchards and market gardens, the Mayor continued. Indeed, said the Prefect. The Mayor sat back and murmured to Bruno, 'That means I've saved your tomatoes.'

And probably saved your own re-election, thought Bruno privately. But he was most struck by what the Prefect had not said. This heatwave and drought was not only a problem for swimming pools and lawns. Perhaps he should have a word with Albert, the chief *pompier* in St Denis, about possible precautions against forest fires.

The gathering of mayors, local police and fire chiefs broke up, grumbling as always about officials from Paris never understanding rural concerns. The Mayor stayed to mingle and Bruno excused himself. He headed for J-J's office to be told that the meeting would be held in the much larger office of Prunier, recently promoted to the rank of *Contrôleur-Général* as the senior police officer of the whole *département*. He and Bruno had first met as opponents in the army–police rugby match. Both men saw this as a firm basis for enduring friendship, however irritating Bruno's loyalty to St Denis could occasionally be for Prunier's much greater responsibilities.

Bruno also thought highly of Prunier's taste in coffee, and smiled as he recalled introducing Prunier to Léopold, the big Senegalese in the St Denis market who imported and sold excellent coffees from Africa. Like Bruno, Prunier had become a convert and bought kilos of the stuff for his home and persuaded the manager of the police canteen to buy it, too. As he entered the police HQ, Bruno's nose caught the familiar and welcome aroma. No police station could run for long without vast quantities of the stuff and Prunier had won the hearts of his force by insisting that everyone should drink the same excellent coffee that he enjoyed, rather than the usual sludge of most police canteens.

'*Bonjour*, Bruno,' said Prunier, advancing from behind his desk to shake hands and pour Bruno's coffee. J-J waved a greeting from one of the comfortable armchairs that faced Prunier's desk.

'I see you escaped from the Prefect's meeting almost as fast as I did,' Prunier said, smiling as he handed Bruno a cup of coffee. 'My secretary has just heard from her counterpart at the General's office that this gendarme, Sabine Castignac, is on her way here, accompanied by Commandante Yveline, and in a state of some distress. Apparently Castignac's superiors in

Metz had neglected to inform her that her only brother was in fact her half-brother. She'd only been told that she'd been reassigned to us and to take all family albums with her.'

'Knowing the gendarmes, that doesn't surprise me in the least,' said J-J. 'They are not always the most sensitive of colleagues.'

Bruno's eyes widened, startled to hear J-J complain of insensitivity in others. He caught Prunier's eye and saw the *commissaire*'s eyelid flutter in what might have been a very discreet wink.

'The gendarme general here is a decent man and he took it upon himself to brief her more fully before she joined us, so at least we're spared that unpleasant chore,' he said. 'He's also authorized her to be assigned to Commandante Yveline Gerlache in St Denis.

'We'll try to take good care of her in St Denis,' said Bruno. 'But won't the family photo albums be back at her family house?'

'We'll find out,' said J-J. 'She's from Bordeaux originally so we might take her home for a family reunion. Obviously we'll need to question her mother about the identity of the real father, and I'm not looking forward to that.'

'So not only Castignac but also her parents are not aware of the DNA findings from her brother?' Bruno asked.

'Apparently not,' said Prunier, pausing as they heard a discreet knock at the door. 'Let's be as professional and as courteous as possible to this young woman. There's no need to make the family drama even worse.' He raised his voice and called out, 'Enter.'

'*Bonjour, Monsieur le Commissaire*, Bruno, J-J,' said Yveline.

'Allow me to introduce Sergeant Castignac of the Gendarmerie Nationale.'

Sabine Castignac marched to Prunier's desk, came to attention with a soft thud of rubber-soled boots and gave a brisk salute. She was wearing full dress uniform, the stripes on her epaulettes gleaming so new that Bruno suspected she'd attached them while travelling from Metz. Her promotion to sergeant must have been very recent indeed. Her blonde hair was tucked at her neck in a tight bun. She was sturdily built with broad shoulders and her skin had a glow of health and fitness that suggested she spent long hours in the gym. Her eyes showed no hint of tears, so whatever shock she had experienced in her general's office had been overcome. Her hands, properly aligned on the seams of her trousers, looked strong and well-kept. To Bruno's eye, she was an impressive young woman whose face was dominated by a determined chin and a nose that had at some point been broken and reset. In a man, he'd have thought it a rugby injury, but more and more women now played the sport. He'd raise the idea with her; it might establish a useful bond.

'Reporting for duty, sir,' she said, still at attention, in a strong, clear voice with no apparent regional accent.

'At ease, Sergeant, and please sit. Would you like some coffee?' Prunier said. 'I gather you now know what this is all about.'

'No coffee, thank you, sir,' she said, taking a hard-backed chair and sitting at attention, her eyes on the wall above Prunier's head. 'Yes, I have been briefed on the situation regarding my late brother Louis. I now know that his DNA shows that he's my half-brother, fathered by an unidentified murder victim some thirty years ago, and not by the man who brought us both up. I'm still trying to come to terms with this news and with the implications for my family.'

'I realize this comes late but please accept my condolences on the death of Louis on active duty in Mali,' Prunier said. 'And my apologies for bringing you this unsettling news about his parentage. Let me introduce Commissaire Jean-Jacques Jalipeau, chief of detectives for the *département*, and Chief of Police Bruno Courrèges of the Vézère valley. I'm sure we can count on your professionalism in helping us investigate this unsolved murder.'

'Yes, sir. We always seek to cooperate with our colleagues of the Police Nationale.' She said the words as if she'd learned them by rote. She glanced at Bruno and added hastily, 'And our colleagues of the Police Municipale, of course.' She paused again. 'I mean, we're all on the same side.'

Prunier said nothing. J-J raised his eyebrows, doubtless thinking of all the turf battles he and every other member of the Police Nationale had waged against the Gendarmes. They liked to think they were the only police who really mattered, with a pedigree that went back far beyond their formal foundation in 1793 as the shock troops of the French Revolution. In fact they had begun as a highly politicized paramilitary force dedicated to the suppression of the Catholic faithful, the monarchists, feudal aristos and their bourgeois allies and all the other enemies of *Liberté, Egalité, Fraternité*. They had found some obscure soldier who died in battle against the English at Agincourt in 1415, the *prévôt des maréchaux* Gallois de Fougières, and adopted him to give themselves an even longer and more impressive pedigree. In 1934, after considerable research, Gallois was officially declared to be the first known gendarme to have died on duty and his remains are buried under the monument to the Gendarmerie in Versailles.

'Your general sent me a copy of your file,' Prunier said, opening a manila folder and glancing through it, turning the pages quickly. 'It's very impressive. I see you are a keen mountaineer and that you volunteer for the ski patrol at Gérardmer. I didn't know the Vosges hills were high enough for skiing.'

'Yes, sir, Gérardmer is only twelve hundred metres high but I've had some good skiing there. It can be icy, which is how I broke my nose, and it's not as magnificent as the Alps. Still, it's only two hours from Metz.'

'Right. I understand you were asked to bring any family photo albums you might have.'

'All the family albums are back home in Bordeaux. I brought with me the photos I had in Metz: two of my parents' wedding photos and one of my brother, I mean my half-brother. They're in my bag outside the door. Should I get them?'

Prunier nodded and she went to the door and brought in a large duffel bag with wheels, opened it and removed three framed photographs. Prunier stood them on his desk so all could see them.

'This first one is my parents at their wedding,' Sabine said. 'The second one is a group photo with my grandparents, my father's témoin and my mother's *demoiselle d'honneur*. This last one is my brother Louis when he passed out of the special warfare training centre at Perpignan.'

The photo of the wedding couple was slightly faded but clear enough. The groom looked some years older than his bride, maybe in his mid-thirties, and each of them looked slightly stunned as they smiled, dressed in clothes that must have been fashionable at the time. The groom's wide lapels and even wider tie matched the exaggerated shoulders of the white wedding dress of a bride whose face had been heavily made up. Bruno suspected she'd have looked more attractive without it. The group photo, in which she was laughing with a slightly taller young woman, showed her to be slim and attractive with dancing eyes, a generous mouth and a long, elegant neck. Bruno was mildly surprised that this young bride had produced a daughter like Sabine, whose physique must have been inherited from her father.

'Is that the *demoiselle d'honneur* standing beside her?' Bruno asked.

'Yes, Dominique, Mum's best friend ever since they were kids. They met the first day of school and remained almost inseparable since. I think of her as my aunt. She was wonderful in Mum's last illness, held us all together even though she was grieving as much as we were.'

'You mean your mother is dead?' J-J asked, in a voice that carried his disappointment at learning that his key witness was no longer available. This was news to him, to Prunier and to Bruno.

'Yes, sir. Last year. Cancer. At least she didn't get to know that Louis had been killed in Mali.'

'Did you have any idea that your mother had this – er – extra-marital liaison that produced your brother?' Prunier asked, trying to use a gentle voice.

'No, sir. I don't think anybody did. Except maybe Tante-Do,

I mean Dominique. That's what I always called her. They lived in the next street so we were always in and out of each other's homes. If anybody can help you, she can. She and Mum were as close as sisters except they never seemed to have a row. They used to go on holiday together. I know they came to these parts for a final girls' fling just before the wedding. I was thinking on the train and I reckon that could have been the time that Mum had her little – I don't know what to call it – accident? Adventure?'

'I think the term "girls' final fling" should cover it,' said Bruno, and then caught himself, wishing he'd remained silent. He was relieved to see Sabine smile.

'I suppose it would,' she said, glancing at him and still smiling, but more to herself than to him. 'Funny how you never think of your mum that way, young and silly and having fun, getting drunk and making mistakes. I suppose we all have to be young once. Even you, *messieurs*.'

Sabine glanced at J-J, a man approaching retirement, and then at the middle-aged Prunier and at Bruno without the least embarrassment at the clear implication that she saw them all as verging on the prehistoric. Behind her, Bruno noticed, Yveline was trying to suppress a grin. He gave her a discreet wink and then leaned forward to get Sabine's attention.

'When you said your mother and her best friend came to these parts for that last fling before the wedding itself, do you mean they came here to Périgueux or somewhere near here?' he asked.

'I'm not sure where it was but it was some kind of local folk festival called a *félibrée* where there was lots of music and dancing. It was Tante-Do's idea to go camping but I forget where it was exactly. Tante-Do would know. It was like a private joke between her and Mum. They'd say to one another, "Do you remember the *félibrée*?" Or sometimes they'd refer to the "Bois de la Vézère", which I think was the name of the campsite. And then they'd both giggle like a pair of schoolgirls and tease me about being far too young for it.'

'The wedding was in July, 1989, and your brother was born, when – in March the following year?'

'Yes, April third, he was a Pisces. I'm a Scorpio. My brother really was a Pisces, always loved the water, swam like a fish.'

The room fell silent for a moment as everyone mentally counted the months of gestation and tried to work out when it was that the unknown Oscar had impregnated Sabine's mother, and just how long that might have been before he had met his own death.

'In the first week of July, 1989, the annual *félibrée* to celebrate the Occitan language and culture was held in St Denis,' Bruno said, knowing that he did not have to explain the event to J-J and Prunier. The city of Périgueux had recently been the location for the hundredth anniversary of the festivity.

'It was long before my time and we haven't had one in St Denis since,' Bruno continued. 'But that's where Oscar's body was buried. Sorry, I should explain that Oscar was the name J-J gave to the unknown murder victim. It's reasonable to suppose that the St Denis *félibrée* was where and when your brother was conceived.'

'It's time we went to your home in Bordeaux to get the family photos, talk to your father and interview this Tante-Do,' said

J-J, lumbering to his feet. 'If anyone can tell us what happened at St Denis it will be her.'

'I'd rather go alone, at least to talk to my father,' Sabine said, her chin thrusting even more forward. 'It's just him and me now and he knows nothing of all this. Coming after Louis's death, it will be quite a blow for him and he's not in good health.'

'No, it's not just you and him. There's also the issue of an unsolved murder and you're a cop,' J-J said bluntly. 'He may be your father but he's the only one I can see at this stage with a motive for murder. He's my lead suspect.'

'You'll have trouble getting much out of him,' Sabine replied coldly. 'He's got early onset Alzheimer's so he's been in a home since Mum went into hospital for the last time. We'll be lucky if he recognizes me or understands what we're asking him.'

8

J-J was sufficiently sensitive to wait with the car while Sabine went in to the nursing home where her father lived, close to the university on the western fringes of Bordeaux and the vineyards of Haut-Brion and Pape Clément. Bruno, who had been in the rear seat between Yveline and Sabine, got out to stretch his legs. J-J, in the front passenger seat beside his aide and usual driver, Josette, clambered out to lean against the bonnet and light a cigarette. He must have craved one, never allowing himself to smoke when others were in the car.

'We might get something from the photo albums even if Sabine's father can't tell us anything useful,' Bruno said.

'I'm pinning my hopes on this Tante-Do, and maybe on that facial reconstruction,' J-J replied. 'It's hard, running into this setback after getting my hopes up with the DNA findings. I was wondering if there's anything to be learned in St Denis. Maybe you can pick something up from the campsite the two girls visited.'

'It's still there, in the same family, and the grandparents who used to run it are still around. I'm sure they'll help if they can but it's a long time ago.'

'You think I'm on a wild goose chase, don't you?' J-J turned to face him.

'No,' Bruno replied firmly. 'I got this started again with the facial reconstruction theory. I know it's a long shot, but this is a murder. We have a duty to press on. And maybe we can at least get a photo or a reconstructed face, enough to help find out who he was.'

Sabine came to the door and gestured for J-J to join her. In the car, they had agreed that squeezing all of them into the old man's room wouldn't be a good idea. Bruno looked at the handsome old mansion that had been recently converted into a nursing home and research centre into senile dementia. It was a fine house, eighteenth century perhaps, with tall windows and surrounded by pleasant gardens. Some patients sat in wheelchairs in the shade beneath a few large lime trees that looked almost as old as the house. Some of the old people had small dogs on their laps. Bruno had read that such pets helped to connect the inmates to the real world and improved their health as well as their moods. That made sense to him.

'Heaven spare us from ending up in a place like this,' said Yveline. 'It seems a sick joke on the part of the Almighty, to grant us longevity but take our brains away.'

'I don't think the Almighty had anything to do with it. Modern medicine, better diets, and maybe doctors are better at diagnosing it, even if they can't cure it,' Bruno said. He recalled what his aunt's doctor at the hospital had said about one in seven in the region being over the age of seventy-five and repeated the statistic to Yveline.

'*Putain*, what's that going to do to our taxes?' she asked.

'Maybe J-J has a point in smoking. That'll probably kill him before he goes gaga.' She looked across the car at Bruno. 'Tell me, do you ever think about euthanasia?'

'Not really.' He was surprised by her question. 'There's no simple answer. I can think of circumstances where it makes sense, but I can also see it opening the way to a great deal of abuse. And it would put a heavy burden on the medics we'd expect to do it.'

'So we stick with the law as it stands, even though we know the law is sometimes an ass?'

'So long as the laws are made by deputies we elect, we stick by those laws. As cops we swore to uphold them. It's not the laws that are an ass, it's us, the people and the deputies who make the laws. The laws change along with us. When we were born, Yveline, both abortion and homosexuality were illegal. Even slavery used to be legal. Maybe we change too slowly, but at least we change.'

The main door opened, J-J holding it for Sabine who was carrying a stack of photo albums. Once she stepped out, J-J offered her a clean handkerchief, took the books from her and came to the car, leaving Sabine standing by the door, her face turned away, her shoulders shaking. Yveline walked past J-J and stood beside Sabine, putting an arm around her shoulder. Bruno heard Sabine tell Yveline that she ought to be accustomed by now to her father's condition but each time it depressed her anew.

'He didn't even recognize his own daughter,' J-J said, his voice solemn. He stood by the back of the car while Bruno opened it so he could put the photo albums beside Sabine's luggage.

'The poor devil is in a different world altogether. He couldn't stop reciting something like a shopping list or an inventory of groceries, over and over. Sabine said he used to be deputy manager of a supermarket. That's where he met her mother who worked on the checkout. I don't think the poor old guy ever knew we were there, not me, not his daughter.'

J-J let out a long breath. '*Putain*, this job. Sometimes it gets to you. It's never the obvious things, the decomposed bodies, not even the women and kids beaten up, those little bloodied faces that break your heart. It's something you just don't expect, like trying to make contact with this old . . . this human vegetable.'

He lit another cigarette, breathed in deeply, coughed hard and spat. 'Right, on to Tante-Do at the beauty parlour.'

Her place was larger than Bruno had expected, filling both sides of a double-fronted modern building on a busy street. The beauty parlour and a hairdresser shared the same entrance and seemed to be two parts of a single business. The hairdresser's premises went back about twenty metres and looked two-thirds full. The beauty parlour smelled of scent and was smaller than the hairdresser's place, little more than a receptionist's desk and a counter where two women were having their nails done. They turned to stare as the receptionist gave a professional smile of greeting that stayed fixed on her face even as the police uniforms piled in behind J-J. Behind her were two doors, one marked *Salon* and the other *Spa*.

'Madame Dominique?' asked Sabine. The receptionist stared briefly at the uniforms and then pointed them to the stairs between the two businesses, saying they'd find her in the office on the next floor.

'Sabine, what a pleasure!' exclaimed the elegant, carefully coiffed woman. She was extremely thin with a complexion that looked as white and smooth as porcelain. She rose from behind a modern desk covered with sheaves of papers. She was wearing a pleated white blouse with a high collar and a neck scarf. She must have kicked off her shoes beneath the desk because she shuffled her feet a little and suddenly seemed five or six centimetres taller when she stood. Bruno had worked out that she must be in her early fifties but to his eye she looked no more than forty, until he looked at her hands. Beside her desk was an old-fashioned wooden hat stand on which hung a medical-style white coat.

'And are these your colleagues?' she went on, as she came from behind the desk to embrace Sabine. She spoke brightly, although she could not have missed the uniforms that meant this was no friendly visit. 'Please, all of you, come into my room at the back. I assume you're here on business.'

Sabine returned her embrace before introducing J-J, who showed his police ID, allowed Bruno's and Yveline's uniforms to speak for themselves and followed Dominique into a comfortable sitting room. A half-open door revealed a kitchen, and some carpeted stairs led presumably to bedrooms. Bruno assumed that she lived here, above the shop.

'Madame, we are investigating a murder that we believe took place during the St Denis *félibrée* that you and Sabine's mother attended some thirty years ago on the eve of her wedding,' J-J began, and went on to explain Oscar's discovery at St Denis and the new DNA evidence. 'It seems very likely to us that you were with Sabine's mother when she had her liaison with the man who was then murdered. We are hoping you can help us discover who exactly he was.'

Tante-Do sat back looking stunned as she stared at J-J, then at Bruno and Yveline before her gaze came to rest on Sabine. Slowly her features relaxed into a sad smile.

'So the family secret finally comes out,' she said, addressing Sabine as if the others weren't present. 'I'm sorry it had to come out like this, Sabine. Your mum never wanted you or your dad or poor little Louis to find out. Not that she ever regretted her brief adventure, and believe me, nor did I.'

Tante-Do gave a grin which made her look much younger and then chuckled with what Bruno assumed was a happy memory. 'I only knew him as Max and he came from somewhere in Alsace,' she said, lighting a cigarette. After her initial shock she appeared unfazed by the police visit and the questions.

'Max was a good-looking guy, a bit of a blond beast, and I might have been interested but I had my own *mec*, his friend Henri. In fact it was Henri who picked me up first and then your mum and Max really took to each other. He was a great dancer. We had a very happy weekend together, the four of us, and then on the Sunday morning they vanished, just disappeared.' She paused, as if suddenly recalling the social niceties. 'Can I offer you some coffee?'

'No, thank you,' said J-J, putting his phone on the coffee table between them. 'I'll take a formal statement later but for the moment I'm recording, if you have no objection. It has no legal status but it will help to jog my memory – and perhaps yours – when you give the formal statement that I'm afraid we are legally obliged to take.'

Tante-Do shrugged and J-J said, 'The witness has signalled her agreement to the recording.'

'I was against the marriage from the start,' she began and then glanced up at Sabine. 'Sorry, Sabine, but your dad was too old and too boring for your mum. I think he represented stability, reliability if you like, and that was what she craved. You may not know this but your grandfather, your mother's dad, walked out on his family when your mum was little. He just disappeared and she never heard from him again. That would have been in 1972, maybe '73. Your grandmother had a hard time raising your mum alone.'

Dominique went on to explain that she understood her friend's need for stability but could never understand her choice of husband. She had tried talking her out of the marriage and it had been her idea to have a last fling before the wedding. Dominique had originally thought of a rock festival but chose the *félibrée* as a suitably wholesome event. She found and booked the campsite, bought the bus tickets and announced it as a surprise pre-wedding gift.

'Which days were you there, exactly?' J-J asked.

Dominique looked irritated and almost snapped out the words, 'Give me a break. It was a long time ago.'

'Please, Tante-Do,' said Sabine, gently.

Dominique nodded, closing her eyes in an effort to remember. 'We got there on the Thursday and spent that evening, the Friday and Saturday and a bit of Sunday at the *félibrée*. Then we caught the bus back to Bordeaux after a late lunch on the Sunday.'

'Thank you,' said J-J. 'Please proceed.'

'My real motive was to give your mum some fun,' she said, looking directly at Sabine. 'That maybe she'd meet another guy, or realize she was too young for this wedding crap. At least I could help her have a really good time for a day or two. And she did. She and Max really hit it off, very passionate, could hardly keep their hands off each other, kept slipping away into the woods for another quickie. Mind you, I wasn't much different with Henri. I really thought it was working. On that last night in our tent she was thinking of cancelling the wedding, but then the next morning the guys had gone. That was the Sunday. Just disappeared, leaving no trace. Your mum had been abandoned all over again so I wasn't surprised when she squared her jaw and went ahead with the wedding. But she regretted it ever after.'

Dominique paused, looking abashed as Sabine gave something like a sob that she tried to cover by clearing her throat.

'I'm sorry, sweetheart,' Dominique said to her. 'But I suppose it all has to come out now.'

'What were the surnames of these two young men?' J-J asked.

'No idea. I've forgotten, if I ever knew them. A family name was hardly important to us.' She stubbed out her cigarette fiercely, as if erasing a memory. 'A lot of guys have flowed under the bridge since then.'

'Can you tell us anything else about them?'

'They were both tall, fair-haired, well-muscled and very fit, bronzed from the sun. Real golden boys. They'd been working in the strawberry fields around Vergt to make some money and were planning to go down to the vineyards to pick grapes before heading back to university in Strasbourg. We were in a proper campsite but they wanted to save their money so they were camping *sauvage* up in the woods. They had a small tent, a sleeping bag each, an army surplus water canteen each and lots of wine they drank from the bottle. They'd sneak into our campsite for a shower.'

'And that was where you – er, connected? Up in their tent?'

'What, in their shared tent? We weren't into orgies.' She laughed. 'Weren't you ever twenty? We did it in the woods, up against trees, in the river, on the bank, in their tent, in ours, everywhere.' She glanced up at Sabine. 'Your mum looked dazed with happiness, Sabine. It might have been the happiest time of her life, at least until she had you and Louis. Just a couple of glorious days, but some people don't even have that to remember.'

'Do you think that was when she became pregnant?' Sabine asked, speaking over J-J who had been about to ask something else.

'We both thought that, but by the time she knew, she was married. And she took that seriously. She was determined to make that marriage work, and she did – after a fashion. She was devoted to you and your brother. But he never looked a bit like your dad, and when he was growing up I kept seeing bits of Max in him, in his eyes and his build. She tried to deny it to herself but we both knew who his father was.'

'So, to sum up: all you know of him is the name Max,' said J-J. 'That he was from Alsace, a student at Strasbourg university and a good dancer. He was with another young guy called Henri from Alsace and they'd been making money in the strawberry fields in Vergt. Did you ever learn what subject they were studying, or their hometowns? You never exchanged addresses or phone numbers?'

Dominique shook her head, but slowly, as if careful of her hairstyle. 'Henri, the guy I hooked up with, was studying something to do with wine. He told me he'd spent some time in the Alsace vineyards as part of his studies.'

'Had they done their military service yet?' Bruno asked.

'I don't know. It never came up.' She shrugged.

J-J jumped in with another question. 'How did you learn they'd gone?'

'We were going to meet at a café in the square for croissants and coffee and they didn't show up. We waited and then went back to the campsite and thought they'd have left a message in our tent but there was nothing. We went up to where they'd been camping and they were gone. Not a sign they'd even been there. Your mum was distraught, looked all around the festival, sure they'd be there. I just thought it was time to move on and put it down to experience. Your mum wasn't like that, Sabine. She took it to heart.'

'Do you have any photos you kept of that trip, anything that might show the faces of these two men?' J-J asked.

Dominique laughed. 'No mobile phones back then, we'd never even heard the word selfie so we weren't taking photos of everything all the time like they do these days. Your mum had a little camera but I don't know that she used it much.'

'These two men, Max and Henri, how would you describe their relationship?' asked Bruno. 'Were they close friends, real buddies, or was there any kind of tension between them?'

'They were just friends spending the summer together,

making some money and chasing girls. We didn't spend a lot of time talking and they seemed to get on just fine. It wasn't like the guys were jealous of each other. They both seemed pretty happy at what they'd found, and so were we.'

'What contraception were you using?' Yveline asked, the first time she'd spoken since entering the room.

'I was on the pill but she wasn't. She wanted to start having babies as soon as she was married, the whole motherhood and nesting thing. I made sure she had some condoms.'

'Do you know if she used them?'

Dominique shrugged. 'She said so but if she did, they didn't work.'

'If you saw either of these guys again, would you recognize them?' Yveline asked.

Dominique gave a mocking laugh. 'You mean even though they'll be going bald and running to fat? Even if I did recognize them I probably wouldn't want to. But yes, I suppose I might know their faces if they hadn't changed too much.'

'I'd like you to do a photofit, work with a police artist to recreate their faces as best you can,' J-J said. 'And if we can find any photos of the *félibrée* we'd want you to look through them. We might also want your help in staging a reconstruction.'

'I've got a business to run here,' Dominique almost snapped. 'I can't just drop everything for some ancient case.'

'Madame, let us understand one another,' J-J said. To Bruno's ears his voice sounded dangerously calm. J-J leaned forward and turned off the recording system on his phone before he spoke again.

'You are a material witness in a murder case, probably the

only one. From what you have said already, you may be the last person to have seen the dead man alive. Inevitably, that makes you a suspect and that gives me grounds to detain you. If you want me to arrest you and make you do as I ask, that's up to you. One way or another, I will require you to cooperate with my investigation. And if I'm forced to arrest you, I will have this house and this business torn apart by a bunch of cops to make sure we miss nothing. I will also be sure to alert the local newspapers and TV stations to send cameras and photographers. You will briefly be famous, or perhaps infamous. And after that, you might not have much of a business to come back to when we let you out. Your choice.'

Dominique stared at him coldly before shrugging again. In a bitter voice, she said, 'For this I pay my taxes.'

'You know our motto, Dominique,' J-J replied calmly. 'Honoured to serve.'

J-J and Dominique glared silently at each other for a long moment before they were interrupted.

'Please, Tante-Do, we really need your help with this,' Sabine said.

Dominique shifted her gaze and her expression changed. She looked fondly at her old friend's daughter and replied, 'For you, sweetheart, anything.'

Mon Dieu, thought Bruno. That was astutely done, one of the most perfectly timed good cop–bad cop routines that he'd ever seen, except that it seemed natural rather than deliberate. It certainly had not been planned.

'By the way,' said Bruno to J-J in a low voice as they all returned to the car for the drive back to Périgueux, 'that young woman, Virginie, working on the skull – she was in the lab alone when we saw her. Can you keep a paternal eye on her? You know what cops can be like.'

As he said this, Bruno suddenly recalled the big guy in uniform who'd made that nasty remark about country cops and sheep shaggers in the police canteen.

9

Back at the *commissariat de police* in Périgueux early that evening, Bruno collected a fat file of photocopies of J-J's original inquiry into Oscar's death and took a lift back to St Denis in Yveline's car. He turned down Yveline's offer to join her and Sabine for dinner, thinking it would be better to let the two women establish their own rapport. It was too late to join the evening ride at Pamela's but he went there to collect Balzac and then drove home. He took Balzac for a long walk along the ridge as dusk deepened. He made himself an omelette and a salad from the garden and called Pamela to say he'd see her the next morning to exercise the horses and he'd bring croissants. After a less than illuminating hour or so with J-J's files, Bruno made a final check of the chicken coop, drank a last glass of red wine from the town vineyard and went to bed for an early night.

He woke just before six after a solid eight hours' sleep and took Balzac for a long run through the woods. In St Denis by seven, he picked up a bag of warm croissants and two baguettes from Café Fauquet just as it opened. Soon afterwards, he was at Pamela's riding school, where he collected a hatful of fresh eggs. He let himself into the kitchen and heard the shower running upstairs. He put the kettle on for coffee, set out cups and plates and began halving and squeezing oranges. The kettle boiled so he made coffee. After a moment he heard her voice from upstairs, 'Is that you, Bruno? I can see Balzac at the stables and I can smell coffee.'

'It's me and breakfast is ready unless you want a boiled egg.'

'I'd love one and I can see Gilles and Fabiola coming up the lane. Better put two more eggs on.'

He put four eggs into a pan he filled with boiling water and set the alarm for five minutes. He took butter and a jar of Pamela's home-made apricot jam from the fridge, added two more cups, plates and egg cups and began squeezing more oranges.

'There's nothing like a breakfast someone else has made for you,' she said, kissing him lightly. 'It feels like being in a hotel.' She sat down and began pouring out orange juice as Gilles and Fabiola arrived. Bruno put the kettle on for more coffee.

'I have news,' he announced. 'Balzac's a father: nine pups, four boys, five girls, all doing well. I went up to the kennels yesterday to see them. I'm going to ask Florence if she'd like one for the twins.'

'Don't mention it in front of them or they'll give her no rest until she gives in,' said Fabiola. 'Gilles and I were saying the other day that we'd be interested but we can't agree whether we want a boy basset or a girl.'

'There's no hurry,' Bruno said. 'Apparently Balzac is a much grander pedigree than I thought and he's been such a success that the kennels want him back again to father another litter in a few months. If you can't agree this time, you'll have another chance.'

They ate quickly and within ten minutes they were trotting

past the paddock, each with an unsaddled horse on a leading rein. Pamela took them along one of the shorter routes since each of the horses would be working later in the day. She restricted them to a canter, a pace so measured that even Balzac could very nearly keep up. But it was also a pace too slow for Bruno to lose himself in the thrill of Hector's speed and the insistent rhythm of his hooves. He found himself thinking of the way Sabine had stood at the door of her father's nursing home, sobbing quietly with her back to them; the way J-J had told Tante-Do that she had no choice but to surrender to his determination to pursue a case that had never lost its grip on him. At what point, Bruno asked himself, does long-delayed justice, inflicting so much pain as it grinds through the innocent lives of others, start to become absurd?

'What is it, Bruno?' Pamela asked when they were back at the stables, after Fabiola and Gilles had departed. 'You're miles away, distracted. I thought you said all the puppies were fine.'

'It's not that,' he said, looking out through the stable door, barely aware of her behind him. 'It's this case that's been on J-J's mind for the last thirty years. There's been a small breakthrough and he's determined to see it through but I fear it's not going to lead anywhere. And it's my fault, really. I had this idea when I saw the exhibition at Les Eyzies of faces rebuilt from the original skull. I got his hopes up and the more I think about it, the more I wonder whether we should have just left it alone. This damn investigation has already started eating away at people.'

He let out a long sigh. 'Sorry, I shouldn't have said all that. Shouldn't offload it all onto you.'

'We're not just friends, Bruno,' she said. He heard a jangling as the bridles dropped to the floor and she came up behind him, wrapped her arms around him and buried her face in his neck. He could hardly hear her, had to strain to catch the muffled words.

'We have a history, you and I, so you can share stuff with me all you want. Lord knows I dumped more than enough on you, about my mother, and about that sad mistake of a husband I had.' She squeezed him hard. 'Let's go and make some more coffee.'

She took his hand and pulled him along behind her, the pair of them clomping over the courtyard, still in their riding boots. There was the sound of a car, and then a cheerful toot-toot of a car horn as Miranda, waving cheerfully, drove her kids off to school.

'I ought to be there, seeing the kids across the street,' he said.

'You know you're probably the last cop in France who still sees children across the road, but you don't have to do it today. Come and have some coffee, and you can just guess what Miranda's thinking we're up to, seeing me haul you across the yard like this.'

In spite of his sombre mood, he laughed and hugged her tightly.

'You're a very fine woman, Pamela. And thank you. But no coffee. Duty calls.' He turned back to the stables, pulled off his riding boots, sluiced his face with water and headed off to see Joe, his predecessor as the town policeman of St Denis, and the man who had called in a very young J-J thirty years ago when a body had been found buried in the woods.

Joe kept goats, geese, chickens and bred pigeons. He fed his large extended family from a vegetable garden that was fenced more securely than some prisons to stop the goats from invading it. He also made the worst wine Bruno had drunk since his days in the army. But he had taught Bruno how to be a neighbourhood cop and he still knew everybody in the town and around it. He lived in a small hamlet a couple of kilometres outside St Denis and Bruno found him in his garden, installing taller sticks to support his tomato plants. He turned at Bruno's call and came to the fence, opened the gate and then secured it, shook hands with Bruno and gave Balzac an affectionate pat.

'What can I do for you, Bruno?'

'Not sure it'll help,' Bruno began, 'but could you take me to that spot where you found the body all those years ago? That cold case has warmed up.'

'I can probably find it if you tell me what this is about,' Joe said, steering Bruno to a chair in the courtyard and then going into the kitchen to bring out two glasses and a murky bottle of his own *eau de vie*. At least it was better than his wine. He poured out two slugs and Bruno explained about the DNA, the dead soldier in Mali, his half-sister and their mother's best friend.

'I want to get a feel for the place where the killing happened, try and bring it into focus in my mind,' Bruno said. 'And then I'd be grateful if you would come with me and talk to the people who ran the campsite at the time. I know their son who runs it now, but the older ones are just acquaintances. Maybe they might recall something.'

'Do you have any photos of these two girls who stayed at the campsite?'

'I can get them.' He pulled out his mobile, called J-J, and asked him to email the wedding photos of Sabine's parents to his phone.

'They aren't very good, a wedding photo of one of the girls, with her *demoiselle d'honneur*.'

'Maybe you should talk to Philippe Delaron, see if his father left any copies of the photos he took of the *félibrée*. It was a big affair for St Denis and the Mairie paid old Delaron to take photos of the entire event, for local press and for the town records. The Mairie made an exhibition of the photos that was very popular and Philippe's dad made a small fortune selling prints of people. Find those old photos and you might find the girls and their boyfriends.'

Bruno sat up, excited to hear this. 'That would be terrific, if they still exist. But when Philippe closed the camera shop I think he cleared out a lot of old stuff so he could rent the place out. Still, it's worth a try.'

His phone gave a double buzz, the sign of incoming email. He opened the attachment and saw the wedding photo. He zoomed in with his fingers to get a close-up of the bride and her maid of honour and showed it to Joe, who first went inside for his reading glasses.

'Pretty girls,' he said, squinting. 'You would think I'd remember them but it's been thirty years and there were a lot of people at that *félibrée*. I can't say they ring any bells but let's go down to the campsite and into the woods.'

They took Bruno's van, Balzac grumbling at his usual place on the passenger seat being usurped, parked at the busy campsite and Bruno went into the office to greet Hilaire, the owner, explain his mission and to ask if Hilaire's parents were around. He was told they'd be at home. Hilaire promised to call them and say Bruno would be coming to see them.

Joe led the way to the back of the campsite which looked full at this time in the holiday season, to be confronted by a sturdy fence and thick hedge. That was new, he observed. In his day it had been more of a token boundary of wooden posts with two planks nailed between each post, easy to climb in or out. They walked back to the entrance and around the side and then up the wooded hillside, Joe moving like a man thirty years younger despite the undergrowth.

'Ten euros a night per person these days, even with a tiny tent, so I imagine there'll still be people camping *sauvage* and finding a way to sneak into the dances,' he said when he paused for breath and looked around, as if hoping to see landmarks.

'We were up here often enough at the time, you'd think I'd remember . . .' he said, and then his eye caught an outcrop of rock and headed for it and paused at the small and soggy hollow below it. 'The stream trickled through there, that's why the ground is damp. But I don't see where it goes out. It just seems to disappear into the ground.'

'It's a hot summer,' said Bruno, wiping his brow and the back of his neck.

'Worse than hot,' Joe said. 'It reminds me of the *canicule*, that heatwave back in '03 when so many old people died in the cities. But I can't think when I last saw a stream just disappear, and this little bog is about the only damp spot I've seen. Look, tiny footprints in the mud, voles and mice looking for water. And the undergrowth is all dry as a bone.'

They clambered up another slope beside the rock, hauling themselves on young trees that wouldn't even have been saplings thirty years ago, and came to an overgrown bank. A large scoop had been taken, or perhaps dug out of it, a place that was now filled with dry bracken. That was another sign of drought, thought Bruno. Bracken normally didn't die off until the autumn.

'That dip in the ground is where we found the body,' Joe said, pointing. They walked along the face of the bank for perhaps twenty metres and came to a sheltered, flat stretch of grass, maybe six or seven metres square. Against the bank was a small ring of stones enclosing charred earth and ashes. Bruno noticed that the ashes were dry but there had been no rain for weeks.

'Looks like that fireplace is still being used,' he said. 'It's a good job they sheltered the fire. It wouldn't take much to set all this dry stuff alight.'

Joe nodded and pointed to a square patch where the grass was paler. 'Somebody had a tent there very recently. Nice to know the old traditions don't change. I remember J-J going all over this area with metal detectors. All he found was an old tin opener and a camping spoon.'

Bruno went back to the spot where the body had been found, clambered up onto the top of the bank and looked around, trying to imprint the scene on his memory, to allow for the increased girth of the nearest big trees and mentally to erase the new growth around the scene. He knew it was hopeless but he kept trying to force his imagination to see the place as it had been. It was a calm but brooding spot, only a few scattered rays of sunlight coming through the thick and multi-layered canopy of the trees.

Usually in a place like this he'd expect the air to be heavy with the smell of moist earth and vegetation. Instead, the air seemed almost dusty. As Bruno moved to one side his foot caught on something and he bent down to find an old stake buried in the ground, the kind that might have been used to secure a tent rope. He pulled it out and it came with a short length of dirty plastic ribbon. He could still make out the stripes of white and red that had been used to mark off a crime scene.

'Where you're standing is where J-J set up his base,' Joe said. He was casting round, poking at the low undergrowth with a stick.

'What are you looking for?' Bruno asked.

'I'm trying to find the tracks. J-J persuaded the gendarmes to let him use a forklift truck. That's how they got the body out. It's hard to find anything after all this time. Thirty years of leaf fall and rotting branches have put a whole new layer of soil over everything.'

'J-J said he found a couple of fireplaces and a latrine. Do you recall where they were?'

'The latrine was off to the side of the campsite and a bit downhill. They found it with the metal detector because they'd put their empty cans of food down there before filling it in. One of the fireplaces was pretty much where you saw the current one but I forget where the other one was.'

'Anything else you recall, anything that strikes you, jogs your memory? It must have been a big moment for you, a lot of press interest, tourists coming to watch all the police activity.'

'Yes, we set up a perimeter at the bottom of the hill for crowd control but the gendarmes did that. After the first day J-J sent me round asking the local hunters and mushroom and truffle pickers if any of them knew the area, if they'd seen anything.'

'I don't see any green oaks or hazelnuts so I wouldn't expect truffles around here,' said Bruno.

'There's the odd hornbeam and you can find truffles around them. I saw one or two on the way up here with the blackened ground around the trunks. I might come up here with the dog, see if there are any *estivales* here. They don't mind the earth being dry.'

Estivales, or summer truffles, were not greatly prized but they could flavour a mild olive oil or make truffle butter. Bruno sometimes used very thin slices on top of a salad or pasta, or to help give some taste to the usually flavourless white mushrooms sold by supermarkets, the *champignons de Paris*.

'Thanks for showing this to me,' Bruno said. 'Let's go back and visit Hilaire's parents. They may have something.'

The old couple, who greeted Joe with affection, had prepared their living room for the arrival of guests. Coffee cups, side plates and small glasses were lined up on a coffee table in the middle of a square formed by the fireplace, a sofa, two armchairs and a big TV set that was screening some daytime soap opera. Hilaire's dad, Antoine, used his remote control to lower the sound and his wife brought in a plate of *gâteau aux noix* and coffee.

'Usually we'd go outside but it's too hot today, even with the parasol,' she said. 'I suppose it's this global warming they go on about.'

'You're very kind,' said Bruno, as Antoine filled the tiny glasses from a bottle of Vieille Prune, a plum brandy that Bruno recognized from Hubert's wine *cave*.

'I don't know how we can help,' Antoine said. 'We spent hours being questioned by that young detective at the time but we really couldn't help him. He went through the list of our bookings for that week but there weren't many credit cards in those days. It was a cash business and the people who bothered to book would call up and often just used their first names. The police tried tracking them down but got nowhere. It wasn't like these days where you have to give a credit card number when you book and give identity cards and passport numbers. It all has to be accounted for and documented now.'

'You can't get away with anything on the taxes any more,' Joe said with a chuckle. 'It's the same with that cottage we rent out to tourists. It all has to be registered with the Mairie.'

Bruno ignored Joe's comment and spoke to Antoine. 'I've read the statement you gave the police at the time. You said you knew that people who were camping *sauvage* would often come in to use your bathrooms and the bar but you never kept track of them. Why was that?'

'It was just me and Mathilde and our peak time was the school holidays so she had her hands full with our children. I couldn't afford extra staff,' Antoine said. 'And the bathrooms were coin operated, a one franc piece to use the toilets, another franc for the communal showers so it wasn't as though it was free. It wasn't just the *sauvage* campers but other tourists would come in to spend money at the bar and buy snacks, and they used the little shop we had for bread and milk and basic foodstuffs. There was no way of keeping track of them all. You didn't have to back then. I think the government was behind all the credit card business so they could track everything to tax it, as if they don't take enough.'

'Did you bring any souvenirs with you when you left?' Bruno asked. 'Photo albums, that sort of thing?'

'The police looked through the ones we had but they were mainly family snapshots, when we were building the site, the children growing up, that kind of thing.'

'Do have some cake,' Mathilde said, pressing the plate on the visitors. Bruno and Joe each took a slice of walnut cake. She turned to her husband. 'Had we started that camper-of-the-week business back then?'

'What was that?' Bruno asked.

'It was something we put up on the noticeboard every week; a photo I took of one the campers doing something,' her husband said. 'There was a guy who caught a big fish in the river, another one who was a bodybuilder and used to lift weights, kids playing with animals or some guy playing a guitar – that kind of thing. It was a friendly gesture, something to give a sense of community and to get the campers to pay attention to the noticeboard.'

'And you'd make a few francs selling prints to people,' said Mathilde. 'Being you, you'd always take a snap of a pretty girl.'

Bruno's ears picked up. 'Did you keep any copies of these pictures?'

'I did,' said Mathilde. 'Nostalgia. I kept them all in a box and then when we retired I started sticking them into a couple of scrapbooks. Would you like to see them? They're all dated. I put the week they were taken on the back of each print.'

'I'd be grateful to see the ones for '89,' said Bruno. 'You remember the time of the *félibrée*? That was when we think the murder took place.'

Mathilde said she'd just be a moment. She went into another room and came back with a large scrapbook, about the size of a tabloid newspaper.

'This is the first year we did these photos of our camper of the week.' She leafed through a few pages. 'Here, that's the week of the *félibrée*, with some pictures Antoine took of the town. You know how they covered the streets with paper flowers, or maybe plastic. It looked so pretty and it gave a bit of shade. It was a hot summer. And Hilaire was starting to use the camera so there are some of his photos in there as well.'

She handed the scrapbook to Bruno, who was sitting alongside Joe on the sofa. Joe immediately found a photo of his much younger self looking rather sour as he stood beside a stage where a woman seemed to be singing.

'I remember that,' Joe said, smiling. 'She was singing some old Occitan song and she had a terrible voice.'

He leafed through photos of people in traditional local dress, surprisingly puritan to Bruno's eye, mainly black and white with the odd scarf or sash to add a touch of colour. There were more photos of peasant dances, and then the campers of the week, each with a tiny pin hole at each corner where they must have been tacked to the noticeboard. There was a young man playing a recorder, a toddler trying to ride on a patient-looking dog, and then a pretty girl whom Bruno recognized.

It was a close-up of the head and shoulders of a tanned, slim and very attractive young woman in a bathing suit, or perhaps the top half of a bikini. She was standing by the side of the swimming pool, some of the bathers visible as they stood in the shallow end, watching her being photographed. Her head was turned a little to one side and she was giving a broad smile or she might have been laughing.

Bruno pulled out his phone, called up the wedding photo J-J had sent him, and showed it to Mathilde.

'Would you say this was the same woman?' he asked her, pointing to the image of Dominique.

'Yes, I think it is. I'm almost sure of it and I think I remember her, always very cheerful, always on the dance floor. I think she was a hairdresser because I remember her showing different styles to some of the other girls. And we nearly used another photo of her, cutting some young man's hair. He was blond but his skin hadn't gone red – he was tanned. A good-looking boy.'

'Would you have any more photos of her, like the one with the young man, or did you keep just this one?'

'Just that one, I think. We didn't keep the ones we didn't use.'

Bruno turned to the next few pages. There was an old man fast asleep in a deckchair, an empty bottle of wine beside him; a toddler looking intently at a hedgehog that had rolled into a ball; a boy juggling oranges. He leafed through to the end of the book but there was nothing else that caught his eye. He turned back to the image of Dominique.

You say you recall her being cheerful. Do you remember anything about her friends, the people she was with?'

'She had a girlfriend she was always with, I think they shared a tent.'

'Do you have a magnifying glass I might use?' he asked, turning back to Dominique's photo.

Mathilde left the room again and came back with a small magnifying glass. 'Here you are. My eyesight isn't what it was.'

Bruno studied the bathers in the pool behind Dominique. There was a young woman who looked like Sabine's mother standing in front of a young man, his muscular arms wrapped around her and his face half-buried in her neck. He had blond hair and was very tanned. He examined the other bathers but none of them looked at all relevant, mainly families with their children.

'Would you mind if I borrowed this to make some copies and blow them up? I'll make sure you get it back but the detective needs to see this. I think this might be the murdered man.'

'Not very good of him, is it?' Mathilde said, taking the scrapbook and the glass. 'You can't see much of his face.'

'It's more than we've found so far,' said Bruno.

'I stuck it down so you'd have to take the whole page,' she objected.

'I think the police can afford to buy you a new scrapbook if you let me borrow this one. I can scan it in the office and then bring it back. It might give me a chance to have some more of your delicious walnut cake.'

10

Bruno dropped Joe off at his house and drove on to the Mairie, scanned the photo of the young Tante-Do and Sabine's mum onto his desk computer and sent a copy to J-J with a note identifying the happy couple in the pool behind Dominique. Yves, the forensics chief, would have some computer wizardry to blow up the detail. He printed out two more versions, one for him and the other for Sabine. Then he called Philippe Delaron, who was on his way back after photographing a couple in Les Eyzies who were celebrating their joint hundredth birthday. They arranged to meet at Fauquet's.

'I'm going to have to install air conditioning if these summers go on like this,' said Fauquet, bringing a welcome glass of cold beer to Bruno's shaded table on the terrace. 'If it wasn't for the ice creams, I'd go broke.'

Bruno had only taken his first, long swallow when Philippe arrived. 'Unless this is urgent, Bruno, I'll have to go to the office to send these snaps back to the paper. They're for one of the pages that gets printed early. Then later this afternoon I have to go and photograph the *pompiers* doing some new training to deal with forest fires. The Prefect has put out an alert.'

'I wanted to see if you can track down those photos your dad took of the *félibrée* thirty years ago. I remember you telling me he kept everything. Time for a very quick beer?'

'Gladly.' Bruno signalled the order to Fauquet. 'That's true, he did. But I didn't. I had to clear out the shop when we started renting it out. I only kept the stuff I knew would make money, like those photo books of old St Denis they sell in the tourism office. Wedding and baptism photos I kept, because a lot of people lose them and want to buy them again. I offered all the rest to the Mairie. You know how the Mayor loves anything historical, but he didn't take much.'

'What about the *félibrée* photos?'

'There was a whole box of that stuff, Dad must have shot rolls. That was one thing the Mayor took but lord knows what he did with it. And if the box was stored in that old basement, you remember it got flooded. They could be ruined.'

'What did you give them, negatives or prints? The prints might be gone but the negatives could be okay.'

'Both, because the Mairie had paid him by the day for covering the *félibrée* so they were the legal owners. Dad was pretty thorough, so the negative rolls were put back into sealed plastic canisters and each of the prints had its own plastic cover. Maybe they survived.'

'Did you hang onto any of the *félibrée* photos?

'Yes, I selected the best because next time we have a *félibrée* here, I'll put out a photo book of the last one. I've saved maybe a hundred and twenty prints, possibly more.'

'I'd like you to look them out for me and I'll come by your office once I've checked with the Mayor.'

'What's this about, Bruno?'

'Can't tell you yet but there may be a good story in it for *Sud Ouest* and you'll be the first to know. I'll give you a clue. Did you shoot that exhibition that's now on at the museum in Les Eyzies?'

'The woman who rebuilds faces from prehistoric skulls? Yes, I was there at the opening reception when you were. I even got a shot of you and the artist and Clothilde chatting together.'

Bruno saw a blank look in Philippe's eyes as his mind began working overtime, looking for a connection. Maybe he'd given Philippe too strong a hint but so far nobody but the investigating team knew of any connection between the dead man and the *félibrée*.

'The beer's on me,' Bruno said, rising and leaving a five euro note on the table before climbing the stairs of the Mairie. The Mayor recalled getting the *félibrée* photos from Philippe but was not quite sure where they had been stored. Claire brought him the registry book for the archives. He leafed through, running his finger down each page before looking up.

'It went first to the basement but when we had the flood alert I had most of that stuff shifted up to the new registry behind the Trésor Public. I'll give the Treasurer a call to say you're coming.'

'Tell him I won't be alone. There are a lot of rolls of film, thirty-six images each, so I'm going to need help from Sabine, the gendarme from Metz whose half-brother was fathered by Oscar. She's been attached to Yveline's gendarmerie.'

'Bring her to the Mairie at some point so I can say hello and give her my condolences on her brother's death. Off you go, and I'll call the Treasurer.'

Bruno called Yveline, who answered brusquely. 'Bruno, where have you been? I've sent you a couple of texts.'

Bruno felt instantly guilty. He tried to be good at answering emails but he'd never yet learned to make his phone an extension of himself and seldom bothered to check for text messages.

'Sorry, I was out in the woods at the murder scene so I didn't get a signal. How's Sabine and what are you up to?'

'We're in Les Eyzies, with your colleague Juliette. I've been showing Sabine around our beat and we ran into her and are having coffee. What's up?'

'Can you meet me at the Trésor Public archive in St Denis? I'm going to need your and Sabine's help. We've a lot of *félibrée* photos to look through but I think we might have a lead. There's no great hurry, the photos will wait, and give my best regards to Juliette.'

'OK, we'll be with you in twenty minutes.'

Bruno went to Philippe's office, the ground floor of a small terraced house at the far end of the Rue de Paris. Philippe lived upstairs, and rented out the neighbouring house that had been his father's and grandfather's camera shop until the coming of mobile phones had overtaken the family business. Fortunately for Philippe, he'd already started taking sports photos for *Sud Ouest* and quickly turned it into a full-time job as regional correspondent for the whole valley, from Le Buisson up to Montignac. He and Bruno had a complicated relationship of mutual dependence that made them part-allies and part-adversaries. Bruno had the stories and Philippe had the means of publicity so each found the other useful. They also liked each other, which helped. Bruno had kept the teenage Philippe out of trouble over a youthful escapade that involved a stolen car that had been crashed. Philippe and his friends had to work for months to pay off the owner and the garage.

'Here are the prints I've saved for the *félibrée* book,' said Philippe, handing Bruno a cardboard box. 'Did you track down the others?'

'Thanks, Philippe. The Mayor saved the others in the archives and even kept them dry. I'll tell you as much as I can as soon as I can. In the meantime, keep this to yourself but if this works out we'll probably be coming to you for a publicity campaign. Have fun with the *pompiers* and give them my best. If I've got time, I might drop by to watch this training for forest fires.'

'Did you see the weather forecast?' Philippe asked. 'They say this heatwave is going to last into August.'

'The tourists will love it. Thanks, Philippe.'

'Here's something you might need,' Philippe said, reaching into a pocket and handing Bruno a loupe. 'Screw it into your eye socket and you get good magnification while your other eye can see the wider context. But I'll want it back and take good care of it – it was my father's.'

The town treasurer, a fellow member of the hunting club, saw that Bruno could hardly shake hands while carrying the box, so he patted him on the back before showing him into the long room at the back of the treasury building that contained the archives. He showed Bruno how to use the catalogue that identified where each item was to be found by row and shelf number. There were copies of registrations for births, marriages and deaths going back to the nineteenth century, property tax records and handwritten annual reports from local officials.

There were even old *cadastre* maps that went back to before the French Revolution, showing who had owned every plot of land in the commune. Testing the system, he looked up the reports by the town policemen that went back to Napoleon's day, when such officials were called *garde champêtre*, a rural guard. Joe's reports were also here, but not Bruno's. Since he was the current holder of the post, Bruno's reports for the past decade were kept in the Mayor's office. Bruno made a mental note to come back and glance through all this stuff one day.

Bruno knew the Mayor had planned the archive system, not only for the convenience of the town administration but also for his own purposes. He was writing the definitive history of St Denis, dating from the Neanderthals who were buried at La Ferrassie seventy thousand years ago and the Cro-Magnons who had engraved bears and mammoths on the walls of a local cave. His account went on through the Bronze and Iron Age peoples, the Romans, the Arab invasion, Charlemagne's visit, the three centuries of the English occupation, the Wars of Religion and all the way through to modern times. The last Bruno had heard, the Mayor was about to tackle the period of the French Revolution.

'You'll find the photographs at the far end on the left,' the Treasurer said and handed Bruno the key. Bruno glanced around, saw a large table with two chairs and more chairs stacked against the wall. That would do. But he'd need a table lamp.

'Commandante Yveline from the gendarmes will be joining me shortly,' he said. 'Might you have a magnifying glass and a table lamp we could use?'

'Of course, Bruno. But what's all this about?'

The Treasurer seemed as keen as Philippe to be the first to pick up the latest gossip. Bruno smiled and said, 'It's a matter of identifying someone. I'm sure the Mayor will let you know the details when he can.'

Bruno first found the box with all the negatives and beside them three larger boxes of prints covering all three weekdays of the *félibrée* plus another two boxes for each of the weekend days. He'd just finished carrying them to the desk at the front of the room when Yveline and Sabine came in, carrying a magnifying glass and a table lamp.

He kissed Yveline on both cheeks and shook hands with Sabine.

'I have a present for you,' he said, and took out the print he'd made of the photo from the campsite. 'Look behind Tante-Do at the couple in the swimming pool.'

'Oh, it's Mum,' Sabine exclaimed. 'And she's looking so happy and beautiful. Can I keep this when we're done?' She beamed at him. 'Thank you, Bruno, that's terrific.'

'See the guy embracing your mum with most of his face hidden?' Bruno said. 'I think that's Max, your brother's biological father. And now I have nearly two thousand photos of the *félibrée* to go through. We're looking for your mum and Tante-Do and hoping to find them with these two men, Max and Henri.

'We need to organize how we do this,' he went on. 'I have a box that contains about a hundred and fifty of the best photos, selected by the photographer's son. I'll start with that. I suggest that you two start on the box with the photos from the weekdays, and one of you skims each print for any sign of your mum and Tante-Do. Then the other looks at it with the magnifying glass to see if there are young men with them. That's what we're looking for, images of Max and Henri. Pay special attention to Thursday evening, when they all met at some dance. And please be sure to keep them in order or we'll be lost. When I've gone through the selection, I'll take the Friday box and you two can take the Saturday.'

They got to work, Bruno with the loupe screwed into his eye, the two gendarmes side by side, Yveline making the first scan and then Sabine examining each chosen print with the magnifying glass. Bruno was halfway through the box of Philippe's selections, with six of the photos to one side for closer perusal, when Sabine said, 'I think I've got something.'

Bruno and Yveline crowded around her to examine a print of a musician in a black hat playing a very old-fashioned musical instrument with a crowd around him, Tante-Do and Sabine's mum in the front row. There was a man behind Tante-Do with his arm around her shoulders, only half of his face visible. Behind Sabine's mum was a man bending down and only his eyes and forehead could be seen.

'That's a good one,' said Bruno. 'Put it to one side.' He handed Sabine a business card. 'Paperclip that to it and note the date it was taken. We'll need a system to identify each of these shots – let's call this one the musician.'

They got back to work and towards the end of his batch, Bruno found an image of people dancing and there was a decent shot of Sabine's mum facing the camera. Her eyes were focused on a taller, fair-haired man who seemed to be dancing with her. His face was in profile.

'Here's one,' he said and the others crowded round. Philippe's selected prints were not dated but he scribbled 'Dance scene, Mum and Max,' on a card as Sabine and Yveline examined the print. Meanwhile, Bruno went through the rest of the selection, picking out two possibles and showing them to the others.

'There's Mum, moving out of the photo but is she holding hands with the blond guy behind her?' asked Sabine. 'I think that might be Max.'

Bruno finished Philippe's selection and began to attack the box of prints for Friday. They worked on together and by the end of their session, they had seven photos with more or less clear images of the two young women with their young men. To Bruno's disappointment, there was no single clear image of either of the men's faces but they had profiles and half faces, eyes and brows, ears and hands for each one.

He suggested they examine the possibles again, one by one, which resulted in one shot of Sabine's mother kissing Max's nose and giving a clear image of his mouth and chin. If he assembled the various photos, Yves at forensics should be able to put together a complete face. Henri, however, remained elusive. They had his eyes and forehead, his profile, his hands and a shot of the back of his head. There were no scars, no tattoos or any other distinguishing marks. Still, Bruno thought, Yves should be able to put something together.

'This is amazing,' said Sabine with a catch in her voice as she scanned again through the various photos of Max. 'That's my brother's chin and his eyes and even his hands. There's really no doubt in my mind that he's my brother's father. I'm sure of it.'

'Let's go through the possibles for Henri one more time,' said

Yveline. 'But this time we'll go through the Friday ones you looked at, Bruno, and you go through the others.'

They went back to work for another hour and came up with one photo that Bruno had missed of a group of people dancing. Tante-Do had her back to the camera with Henri facing her, his nose and eyes obscured by one of her arms but his mouth and jaw were clear.

'That should be enough for forensics to put together images of each man,' said Bruno, much relieved.

'This calls for a drink,' said Yveline. 'The Gendarmerie is a stone's throw from here and I have some wine in my apartment there.'

'Good idea,' said Bruno. 'Just let me draft a receipt for each of the photos I'm taking. I could do with a drink after that intense concentration. Do you realize we've been at it for nearly four hours? No wonder my eyes feel tired.'

'It's not like we've cracked the case,' said Sabine. 'We can put together a couple of images of two unknown guys, one of whom was murdered by a blow to the head, probably on the Saturday night. But we aren't sure that it was then that he was killed, rather than later. We don't know his real name nor where he was from. And if we can't prove when exactly he was killed, we certainly don't know by whom. There's no proof Henri was the killer.'

'You're right,' said Bruno. 'But Max was buried here near the St Denis campsite so he was probably killed there. And if it wasn't Henri who killed him, why didn't Henri report the death instead of just disappearing? Even if Henri was not the killer, we need to talk to him.'

'We're a long way further down the trail, Sabine, than we were when you arrived from Metz,' said Yveline. I thought then that this was the longest of long shots and that we were simply indulging J-J's obsession. Now we have a possible suspect, a face, a name, and a witness who can place him at the right place and probably within the relevant time frame.'

'We have thirty-year-old bits of a face, a false name, and a witness who saw no crime being committed,' said Sabine.

'We have more than we started with but a lot less than we need, which is not unusual for this stage of an investigation,' said Bruno, who was still sorting prints. He swivelled in his chair to face them. 'But we know the next step, which is to wait for forensics to put the photos together and then see where we are.'

'If Tante-Do says the face looks right,' Yveline was saying, 'then J-J can run it through the facial recognition software against known offenders, ID cards, driving licences, passports, the lot.'

'We'll need a magistrate and a court order to do that,' said Sabine.

'That's for J-J to handle,' Yveline replied. 'This is his case and he really wants it wrapped up and done. He can fix it.'

Bruno watched this exchange, struck that he'd never seen two women cops thinking through a case before, arguing but in an amiable and positive way without regard to their different ranks. It was refreshing when he compared it to the close but often stormy relationship he shared with J-J. Bruno knew his friendship with J-J could never have prospered if he'd been in J-J's chain of command, as Sabine was under Yveline. Knowing that Sabine had already qualified for the two-year course that would make her an officer, Yveline had treated her as such, even though Sabine had been a simple gendarme only a week or so earlier; whereas Sabine treated Yveline more as a slightly older sister than a superior.

Over the past year or more, Bruno had watched Yveline rebuild the small squad of gendarmes at St Denis after her predecessor, a pompous but incompetent officer, had almost destroyed their morale. Yveline had had the good sense to make an ally of the veteran Sergeant Jules, whom Bruno had long befriended through the hunting club. Overweight and close to retirement but experienced and a shrewd judge of people, Jules was loyal to those superiors he judged deserving of his support. He gave Yveline his full backing and a great deal of discreet advice. In return, Yveline had helped Sergeant Jules maintain his long rearguard action against being posted elsewhere. Bruno knew that without Sergeant Jules's friendship, his own task in St Denis would have faced many more obstacles. These days in St Denis, Yveline's gendarmes, Bruno as the town policeman and his Mayor, along with the Police Nationale represented by J-J at Périgueux, all worked together in unusual harmony.

'I think we have to wait and see what J-J says when Yves has done his work with the photos,' Bruno said. 'We may not have a murderer, but we've come a long way towards identifying the victim, which J-J has been trying to do for three decades. Let's see where we go from there. Yveline is right. We've certainly earned a drink.'

They returned the key and receipts to the treasurer and Bruno took the cardboard box of negatives. The three of them walked up the slight rise to the stucco-fronted building with the flaming grenade escutcheon of the gendarmes. Yveline told the duty officer she'd be in her rooms. Then she led the way through the yard to the apartment block behind, where she punched in the access code at the entrance door. Gendarmes had traditionally lived in barracks, but since the 1960s they had been housed in these newly built blocks where married gendarmes could live with their families.

Yveline, as *commandante* was housed in a two-bedroom apartment with a balcony on the first floor. The rooms weren't large, but she had made her home cheerful with sunny yellow walls covered with batik prints and masks from a holiday in Indonesia. The wooden floors of her living room had been sanded and covered with Persian rugs. Two Wassily armchairs of leather with chrome tubing faced an antique chaise longue. The rear wall was filled with shelves containing books, framed photos of her family and sporting career and a bar. In one corner was a TV set, in the other a small desk.

'Scotch, wine or beer?' she asked, taking glasses from the bar.

'White wine for me,' said Sabine. Mopping his brow from the heat, Bruno asked for his to be mixed with mineral water as a spritzer. Sabine then said she'd do the same, told Yveline she admired the way she'd done the room and asked to use the bathroom, adding that she knew the way. All gendarme housing was the same.

As Yveline poured the drinks, Bruno's phone buzzed. He opened it to find an email from Claire at the kennels, with three photos attached of Diane de Poitiers and her puppies. He examined them with delight. The first one was as he had seen them on the day of their birth but the next two were a day or so later and he could get an impression of their new energy and curiosity from the way they sprawled over and around, and crawled away from their mother. One was so near to the camera it was almost a close-up. He showed them to Yveline, and then to the returning Sabine and they cooed and enthused over the playful charm of the baby bassets.

'You remember I said I wanted one from when you first took Balzac to the kennels,' Yveline said. 'I looked up the kennel website and I know they cost about fifteen hundred each so I've been saving.'

'Boy or girl?' Bruno asked.

'I want a girl.'

Bruno gave her a broad smile. 'Done! But I'm not looking to make money out of this. I'm really happy that the puppy will be going to a good home and I'm sure Balzac will enjoy having his daughter around. I think I'll get a great deal more pleasure from seeing these happy bassets pottering around St Denis with equally happy owners.'

'It's a deal, so we can drink to that, even if Sabine's right and we're being premature about identifying Max and Henri.'

11

Just after dawn the next day, Bruno reached the tree at the top of the hill near his home. It was the point at which he usually turned on his morning run, pausing for a moment that allowed Balzac to catch up and for him to look across the Périgord landscape. From this vantage point there was not another house to be seen. Ridge succeeded valley and then more ridges all the way east as the land steadily rose to the extinct volcanoes of the Massif Central, the very heartland of France.

A snuffling at Bruno's feet made him bend to caress his dog, which reminded him that he should consult Florence about one of Balzac's puppies. He set off again down the long, shallow slope leading to a track that gave him an easy kilometre along level ground back to his home, to a shower and breakfast. Twenty minutes later he left for St Denis, to be ready to patrol the crossing over the main road from the post office to the Ecole Maternelle.

He was there some minutes before eight, chatting with various young mothers he'd known since they were schoolgirls and ruffling the hair of their toddlers as he saw them across the road. Florence and her children were among the last to arrive. Once they had crossed, he waved thanks to the cars that had stopped and then joined them, kissing Dora and Daniel first, then Florence. He took care to embrace her in the brief, courteous and evidently unromantic way customary among friends. As a highly eligible bachelor in St Denis, whose relationship with Pamela was rumoured to be ending, he did not want to excite any new speculation, even as his mind wandered back to that enthusiastic embrace she had given him when he taught her twins to swim. He would not easily forget that entrancing sight of her in her green bikini, and far less the feel of her body against his.

'Lovely to see you, Bruno,' she said, with an eager smile. 'But I'd better take the kids inside.'

'I'll wait,' Bruno said. 'I want to have a word, if you have a moment.'

'It's about Balzac,' he said when she returned. Her smile faded a little and she glanced at her watch, a reminder that the classes she taught at the *collège* started in a few minutes. They began walking to the bridge. 'You know I took him up to some kennels for a mating. Well, the puppies have been born and I wondered if you thought it would be a good idea for Dora and Daniel to have one.'

'That's very kind but I don't think I could afford—'

'It would be a gift, Florence. Christmas and birthday combined for both of them,' he said swiftly. 'I thought I'd consult you first, before saying anything to the children. I don't want to get their hopes up.'

'That's thoughtful of you, Bruno, thank you. Would you let me think about this for a day or two?'

'Of course, I know you have quite enough on your plate without having a puppy to housetrain.'

'It's not that, but I'm wondering whether we have enough space or garden, or the time to give him the attention he needs. It's quite a responsibility and the children are still rather young for that. But of course they'd love to have a basset puppy and so would I. You know how they adore Balzac.'

'That's why I suggested it,' he said. 'But it's up to you, and it does mean walking duties twice a day. Take your time. Balzac will have more puppies in the next few years so there's no hurry.'

'I understand but I'd hate to deprive the children of such a gift and it might even be good for them. I'd better sleep on it.' They'd reached the *collège*. 'I'm really touched that you thought of this.' She hugged him and went inside.

Bruno's eyes followed her and he thought he had not handled that well. But then his phone buzzed with an incoming message. As he pulled it from the pouch he felt the different vibration of an incoming call. He looked at the screen. It was J-J.

'I just sent you a copy of Yves' two composite pictures, one of Max and the other of Henri,' he said. 'They look very convincing to me. I'm waiting to hear back from Tante-Do to see what she thinks. If she says they're good, we can prepare to launch the media campaign. And Virginie says she should have Oscar's reconstructed face in a few days. The funny thing is, she refused to look at Yves' picture, saying it might influence her.'

'Good for her, and please send copies to Yveline and Sabine,' said Bruno. 'If you're going to release the photos through your press office, maybe you should send copies to Gilles. He said he'd try to do a piece for *Paris Match*.'

'Right. And let me know what you think when you see them.

For the moment I won't stand down the Strasbourg cops who've been going through old university records and class photos from the late 1980s, looking for two students called Max and Henri.'

Bruno called up the pictures, first Max and then Henri. He recognized in each parts of the various photos he'd sent to Yves but the compilations looked dramatically better, like real people. And the more he looked at Henri, the more he had a sense that he'd seen this man before, but when he was much older. The shape of the face and head and something in the eyes and mouth rang a distinct bell in Bruno's memory, and it was linked to St Denis. The man wasn't a resident but he'd visited the town within the last two or three years, Bruno was sure of it.

When could it have been? A market day, perhaps? Or at some cultural event or political meeting? As he closed his eyes to remember, Bruno could almost imagine hearing the man's voice, as though he'd exchanged words with him rather than just seen him passing by.

'What's happening to you?' came Pamela's voice and his eyes opened. 'You looked like you'd gone into a trance.'

She was carrying a shopping bag and he saw a big baguette and caught the delicious smell of fresh croissants. She must have been to the Moulin bakery nearby.

'I was trying to remember someone I know I've seen but I can't remember where.' He showed her the photo on his phone.

'I know what you mean,' she said. 'I get the same sense that I've seen him before, maybe at a market stall, or a *brocante*, trying to sell antiques, or a jumble sale – that sort of thing.

There are so many of these events it's hard to place him. Could it have been one of the antique book sales?'

None of them felt quite right to Bruno. He sent the Mayor a copy of Henri's photo, suggesting that he print it out and show it around the Mairie. No sooner had he done so than his phone buzzed again. Once more it was J-J to say that Tante-Do had declared Yves' composite photo to be the very image of her lover of thirty years ago.

'See if your friend Gilles can get that photo into *Paris Match*,' J-J went on. 'We've got our press office trying to get it on the TV news bulletins and promising them photos of Virginie's skull. And now is the time to use that local reporter of yours, Philippe. This is going to work, Bruno!'

Bruno thought it best to coordinate all this from his office so he kissed Pamela goodbye and went to the Mairie. There he called Gilles and Philippe before printing out an image of Henri larger than the one he had on his phone.

'Here's that story I promised you, Philippe,' he told Delaron. 'We've called in an expert who works with that woman you photographed at the museum who rebuilds faces from prehistoric skulls. She's currently building a face from the skull of a man who was murdered in St Denis thirty years ago. I can let you have a photo of the man and of a friend of his we very much want to interview, and we want you to run it in the paper tomorrow to see if anyone recognizes him. How does that sound as a story?'

'You mean you think he was the killer?'

'No, that would be premature. Let's just say we want to identify him very urgently.'

Philippe nodded and asked Bruno to make sure J-J let him into the police lab to photograph Virginie and her skull. He would leave for Périgueux right away.

No sooner had Bruno put down his desk phone than his mobile buzzed again. This time it was his cousin, Alain, saying that he'd managed to obtain a weekend leave pass for him and Rosalie. Would it be convenient for the pair of them to visit Bruno, arriving late this afternoon? Of course, Bruno replied automatically, not letting himself worry about what threatened to be a weekend consumed by the hunt for Henri. He'd make it work somehow. They had a car, there were caves to see and it was perfect weather for Alain and Rosalie to take a canoe trip down the Dordogne. He would prepare a welcome dinner Friday evening and on Saturday maybe visit the *marché nocturne* at Audrix, where they could buy their food and wine at the stalls and dine in the open air in the medieval square. The next call that interrupted him came from Sabine on her personal mobile, not from the Gendarmerie. She had just heard from Tante-Do about the photo of Henri. Had Bruno seen it? He told her he had. She sounded excited.

'The thing is, Tante-Do says it's him for sure. So what happens now?'

'J-J is organizing a media blitz, TV and newspapers, national and local, millions of eyeballs and all being asked the same question – do you know this man?'

'But do these things work? We'll get hundreds of false leads, all over France. The chances of this working can't be good.'

'It's a standard tool of police work and it has worked before. All those false leads will be checked, certainly, but we might just get the one we want. It's the best chance we have, Sabine.'

'What happens then?'

'Any good prospect will have to be seen in person by Tante-Do. If she still says this is the man, J-J will not only interrogate him round the clock, he'll go through the guy's life with a fine-tooth comb. J-J has been looking for this murderer for thirty years. He's got almost as much invested in this as you do.'

'Could this put Tante-Do in danger?' Sabine asked. 'I really wouldn't want that to happen. I couldn't live with myself . . .'

'J-J can organize a police guard for her, but we're not at that point yet, and you'll be with us every step of the way. J-J will listen to you. He's a good cop and a decent man.'

'There's something else. I'd like to know what I'm expected to do next, beyond introducing you to Tante-Do.'

He picked up Sabine's frustration; she was feeling under-used. 'I'll talk to him. I'm sure he has you in mind for the crucial phase, checking out the leads we get from the public and being there with Tante-Do when she verifies Henri's identity.'

'Right, I get it. I'm babysitting the key witness.'

'We wouldn't have her, if not for you, Sabine. Remember that.'

'Okay, Bruno, thanks. If there's anything I can do . . .'

'I'll let you know.' He stayed on the line for a moment, hoping for some clue as to her mood. He heard her sigh before she put down the phone. He must keep an eye on her. With a team of gendarmes to run, Yveline had only limited time for Sabine.

Bruno sighed too, making a note to call J-J about it. Then he sat back and considered what to cook for dinner with Alain and Rosalie. Since it was still so hot, he'd start with a cold soup and then a light main course. It was Friday and although he had no idea whether Rosalie was religious or not, French tradition still called for fish. They'd be eating outdoors so he could barbecue some trout or red mullet, or perhaps make something more ambitious with scallops and a creamy risotto flavoured with a grating of summer truffles. Bruno had all he needed in the garden for a salad but he might crumble some Roquefort over it instead of a separate cheese course. Nobody would want a heavy meal in this weather. For dessert he had some peaches in his garden.

This should be a family dinner, just the three of them, to give Bruno and Rosalie a chance to get to know each other. They were staying with him so nobody had to drive which meant they could enjoy the wines. He'd serve a kir royale for the apéritif, crème de cassis with a lovely local sparkling brut from Lestevenie that was in his fridge. Then a really good white wine, a cuvée Quercus from Pierre Desmartis at La Vieille Bergerie, ending with some Monbazillac that would match the strong cheese in the salad and would also go splendidly with the dessert.

If the Baron had been out fishing that morning he'd have told Bruno if the catch had been good. Today's market was in Le Buisson, just down the road, so Bruno drove there, removed his *képi* and went to the fishmonger who he knew had bought his stock that dawn at the Arcachon quayside and driven directly to the market. Standing in line, Bruno studied the fish spread out on the long, ice-packed counter with the centrepiece of a big fresh tuna, about twice the size of Balzac. He considered the cod and the plaice, the red mullet and the mackerel, thought briefly about the still-squirming crabs and scallops before finally deciding on the écrevisses.

They were the red American crayfish, originally from Louisiana, and they had almost completely replaced the traditional white-foot crayfish that were native to the Périgord. He selected two-thirds of a kilo and also a half-litre of the fishmonger's own fish stock. Then he went over to Stéphane's stall and bought some Roquefort and fresh cream. On the way back, he stopped at the Moulin bakery for a fat, round *tourte* of bread. Everything else he had already, either in his kitchen or in his garden. He was just parking outside the Mairie when his phone buzzed. It was Isabelle, calling from Paris.

'Thank you for the photos of the puppies,' she said. 'I think we can be very proud of our handsome Balzac. There's one that looks just like him when I first saw him at the kennels, and I don't know if I can resist getting him.'

'Not while you're in your current job, you can't,' he said. 'You'd spend half your time trying to find a puppy-sitter while you're off in Brussels or Berlin, and the rest of it worrying about whether he was eating right or getting enough walks. Still, it's good to hear your voice – it reminds me of that lovely weekend when we saw him start these puppies.'

'Yes, I know, and the same goes for me. That's not why I'm calling, though. A little bird in the media here tells us that *Le Monde* is running what could be a rather embarrassing op-ed on Sunday written by your friend Jacqueline. Do you know anything about it?'

'What's embarrassing about it?' he asked. 'It's no secret that the Americans don't share with us like they do with the British. And the Stasi business was a long time ago.'

'We have very long institutional memories,' she replied. 'And I see you know exactly what I'm talking about. Is there anything you can tell me?'

'Only that she and Jack Crimson were in Washington at a Cold War historians' conference on some East German intelligence dossier. Jacqueline is upset that the files were shared with the Germans and Scandinavians but not us. She thinks some French agents might have been recruited when they were young enough to still be in place today. There's a risk that they could have been blackmailed to work for the Russians, or even the Americans.'

'*Merde*, she must mean the Rosenholz dossier, so it's as bad as I feared.'

'Jack Crimson didn't seem too concerned about it.'

'Jack doesn't have a prima donna president who likes to think that he can have a special relationship with Washington, just like the Brits. Ever since Brexit, the Elysée has been dreaming of France becoming the Americans' key security partner in Europe, a geo-strategic coup that puts Paris back in the top rank.'

'With him as the essential go-between,' said Bruno. 'It's a fantasy. The British haven't been in the top rank since the end of World War Two.'

'Ah, but the British never claimed that they could speak for Europe. The Elysée thinks that we can.'

'And you?'

'I'm still a cop at heart, Bruno. I've learned to deal with

things as they are, not as they could be. Putting all that aside, Jacqueline's op-ed means that I have a problem. We've been talking discreetly with the Americans about sharing with us the Rosenholz dossier, and discussions are at a critical stage. If a political row blows up in Paris we'll go right back to zero. And don't tell me that it's just the price we pay for the benefits of a free press.'

Bruno sighed. 'Knowing Jacqueline, I really don't think there's anything I can do here that would not make matters worse. In fact, I'm going to add to your troubles. Gilles was there when Jacqueline spoke about it and he's doing a piece for *Paris Match*.'

'*Merde*,' she said. 'I guess we have to live with it.' Then her voice changed. 'It's good talking to you. Why not come up to Paris to see me this weekend with Balzac and forget all that. We can all curl up together and look at pictures of his puppies.'

'There's nothing I'd like more,' he said. 'But my cousin Alain, the only member of the family I'm close to, is arriving this evening with the woman he plans to marry.'

'Is that the one in the air force?'

'That's right, but he's getting out in a year or so, getting married and moving somewhere near here to start a new life as a teacher.'

He kept his voice cheerful, not mentioning that the key to the new life that Alain was hoping for was settling down with Rosalie to raise a family, something that Bruno increasingly feared would never happen to him. Listening to Isabelle's voice made it all the more poignant.

'You'll like that,' she said. 'I remember thinking when we

met him for lunch that day how close the two of you were, how much of a childhood you'd shared. So if we can't enjoy Paris together this weekend, let's plan one when this business with Rosenholz and with Oscar is all over. Promise?'

'Promise,' he said, thinking of her apartment just off the Boulevard Voltaire and recalling breakfasts in bed and later a light lunch by the Pont Ste Marie and taking the Metro to her favourite museum. She had shared it only with him, she had said; the Marmottan by the Bois de Boulogne, home to the paintings owned by Monet's family. 'I'll count the days.'

'Me too, and please send me lots more photos of the puppies.'

With the sound of a kiss, she ended the call. Bruno sat immobile for a long moment, hoping as he so often did, that there might be a crack in the wall that kept them apart; her craving for Paris and the promise of a glittering career, and his for the peace of the Périgord, his horse and dog, his home and his garden, and the embracing sweep of the Vézère as the river wound its way through the gentle hills and ancient caves around St Denis. But she would no longer be the vibrant, ambitious Isabelle if she came back here and he would no longer be Bruno if he left.

He took a deep breath, climbed out of the van and strolled halfway across the bridge to look down at the river. He could never remember having seen it so low, its flow feeble, its sandbanks filling more than half its width. He went back to the van and took out the crayfish, cheese and fish stock. They'd be spoiled if he didn't put them into the fridge at the Mairie while he went through his paperwork before going home to cook.

He turned, looking across the square at the Hôtel de Ville,

standing on its thick stone pillars, and known to all as the Mairie rather than by its formal name. The familiar noticeboard carried its usual announcements of forthcoming events, from the anglers' competition to the *bouquinistes*, the old books sale, from the Noir Vézère, the annual book fair of *polars*, as the French called crime novels, to the *vide-greniers* – the jumble sales. It was when he thought of the *foire des vins* that suddenly the gods of memory smiled upon him.

With a start he suddenly remembered that it was under those same arches that he'd seen an older version of the young Henri in the photographs. It had been at a *foire des vins,* two or three or perhaps four years ago. The man had been standing behind a stall, selling his own wine. Had Bruno tasted a glass or two? He could not remember, but he distinctly recalled the face, the light cotton jacket the man was wearing over a black T-shirt, his height and his heavy build.

Bruno raced up the stairs to his office, took from the printer the enlarged photo of Henri and put the food into the fridge. He got back into his van and drove the five hundred metres to Hubert's wine *cave*, thinking he had not a moment to lose. He burst into the store, ignoring the greetings of '*Bonjour*, Bruno' from the staff, went behind the counter and barely knocked before thrusting his way into Hubert's private lair at the back.

'Bruno, what a pleasant surprise, but why the rush?' Hubert asked. 'I'm just about to taste a charming Riesling I have high hopes of. Do join me.'

Bruno ignored this and pushed the photo at him. 'This man's a winemaker, he was at one of our *foire des vins*. This photo was taken thirty years ago but do you know him?'

Hubert put the photo under his desk lamp and donned the spectacles he was too vain to wear in public. 'I'm pretty sure it's Henri Bazaine. Mostly he makes a run-of-the-mill Bergerac from an old family property near St Laurent les Vignes. He married into it, as I recall, and almost all the wine he makes goes to the cooperative. It's all that most of his wine is fit for. But you know winemakers and their little vanities. He makes a small amount of a reserve red wine which is pretty good, not as good as he likes to think but certainly very drinkable. I'd like to offer some here but Henri likes to sell his special wine privately. He's a bit of a recluse, lets his wife and son and daughter do most of the marketing. He likes to stay in the *chai* and the vineyards. Why do you ask?'

'Are you sure?' Bruno asked, the urgency almost painfully evident in his voice. 'Would you swear to it?'

'I don't know about swearing but it's him all right. I think he was from Alsace originally and came down here for the *vendange* as a student, picking the grapes all over the Bergerac to earn a bit of money. He caught the eye of old Mathieu's pretty daughter, Mathilde, and soon a baby was on the way. Mathieu grumpily consented to the marriage and took him into the vineyard. Of course, if Mathieu had any sons, it would have been a different story. But the marriage worked out well, it must be thirty years ago or so.'

'What's the name of the vineyard?'

'Le Clos Bazaine, the old family name.'

'And that's his name, too?' Bruno asked. 'That's quite a coincidence.'

'I think he might have taken on the name when he married

to please Mathieu, God rest his soul. And now can you tell me why you're so interested in Henri Bazaine? It certainly can't be because of his wines.'

'Sorry, but at this stage, I can't tell you. When I can, let's sit in this room, enjoying a decent bottle, and I'll give you the full story from its beginning here in St Denis. In the meantime, I'm afraid I have to swear you to silence.'

'There you go, wanting me to swear again,' said Hubert, smiling. 'After that tasting glass, let's have a proper glass together of this wonderfully refreshing Riesling while the world outside bakes in the heat. And you can tell me how seriously we should take this sudden alarm over forest fires.'

12

Bruno could not explain the instinct that told him not to alert J-J to his discovery, or at least not yet. It was partly because he was far from sure that he had the right man. He'd have to see if the family name had been formally adopted and if he could find his original surname. Also he wanted to get his own sense of this possible murderer, to look into his eyes and see how much of Hubert's story he could discreetly verify. The last and most cogent reason was that Bruno felt that he shouldn't alert Henri that the police were on his track. Someone with the nerve to commit murder, to keep it to himself for three decades, to marry and create a new life for himself and build an apparently successful business, was not a man to be trifled with. And of course, even if he had been Tante-Do's lover and Max's friend, he might still be innocent of the killing.

In the meantime, he could do his own research. Back in his office, where a bottle of Hubert's Riesling now lay in the Mairie's fridge alongside the crayfish, Bruno fired up his computer. He rubbed his hands together and began by searching for the vineyard's website. It was disappointingly thin. Unusually, it did not seem to welcome visitors for tastings and there were none of the usual vineyard photos, family histories, press reviews and price lists. The place seemed deliberately to be running under the radar. The police data bank showed no criminal record for Henri Bazaine, just some minor speeding offences. He hadn't accumulated sufficient penalty points to put his driving licence in danger.

The website of the Conseil Interprofessional, the overall administrative body for the Bergerac *appellation*, was more helpful, showing that it was now a relatively large property for the region with forty hectares of vines, more than double the size it had been twenty years earlier. For somebody making wines mainly for the co-op, where prices were low, that was unusual. Most successful vineyards in the region depended on the higher prices they could command for premium wines like Monbazillac or Pécharmant, or by gaining a reputation for their better wines through winning medals and prizes.

By contrast, there was more to be found on Henri's father-in-law, the late Mathieu Bazaine, in a newspaper obituary. He had been a local councillor and served one term as Mayor of his commune. His family vineyard had been devastated, like so many others, by the great frost of 1956 when the temperature had been so cold for so long that the vine roots had died. Mathieu had returned from serving in the Algerian war to rebuild the vineyard, becoming active in the cooperative and producing cheap wines for the new supermarkets. He had also been on the board of the local Anciens Combattants, the veterans' association. That was interesting, Bruno thought. He had contacts among them.

He called the Baron, another Algerian war veteran, who laughed at the mention of Mathieu's name.

'He was a *fainéant,* a real poser, always turning up at Remembrance Day parades with his medals. He spent his entire time in Algeria working in the motor pool at the big base in Oran, never on what I'd call real active service,' the Baron said. 'Certainly, he never saw combat. He spent most of his time wooing the very plain eldest daughter of a rich *pied noir*, married her and then used her dowry to rebuild his vineyard here. She must have been at least ten years older than him and obviously on the shelf. Her family must have been grateful to get her married off. He inherited a small place from his dad, just seven or eight hectares. But when Algeria became independent in '62 all his wife's family came to France and put more money into the business, doubling the size of the place.'

'How well did you know him?'

'Well enough to have lunched with him a couple of times at Anciens Combattants events. I think I even dandled his little girl, Mathilde, on my knee once, and I recall one ceremony when she came along with him dressed like she was going to her first Communion. She was no beauty, just like her mum. But she got herself a good man who did wonders for that vineyard.'

'Did you meet him?'

'Just at the wedding. I think I was only invited because Mathieu wanted to get close to my father, who was president of the Société des Gastronomes de France. We were both invited and my father said I should go, just to show the flag.'

'Are you at home?' When the Baron said he was, Bruno asked him to stay there and drove directly to the old *chartreuse* that he knew so well. He found his friend mowing his extensive lawn and showed him the composite photo of Henri that Yves had prepared.

'That's him, sure enough, a good-looking guy,' the Baron said. 'I think his name was Henri. I could never work out what it was he saw in little Mathilde, except maybe for the family vineyard. Still, I gather the marriage has lasted, which is more than you can say for a lot of marriages these days.'

Bruno thanked him and then apologized, saying he had to go, explaining that he would tell the Baron about Henri when he could, but now he had to go and cook for the visit of his cousin, Alain.

'Was that the one I met when he came here before, the one in the air force?' the Baron asked. 'I remember him, a decent guy. Bring him round for a drink if you have time.'

Bruno nodded and said he'd try to drop by, but maybe the Baron would like to join them at the Audrix night market the following evening. He made a mental note to call some other chums about Audrix.

'Good idea, I haven't been there yet this year,' the Baron said. 'Let's invite the whole gang. We can all meet for a drink here at six, and then get there by seven. I know the village Mayor so I'll call to make sure he holds a table for us.'

Once back home, after greeting and feeding Balzac and the chickens, he called Pamela, Jack, Gilles, Florence and the Mayor to suggest they all gather at the Baron's house and then go up to Audrix and meet his cousin and his bride-to-be. Then he called Sabine on her personal mobile to invite her to join them, to meet his friends and experience the local tradition of the night markets. With a touch of guilt he then recalled Virginie, the young woman working on Oscar's skull at the police lab in Périgueux. He called her mobile and invited her for the weekend, but she had already bought a ticket for an open-air concert in the Parc des Arènes, the old Roman amphitheatre. Could she come the following weekend instead? Of course, he replied.

It was time to start preparing the meal and for such a warm evening, he'd start with the classic cold soup of vichyssoise. In the garden, he dug up a single potato plant, which gave him four fat ones, nearly half a kilo. He pulled out two medium-size leeks, two small onions and snipped off a bunch of chives. Back in the kitchen he peeled the potatoes and onions and stripped off the outer leaves and tops of the leeks, keeping only the whites. He sliced and chopped them into small dice, then began to fry them in duck fat over a very gentle heat. Ten minutes would let them cook without browning as long as he kept turning them.

He returned quickly to the garden with a wicker basket, loaded it with three fat carrots, a head of celery, eight shallots, a large lettuce, a cucumber, parsley and some cherry tomatoes and darted back to turn the vegetables. When the onions and leeks were soft, he slowly added a half-litre of his own chicken stock and a wine glass full of water, bringing the vegetables to a simmer until he was sure the potatoes were cooked through. He thought there would be enough salt in the chicken stock but he'd test it later once the dish had cooled.

Suddenly his ears pricked up as the radio, tuned to France Bleu Périgord, began reporting 'sensational developments in a murder inquiry that has been unsolved for three decades. The victim of the murder, which took place in the woods near St Denis, has never been identified – until now. The crucial breakthrough in the case came thanks to the Museum of Prehistory at Les Eyzies, where an exhibition of prehistoric faces that had been reconstructed from their skulls inspired local police to bring in an expert to reconstruct the face of the murder victim. Here's the chief of detectives in Périgueux, Jean-Jacques Jalipeau.'

'For the Police Nationale, a murder inquiry is never closed,' J-J said. 'We have new information and new tools so we are working hard now to push this to a conclusion.'

That was it. Bruno looked up at the radio in surprise as it moved on to the next item. There must have been a leak. That was a non-answer from J-J, framed with unusual caution for a man normally so outspoken. Could the leak have come from Philippe, who regularly worked with the radio station? Bruno thought not; Philippe knew a lot more about the case than just Virginie's work on the skull. The leak could have come from a cop who knew of Virginie's work. But did this mean that Bruno should contact J-J at once with the news of Henri Bazaine?

Bruno paused to think, wooden spoon still in his hand. If Henri had heard that news bulletin, might he try to flee, to disappear again as he had thirty years earlier? That was not a risk Bruno had any right to take. He put down the spoon, picked up his phone and called J-J, only to reach his message service. Bruno reported that the man in the photo had been identified as Henri Bazaine, winemaker of Le Clos Bazaine near Bergerac, by Hubert and by the Baron, both of whom J-J knew. He recommended that J-J arrange for Tante-Do, suitably escorted, to be taken to verify the identification.

He washed and chopped the lettuce, peeled and sliced a cucumber and put them into a salad bowl with the cherry tomatoes, then crumbled and added the Roquefort cheese. He cut two slices of bread from the *tourte* and toasted them, ready to be cut into cubes to go into the salad once he'd added the vinaigrette. The bowl for the walnut oil and white wine vinegar for the dressing stood ready by the chopping board.

He peeled and chopped the shallots, then cut a head of garlic from the braided rope that hung from a kitchen beam. He peeled and sliced two cloves and began peeling the carrots and celery before slicing them into a julienne of fine strips with his mandolin. He was planning écrevisses à la nage, crayfish that would seem to float atop the julienne of vegetables.

He put a hundred grams of butter into a pan over the lowest possible heat and went to the garden for a sprig of thyme, three sprigs of tarragon and a bay leaf and tied them together as a bouquet garni. He put the shallots and garlic into the pan with the now-melted butter, half a dozen halved walnuts and two spoonfuls of tomato paste and softened them slowly for about ten minutes. He added the crayfish and sautéed them until they were bright red. Then he poured a glass of pastis, struck a match and flambéed the dish. Once the flames died down he removed the crayfish and began slowly adding a bottle of Bergerac Sec to the sauté pan. He added the bouquet garni, sea salt and *piment d'espelette*, the red pepper from the Basque country, and raised the heat for five minutes to reduce the liquid.

The vichyssoise was now cool enough to go into the blender

to become a smooth purée. He stirred in the two hundred grams of Stéphane's cream and put the bowl into the freezer to chill. He went out to the rear garden, picked three plump, fresh peaches from his tree, washed them, peeled and halved them, removed the kernels and put them into the fridge on a plate, cut side down. He would leave the last stage of cooking for the arrival of his guests.

He'd already prepared the bedroom for Alain and Rosalie, putting fresh sheets on the double bed and fresh towels in the bathroom when he'd cleaned it that morning. On impulse he went to the garden, plucked two red roses with long stems and put them into a long-necked wine decanter that he took upstairs and placed on the bedside table. He checked his watch and saw that he was in good time so he took a quick shower and changed into khaki slacks and a polo shirt. He'd need about twenty minutes for the risotto so he could serve the chilled soup first.

He was putting new candles into his two terrace lanterns when his phone buzzed. It was J-J, to say he'd got Bruno's message and Tante-Do and Sabine would be calling at Henri's vineyard in the morning. Sabine had been given an unmarked police car and Yves would go with them for security. They'd pick up Tante-Do in Bordeaux at nine, and should be at the vineyard soon after ten. Tante-Do had been instructed to wear dark glasses and leave the talking to Yves and Sandrine, who would say they'd heard from Hubert's wine shop that they should try a bottle of Henri's Reserve red. J-J himself would first be calling at the Bergerac wine cooperative to get further confirmation of the photograph. Did Bruno want to be there?

He explained about his cousin's visit. He'd arranged tickets for Alain and Rosalie to visit the Lascaux cave at ten the next morning which meant they would be leaving about nine. They could have lunch in Montignac then he'd urge them to take a canoe trip in the afternoon from the fortress of Castelnaud down the Dordogne river to the next fortress of Beynac that loomed above the river from its clifftop. Bruno said he could be at the Bergerac vineyard by ten to meet Tante-Do and Sabine. Being in the military, Alain and Rosalie would understand if he pleaded urgent and unexpected police duty.

'Right. I'll tell Yves to expect to see you at the vineyard. You'll be in civilian clothes, of course, but carrying your police badge, just in case. It's up to you but I don't think you need to go armed. Yves will be wearing a concealed weapon in a holster and I'll be nearby. I don't expect to be long at the co-op and I'll have a couple of my men with me. I'm not planning an arrest at this stage, just starting with a few questions. I've checked his ID with his local mairie, which says he was born in '69 in Belleville, in the old Red Belt of Paris. By the way, he lied to Tante-Do about being a student – Strasbourg university never heard of him. Still, let's not forget this could be a case of mistaken identity. He might not be our guy.'

'This is how we find out. By the way, I heard you just now on the radio. Was there a leak?'

'We're looking into that but I think the press office may have thought it would help stir up public interest. Thanks for getting Hubert and the Baron to confirm the photo. See you tomorrow.'

Bruno sat in his garden, thinking about the confrontation that would be coming in the morning at the vineyard and whether Tante-Do, Hubert and the Baron could all be wrong about Henri. It was just possible. He got up, remembering to pick some parsley, and was heading back to the kitchen when Balzac gave his customary bark of warning a moment before Bruno heard the sound of Alain's car coming up the lane.

Rosalie was even more attractive in person than in the photo on Alain's phone. She greeted Bruno with a broad smile that came from her eyes as well as her lips. He got the immediate impression that she was one of those fortunate people who'd been born with a positive attitude to life that they never lost. Almost as tall as Bruno, she was wearing flat ballet shoes and a short-sleeved summer dress in broad vertical stripes of white and light blue. She shook Bruno's hand and then gave him a smacking kiss on each cheek as Alain stood by, beaming proudly. Then she bent down to greet an enthusiastic Balzac, finding just the right spot to make him kick a rear leg in delight. Bruno warmed to her at once.

He took Rosalie's overnight case from Alain and led the way upstairs to show them their room, said there was plenty of time if they wanted to freshen up after the journey, adding that drinks would be served outside when they were ready. He took three champagne flutes to the small table on the terrace and went back for the *brut* and the cassis.

When they came downstairs, Alain presented him with a bottle of champagne and Rosalie gave Bruno a small, wrapped parcel, saying, 'Alain tells me you were always a great reader and that as a boy you loved Sherlock Holmes, as did I. Here's a modern writer's attempt to do a Sherlock, but it's about his brother, Mycroft. I read it when it was first translated and I thought you might enjoy it as much as I did, unless you get enough detection in your day job.'

'That's very kind of you,' he said, hugging her in thanks and catching a hint of roses from her newly applied scent. 'Thank you for the champagne and the book. I'll look forward to both. Meanwhile, here's some Bergerac champagne. Of course we're not allowed to call it that, even though it's made by the method invented by Dom Perignon long before he went north to teach the people of Champagne how to do it. Would you like it with cassis or without?'

Alain chose it with and Rosalie asked to try it without. She stood a moment to sweep her eyes across the vegetable garden, the avenue of truffle trees, the chicken run and the roses that climbed up the front of the house.

'It's lovely here, a charming spot,' she said. 'Did those roses by our bed come from the climbers beside the door?'

Bruno shook his head and pointed to the cluster of rose bushes at the corner of his driveway, pleased that she had noticed the roses in their room. He then told them of their booking for Lascaux in the morning and of his own police business.

'I have to leave here soon after nine,' he said, 'and I need to make my usual patrol of the Saturday market tomorrow morning at about eight so I suggest we go down to St Denis for coffee and croissants in my favourite café, then you can go to Lascaux and I'll head for Bergerac. And I really recommend you take a canoe ride on the way back from Lascaux. Tomorrow evening we're having drinks at a lovely small chateau that belongs to a good friend and then we'll head to a tiny village with some more friends to have dinner at a night market.'

He explained that they could park at Beynac and the canoe rental people would drive them upstream to Castelnaud, from where they could launch their canoe into the river and paddle gently downstream to Beynac with the current. Two formidable medieval castles, Castelnaud and Beynac, had changed hands several times but usually one was held by the English and the other by the French.

'If you have time, it's worth visiting Castelnaud and the museum of medieval warfare there,' Bruno said. 'At this time of year they have fencing exhibitions and you might see them fire one of the trebuchets, the heavy artillery of the middle ages. Amazing machines, they can toss an eighty kilo rock as far as two or even three hundred metres. The Crusaders learned to use them from the Saracens and brought them back to Europe.'

Aware that he was prattling, Bruno gave Rosalie a rueful grin. 'Sorry, but this kind of thing captivates boys of all ages and I think Alain might like it.'

'Not just boys,' she said, returning his smile. 'Why do you think I joined the military? That sounds great and thank you for arranging all this.'

As Bruno refilled their glasses she asked, 'How far does your land go?' He pointed to the top of the hill behind the house and said it ran from there down to the hedge in the lower field, where some cows were grazing.

'Do those Blondes d'Aquitaine belong to you?' she asked.

'You know your cows, Rosalie. No, they belong to a neighbouring farmer. He uses my pasture and gets a dozen of my eggs each week and I get a lot of free veal in return.'

'Are we eating veal tonight? Alain tells me you're a good cook.'

'No, I thought in this heat we should have something light but a lot of it will have come from this garden.'

'I can't wait until Alain and I have a garden of our own but I think we'll be turning to you for advice. And what are we eating?'

Bruno suggested they move to the larger table he had laid for dinner and brought out on a tray the bowls of chilled vichyssoise to which he'd added some fresh parsley. He poured out glasses of the cuvée Quercus, cut some bread from the *tourte* and said, '*Bon appetit.*'

'Delicious, and I suspect these are your vegetables,' she said. Bruno thanked her for the compliment, aware that she was working hard to make friends with the cousin of her future husband. This was an interesting aspect of etiquette. Here were two people who might in other circumstances have been attracted to one another, each trying hard to please the other out of their mutual affection for Alain. Bruno could foresee many Christmases, birthdays and New Year's Eves being spent together. The thought of such shared family events pleased him.

'Would you like to come into the kitchen while I finish the next course?' he asked, and they joined him with refilled glasses once the plates had been cleared.

He boiled a kettle, put the julienne of carrots and celery into boiling water and reheated the white wine sauce, adding the crayfish once it began to simmer. He drained the julienne, thoroughly mixing the carrots and celery together and spooned a generous portion into each of three warm bowls, added the crayfish, and then offered Rosalie a teaspoon of the sauce to taste. She nodded her approval and he poured the sauce into the bowls.

The evening was still light enough for them to eat without candles and, with the odd word and murmur of appreciation, they devoted their attention to the food and wine. When the écrevisses à la nage had gone, Bruno brought out the chilled Monbazillac to go with the Roquefort salad. Finally, Rosalie pushed back her plate, wiped a last chunk of bread around the bottom of her salad bowl, popped it into her mouth and closed her eyes.

'That was bliss,' she said. 'I'd never have thought of a dessert wine with the salad, but the Roquefort made it just right. Brilliant, Bruno, altogether a lovely meal.'

'There's a small dessert to come,' Bruno said, smiling as Rosalie gave a mock groan of pleasure. 'I'm delighted that you enjoyed it.'

He lit the candles as they enjoyed their peaches, topped with Stéphane's cream. Alain and Rosalie declined coffee and they sat with the Monbazillac until the last glow had faded from the distant ridge. Bruno blew out the candles in the lanterns and the stars all seemed to explode into view overhead, so they watched them, trying to trace the more familiar galaxies until the moon rose and it was time for bed.

13

Before seven the next morning, Bruno stepped out of his front door in his running gear and was surprised to see Alain and Rosalie, similarly dressed, limbering up in the garden.

'I told Rosalie you were a jogger,' said Alain, embracing Bruno. 'So are we, along with most of the airbase.' Rosalie embraced him in turn, saying that after the dinner of the previous evening she felt she really needed to run. Airbases were flat places, thought Bruno. Perhaps he should spare them the path up the hill through the woods. He led the way at a moderate pace down the driveway and into the lane that led up a gentle slope, starting to lengthen his stride on the long ridge that stretched for three – usually windswept – kilometres until the land dropped to the Vézère valley below.

The earth was so dry that Bruno saw small puffs of dust rising with each step. They ran side by side, Rosalie between him and Alain, each of them moving easily and running well within their limits but still outpacing Balzac. It was, thought Bruno, even more companionable than the dinner they had shared the previous evening. The only animals up here were sheep with their lambs. Balzac had been taught not to bother them and the sheep in turn ignored the visitors but edged away from the ridge itself, seeking some shade on the western side of the hill while the sun was still low in the sky.

Bruno increased the pace on the way back and the two others stayed with him. Balzac, who was by now way behind, stopped in his tracks as they approached and gave a happy bark of greeting until they raced past him and he had to start chasing them all over again. Bruno glanced at the others when he trotted the last fifty metres up his driveway to the terrace. Like him, they were sweating only slightly, their chests not heaving. They obviously ran as much as he did.

'I'll put some coffee on, then take a shower before we head down for the best croissants in the district,' he said, as Balzac finally trotted up the driveway to rejoin them. 'By the way, do either of you like riding horses?'

'I do,' said Rosalie. 'But then I grew up on a farm near Lisieux, which is why I recognized those cattle last night. We didn't have horses but some of my friends did. Alain told me you have a horse of your own. Where do you keep him?'

'He's called Hector and he stays at a nearby stables, a riding school run by friends of mine,' Bruno said. ' I only started riding quite recently and I love it.'

Alain was making friends with Balzac, who was lying on his back, the flesh of his lower jaw hanging down from his teeth in what looked like an extremely happy grin. Alain was running both hands over his chest and flanks. He looked up. 'Didn't you tell me you were breeding him?'

Bruno nodded. 'The first litter of his pups was born just a few days ago. I went to see them and they're enchanting.'

Alain looked at Rosalie, who was smiling broadly. 'We've been thinking about getting a dog when we're married,' he said.

'That solves the problem of your wedding present,' said Bruno. 'Tell me the date and I'll not only be there, I'll time Balzac's future matings so you get a puppy once you're hitched.'

'That's far too generous,' said Rosalie. 'I know how much a basset like this one can fetch.'

'Alain is the only real family I've got. And I think the two of you would count as a very suitable home for one of Balzac's pups.'

Twenty minutes later, fresh from their showers and coffee mugs in hand, Bruno was introducing them to his chickens and his cockerel, Blanco, named after a legendary French rugby star. They were suitably impressed by the two geese, Napoleon and Joséphine and their latest brood of half-grown goslings. He explained the three kinds of truffle trees and the different varieties of mushroom he found in the woods that rose up the slope behind the cottage.

'I see you have apple trees, pears, plums and cherries,' Rosalie said, looking at his small orchard behind the chicken run. 'Where did you get the peaches we had last night?'

'Come see.' He led them to the back of the house where he had a peach and an apricot tree espaliered against the rear wall with a fig tree at each end. Rosalie nodded approvingly and then looked into the barn where he kept his tools, a big freezer and shelves filled with glass jars of his various preserves of jams and pâtés, confits of duck and *enchauds* of pork.

'The only thing you're missing is beehives and goats,' she said thoughtfully but in her good-natured way. 'Then you could be entirely self-sufficient.'

'I'm not sure I'd want that,' Bruno replied. 'Not having them means I can swap my jams and confits for someone else's honey, or for their fresh trout from the river. And I prefer cheese made by people who really know what they're doing, like my friend Stéphane whom you're about to meet in the market.'

After enjoying Fauquet's croissants and some of his gossip about the strange business of J-J and the reconstructed skull, Alain and Rosalie joined Bruno on his tour of the market. They bought some cheese from Stéphane, Mara des Bois strawberries from Marcel and fresh foie gras from the stall of the Lac Noir farm. When Marcel asked why he was in civilian clothes, Bruno explained that his cousin's visit was the reason. After briefly showing them his office, he waved them off on the road to Lascaux, then set off in his Land Rover in the other direction for Bergerac.

Henri's vineyard, Le Clos de Bazaine, was south of the city, mostly on the plain. But part of it was on rising ground on the far side of the road that ran along the flank of the north-facing slope dominated by the tall towers of the castle of Monbazillac. Despite the conical roofs that topped the towers, the place looked like a medieval fortress until one was close enough to see the Renaissance windows. Bruno drove slowly past the entrance to Henri's traditional farmhouse with its outbuildings and barns. One of them must be the *chai* where he made his wines and another where he stored it.

Henri's vineyard looked old-fashioned to Bruno's eye. Well-drilled rows of vines, separated by strips of mown grass and gravel, were all of the same height and bulk. That meant the vineyard wasn't organic. Bruno wondered just how many chemicals Henri used to get that disciplined but unnatural effect. Few of the Bergerac vineyards looked like this any more as more and more winemakers joined the organic revolution. He glanced up the slope, where most of the vines straggled and looked wilder, as nature intended. He wondered whether Henri's better wines came from these slopes, although they would have little protection from the chemicals that were pumped over the vines on the flat side of the road.

Outside Henri's farmhouse were a dusty Toyota Land Cruiser, a Mercedes saloon that looked new and an older Renault Twingo. Bruno parked in the entrance to a farm lane and kept an eye out for the grey Renault Sabine would be driving. His phone buzzed.

'Is that you, Bruno?' came her voice. He explained where to find him. She had just turned off at Gardonne, on the main road from Bordeaux to Bergerac. She'd be with him in little more than five minutes. While waiting he tried to work out how best to handle the coming confrontation. It would have to be fast, just a simple and friendly question about his wine to ensure the real prize, a chance for Tante-Do to get her eyeballs on him. She should stay by the car while Yves and Sabine knocked on the front door and Bruno tried the barns in case Henri might be there. He'd better stay in the background since Henri might possibly remember him wearing police uniform at the wine fair in St Denis.

When Sabine's car arrived, Bruno waved her down, got into the back seat and explained his plan. They drove into the courtyard and parked. Sabine and Yves walked slowly to the main door while Tante-Do leaned against the car. Bruno tried the barn on the left, which had double sliding doors, slightly open. He squeezed through, calling out Bazaine's name, and saw that this must be the *chai*. Six tall stainless steel vats stood on one side, four on the other, everything spotlessly clean. There was no reply to his calls. A locked door on one side of the barn had a glass panel and seemed to lead into what looked like an empty office. He went across to the other barn, which was locked, before walking back to the car. Yves and Sabine were still waiting at the front door until it was opened by an overweight young woman with short blonde hair, who said, politely and loud enough for Bruno to hear, 'We don't take visitors here at the vineyard.'

'We heard from Hubert de Montignac in St Denis that you make a very good reserve wine and we'd like to buy some,' Sabine said. 'He told us you only sold it here.'

'*Bonjour*, Mademoiselle Bazaine?' said Yves, smiling and with a hand outstretched. 'We've come here specially because Hubert told us your wine was worth the trip. Is Monsieur Bazaine here?'

'Sorry, but we don't—' she began and then a tall, well-built young man with fair hair appeared behind her.

'I'm Monsieur Bazaine the younger and my sister is right,' he said. 'We don't sell from here, only from the cooperative, and you can find our wines in most supermarkets.' He began to close the door.

'Excuse us for interrupting your day,' Sabine said in friendly tones. 'But it's not the co-op wine we want, rather your special reserve. Perhaps your father could help us. Is he here? Monsieur de Montignac told us your father was very proud of his reserve.'

'We're all proud of it,' said the young man. 'Dad's not here right now.' He paused, looking uncertainly from Yves and Sabine to Tante-Do and Bruno waiting by the car. Then he seemed to make a decision. 'I'm sorry you had a wasted journey. Just wait here a moment.'

He ducked back inside, leaving his sister on the doorstep, and Sabine asked her brightly, 'Are you a winemaker, too?'

'I'm learning,' she answered curtly. Her brother reappeared, a bottle of red wine in his hand. He thrust it at Sabine and said, 'Here, sorry, we're busy, but this is the wine.'

'How much do we owe you?' Yves asked, pulling out his wallet.

'Ten euros will do it,' said the young man, and almost snatched the note from his hand, pulled his sister back and began to close the door.

'If it's as good as I hope, how do we buy more?' Sabine asked.

'Write to us. We sell mainly by mail. Thanks for coming.' The door closed.

Yves and Sabine stared at one another, shrugged and returned to the car, displaying the bottle. It was labelled as a Special Reserve from four years earlier. Bruno knew it had been a decent year.

'That's a very strange way to treat customers,' Bruno said loudly but there was no reaction from the house. Tante-Do was already back in the passenger seat and, as Sabine drove out, she turned to Bruno.

'That young man is the spitting image of his father thirty years ago. I'm sure of it,' she said.

'Look at this,' Sabine said, handing Bruno a photocopy of a newspaper article with the headline, 'Love blooms among the vines.' It showed a photo of a bride and her new husband, who was very clearly Henri but it could have been the son they'd just met.

'I spent hours at a microfilm reader yesterday going through old newspapers for the relevant time period,' Sabine went on. 'I started searching from three months after the murder and the first six months of the following year. That's what I eventually came up with.'

'Well done,' said Bruno, impressed, knowing that he should have thought of that. The caption to the photo gave Henri's original name, before he changed it: Henri Zeller. The name reminded Bruno of one of the Alsatian brasseries in Paris where he'd eaten a fine *choucroute royale*.

'What do we do now?' asked Tante-Do.

'We find J-J and check with him. It's his inquiry,' Bruno said, wondering if the radio news story the previous evening had alerted Henri and induced him to disappear again. Yves called J-J, who told them he was waiting in the car park at Monbazillac. Yves explained what had happened and J-J suggested they meet up. Bruno gave Sabine directions.

'D'you think he's done a bunk?' J-J asked once they'd joined him.

'I don't know. He could have been inside the house or just out shopping. I didn't see anyone working in the vines,' Bruno said. 'What did you learn at the co-op?'

'They confirmed that it was him in the photo but that was all. He's a member of the co-op in good standing but seldom appears at meetings, and he refused all requests to go on the board or take any part in management. They called him a bit of a loner and said they used to deal with his wife. Now they deal mainly with his son who's well-liked and respected and knows the business – he did the wine course at Bordeaux university. Apparently, Henri travels a bit as a wine consultant, they call it an oenologist. Maybe that's how he earned the money to expand the vineyard.'

'Unusual for people to pay for a wine consultant who mostly makes wine for a co-op,' Bruno said. 'Customers usually want better credentials than that. Did they say where he consults?'

'Canada was the only place they mentioned,' J-J replied. 'We've started checking on his passport and movements. I have his bank account details from the co-op so we'll soon have his credit cards, mobile phone, all the usual data. And one more thing, now that we have a photo for Max, I'll ask Interpol to try again on medical records for that unusual break in his leg. I'm told those data banks are a lot more complete than they used to be. Maybe we'll get lucky and get a surname for him, too.'

'Let's hope so,' said Bruno. 'What about his income? Did you get to see the co-op accounts?'

'Yes, he seems quite wealthy. The co-op said he was the first of them to push for the bag-in-the-box and almost all his wine is now sold that way. You know the things, fifteen euros for a five litre box. He gets just over a third of that, one euro ten per litre, and he usually produces about a quarter million litres a year. The co-op pays for the boxes, delivery and marketing and he also gets a share of the profits the co-op makes, which netted him another nine thousand euros last year.'

'He has to pay for labour, the picking, his wine-making equipment, insurance, social costs, fertilizer and taxes,' Bruno said.

'And don't forget that every few years there's a hailstorm or some expensive blight or a drought. If we don't get some rain soon he won't have much of a harvest this year. Still, he must usually clear close to a hundred thousand a year.'

'More than you and I make combined,' said J-J, shrugging. 'He has no labour costs. His family helps him work the vines and the grape-picking is all done by the co-op machines. What's more, he drinks for free.'

'We're in the wrong business,' said Bruno, laughing. 'If it wasn't for the company, J-J . . .'

'Very funny. Sabine can take Tante-Do back to Bordeaux. I'll get the Paris police looking into Henri's background, now that we have his real name. He was born there so they'll check his school records, get the address where he grew up and the names of any relatives. They should have something for me on Monday.'

'You still running a media blitz with the photos on Monday?' Bruno asked.

'We might as well. It can't hurt and it puts a spotlight onto him. And if it panics him into doing a runner, all the better. We'll have his credit card numbers, his passport and the details of his cars. He won't get far.'

'What if he just uses cash to buy a train ticket to Italy or Spain?'

'And then where does he go?' J-J replied. 'Henri's found a safe harbour here that has sheltered him for the last thirty years. D'you think he's the type of professional criminal to have fabricated a second identity with a false passport, secret bank accounts, all that?'

'I don't know. It's unlikely but possible.' As Bruno spoke, he knew that J-J was thinking aloud. He was at least a step behind but he followed the direction of J-J's mind. He knew better than most that J-J's bullish manner and appearance concealed a profound and subtle intelligence. He'd been a successful detective for thirty years and had navigated the complexities of police politics to reach his current job. Bruno would never underestimate him.

'Do you think Henri's going to stay here and brazen it out? Plead that all your witnesses are mistaking him for someone else?' Bruno asked.

'I believe Tante-Do. I don't think she'd be mistaken in identifying him after that passionate weekend together. Guilty or innocent, brazen denial could be his best bet, if he can bring forward someone who gives him an alibi for the time of the *félibrée*.' J-J's voice sounded almost detached, as though he were thinking of something else entirely. 'Even if he admits to being Tante-Do's Henri, we still need evidence that he killed Max.'

Bruno nodded. Identifying Henri was one thing. Proving that he was the one who had killed Max was something quite different.

'But if we can't prove that he was Max's killer, maybe if we look hard enough we can find something else.' J-J turned to look at Bruno directly. 'Any ideas?'

'None at all.'

'You're the hunting club man, Bruno. I'm surprised you didn't know that Henri is a member of the Pomport club, just a few kilometres from here. And he's a crack shot, they tell me.'

'You've lost me, J-J. Where are you going with this?'

'Where did he learn to shoot? What was his military service? You still have that friendly contact in army records?' When Bruno nodded, J-J said, 'Give him a call on Monday and see what you can find out.'

'Will do. What's your next step?'

'I'll do the obvious. Go to Henri's house, show my police ID and ask for him. If he's not there, I'll ask where he is and when he'll be back. I'll leave my card and request that he calls, that I have some questions for him.'

'You're a *commissaire*, the top detective in the *département*,' Bruno said. 'That would scare anybody.'

'You could be right, but it makes no difference if I send a junior. Henri will still end up talking to me. The sooner he learns that I'm interested in him, the more time he has to worry, perhaps even to panic. Always take account of the panic factor in police work, Bruno. Over the years it's probably caught as many criminals as fingerprints.'

14

Alain and Rosalie had caught the sun on their canoe trip, their faces glowing red. Nonetheless they were beaming with delight as they came from the car to join Bruno on his terrace. Balzac darted from his spot by Bruno's feet to welcome them, circling around them twice and then standing before them appealingly, one paw raised, until Rosalie bent down to stroke him.

Bruno had spent two calming hours weeding his garden, scything some long grass behind the house and deadheading the faded roses. He feared for his flowers if some rain did not come soon. For the past few days he had watered only the vegetables, following a tip he'd learned from Marcel in the market. He had planted discarded plastic bottles upside down at strategic points, having pierced small holes in the caps, screwed them back on, cut off the bottoms and half-filled each one. From the healthy look of his tomatoes, peas and lettuces this primitive drip irrigation seemed to work.

'Lemonade, coffee, tea?' he asked his guests. 'We should leave for the Baron's place in about half an hour if you want to shower first.'

'That's okay,' said Rosalie. 'We took a dip in the river before we handed the canoe back. It was spectacular, those amazing castles, one after another, and that little village that clambered up the cliff was too pretty for words. And at Castelnaud we saw them fire the smallest of the trebuchets. Very impressive. They said some of the damage to the castle was done by catapults like that.'

'And how was Lascaux this morning?'

'Amazing,' she said. 'I had no idea that it was so beautiful and that those prehistoric people were so smart. The only way they could get enough light inside the cave to paint was to invent a special kind of lamp that used a juniper twig as a wick in rendered reindeer fat. Any other kind of flame would have covered the white chalk walls with soot. How long did it take to develop that? I'll never think of those people as primitive again.'

Bruno was used to the enthusiasm of visitors, but it always pleased him. 'There are many more caves worth a visit, twenty-four painted caves and over a hundred with various engravings. One is so big you take a train to get deep inside and the walls are covered with mammoths.'

'I told you we'd need more time here,' Alain said, putting his arm around Rosalie's waist.

'Should we dress for this evening with your Baron friend?' she asked.

'Not at all, I never do and nor does he, you both look fine as you are. We'll stop to pick up a friend called Sabine, a young gendarme who's on temporary assignment here.'

'I'm getting out of these bathing trunks under my slacks,' said Alain. 'We'll go up and change but we won't be long.'

The eyes of Sabine and Rosalie widened when they drove

along the Baron's driveway and saw his four-hundred-year-old home. It was a *chartreuse*, the local name for a building that was smaller than a chateau but larger than a manor house. The rear looked like a fortress, a fifty-metre stretch of stone wall with a tower at each end, a bleak façade broken only by a few windows, recently added. It formed one side of a square in the small hamlet that had grown up around the building, mainly cottages and smallholdings for families who had worked the land of the Baron's ancestors.

By contrast, the front of the *chartreuse*, framed by a long avenue of apple and walnut trees that led up to a wooded slope, was open and welcoming. Tall windows suggested the height of the rooms within, and stone steps, wide at ground level but narrowing as they rose, led up to a venerable set of double doors studded with iron. The bottom half of the doors was darker and the Baron claimed they were scorch marks from an attempt to burn out his ancestor in the turbulent years after the Revolution. Since that same ancestor had survived to become one of Napoleon's generals, the attack had been briskly defeated.

At some point large French windows had been installed on either side of these steps, and from one of them the Baron emerged, carrying a tray of drinks and glasses, to welcome his guests. He put the tray down on a round metal table, painted white, which stood on a stone terrace that stretched along the whole front of the building. Big terracotta urns that reached above Bruno's waist were filled with bright red geraniums.

'Welcome,' he said, advancing to greet them with the stride of a much younger man. 'Alain, it's good to see you again, and

Bruno, please introduce me to this charming young woman. If you are marrying Alain, my dear, then he's a lucky man. And Sabine, you must be the gendarme of whom Bruno has spoken.'

Then he sat on one of the garden chairs to greet Balzac, who seemed to assume that the Baron was a member of the family, along with all the other friends of Bruno that Balzac saw almost every day.

'Your welcome is as courtly as your home, *monsieur*,' Rosalie said, as a car horn tooted. Fabiola's Twingo swung into the driveway and parked to disgorge the doctor, her partner, Gilles, and Florence. Pamela's elderly *deux-chevaux* then hove into view, followed by the Mayor, bringing Jacqueline. Balzac at once raced off to greet each of them, and Bruno wondered, not for the first time, whether his dog's hearing was so acute that he recognized people by the sound of their car engines.

'Looks like we're all here,' the Baron said. 'Bruno, would you take care of the drinks while I greet the others?'

Three bottles, white, red and rosé from the town vineyard, stood on the tray with bowls of nuts and olives and a bottle of cassis. Bruno began to serve, thinking it might be time for Hubert and Julien to add a sparkling wine to the town's production. There were chairs enough for all on the terrace but they gathered instead under the shade of a cypress tree. Balzac snuffled around the feet of each one of them, waiting for the inevitable snacks that would come his way.

'Make a note in your diary for Monday afternoon, Bruno,' said the Mayor. 'We're having the forest fire rehearsal that was postponed, but it's going to be much bigger with some *pompier* experts, people from other communes and the Préfecture. Your colleagues from Les Eyzies and Montignac will also be there. It starts at two.'

'I'll be there,' said Bruno, handing the Mayor a glass of kir. 'Let's just hope the rehearsal is never needed.' He made sure everyone had a glass, then managed to have a quiet word with Gilles.

'Have you and Jacqueline conferred on those articles you're each writing about that spy business?' Bruno asked him. 'It's tomorrow they come out, isn't it?'

'Yes, Jacqueline's is in Monday's *Le Monde*, which will be available in Paris late tomorrow afternoon. My piece goes up on the website at five tomorrow, with a longer piece plus photos in next week's print edition.'

'What photos have you found?' Bruno asked.

'Gisela, of course, sometimes called the spy of the century. Her real name was Gabriele Gast. She went from think-tanks into West German intelligence, the BND.' Gilles explained that Gisela was an attractive woman and there was a romantic angle, too, with her Stasi handler. That made her story perfect for *Paris Match*.

'Then there was the biggest spy of all, Rainer Rupp, code name Topaz,' Gilles went on. Rupp had worked at NATO HQ in Brussels and photographed secret documents in his wine cellar at home and had a British wife who tried to persuade him to stop but stayed loyal to him. He gave over the crown jewels, the locations of the Cruise and Pershing missiles, NATO's strategic plans and its assessment of what the Warsaw Pact could do. A lot of that material was given the 'Cosmic Top Secret' classification, NATO's highest, and was copied at once to Moscow.

'Then I list some of the spies exposed in the Rosenholz dossier in various countries,' Gilles went on. 'This raises the obvious question: why would there not be Stasi spies in France? Rupp was recruited when he was a young student leftist in 1968, when our own student revolt would have been a happy hunting ground for Stasi and the KGB. Most of this stuff is available if you know where to look for it.'

'What about Jacqueline's article?' Bruno asked.

'As you'd expect, hers is much more policy based, on the implications of the continued lack of trust between Paris and Washington, with the Rosenholz dossier as Exhibit A. Predictably for *Le Monde*, her piece is aimed at the policy-makers whereas mine is aimed at ordinary people, the office worker on the Metro. It's the same story but with different targets and you know how people always love to read spy stories. I threw in some stuff about how we expelled Dick Holm, the CIA station chief in Paris during the Clinton years, for running an operation against France.'

He gave Bruno a shrewd glance. 'Are these questions just for your own interest or are you asking on behalf of somebody?'

'A bit of both,' Bruno acknowledged.

'I can guess who's interested,' Gilles said, grinning. 'It's not a problem for me if I email you my article tonight. It's already ancient history, anyway. I filed my final version minutes before I came here.' He took out his phone, tapped a few buttons and said, 'There you are. On its way to your private inbox. Give Isabelle my compliments.'

Bruno strolled discreetly into the Baron's kitchen, read what Gilles had sent and forwarded it to Isabelle, with a note saying

Gilles sent his regards. That was how it worked. Gilles had done Isabelle a favour and would doubtless expect one in return. Jacqueline would probably not be so helpful. Back in the garden, Bruno went up to where she was chatting with Rosalie, Sabine and Pamela and offered to refresh their drinks. As he handed them back, he managed to steer Jacqueline aside and ask if her *Le Monde* piece was running the next day.

'So they tell me. I hope it makes a stir,' she said.

'If it's anything like your remarks over dinner the other day, I'm sure it will,' he said. 'I never cease to be surprised at the way history thrusts its claws into our present. It must be even stranger for you, a historian of the Cold War, to find it here again thirty years after it ended.'

'If it has ended – that's the question,' she said. 'Every one of us here is a child of the Cold War, Bruno. It shaped us, defined our politics and reshaped our economies and our systems of government. Not just the Russians and Americans but we Europeans in our own way also became national security states. The past always lives on in profound ways, particularly in our security agencies, arms industries and defence bureaucracies.'

'I remember once in Sarajevo, taking shelter in a slit trench at the airport when the Serbs were shelling it, and I was reading a piece in *Le Monde* about the Cold War being over. It certainly didn't feel like it.'

'Yes, I can recall articles like that in those days,' Jacqueline said with a chuckle. 'I may even have written one or two suggesting that the Balkan wars were the sign of a return to the traditional wars of national interests. I even called it the first war of the Soviet succession.'

'National interests never go away,' said Bruno. 'Just look at this Franco-American suspicion you're writing about.'

'I think you might enjoy my *Le Monde* piece,' she said. 'I make the point that the Americans still assume that their interests are the same as those of the other members of the NATO alliance, particularly with Russia making trouble again and China playing its own superpower games. In reality, most of us NATO allies have moved on, not just to our traditional national interests but to the new interest of this Europe of ours after Brexit. The British were always the linchpin of the Atlantic alliance. Without them in Europe, who knows?'

'Too soon to tell,' he said.

'We'll see. But would you not agree that it's better to be early in thinking publicly about these things than too late?'

'You're probably right. But there's such a thing as being right too soon. Didn't you write a book about the people who went to fight in Spain against Franco? Premature anti-fascists, you called them.'

'I did indeed, and if you recall my conclusion, I noted that some of those Spanish war veterans who came to France as refugees became the hard core of our own Resistance in France.'

Suddenly their exchange was interrupted by the Baron, clapping his hands and announcing, 'Drink up, it's time to go to Audrix for the night market and dinner.'

The tiny hilltop village of Audrix clustered around a small square that was dominated by a simple twelfth-century stone church on one side, facing the Mairie on the other. On a third side stood the local inn, the precisely named Auberge Médiévale, with a good restaurant where Bruno liked to eat on the terrace. Opposite this was a road that was wide enough for a row of stalls, selling the usual range of wines, cheeses, strawberries, grilled meats, ducks and chickens, salads and pastries, that were common to all the night markets of the region.

Some night markets liked to offer different foods, like St Denis's stalls of Vietnamese, Caribbean, Moroccan, West African and Indian-style food from Mauritius, gifts of the old French colonial empire. Audrix remained proudly traditional; the specialities were dishes based around roast chicken and barbecued steak, along with snails from a local farm and raw foie gras sautéed with a sauce of honey and balsamic vinegar. Then there was the village bread oven, a beehive-shaped structure of stone which baked fresh bread and pizza, all surrounded by a paved space without walls but covered by a wide roof supported by wooden beams. This was where the musicians played while visitors danced. Thanks to the passionate Greens on the local council, the village had banned the use of plastic plates and utensils, so beneath the Mairie was a stall where crockery, glasses and cutlery could be hired for a modest deposit.

Having waited for Pamela, who always took longer in her trusty but ancient *deux-chevaux*, Bruno and his group strolled up from the car park in the fields, pausing to admire the gigantic straw sculptures of a mammoth and a warrior of ancient Gaul, at which Balzac always paused to lift his leg. Bruno assumed it was his dog's way of paying respect to such magnificent structures. The Baron and his friends had secured a large table on a patch of higher ground beside the

Mairie and had spread out plates, glasses and cutlery from their various picnic hampers. Bottles of wine had already been bought and opened. Florence was standing in line for salads, Fabiola for cheese, Gilles for roast chicken and lamb chops, Jack Crimson for bread and pizza and Jacqueline for the foie gras. Everybody had put twenty euros into the communal pot and planned to spend any remainder on dishes of strawberries and cream.

The band was a local favourite, composed of an accordion, guitar, drums, saxophone and a woman in a blonde wig who dressed and performed like a pre-war torch singer. They made a living in summer by playing each night at a different market in the region, offering popular French cabaret classics mixed in with *bal musette* dance music and romantic ballads. Bruno enjoyed it hugely, making a point of dancing with each of the women in their group, and with several more, friends whom he came across while strolling past the food stalls.

After his first stroll, trying to decide which of the foods on offer he would choose this evening, Bruno went to the rear of the church. Balzac followed him and at once joined some children playing on the grass. Bruno waved at two of them whom he recognized from his tennis classes. He then used his burner phone to call Isabelle on her private number.

'Thanks for the *Paris Match* piece,' she said. 'And give my thanks to Gilles. There's nothing much that's new in it but he certainly makes it all sound sensational. Maybe he should try a new career as a spy novelist. It's Jacqueline's piece I'm more worried about.'

'It's all policy-based, Franco–American relations,' Bruno

replied. 'But it all hinges on Gilles's point that the Stasi were recruiting among the student left in Germany in '68 and they'd almost certainly have tried the same in France. It seemed a bit odd to me since any of that generation would be in their seventies by now and long since retired. Other than some cerebral stuff about the new Cold War and national versus European interests, that seems to be it. I shouldn't imagine that it will cause you any real problems.'

'That's not what they're saying in the Elysée Palace,' she said. 'Anyone recruited back in the sixties could have recruited promising candidates from the next generation they were meant to be training and supervising. There are already people warning that this could lead to a witch-hunt, sniffing out suspected spies and sleeper agents among the énarques,' she added, referring to graduates from the elite ENA, the *Ecole Nationale d'Administration*, who filled the higher ranks of the state bureaucracy and the boards of directors of France's top corporations.

'But all these people are routinely vetted by our own security people, just in case,' Bruno replied.

'Yes, but the point Gilles missed about Rainer Rupp was that the guy was an idealist. He wasn't a passionate supporter of East Germany, far from it. He just thought that the Cold War arms race could be made less dangerous if each side knew what the other was doing and thinking. He convinced himself that he was in the right place to do that. He even claimed that he helped prevent World War Three by reassuring the Warsaw Pact that NATO was not planning a surprise attack back in '83, when Ronald Reagan was talking about the Evil Empire and Star Wars and scaring the pants off the Kremlin.'

'These are very different times,' Bruno said.

'Up to a point, Bruno, but the current American administration is not exactly reassuring. It's no secret that most European capitals worry that we're all skating on thin ice, whether we look at trade, security policy, arms control, relations with Russia, the Middle East . . . I could go on. Some of the advisers around our President are almost panicking about it.'

'This is all way above my head,' Bruno said.

'Yes, but you can understand why the Rosenholz dossier has suddenly become a hot topic here in Paris. I have to go but thanks, and kisses to you and Balzac.'

Bruno stood for a moment looking out over the valley, the sounds of some old dance music drifting to him from the far side of the church, accompanied by the scents of different foods from the night market stalls. The contrast between the innocent pleasures of this peaceful village and the mood and politics in Paris that Isabelle had described disturbed him deeply. It suggested a huge and dismaying gap in perceptions and concerns between the Parisian elite and the people who voted them into office and entrusted them with power.

As a very minor cog in the vast machinery of French administration, the scale of this gap scared him. Nor was Bruno comfortable at having shared his friends' articles and views with Isabelle. He told himself that he'd passed on Gilles's piece only with his tacit permission, for Gilles was familiar with this game of complicity between media and officialdom. And while he had shared nothing of what Jacqueline had written, he'd passed on her views, not that they were secret. Everything would soon be available to anyone who bought *Le Monde* or *Paris Match*.

That did not stop Bruno from feeling he'd participated in something underhand. It was not so much guilt as feeling rather shamefaced at making use of people he considered his friends. These were people who had reason to trust him, to assume that they could converse with him in confidence. And he could not fool himself by claiming to have acted from patriotism nor from some sense of duty to the French state. Not at all. He had acted simply to render a small service to Isabelle, a woman he would rather not disappoint.

Putain, it was a lot more than that. He still loved her, still thrilled like a schoolboy at the sound of her voice, still dreamed of somehow squaring the impossible circle of contrasting ambitions that kept them apart. Even in those blissful moments when they shared the same bed, they had different dreams. Perhaps he should force himself to end it, to refuse to run at her bidding. It would hurt, he knew, but pain eases with time. He'd be bruised but free to look elsewhere and perhaps to give his heart fully and honestly to another.

He breathed out a long sigh. As he'd told Isabelle, this was all far above his head. Also he was hungry. He went back to buy another bottle of wine from the woman from the Domaine de la Voie Blanche, who made the wine the Baron had offered for his blind tasting. And that, Bruno recalled, as he tried to decide between the foie gras and the lamb chops, had been the dinner when Jacqueline had first talked of the Rosenholz dossier.

Enough of that, he told himself. This was a Saturday night.

He went back to the table to invite Pamela to dance. Then he should also dance with Rosalie again, he thought. Nor should he leave out Sabine, Florence and Fabiola. The thought of more dances made him feel better. Food could wait.

15

The next morning there was no sound from the guest bedroom upstairs when Bruno rose and took Balzac out for their morning run. He'd bought a couple of extra loaves from the Audrix bread oven the previous evening so he could make breakfast here at the cottage. Looking in at the chicken coop on his return he saw that his hens had been particularly generous that morning. He left six out and put four into the large crockery duck he kept in his pantry. He then went out with Balzac, his wand and a trowel to his row of truffle trees and began tapping as he watched for the shimmering dance of a rising fly.

'*Cherche*, Balzac, *cherche*,' he said and the hound padded forward to sniff at the point where Bruno had placed his wand and began to paw gently at the ground. Bruno moved him to one side and scraped with his trowel until a summer truffle, perhaps the size of a golf ball, emerged. That would do. Usually he'd have put it with the eggs in his pottery duck for a couple of days so the scent could seep through the porous eggshells but he'd grate this one onto the omelette he was planning.

He showered and dressed, set the table on the terrace and brought out butter, home-made apricot jam and freshly squeezed orange juice. As he went back inside to make the coffee, he heard the shower running upstairs. He went to the garden to pick a small bunch of fresh parsley before peeling and chopping two cloves of garlic, brushing the truffle clean and shaving off half a dozen slices. He waited until his guests had descended before cracking the eggs and announcing that their breakfast would be an *omelette aux truffes* outside in the garden. He whisked the eggs, added salt, pepper and the remainder of Stéphane's cream before pouring a little olive oil and a large pat of truffled butter into the frying pan. He tossed in the garlic and as it sizzled he added the egg mix and began to make the omelette, lifting and then lowering the pan to spread the liquid and running a wooden spatula around the sides to stop it sticking.

When he judged it to be almost done, Bruno grated the remainder of the truffle onto a surface that was still slightly liquid and folded the omelette over. He added the slices of truffle he had shaved earlier and took it out to the terrace, where he tore apart the parsley leaves and sprinkled them on top before serving. Alain broke off chunks of bread for them while Rosalie poured out the coffee.

'A perfect country breakfast,' said Rosalie, tapping her tummy when the omelette had gone along with all the bread and a third of a jar of Bruno's apricot jam. 'I'll go on a diet when we get back.'

'And we missed our morning run,' said Alain.

Rosalie smiled and put her hand on his, giving him a dreamy, loving look that suggested to Bruno that they'd enjoyed a rather different form of exercise this morning already. He smiled at the thought.

'I think you're well suited, you two,' he said. 'I look forward to seeing more of you when you're out of the air force and settled somewhere nearer.'

'We've been talking about that, whether we want to settle down in the Bergerac area as we first thought, or somewhere near here. It seems there's a vocational school in Sarlat we might consider, as well as the one in Bergerac. We heard about it from Florence over dinner last night. She said we might be able to do as she did, get the teaching diploma while actually working.'

'But Florence already had a university diploma,' Rosalie added. 'Still, she said vocational schools were more interested in craft skills and she asked me to send her the qualifications we got from the air force. And since she's on the executive committee of the teachers' union, she'll try to make it work. Your Mayor said he'd help if he could.'

'It makes sense to have a good look around,' Bruno said. 'You know what they say in the army – time spent in reconnaissance is seldom wasted. Sarlat will be full of tourists but if we set out now, we'll beat the rush. It's a handsome old town and worth seeing for its own sake.'

Soon after, they set off in Bruno's Land Rover, Rosalie on the back seat with Balzac. At Les Eyzies they looked up to admire the great overhanging cliffs that sheltered the town. They were in Sarlat not long before nine. The town was starting to stir, with stalls of cheese, *saucissons* and souvenirs being set out in front of shops. The streets weren't yet crowded so they could admire the heart of old Sarlat.

Other than the shop windows, it was a place that seemed

barely to have changed over the past four hundred years. Its centre was filled with Renaissance townhouses, a grand square and cathedral, interspersed with narrow alleys filled with restaurants and shops selling local delicacies. Bruno took them around the back of the cathedral to see the Merovingian tombs from the centuries after the Roman empire fell, and to the Lanterne des Morts, a tall, conical tower built eight centuries earlier from whose top a lantern glowed each night to mark the place of the dead.

'St Bernard came here to preach the Second Crusade,' Bruno said, warming to his role as guide. 'And there are Knights Templar signs engraved inside the tower. This was where the rebellion against English rule began in the Hundred Years' War. And the town was a Catholic stronghold in the Wars of Religion. It went through a bitter siege but held out. There's a lot of history here.'

Alain stopped to look at an estate agent's window and Rosalie picked up a photocopied leaflet that offered local houses for sale. They stopped for coffee at a place Bruno saw had a bowl of water outside for customers' dogs so Balzac could drink, too. Bruno glanced at the copy of that morning's *Sud Ouest* that lay on the counter. A third of the front page was covered with the composite photo of Henri under the headline, 'Unsolved murder – Do you know this man?'

Inside was Philippe's photo of Elisabeth Daynès at the Les Eyzies museum standing beside the Neanderthal skull she had reconstructed. Alongside it was a photo of the skull Virginie had worked on. Although it was unfinished, to Bruno's eyes it was already uncannily like the composite photo of Max that he had helped put together. The caption read, 'At last – after thirty years, we reveal the process of rebuilding the face of the unknown victim.'

Bruno nodded approval, thinking that J-J's media blitz seemed to be going well. He wondered if he'd had similar success with the national press and TV. He called Virginie to tell her how impressed he was but had to make do with leaving a message on her answering service. Just as he'd done so his phone rang again. It was J-J.

'I was just thinking about you,' he said. 'I'm in Sarlat, admiring your coverage in *Sud Ouest*. Did you have any luck with Henri?'

'Yes, he's coming to the Bergerac police station for an interview tomorrow at ten,' J-J replied, sounding very cheerful. 'Do you want to be there? Sabine is bringing Tante-Do for the confrontation. And our hotline has already had two calls saying it's Henri Bazaine. I think we'll get a few more after the responses come in from the TV bulletins.'

'Great, and well done. I'll see you before ten tomorrow in Bergerac.' He ended the call, picked up his coffee and joined his friends outside.

'I mean it about wanting one of Balzac's pups when we find a place of our own,' Alain said. He scratched the area where Balzac's silky ears joined his pointed skull and the dog groaned softly with pleasure as they sat on spindly chairs outside the coffee shop.

'That's agreed,' Bruno said. 'I thought I'd show you one or two more sights and then take you to the town vineyard outside St Denis that we're so proud of. We can have a light lunch there and taste our wines before you have to get back to the base. Have they got you on some kind of curfew?'

'No, it's not that, but it's at least a three-hour drive and we want to be back at the base in time for the evening meal, which means putting on our uniforms. The town vineyard sounds like a good plan.'

'I could stay around here for ages,' said Rosalie. 'It's lovely. Still, we haven't quite ruled out moving to Bordeaux, where we'd have a lot more options with technical schools but the house prices look steep. And with you nearby, we'd have a ready-made social life if we moved here.'

'You don't want to go back to Normandy?' Bruno asked.

'No, the weather's better down here. The farm was sold when my parents split up and the family is spread out all over the place. I've got a sister who's a surgical nurse in the South Pacific, in Nouvelle Calédonie, where we're planning our honeymoon, and a brother who works in insurance in Paris.'

'Well, you'll both be very welcome if you want to move to this area.' Bruno looked at the groups of tourists gathering behind guides holding up coloured ribbons on poles. 'The crowds are starting to move in so let's head back and I'll show you one of my favourite castles on the way.'

He took them to Commarque, a medieval fortress founded by Charlemagne and built up over the centuries to become one of the largest castles in Europe. They walked down the lane and through some woods until they reached the valley floor. Suddenly there it was, the great walls and tower standing proudly against the sky. Children were trying their hand at archery butts further down the valley. Beyond them, a special breed of cattle that thrived on marshland was grazing among the rivulets to which the River Beune had shrunk in the drought. Bruno told them the story of the dead woman he'd found at the bottom of the cliff on which the tower stood, and the Templar remains that had been unearthed in one of the caves beneath the castle.

'I think that was in the paper, with those Arab terrorists. I remember reading about it, around the time Alain and I were getting together,' said Rosalie. 'They had your photo in the paper and that was when Alain told me you were his cousin.'

'It's quite a place,' said Alain, looking up. 'I'd like to come back here and take a good look, climb up to the top of that tower. There must be a terrific view.'

'There certainly is,' said Bruno. 'It was built to be high enough to send signals by beacon across to Sarlat. The hills were bare of trees in those days. They were all cut down for charcoal to feed the forges in the area, busy making swords and armour for the knights. Much of the land around here is full of iron ore. Those cave paintings you saw used the iron-bearing clay to get the red pigments, and around St Denis they were still making cannon for warships in Napoleon's time. They used to ship them down the river to Bordeaux.'

They drove back to Les Eyzies, crossed one of the great bends of the Vézère and then a second at Campagne – 'Another chateau,' Rosalie announced – and through St Denis to the town vineyard.

The vines spread out along the hillside, hectare after hectare. First Bruno pointed out the small chateau that was at the heart of the place, where Julien had lived when trying to make a success of it as both vineyard and hotel. Overstretched and in debt, and distracted by his wife's terminal illness, Julien had been rescued by the Mayor, as well as by Hubert and other local businessmen who had bought out his debt and knuckled down to make the new town vineyard a going concern. Bruno had played a minor role in the saga, sufficient to get him awarded some shares and an appointment to the board of directors. He had used his savings to buy more shares and took great pride in its progress.

They found Julien and Hubert in the big barn that was now the *chai* where the wine was made and bottled. They were looking worried but cheered up at the sight of their guests, and led them to a modest table that served as a tasting counter. Despite the Mayor's best efforts, the plan for a vineyard visitors' centre was still on the drawing board.

After giving a special pat and a bowl of water to Balzac, Hubert poured out small glasses of the previous year's dry white for each of them, explaining that it was a classic blend of Sauvignon Blanc and Semillon grapes.

'It's three euros twenty a bottle but you can have Bruno's discount, three euros even,' said Julien. 'Or we offer a five litre box at fifteen euros, with Bruno's discount. That's a good buy.'

'I could drink a lot of this,' said Rosalie. 'It feels very refreshing and has a lot of fruit without being sweet. And I like the name, Demoiselle de la Vézère. Tell me, what's this dry weather we've been having doing to the vines?'

'It varies,' Julien replied. 'The old vines have sunk deep roots and can take water from far below the surface. And a bit of stress makes for better wine. But a lot of the young vines we've planted over the past few years are really suffering. Hubert and

I have just been talking about it. We certainly need rain, the sooner the better.'

'What kind of wine do you usually prefer?' asked Hubert.

'I'm no expert,' Alain replied with a smile. 'Red with meat, white with fish and after the first couple of sips of the stuff they serve us in the air force, I'm damned if I can tell the difference.'

'*Mon Dieu*, Bruno, your cousin's an honest man,' said Hubert. 'Not many of our customers would admit that. See what you think of this one, Alain. We call it Seigneur de la Vézère, and it's our standard red. It's two years old, half Cabernet Sauvignon with a quarter each of Merlot and Malbec. The same price as the white.'

'It's a lot smoother than what they serve at our canteen,' Alain replied after taking a sip. 'I like that.'

'Now try this one, the same blend of grapes but from our older vines and it has spent six months in oak barrels. See if you can taste the difference.'

Rosalie and Alain sipped and nodded. 'It leaves a lovely taste in my mouth,' she said.

Alain nodded, adding, 'I agree, and it has more flavour. How much is that?'

'Four euros fifty a bottle but you can buy five litres in a box for twenty-five euros and it stays in top form for six weeks, two months if you keep it somewhere cool.'

'Why is it more expensive?' Rosalie asked, reading out the name on the bottle, Chevalier de la Vézère.

'Oak barrels are expensive,' said Julien. 'Even the cheapest ones are more than six hundred euros each and the really good ones from old wood with a tight grain are a thousand upwards. What's more, you don't want to use them for more than three years, four at most. Then we sell them second-hand to Scotland for their whisky.'

'Really?' Rosalie asked. 'But whisky's a spirit. Does it change in the barrel?'

'The colour changes most. Like most spirits, whisky is colourless at first. The colour comes from the wood but you get a slightly different flavour from a sherry barrel from Spain than you do from one of our barrels. And that's not just the wine, it's the toasting. Look,' he said, pointing to a row of barrels. 'These are marked *noisette*, but they're made of oak, not hazel wood. The term comes from the colour of the toasting. All barrels are toasted on the inside. It used to be done over an open flame but these days they use a blow-torch. *Noisette* is a very light toasting but some heavy wines like a Syrah or a Malbec from Cahors benefit from a much darker toasting.'

'Well, we've learned something today and I think we've found the wines we'll serve at our wedding,' said Alain. 'I'm driving, so no more tasting for me, but we'll buy a box of the white and another of the good red.'

'When's the happy day?' Julien asked.

'As soon as I get my promotion which should come through within the next month or two,' Rosalie said. 'Then I'll be the same rank as Alain and we can marry and move into married quarters. These wines are for our engagement party. You'll come, won't you, Bruno?'

'Certainly, and we look forward to your being regular customers in the future,' he said.

'And I'll send along a bottle of champagne with him to help you celebrate, with my compliments,' Hubert added.

'Good luck with the rain,' Rosalie said. Bruno told Hubert and Julien they were heading for lunch.

'We only want something light,' she added. 'Bruno made us one of his truffle omelettes for breakfast.'

They ate on the terrace behind the small chateau that was attached to the Domaine, with a view over the swimming pool and tennis courts to the river beyond the gardens and parkland; *salade aux gésiers* for her, a *confit de canard* with salad for Alain, and Bruno chose a *salade chèvre* with goat cheese. He and Rosalie shared a small carafe of the town white and Alain drank mineral water.

'What does it mean, your being a director of the vineyard?' she asked.

'Lots of meetings, at least once a month,' he replied. 'Keeping an eye on the finances, and last month we agreed to postpone building the new visitors' centre until we see how this year's *récolte* comes out. If we get no rain, we'll need to economize. The best meeting was when we chose the names for the wines. Then there's the marketing strategy to discuss, which I don't know much about. But I did push hard for our wines to be on sale at all the *marchés nocturnes* in the region because they're less expensive than most. We only charge six euros a bottle, when most vineyards want eight or ten. And we now provide the house wines for several of our local restaurants.'

'It's a real surprise, Bruno. I never thought of you as a businessman.'

'I'm not,' he replied, laughing. 'I'm a country copper trying to do what's best for our town. Hubert and Julien really run the show.'

Back at Bruno's home, their bags packed and loaded in the car with their wines, Bruno embraced them both, saying that they would always be welcome in St Denis and promised he'd keep an eye out for possible houses. Rosalie crouched down, followed by Alain, to say their own farewells to Balzac. To Bruno's approval, they seemed to enjoy the generous lick of affection the hound bestowed on each of them. Being Balzac, he gave Rosalie a second enthusiastic slathering and watched with Bruno as they drove off.

16

The next morning at Bergerac police station, Bruno was drinking coffee with J-J, Sabine and Tante-Do, and leafing through the national newspapers. They found only some small stories with photos of Henri on the inside pages. Save for the local and regional press and TV, J-J's vaunted media blitz had been more of a fizzle. Most of the papers focused instead on the new scandal of possible German spies in France, following up on Jacqueline's op-ed article. The reports usually began by citing *Le Monde* but then went on to pillage Gilles's post on the *Paris Match* website, repeating the names of spies and even printing the photo portraits he had used.

'Do we need a new witch-hunt against the Left?' demanded *Libération*, the daily that seemed to Bruno to have one foot in the socialist centre-left and the other waving towards the various anti-capitalist sects, militant feminists and even more militant vegetarians and environmentalists. 'Better late than never for a house-cleaning of security risks,' suggested the centre-right *Le Figaro*. 'Reds under our beds?' asked the populist *Aujourd'hui*.

'Those damn friends of yours have stolen my media campaign, Bruno,' J-J grumbled, but his heart didn't seem to be in it. He kept glancing at the clock in the borrowed office and his eyes were bright at the promised confrontation of Tante-Do with Henri. He was also pleased when Bruno informed him that his predecessor, Joe, had called to say he recognized Henri's photo and was prepared to testify that he recalled seeing Henri, Max and Tante-Do together at the *félibrée*.

J-J had already made them rehearse his opening gambit twice. The moment the desk sergeant downstairs announced Henri's arrival, Sabine and Tante-Do were to stroll slowly and casually down the long corridor. That would give her twenty seconds to take a careful look at Henri to confirm his identity and then to greet him by name as an old friend. J-J would take it from there.

But the plan did not work out that way. Henri wasn't alone. He came with a lawyer. And not just any lawyer but one of a new breed, Pierre Perle, who liked to be known as the People's Pierre. A bouncy and aggressive advocate who seemed to have learned his trade from American TV courtroom dramas, he had a genius for publicity. He also had formidable legal credentials from the University of Bordeaux as one of the top law graduates of his year and as the author of a best-selling book, *It's Your Law – how to make it work for you.*

'This is outrageous!' Perle almost shouted the words following a moment of shocked silence after Tante-Do marched up to Henri, embraced him and said, '*Salut*, Henri. It may have been a long time but you haven't changed a bit. You're still a handsome devil.'

'This is a trap, a shameful ambush of an honest citizen who has come here to perform his civic duty,' the lawyer shouted while Henri looked stunned, trapped in Tante-Do's embrace. 'I shall complain to the courts. Commissaire Jalipeau, you should be ashamed of yourself.'

Bruno saw with a start that Philippe Delaron, obviously tipped off to attend this moment, was standing on the stairs, putting aside his camera to start scribbling in his notebook. J-J merely smiled and then brought his hands together three times, very slowly, in a mockery of applause.

'There you go again, Pierre,' he said. 'Making it all about you instead of about your client, and whether he can help in our attempt to find out how a young man was murdered thirty years ago.' He turned to Henri. 'Monsieur Bazaine, thank you for coming to see us. I hate to interrupt that touching reunion with an old flame of yours, but perhaps you would be happier discussing this in the privacy of an office.' J-J paused and then threw the People's Pierre a contemptuous glance, adding, 'Although I'm sure your lawyer would prefer to have it in the middle of the market hall.'

J-J opened the office door and gestured to the others to precede him. When Henri and his lawyer were seated before the desk, he stood facing them. 'Again, thank you for being here. Allow me to introduce the chief of police of the Vézère Valley, Bruno Courrèges, on whose turf the murder took place, and Sergeant Castignac, our liaison with the gendarmes.'

'And what have the gendarmes to do with this?' the lawyer asked.

'They helped disinter the body and examine the scene of the murder, and Sergeant Castignac has unearthed their contemporary reports. She has also assisted in our research into the

St Denis *félibrée*, during which we believe the murder occurred. You recall the *félibrée*, Monsieur Bazaine?'

'My client has no recollection of the event,' said Pierre.

'Despite the photographic evidence that he was present and in the company of the murdered man, and all this confirmed by contemporary witnesses,' J-J said calmly, taking his seat and opening a bulging file that Henri was eying with some concern. Bruno suspected that J-J had padded it with pages of less than relevant material.

'Photographs that were obviously concocted long after the event,' Pierre shot back. 'I shall ask the court to rule against their being admissible as evidence.'

'How fortunate then that we have some living witnesses, one of them a successful businesswoman of unquestioned probity who has identified him,' J-J said.

'You mean that harpy you launched at us in the corridor?'

'Harpy?' J-J raised his eyebrows. 'Tut-tut, Pierre, such outrageously sexist terms discredit you. I'm appalled to hear you speak that way about a woman who obviously cherishes some tender memories of your client in his younger days. I think you should apologize to Sergeant Castignac here.'

'I fear the woman must have mistaken me for someone else,' said Henri, the first time he'd spoken. He had a harsh, almost hoarse voice but his face was expressionless. 'I have no recollection of her.'

To Bruno, who had trawled through so many photos, this was evidently the same man. His hair colour and eyes, the set of his mouth and jaw, his height and build, all matched those of his younger self. And as Bruno studied him, he noticed that his ears were unusually large and set very close to his head, something that also matched the photos he had picked out.

'May I see your identity card, *monsieur*?' J-J asked, raising a hand when the lawyer made to object. 'We can hardly eliminate your client from our inquiries if we can't verify who he is.

'Henri Thorez Bazaine, born October fifteenth, 1968, in Belleville, Paris,' J-J read aloud as he copied the details onto a sheet of paper in the file before him. He looked up and said casually, 'Thorez is an unusual name. Would it have any connection to Maurice Thorez, the old Communist Party leader?' There was no response from Henri. 'Ah well, Belleville used to be the heart of the Red Belt even though these days it's become very trendy and gentrified, I'm told. What was your address there?'

'I was raised in a municipal orphanage named for Paul Lafargue, on the Rue Jean Jaurès,' Henri said.

J-J asked for the name of each school Henri had attended, primary, *collège* and so on. Henri had not gone to a *lycée*, which would have put him on a university track. Instead he'd attended a vocational school, learning general construction and electronics, and had been an apprentice with the works department of his local Mairie in Paris. J-J asked for more details: how long he'd been an apprentice; who were his teachers and who supervised his work; how much he was paid by the Mairie; when and why he'd stopped working for the Mairie and so on.

'Are you sure all this is necessary?' the lawyer asked.

'One never knows what is and isn't relevant until we check,' J-J replied blandly. 'And now, Monsieur Bazaine, can you tell us where you were in the first days of July of 1989?'

Henri looked at his lawyer who shrugged. 'I don't recall

exactly. It was too long ago. Probably hitch-hiking somewhere in central France, heading for the vineyards to get some work picking grapes. I was aiming for the Bordeaux region but got a lift to Bergerac so that's where I stayed.'

'The first few days of July would have been a couple of months too early for picking grapes.'

'I earned some money washing cars for tourists on the quayside until it was time for the harvest. I worked with a guy called Gérard Follet and we're still friends. These days he runs half a dozen automatic car washes in Bergerac and Sainte Foy and he remembers working with me.'

'One of our witnesses, a farmer near Vergt, recognised you from the photo in *Sud Ouest*. He distinctly recalls you and your friend Max picking strawberries with him on his father's farm in the last week of June. Is he making it up?'

'Must be mistaken identity,' said Henri. 'I never knew a guy called Max. But I can understand people making mistakes if this Max was around the area with a guy who looked like me. And I accept that there's a resemblance from the photos in the newspapers. But that's all it is, a resemblance from three decades ago.'

'I think we're finished here, *Monsieur le Commissaire*,' said the lawyer. 'My client came here voluntarily, answered your questions and very generously accepted that he bears a resemblance to your suspect. We conclude that you and your witnesses have all made an honest mistake and that should be the end of the matter.'

'Not so fast, Pierre. Naturally, we'll have to check out some parts of your client's story and I find it hard to believe that so many witnesses have all made the same mistake. Bruno, do you have any questions for Monsieur Bazaine?'

'Yes, one or two. The first one was where you performed your military service.'

'I was excused for medical reasons as asthmatic. The illness still troubles me. What else?'

'Your work as a wine consultant surprises me,' Bruno added. 'It's very unusual to be a professional oenologue whose own vineyard mainly makes cheap wines for a co-op. How do you explain that?'

'That's not the only wine I make,' Henri retorted, clearly stung by Bruno's mocking tone. 'And it's not as easy as you might think to make a consistent and decent wine year after year for the mass market. That's a skill people want to learn and they're prepared to pay me for it.'

'And where are these clients of yours who are willing to pay you to teach them how to succeed with mass market wines?'

'I protest,' interrupted the lawyer. 'These questions are entirely irrelevant to the matter before us.'

'I have an important client in Canada,' Henri said, raising his hand to silence his lawyer. 'I'm advising him on which wines he should plant on the northern shores of Lake Ontario which is becoming interesting wine country, thanks to climate change. More and more of us here in the Bergerac have been experimenting with different varieties of grapes so we have built up a lot of expertise that clients are prepared to pay for.'

'I think that's enough of these irrelevant questions,' said the lawyer.

'Who is your doctor?' Bruno went on, ignoring the lawyer's

objection. 'We should check on this asthma condition. I'd have thought the chemicals you spray on your grapes could be a problem for you.'

'That's more than enough,' said the lawyer, rising. 'Since you have evidently exhausted your relevant questions I see no reason to waste my client's time further with these irrelevant ones. And in future, any questions for my client should come first to me. Come along, Monsieur Bazaine, we're leaving.'

'I'll be in touch,' J-J said cheerfully as they left. Once the door closed behind them, he looked at Bruno and Sabine. 'That went rather well. Did you note that he swallowed my suggestion that he was here in the first few days of July? I'd expected him to say he wasn't even in these parts at that time. He slipped up there but maybe he knew we had enough witnesses who recall seeing him. And he's clearly nervous about this, otherwise he wouldn't have hired the People's Pierre.'

'I'm sorry, sir, but I can't understand why you're so confident,' said Sabine, a little hesitantly. 'He just stonewalled you.'

'But he gave us enough to start checking and verifying. We'll find people he was at school with and at the orphanage. We could well find that was where he met Max, even though he denied knowing him. Detective work is mainly about this sort of detailed work, slow but sure, Sabine, that's my watchword, so cheer up because we have lots to check. Once you've taken Tante-Do back, perhaps you could start with those schools he attended, see if there are any class photos and if any teachers are still alive. Then track down his old classmates. Bruno, have a word with that Belleville Mairie, if you would, for the orphanage records. I'll have my team check his car-wash story and the local doctors for his claim to have asthma, although I don't believe a word of it. I'll see how many more identifications we have from the media blitz.'

'I can't stay long, J-J,' Bruno said. 'I have to attend a forest fire rehearsal in St Denis this afternoon.'

Bruno found a spare desk with a phone, found a number for the Paris Mairie and asked for the Mayor's secretary, explaining his task.

'I don't think we can be much help,' she said. 'Ever since the old Communist neanderthals lost control of this *arrondissement*, we've had dreadful trouble trying to make sense of the old files. They destroyed a lot, deliberately burning whole sections of the archive trying to cover their tracks or making it difficult for their successors. That included a lot of budget accounts, school records, all sorts of special funds for labour relations, international links, so-called summer schools that seem to have been Communist holiday camps. Even the births, deaths and marriage registrations had huge gaps.'

'What about the Paul Lafargue orphanage?' he asked. 'We're trying to check the background of a suspect in a murder inquiry who claims he went there.'

'I've never heard of it, which doesn't mean it didn't exist. Hang on a minute, I'm just calling up on my computer the index we made of the archives and I've found a reference to it but the note says all the files are missing. Shall I pass you on to our archives department? They may be able to tell you more.'

The archives people were friendly but unable to be of much help. They did check on the apprenticeships record and found the name of Henri Thorez Zeller. He was listed as attending the local vocational school for four years after 1985 when he'd have been aged sixteen. He'd started doing three days a week of studies and two days working as an apprentice. In his fourth year he was doing one day a week at the school and the rest at his apprenticeship at the public works department. The file said his marks had varied between good and very good and that he'd graduated as a qualified construction electrician in June of '89.

'Do you have an address for him? Bruno asked.

'The Lafargue orphanage,' said the archivist. 'We think it closed a couple of years after Zeller left, when Jacques Chirac was Mayor of Paris and began cleaning up some of the old Communist strongholds. We have no files at all on the orphanage.'

'Any health records for this guy? He's supposed to have been spared military service because of asthma.'

'I doubt if these guys would have put an asthmatic into public works, even as an apprentice, but we don't have those records. Maybe the army can help you.'

'Why would all these archives have been destroyed? Any idea?'

'Some of it was inefficiency. But a lot of it was covering up corruption, jobs for the boys that didn't involve any actual work except what they called political organization. There were solidarity funds which filed no accounts, public housing for Mairie workers who never seem to have paid rent, that kind of thing. And a lot of incompetence was involved as well. Still, your man Zeller was at the vocational school so at least you have that.'

'What about his classmates? Do you have registers for them? I'm particularly interested in the murder victim, first name

Max. We know the two of them were travelling together around here in June and July that year.'

'I can have a look and get back to you.'

'Many thanks, and good luck with cleaning up those archives.' Bruno gave his phone number and email address before ending the call. He wrote a note for J-J on his findings and set off on the return to St Denis. He went home first to check on Balzac, then to his office to run through his emails. Shortly before two, he joined the large group of people already gathered in the hall of the fire station. The fire trucks had all been moved outside to make room. Half the Mairie staff was there along with Yveline and Sergeant Jules for the gendarmes, Fabiola and Dr Gelletreau, the *collège* director, and officials from the communes up and down the entire valley. He found his police colleagues, Louis from Montignac and Juliette from Les Eyzies.

'This would be a good time to pull off a bank robbery,' he said. 'Half the cops are tied up here.'

'Not to mention the TV news cameras,' said Louis, nodding at a separate stand filled with cameras and reporters, Philippe Delaron included.

'And the military,' said Juliette, pointing to a tall officer in air force uniform who was chatting with Albert, the chief *pompier* of St Denis, along with his boss, the woman who had recently taken over as head of the fire service for the *département*. She mounted a small dais, tapped the microphone to check it was working and began.

'We are now at a very high risk of forest fires and in a highly wooded region like this with lots of scattered housing we could lose dozens of lives, not to mention many millions in property, unless we take some very serious precautions. Each of your Mairies has been sent checklists of things they have to do, from preparing evacuation centres and emergency food and water supplies to mounting round-the-clock fire-watch stations on all the water towers. Doctors, pharmacies, medical centres and social work teams are being sent their own checklists on supplies that could be required and plans for preventive evacuation of at-risk individuals.'

She stepped down and handed the microphone to the Prefect, who began by saying he supported everything the chief *pompier* had said. 'If we get a major fire, I will at once declare a state of emergency under which supplies and key personnel can be requisitioned to deal with the challenge. Any disobedience of evacuation orders will result in an arrest. I should stress now that if such a fire occurs, human life will be our priority so we may suffer heavy losses in livestock. Paris has agreed that special compensation funds will be available and that *pompiers* from other regions which are not at risk can be drafted here. Mairies will have to make arrangements for their housing and upkeep. From midnight tonight, a special operations centre will be manned at the Périgueux Préfecture around the clock. And just so you know how seriously we are taking this, I will be on the first night shift. Now let me introduce Commander Yvelot of the *armée de l'air* who will be in charge of water-bombing operations.'

Commander Yvelot took the microphone. 'My team will be based at Bergerac airport,' he began. 'We'll have a flight of four dumpers, as we call the water-carriers, on permanent standby at Bordeaux for the region. We'll also be flying in chemical fire-suppressants. My colleagues are currently building a master map of the region, giving each square kilometre its own identifying code so we can steer the dumpers quickly to threatened points. We plan to issue stacks of these maps for each commune for your fire-watchers, Mairies, police and *pompiers*. We'll also have meteorologists on-site to warn us of prevailing winds, which are the real danger to the fires spreading. The bad news is they are predicting warm, dry winds from the south for the coming week, which is why this emergency practice has been called.

'Now, I have to speak in the name of my colleague from the army, Colonel Rostin, a signals specialist who is currently meeting in Périgueux with the local directors of all the telecommunications companies about their roles in maintaining phone links even if we lose some mobile-phone towers. They are setting up a dedicated communications centre at the Préfecture, with direct radio as well as phone links to every Mairie, Gendarmerie and *pompier* station. Expect one of those teams to be setting up links in your own communes over the next two to three days.'

'One more thing,' said the Prefect, climbing up onto the platform once more. 'In terms of handling any fires, local chiefs of *pompiers* will have absolute authority. If they demand public works staff and equipment to build firebreaks, they must be obeyed. If they have to drain swimming pools to get water or requisition civilian vehicles for evacuation purposes, so be it. All fires in the open air are now banned, which includes domestic barbecues. I hope you now realize how seriously we have to take this threat. Thank you.'

He stepped down to a long moment of stunned silence.

'Well, at least the schools are out so we have some evacuation centres available,' said Bruno to his two colleagues.

'We don't even have our own *pompiers* in Les Eyzies,' said Juliette.

'Christ, what about Lascaux?' said Louis, in whose district the prehistoric cave stood, surrounded by woodland. I'd better find my Mayor and see if we should close it.'

'All St Denis *pompiers* to me,' called out Albert. 'And you, Bruno, and Yveline and Jules and Monsieur le Maire.'

When they had all gathered, he began, 'I've spent the weekend with some of the lads from the hunting clubs trying to identify the highest risk zones, those woodland areas that appear to be most dry and flammable. There are three that really worry me. The first is the wood along the ridge above the town vineyard and all the way past Limeuil to Terrasson. The second is on the road up to Audrix along to the road that leads down to the forest of Campagne itself. The third is the woodland north of St Denis up to the Miremont crossroads and east to Les Eyzies. We'll need fire-watch volunteers, at least two people at each post, with binoculars and fully charged mobile phones running shift systems night and day. Bruno, can you round up some volunteers from the tennis and rugby clubs? And anybody who has a drone. They could be useful.'

'I'll do that as soon as we're finished here,' Bruno replied.

'If you could do the same for Les Eyzies, Juliette, I'd be grateful,' Albert went on. 'Fire-watch volunteers can use phone and church and water towers, whatever gives us good views. We'll have helicopters available to check out each warning.

And one last thing – beware of broken bottles. Fires are easily started by glass. At the right angle, it can become a lens that concentrates the sun's rays.'

As he turned to go, Albert paused. 'Oh, and finally, everybody. Double check your fire insurance.'

17

Bruno had to excuse himself from the usual Monday evening dinner with his friends at the riding school. He worked late into the night collecting keys to church and water towers, rounding up volunteers to watch for fires, his only meal a cold half-pizza from a stack of boxes delivered to the *pompiers*. His own home was in one of the high-risk zones so when he got home after midnight, he collected a box full of essential documents. He filled another box with his most cherished books and bottles of wine. He would leave them and Balzac at the Mayor's house in town. Then he fell into a deep sleep as soon as his head touched the pillow.

He woke with the cockerel's crow, skipped his usual run, and packed a suitcase of clean clothes. He went out to load up his Land Rover and felt the heat of the day building unusually early. The wind was from the south, warm but now menacing, and there was not a cloud in the sky. He sent a blanket email to all members of the rugby and tennis clubs calling for fire-watch volunteers, adding that they could sign up at the fire station. Then he cooked himself a hearty breakfast, a cheese omelette with cherry tomatoes on the side and two big slices of toasted bread from the *tourte* to go with it. This might be his only meal for some time. He squeezed his remaining oranges and made a big pot of coffee, sufficient for a mug with his breakfast and to fill his vacuum flask for the day to come.

On the radio, France Bleu Périgord was reporting the emergency, the Prefect's speech and the new fire regulations. The final item on the morning news made him sit up when he heard J-J's name and the familiar voice of the People's Pierre claiming that the veteran detective had developed a pathological obsession with a case he failed to solve at the start of his career.

'Now as this elderly policeman's career approaches its end, Jalipeau is riding roughshod over human rights in a desperate bid to find a plausible victim for his personal vendetta,' Pierre said, sounding as though he were addressing a public meeting. 'He is even using doctored photographs and dubious evidence of witnesses claiming to recall events that happened thirty years ago.'

'You are representing one of the suspects in the case, and I understand you took him to meet Commissaire Jalipeau,' said the interviewer.

'That's right. My client went to the police station voluntarily only to be ambushed by a woman he'd never met who was claiming some kind of relationship with him around the time and place of the murder. This farce was staged by Commissaire Jalipeau for reasons best known to himself. I can only presume he was hoping to shock my client, heavens know why.'

'These are serious allegations against a well-known and much admired senior police—'

'I quite agree,' Pierre interrupted. 'I have had great respect for him in the past, but his latest antics are beyond belief. Do you know he is using some unqualified young archaeologist to try to rebuild the face of the victim from a thirty-year-old skull? This is crazy, it's close to witchcraft. No serious lawyer could stand for it.'

'So what are you going to do?'

'I'm filing a formal complaint with the Commissioner of Police requesting that Jalipeau be suspended or at least removed from this case. Moreover, I will today petition the court on my client's behalf for relief from vexatious abuse. In a free country, the police cannot be allowed to get away with this kind of behaviour.'

'And now, it's going to be a hot day and watch out for those forest fires. If there's a pool or river near you, this might be a great day for it. But remember folks, no barbecues. By order of the Prefect. Turning to sports news . . .'

Bruno turned it off, finished his breakfast and washed up. He loaded Balzac into the Land Rover, drove into town and left Balzac in his office. It was too early to deliver him to the Mayor. Passing the *maison de la presse*, he saw Gilles emerge with the day's newspapers.

'Can you spare me ten minutes?' Bruno asked him. 'My house is in the danger zone so I'd like you to drive up there with me, and you bring back the Land Rover to park by the Mairie and I'll bring the police van back.'

'No problem,' said Gilles. On the drive there, he said that Fabiola was already at the medical centre but at least their house should be safe.

'I'm worried about Pamela's place,' Gilles went on, and Bruno realized with a sudden sense of guilt that he hadn't thought of that; not only of the danger to Pamela, Miranda and her children, but that Hector and the other horses might also be at risk.

'Have you spoken to her about it?' Bruno asked.

'Not yet. I was going to call her when I got home. Maybe she can at least move the horses to another stables.'

'The stables aren't that close to the woods, but Pamela's house could be in danger.'

'Don't forget about her gîtes. Right now they're full of tourists, probably all Brits.'

'I'll go up and see her after we get back to town,' Bruno said.

Twenty minutes later, he parked the police van at the stables, went to visit Hector and give him his usual carrot and greeted Beau and Bella. He walked up to the house to find her in the kitchen. She was speaking on the phone. She blew him a kiss before saying into the phone, 'I don't think anybody really knows how high the risk is. Ah, here's Bruno. I'll ask him and call you back.'

'*Bonjour*, Pamela,' he said, embracing her. 'Your stables should be okay, but this house could be in trouble if there's a fire in the woods behind. This south wind could sweep the flames right down. Let's take a look.'

There were twenty metres of garden behind the house, mainly her croquet lawn and flower beds, then a low hedge and another thirty or forty metres of grassland that linked to two big paddocks to left and right. So the woods were probably fifty or more metres from the house, a distance wider than the usual firebreak. The outbuildings that had been converted into four gîtes were even further from risk.

The house and gîtes were all stone with tiled roofs so there was little danger of sparks.

'You should be fine,' he said. 'But if you have to get out, make sure you and Miranda prepare boxes with all your essential documents and things you don't want to lose, and tell your guests to do the same.' Bruno checked his watch. 'May I take Hector out, go up to the ridge and see just how dry those woods are?'

'I'll come too, on Primrose, we both need some exercise.'

Ten minutes later, Bruno dismounted, handed his reins to Pamela and plunged into the woods, the vegetation was dry and crunchy beneath his feet at first, but as he went deeper the trees were older and the canopy more dense. The grass beneath his feet gave way to the mulch of a forest floor and he saw new shoots and some ferns, all still green. He bent down and brushed away the top layer of mulch, feeling a slight but reassuring dampness below.

'It's not too dry so it won't catch fire easily,' he said. 'Have you looked at your spring lately?'

She said she hadn't so Bruno rode further along the ridge and then diagonally down to the rocky outcrop from which water bubbled throughout the year. It fed a small stream that ran down through the riding school to a pond that housed colonies of toads whose croakings always fascinated Balzac. The water was invariably cool and clear, and Bruno found it delicious to drink, usually filling a twenty-litre *bidon* before the regular Monday night suppers. He dismounted again and clambered through the rocks to find that the spring was still giving water, not much but the flow in summer was always more feeble. Still, if the water table on the ridge and plateau were still feeding the spring, there would be water underground for the tree roots.

'It's still flowing, so the woodland above should be moist enough to resist anything but a massive fire,' he told Pamela.

The further they rode along the ridge, the drier the woodland below appeared to be, and when they came to the bridle trail they so often took, some of the trees were so dry that they had lost many of their leaves. Land that he knew to be usually boggy was now dry cracked mud. When they reached the hunters' cabin and took the track back to the valley, the stream that usually fed into the Vézère was barely a trickle. The horses cantered easily but even Hector seemed reluctant to increase his pace, as if drained by the heat. How, Bruno wondered, had Arabian horses won their historic reputation for speed when they must have endured heat like this? Perhaps their breed had grown used to it.

Back at the stables, they unsaddled and rubbed down the horses. Bruno sluiced himself down in the sink and drove back to town where he entrusted Balzac and his boxes to the Mayor. After this he made his usual patrol of the Tuesday morning market. Everyone he knew asked him about the fire emergency and he told them all of the need for fire-watch volunteers. One of the stallholders Bruno knew slightly, who sold novelty T-shirts and only came in the tourist season, brandished a mobile phone at him and said, 'You know this cop they're talking about.'

Bruno peered at the Twitter feed on the small screen. It read: '*Flic* should be locked up,' followed by '#CrazedCopPerigord'. He took the phone and scrolled up, seeing insult after insult against J-J, all with the same hashtag. Calling for him to be locked up was mild. Others claimed it should be '#CorruptCopPerigord' and that led to a second stream of different insults. There was one, referring to a long-ago gunfight when J-J had been hit by a bullet, that said, 'Shooter should have aimed higher, #CrazedCopPerigord.'

Feeling a cold anger at this vicious and anonymous attack on his friend, Bruno handed back the phone, and said curtly before turning away, 'He's a brave, honest guy and a friend of mine. If you get robbed or your kids get snatched, you'll want him on your side.'

'Aw, come on, don't take it so seriously,' the stallholder called after him. 'It's just a joke.'

Bruno turned on his heel, controlling his anger but his eyes were blazing. 'How would you like it if somebody burned out your stall and I said that was just a joke? Or if somebody held you up at gunpoint and I just shrugged and said you shouldn't take it seriously? We're cops. We're not supposed to back away and say it's all a joke. It's not a joke to me when some cop-hater trashes the reputation of a good man.'

He stared around at the people who had gathered to watch this confrontation, and one by one they dropped their eyes. As they began to move away, Bruno felt a hand land heavily on his shoulder and heard Léopold's deep voice.

'I was right here in this market just before Christmas when some young thugs trashed the Vietnamese stall that sells those *nems* we all like,' the big Senegalese said quietly, looming over the T-shirt seller. 'This cop here, Bruno, was dressed like Santa

Claus, raising money for kids. And he went for those thugs, knocked them down and took them out. Alone.'

'I didn't mean anything,' mumbled the T-shirt man, backing away to the shelter of his stall. 'Sorry.'

Bruno nodded at him coldly, turned, and Léopold shook his hand. 'My boys and I will be going to the *pompiers* to sign up for the fire watch after the market closes,' he said.

'Thanks, Léopold, See you there,' Bruno said, and walked on to the fire station. Ahmed was holding the fort, Albert's deputy and the only other professional firefighter in the St Denis team. The rest were all volunteers.

'Albert is getting some sleep,' Ahmed said. 'He'll be on watch all night. We've got some more professionals coming up from Bordeaux later today, bringing water tenders. You ought to go home and get some sleep. We might need you tonight.'

Instead, Bruno went back to his office and called an old contact in army records to see if there was any record of Henri being excused military service for asthma. He gave Henri's details, and was promised a call back. Then he called the Belleville archives again, to see if they had any medical records of children at the orphanage suffering from asthma. They would check. Almost as soon as he put down the phone on his desk, the mobile at his waist buzzed.

'What's this crap on Twitter about J-J?' came Isabelle's familiar voice.

'*Bonjour*, Isabelle. It's good to hear your voice,' he replied. 'There's a publicity-hungry lawyer playing games over the Oscar case.'

'That's clear from the Twitter feed but is this guy that J-J interrogated really a suspect?'

'His name is Henri Bazaine and his identity was visually confirmed by an old girlfriend who knew both him and Max – that's Oscar's real name. The guy says she's mistaken, so we're double-checking his background at an orphanage in Bellville that was long since closed and the local records were left in a mess, lots of files missing or destroyed.'

'Belleville? In the old Red Belt?'

'Yes, an orphanage named after someone called Paul Lafargue.'

'That doesn't surprise me. Lafargue was Karl Marx's French son-in-law. He founded the Workers' Party in France and wrote a book with the brilliant title, *The Right to be Lazy*. No wonder they liked him in Belleville. Still, it's convenient that this Henri claims to be from somewhere where the archives are a mess.'

'I'm checking his military service records. He claims he was excused because of asthma.'

'Would you like me to have someone take a look at the old RG files?' she asked. The Renseignements Généraux was the old police and security intelligence network which devoted much of its time to watching French political activists of left and right. Some of its employees were once famously discovered planting microphones in the offices of the investigative weekly *Le Canard enchaîné*. The RG had long since been merged into a new Directorate of Internal Security but its files and its work continued.

Hoping the RG might turn up something useful, Bruno gave her Henri's details, including his original surname, and then ended the call as his desk phone rang again. It was J-J, announcing himself by saying, 'Your mobile line was busy.'

'It was Isabelle, worried about your Twitter attack.'

'A man is judged by the enemies he makes,' J-J replied, his voice calm. 'Enough of that. I seem to recall that you had a contact with the Quebec cops in Canada. Are you still in touch?'

'I can be. Why?'

'I'm interested in Henri's wine-consulting business. Don't ask how I know but there are hefty annual payments to Henri from a Montreal-based corporation that owns vineyards and distilleries in Quebec and on the west coast. It all looks legal – a friend in the *fisc* tells me the money was declared and tax paid. It's a lot, ten grand a year going back as far as we can track – over ten years – and rising to fifteen the last two years. We looked at the firm's website and it seems real but maybe the local cops know something different.'

'I can try. What have you got?'

'It's called Vins de la Nouvelle France, and it's run by a guy called Laurent Loriot, and guess what? He was born in Belleville, just two days before our Henri. It seems a hell of a coincidence. He emigrated to Quebec from France in '91 and made good.'

'You have to be joking.' Bruno scratched his head, thinking hard, and said, 'I just talked to Isabelle. She's looking into old RG files about Belleville. You could ask her to try Loriot's name along with Henri's and I'll do the same with army records and a helpful guy at the Belleville archives. And she's the one with the Quebec police contacts.'

Bruno tried his army records contact first, a retired *sous-officier* who had helped him in the past, who began by saying he was about to call Bruno.

'There's nothing here in the Henri Zeller file about asthma or any medical condition. He got a deferment to finish vocational school and the next thing we knew was that we were informed that Henri Zeller had died in a road accident. We received a death certificate from the Belleville Mairie along with another one who died at the same time, Max Morilland, who was also on a vocational school deferment. They each had the same address, the Lafargue orphanage in Belleville.'

Bruno suppressed his excitement. 'What was the date on the death certificate?'

'December tenth, '89. Both men were supposed to turn up for military service the following month, January.'

'Thank you, my friend. This is very important. Could you email me a scan of those death certificates, please? We're into a murder inquiry involving a man who's been using that identity of Henri Zeller, changing his name to Bazaine. And the murdered guy was called Max.'

'I'll do it now. Let me know how this turns out. You've got me interested.'

Forgetting his promise to check army records for Loriot in Quebec, Bruno immediately called J-J to convey the news that Henri Bazaine had officially been dead for three decades, supposedly in a car crash with a man from the same orphanage named Max Morilland. As they spoke, his desktop computer pinged to signal an incoming email. It was the scans of the two death certificates that he at once forwarded to J-J and to Isabelle. The printed form itself looked straightforward, with the official stamp of the Mairie, the date, and the name of the doctor who certified the cause of death as a traffic accident.

'I suppose this means I can arrest him for identity theft, or for forgery to evade military service,' J-J said, sounding hesitant.

'I've never come across anything like this before. I'd better have a word with our police lawyer. And this other guy, Max Morilland, do you suppose he's the murder victim?'

'I presume so,' said Bruno. 'It could be a coincidence. I'm as confused as you by this. Either Henri forged the death certificate or, more likely, got somebody in the Mairie to do it for him and sent it to the army. But the record of Henri's death should have gone automatically to other official databases like the electoral roll and the social security register. You'd better check whether this supposed death was recorded elsewhere. And before you arrest him, do you have any evidence that he was involved in this fake certificate? He could claim he was the innocent victim of some bureaucratic mix-up – and given what I've been told about the state of the local archives in Belleville, that's entirely possible.'

As Bruno spoke, his computer pinged again. The new email was from the archives in Belleville, informing him that Henri had a classmate in vocational school called Max Morilland. He immediately passed on the news to J-J.

'It all seems too convenient,' J-J replied.

'It reminds me of something I read about the Resistance during the war,' Bruno said. 'They always wanted to have somebody inside a Mairie who could arrange to concoct apparently genuine identity documents, working papers, coupons for food rations, justifications for travel. Maybe there was somebody doing that in Belleville and making money out of it. This was back in the eighties, when it must have been easier to get away with it. Registers were filled in by hand and kept in filing cabinets, before everything became computerized.'

Bruno's computer pinged yet again. This time it was an email from Isabelle, with a copy to J-J. It read, 'Have passed this to Paris police and to RG. It smells fishy. We'll also take a look at Malakoff, which has had a Communist Mayor since the 1920s and a sports stadium named after Lenin. RG suggests no arrests yet. We'll talk.'

18

Bruno had hoped to catch a few hours' sleep at home before heading out at around ten to his fire-watching post on the church tower of Audrix. Now he wondered whether he'd make it. He felt almost overwhelmed with all the balls he was juggling – the fire precautions, worrying about Pamela's house and Hector as well as trying to keep straight all the aspects of the murder case. He called his friend at army records and asked him to find what he could of the military service of Laurent Loriot, the Quebéc winemaker who'd been born in Belleville and had become the main customer of Henri's wine consulting business.

His phone rang again almost at once. It was Florence to say that she had thought about his offer of one of Balzac's puppies and she was very grateful, but her children were still too small to take proper responsibility. Bruno said he understood and promised to save one from a future litter. Then he called Rod Macrae, a former rock musician who lived nearby. He'd told Bruno months earlier that he wanted one of Balzac's pups and now he could have one. Macrae was delighted and they agreed to visit the kennels at some future weekend and he invited Bruno to drop by to seal the deal over a drink.

The next call came from Sabine, saying that Tante-Do was

becoming increasingly nervous for her own safety as a woman living alone and had asked if Sabine might come and stay with her. Bruno, feeling instantly guilty at not thinking of this, said he saw no objection but she'd better check with J-J. Moments later, Isabelle was calling again, this time to say that the latest edition of *Le Monde* had just arrived on her laptop and the expected counter-attack of the French establishment had begun. As she spoke, a copy of the article appeared in Bruno's inbox.

> The new 'Finlandization' and the danger to France [ran the headline]. As France considers how to deal with the latest eruption of the East German spy scandal of the Rosenholz dossier, a timely warning comes from Finland. During the Cold War, the term 'Finlandization,' deployed in the American capital as a term of abuse, described the way that the small Nordic country felt the need to remain neutral to appease its giant Soviet neighbour. Now France is threatened with a new kind of Finlandization, following in Finland's footsteps into a dangerous witch-hunt that could target many innocent officials

The article went on to explain that on the basis of the Rosenholz files, Finland's SUPO (security police) had begun to investigate one of the country's ambassadors, Alpo Rusi, a former adviser to the country's President Martti Ahtisaari, as a possible Stasi agent. SUPO had judged him to be the Stasi agent called Pekka in the Rosenholz dossier, and Rusi had strenuously denied the charges brought against him. He'd won his case, and then sued the Finnish state for slandering his good name and won again, securing a compensation payment of twenty thousand euros. As a result, the Finnish high court decided that the Rosenholz files were inadequate as proof and that they should remain classified in future.

So why is France now trying once again to obtain these dubious records, whose validity has been publicly questioned, and to what end? Do we seriously wish to inflict on our own public servants the ordeal inflicted on Ambassador Rusi? Do we want to stage our own McCarthy-style witch-hunt when such an act of anti-Communist hysteria is now widely and rightly condemned in the country that suffered it?

'The key point, Bruno,' Isabelle said, 'is that this article is signed by a member of the Constitutional Council, which sounds to me like a shot across the bows from the legal establishment. I've already had a couple of worried calls from the Elysée, and the President himself is concerned. On top of that we have French diplomats saying that this is damaging our relations with Germany, and I'm getting some snide remarks from my own German counterparts. This is becoming a very unpleasant political mess.'

'I sympathize, but I don't see what I can do about it.'

'You could try to persuade Jacqueline and Gilles to shut up.'

'You and I know them well enough to be sure it would have the opposite effect and make them redouble their efforts,' he replied. 'And it's too late.'

'You may be right, but at least give me warning of any new intervention they're planning.'

'I shall. You can do something for me,' he said. 'Another of the Belleville orphans, Laurent Loriot, born in the same week as our Henri Bazaine, went to Canada thirty years ago and made good in the wine business. He's been paying Henri large sums for alleged wine consulting – ten or fifteen grand a year for many years. Could you check with your contacts in Ottawa and Montreal if anything is known about him and his group, Les Vins de Nouvelle France?'

'I'll make a call,' she said. 'And please keep me informed.'

Bruno sighed and went back to his task of listing all the elderly and handicapped people living in remote locations in the commune who might be at risk from a fire. He had still to check it against separate lists for emergency evacuations drawn up by the medical centre, the pharmacists and the social services. Then there was the list of volunteers who offered to use their cars to pick up people who would not need a special vehicle. His phone rang again.

'Where are you?' came the voice of Albert, the chief *pompier*.

'In my office at the Mairie. Why?'

'You ought to be getting some rest,' Albert said. 'You're on watch tonight at Audrix from ten, according to the list you drew up. So where are you going to sleep?'

'Back at my place.'

'Forget it, Bruno. Your house is too much at risk and I'm not in a position to drop everything and come to rescue you. You'll sleep at the Mayor's house. He's expecting you, and I mean now. Sweet dreams.'

Bruno shrugged and decided he could make one more call. He phoned the Belleville archives, who'd been helpful before, to inform them that the Henri Zeller he had asked about was supposed to have been dead for three decades.

'I'll send you a copy of the death certificate,' Bruno told the archivist. 'It was one of two sent from the Belleville Hôtel de Ville to the army to explain why Bazaine and another local young man called Max Morilland would not turn up for military service.'

'That's interesting,' the archivist replied. 'But this Zeller is the guy who's supposed to be still alive and the subject of your investigation, is that right?'

'Correct,' said Bruno. 'Zeller was his original name. He changed it to Bazaine when he married a woman with that name who was going to inherit a vineyard. I thought you'd like to know. And we think the man he might have killed was Max Morilland, Henri's classmate at vocational school. You sent me that email about him.'

'Wow, I've never been involved in anything like this.' The archivist's voice was excited. 'I'd better check this with the last survivor.'

'Who's the last survivor?'

'Sorry, I was thinking aloud,' the archivist replied. 'There's an elderly woman, the last living member of the Mairie staff under the old regime. She is sometimes helpful. A veteran Communist, of course, but she's seen the light. She's retired, getting on for eighty and living with her son somewhere near you, a place called Carlux. Do you want her number? She goes by the name of Rosa Luxemburg Delpèche, which is a giveaway to her parents' politics.'

Bruno nodded. Rosa Luxemburg had been a leader of the German Communists, assassinated at the end of the Great War. He took down Madame Delpèche's address and phone number, toyed with the idea of driving there at once, less than an hour away, but then thought of Albert's call. The fire chief was right. Bruno needed some sleep. And he'd see Balzac. He picked up his cap, strolled down to the Mayor's house, and greeted Balzac who raced from the far end of the garden where Jacqueline was weeding.

'*Bonjour*, Bruno, you're in the spare room,' Jacqueline said, presenting her cheeks to be kissed after the first flood of Balzac's welcome had receded. 'I'll wake you before ten. I have my orders from Albert along with a set of very impressive binoculars for you and a map that's far too complex for me to read. Balzac stays with me, otherwise you'll get no sleep. Your case is already in the room along with towels and some mineral water. Sleep well. Oh, and the last news bulletin reported two new forest fires, one in the Lot, east of Cahors, and the other south-west of us at Casteljaloux. The *armée de l'air* sent planes dropping water.'

In his days in the army, Bruno had been able to fall asleep almost at will, seizing any opportunity to doze off. Perhaps because he was older, it was no longer so easy, or perhaps his life was now more complicated. Thoughts of Henri Bazaine, the dead Max and the frightened Tante-Do danced in his head. He was also surprised that Isabelle took so seriously the little flutters of panic that arose in the bizarre, self-absorbed world of French presidential politics. None of that was as important as protecting his valley from the threat of forest fire.

He must have drifted off for when he heard a knock on the door and Jacqueline's voice, his watch showed twenty minutes to ten. He called out that he was up, took a quick shower and went out to the smell of fresh coffee. Places were set for three at the kitchen table and Jacqueline was mixing a salad while the Mayor pulled toasted cheese sandwiches from beneath the grill.

'I'm not sure if this is breakfast or dinner but either way I'm looking forward to it. *Bonjour et bonsoir* and thank you,' Bruno said. At the sound of his voice came a scratching on the kitchen door and the Mayor used the hand bearing the spatula to open it, allowing Balzac to rush in to greet his master as if they'd been separated for weeks.

'If you could pass that Worcestershire sauce, it's time to add it,' the Mayor said. 'I'll always be grateful to Pamela for introducing us to this. Grilled cheese would not be the same without it.' Bruno complied and then began squeezing oranges from the bowl on the table as the Mayor brought the plates to the table. Ten minutes later, refreshed and for-tified, with a thermos of fresh coffee, a bag of fruit, *saucisson*, water and a baguette, they were in Bruno's van and heading for Audrix. There were still some customers dining on the terrace of the Auberge when they arrived, and the village's own Mayor, Jolibert, was standing on the steps of his tiny Mairie to greet them.

'My turn tomorrow night,' he said by way of greeting as they shook hands. 'We had three or four small outbreaks today, nothing the lads couldn't handle. But this is the first evening when that damned southerly wind hasn't died down. It could be a bad night. Be sure to call me if things start looking rough.'

'I heard the planes were busy dropping fire retardant down south in the Lot,' said Bruno. 'But that was hours ago.'

'Rocamadour and Biron were the nearest the fires came to us today,' said Jolibert. 'Now you're here, I'm off to bed. But please wake me if you see a big one.'

Bruno and the Mayor walked slowly around the hilltop village, able to see for at least ten kilometres in all directions except east, where the nearest skyline was dominated by a tall aerial mast. It was owned by the Defence Ministry and said to be a key link of French military communications.

'Has anybody suggested we should have a watching post on top of that?' Bruno asked. The Mayor shrugged and said, 'Ask Albert.'

Bruno phoned in, to be told the request had been dismissed on grounds of security.

'Understood. But have we suggested that the military put their own fire-watchers up there? They'd have a much better view than we do. It's crazy if we work with the air force to drop water but can't use their facilities to check for fires.'

'You're with the Mayor,' Albert replied. 'Ask him. He's the politician.'

The Mayor agreed. 'That makes sense. I'll call the Minister tomorrow. Now you can tell me what's going on with this old murder inquiry that's made J-J so unpopular on social media.'

Bruno did so as the Mayor made a slow scan of the horizon with the binoculars.

'You and J-J seem very focused on collecting evidence to charge this Henri Bazaine with murder,' the Mayor said once Bruno had finished. 'I'm more worried that we've had a Communist mairie in Paris that's been forging documents, creating fake identities and killing them off, and has since managed to destroy most of the evidence.'

'That's why Isabelle has brought in the internal security people. They're trawling through the old RG files.'

'Renseignements Généraux? I never liked the idea of that kind of political police, neither the files they kept, nor their methods or the use that could be made of them. But in this case, I might make an exception. The idea that a French mayor could preside over a system where foreign agents could be provided with apparently genuine French identities in order to conspire against an elected French government is sickening.'

'They were hardly discreet about it,' said Bruno. 'You remember the old Communist Party slogan, that my true homeland is the international working class?'

The Mayor made a sound halfway between a grunt and a sigh and handed Bruno the binoculars.

'Very distant red glow to the north-west,' said Bruno. 'Better call it in.'

The Mayor called the control room in Périgueux and reported the glow.

'A fire in the woods north of Cendrieux,' he told Bruno. 'The *pompiers* are there. You know,' he went on, 'we're going to need a better system of forest management to deal with this climate change. We can't continue just cutting timber and leaving loose brush and branches all over the ground. It's an invitation to fire.'

'Yes, but it also provides a habitat for the insects and wildlife that regenerate the ground,' said Bruno. 'It's complex. Maybe you should get our local agricultural research station to make some recommendations.'

'I did a little research into this recent surge in forest fires,' the Mayor explained. 'A hundred dead in Greece three years ago and eighty in California, parts of Los Angeles evacuated and insurers losing more than twenty billion euros. And then there's Australia with eleven million hectares burned, that's about the size of England. What we're doing here with fire watches, we're just reacting. We need to think ahead.'

'But how far ahead?' Bruno asked. 'When trees can live for hundreds of years we need a special kind of long view.'

And so the night went on, the two men chatting while eating their bread and *saucisson* and drinking their coffee from the thermos, breaking off to report a red glow suddenly in the sky to the south-east, towards Cahors. Nearer to dawn they reported another, due south near the old abbey of Cadouin. Each time the control room had already been alerted.

'How does a fire suddenly break out at three in the morning, when there's no lightning, no tourists dropping cigarette ends, no sun to start a flame through a piece of broken glass?' the Mayor asked.

'Albert says fire can lie dormant, just glowing for hours if there's the right amount of fuel, until a sudden gust of warm wind licks it into life.' Bruno upended the thermos. 'There's no more coffee and dawn's coming. What's your schedule today?'

'I shall write a letter to the Minister of Defence and call him, the same for the Environment Minister. Since French law allows me the privilege of an immediate audience with all ministers I'd be failing in my constitutional duty as a former Senator if I didn't take advantage of such access. I'll also talk to the head of the research station. And you?'

'I have a meeting with J-J and Prunier with a police lawyer in Périgueux to see if we have enough of a case for the Procureur to bring charges against Henri. There's a text on my phone saying I should be there. I'll also want to arrange a police guard for our main witness, the one we call Tante-Do. Then I ought to call in on Virginie, the young woman who's making a face out of J-J's famous skull. I feel a bit guilty about not doing more to make her welcome so I've invited her down to St Denis for the weekend. Fabiola is interested in the project and said she'd gladly let Virginie have her spare room and you ought to meet her. Then at some point I'll go to visit an old lady who used to work at the Belleville Mairie who may be able to tell me more about these fake death certificates.'

'I hope you'll get some time to sleep.'

'I slept well at your place and I might take a nap for an hour or so when we leave here. After the military I'm accustomed to a few broken nights. These night duties are probably worse for all the volunteer *pompiers* but we wouldn't have a fire or rescue service without them. And it's the same for you, taking your turn on fire-watch.'

'If I didn't, not a single volunteer *pompier* would ever vote for me again,' the Mayor replied. 'And they'd be right. When I think of the hours they put in . . .'

'It's not just the *pompiers*,' said Bruno. 'We have more than two hundred people from St Denis who've volunteered themselves and their cars to go pick up any old folk at risk. These are decent people that we work for.'

19

By nine in the morning, after a nap, a brisk ride of Hector with Balzac trotting behind, a shower and breakfast, Bruno arrived at the address of the woman with the unforgettable name of Rosa Luxemburg. He had to work at his memory to recall her surname, Delpèche. She lived in a small cottage outside the hilltop village of Carlux, close to the bridge over the Dordogne. The far side of the river was heavily cultivated but this side was so thickly wooded that the whole area looked to Bruno like a fire risk, threatening even the lavishly restored Château de Rouffillac on the slope dominating the bridge.

He parked his police van, put Balzac on a leash and approached a wooden gate that led to a well-tended garden. He stood for a moment admiring the neat rows of lettuces, peas, aubergines and tomatoes before wondering how on earth she watered them. Then he saw the large cistern, rather like his own, into which the cottage gutters fed. Interspersed between the rows he saw the tell-tale glint of inverted plastic bottles. She was using a drip system of irrigation, not unlike his own.

'*Bonjour*, Madame Delpèche, and my congratulations on your watering system and the splendid potager you've made,' he said, touching the brim of his cap as a tall, thin, elderly woman came briskly around the corner of the cottage. She was wearing baggy khaki pants, a blue denim shirt and an enormous straw hat. She carried a plastic bowl that looked half full of muddy water and she poured it into the cistern before turning to reply politely to his greeting and to stare at him with a confused half-smile as if trying to remember when and where she might have met him.

'I assume you save the water from rinsing your vegetables,' he said. 'I do the same, but I don't think you learned your gardening skills in Belleville. I'm Bruno Courrèges, municipal policeman from St Denis, and I'd be grateful for a few minutes of your time. The people at today's Belleville Mairie tell me you're the only person who can help make sense of what's left of the old archives.'

'I'm saving water because my cistern is nearly empty and I don't see this heatwave ending soon,' she said, coming forward to open the gate before shaking his outstretched hand. Her face widened into a broad smile when she saw Balzac. He always helped to break the ice.

'What a splendid dog,' she exclaimed. 'Do you work with him?'

'I'm training him to find truffles but he's a wonderful guard for my geese and chickens.'

'I had a little terrier who passed away last year and haven't had the heart to replace him,' she said, going down on one knee to fondle Balzac's ears. She was spry for her age. The archivist had told him she was nearly eighty but she looked to be in her sixties. As she rose again and took off her straw hat, he saw she had iron-grey hair, cut short, and watchful brown eyes.

'Would he like a drink of water?' she asked, looking down again at Balzac. 'I was about to make myself some coffee. You're welcome to join me. It's cooler on the terrace at the back, and you can tell me why you're here.'

'It's about a man, born in Belleville, called Henri Zeller,' Bruno began as they sat in the shade of an awning behind the house. Chickens pecked in the small fenced area of land that gave way to a steep and wooded cliff that rose to Carlux on the hilltop. The slope was too steep to see the ruins of the old castle at the heart of the village.

Bruno explained that Henri had failed to appear for his military service because the Mairie sent the army his death certificate in December of '89. But he was alive and well and running a vineyard in the Bergerac under the name of Bazaine. Bruno was helping to investigate the long-ago murder of a friend of Henri's that same summer while the two men were camping near St Denis. The dead man, also from Belleville, was called Max Morilland. The Belleville Mairie sent the army a death certificate for him at the same time. They had both grown up in the Lafargue orphanage in Belleville. Could she help?

'Have you been to Belleville?' she asked, after studying him for a moment.

'I walked through it once, from the cemetery of Père Lachaise to the park of the Buttes Chaumont. I was in love at the time and only had eyes for the girl. We failed to find the lamp-post on the Rue de Belleville that marks the spot where Edith Piaf was supposed to have been born.'

She smiled and said, 'I know you look the part, but it's hard to believe you really are a municipal policeman.'

'You could call my friend Montsouris in St Denis, a train driver and a party member. We play tennis together.'

'I don't think I've believed a word any party member said to me for thirty years. But don't worry. I read *Sud Ouest* and I remember seeing a photo of you and your dog when you arrested those IRA people.'

'So you know I'm genuine. What can you tell me?'

'The Lafargue orphanage was very small for the number of children it was supposed to house, because most of those registered were never there. We all knew it, even though I wasn't in the registrations department which managed such matters.'

'How do you mean, they were never there?'

'They were invented, just names on lists. I assumed it was a way of getting more money from the central government, welfare payments for non-existent orphans.'

'Which department did you work in?

'I was in a section known as "Fraternité", which dealt with relations with comrades elsewhere, from Italy and Britain to Poland, Cuba and above all East Germany.'

'Why above all?' Bruno asked.

'Many of our senior party cadres had been conscripted to Germany as forced labour during the war and had learned the language. The German comrades were keen to maintain the connection, inviting us to their holiday camps and so on. I went twice, although I was most useful for my English and my Spanish. First time I visited Schwerin, a beautiful place, a lovely castle on a lake and a fine old town. That was in the late seventies. The second time, in '86, I was invited to Radebeul, near Dresden in the Elbe valley, an area of vineyards. It was sad. They had no corks so used bottle caps instead. Their old barrels were rotting and they couldn't afford stainless steel vats so they used enamel ones, designed for making beer. Still, the people were very welcoming.'

She smiled. 'The wine wasn't bad. And we had to sit through a lot less folk dancing than we did in Cuba and Bulgaria.'

'Did you make friends?' Bruno asked, genuinely curious.

'Yes, there was a French couple from Belleville, Jacques and Sylvie Lefort, who'd emigrated there in the fifties. They taught French and helped run a local orphanage, named for Clara Zetkin, a famous German Communist. She's buried in the Kremlin wall. We met some of the youngsters and were amazed at how good their French was and how much they knew about France. They would listen to French radio, watch French films and there were up-to-date French papers and magazines in the library.'

'Did you conclude that these German youngsters were being trained to merge into French life?'

'Yes, but I didn't think that was sinister at the time. I just thought it was a marvellous way to educate these young people.'

'How much of their education did you see?'

'How do you mean?'

'Did you see anything special that might have been espionage training, in codes, communications, that kind of thing?'

'There was a lot of gymnastics, judo, cross-country running and hikes – at the time I just thought it was very healthy. But we didn't sit in on the classes. They could have had espionage training and I wouldn't have known.'

'Did you talk politics with the kids?' Bruno asked.

'Not really, except bland clichés about the struggle for peace, racism in America, the Vietnam war, that kind of thing. Our meetings with the youngsters were mostly organized and scripted, except when we went off for picnics in the vineyards when we realized they were very well informed about France and French politics. They were bright kids. They clearly saw the difference between what they read in the French media and the spoon-fed propaganda in their own East German press. Looking back, there were some clues that their thinking was a bit dissident.'

'Did Jacques and Sylvie encourage this kind of free thinking?'

'Yes, I think they did but not in any subversive way. They had no children of their own but they were really proud of the kids they taught and loved to see the way they interacted with us.'

Jacques and Sylvie had kept a scrapbook with sections on each of the youngsters, growing up, playing sports, their school reports, their work in the vineyards. Leafing through it one day with Sylvie, Rosa said she'd seen photos of a couple of boys, almost young men, whom she recognized.

'I'd seen them in the Mairie back in Belleville where they were working in registrations,' she said. 'I'd thought they were French. I assumed it was some sort of exchange scheme. It took some time for me to realize what their presence really meant.'

'Which was . . .?' asked Bruno.

'To insert them into French life as French citizens, presumably while still taking their orders from East Berlin.'

'What year was that?' Bruno asked.

'Nineteen eighty-six, a time of great controversy in the Belleville Mairie with most of the younger people thinking

Gorbachev was wonderful and most of the old guard fearing that he was betraying the Revolution.'

'What did you think?'

'I was confused. Gorbachev was such a breath of fresh air, an idealist, a believer in peace after all those dreadful old men in the Kremlin. But I was worried that he was naive and that he could end up destroying the good things about socialism along with the bad.'

She sat forward and tapped Bruno on the knee. 'You have to understand that I was born in the war. It was clear to me that the Nazis had been defeated in the field by the Red Army and in France by the Resistance, which was mainly Communist. You're too young to remember but the Party used to call itself the party of *les quarante milles fusillés*, the forty thousand martyrs, executed by the Nazis for their courage. That was how I was brought up – that it was Communism that beat Hitler, not American capitalism and British imperialism. And without the Soviet Union, what would save us from the new fascism that we could all see at work in the Vietnam war?'

'So you were torn,' Bruno suggested. 'You were trying to believe two contradictory things at the same time, that Gorbachev was great but that he could imperil everything the Soviet Union stood for.'

She nodded. 'Yes, that's right. And everything in my life, all my friends, my workmates, even friends who were not in the Party, we were all instinctively on the left. We'd all been thrilled by '68 in Paris, the general strike, the state giving in to the workers' demands, the Americans getting a bloody nose in Vietnam. I got married then to a comrade who worked on l'*Humanité*, the party newspaper. We had our son. It seemed we were on the right side of history. And yet at the same time, Belleville was changing. New housing estates, new people, a lot of hostility to the Algerians and you could feel the Party's grip on the working class start to weaken. You could see the old working class starting to dissolve, just like my marriage. We divorced in '84.'

'How long did you stay at the Mairie?'

'My department was closed at the end of '89 after the Berlin Wall came down. I got a job in a travel agency and then an old comrade helped me into a better job on the railways, the international office where my languages were useful. When I retired, I came down here where my son works in the tourism office. He married a woman from Sarlat, so I have my son, my grandchildren, my garden.'

'Did you ever hear again from Jacques and Sylvie Lefort at the orphanage?' he asked.

'No, although I wrote to them a couple of times, but never had a reply. I tried to telephone the orphanage but it had been closed.'

'How many French-speaking youngsters did you see at this orphanage?'

There had been at least twenty that she had seen but there may have been more, Rosa explained. The Leforts had been running the orphanage for more than twenty years, for girls as well as boys. There had been a separate small house for girls.

'And those faces at the Mairie whom you recognized from the Leforts' scrapbook, did you ever see them again?'

'No, and the Party was dying along with the old guard. So

many Mairies were lost as the Party shrank. Mitterrand killed it. He brought the Party into his government in '81. We thought it was the start of great things but he slowly embraced us to death. No, I never saw the Leforts again, but I often wondered what had happened to those young German boys with their perfect French and French identity cards. What on earth they must have thought as their own country dissolved and they were stuck in France.'

'Did you recognize those names, Henri Zeller and Max Morilland?'

She shook her head. Bruno pulled from his small briefcase a file with the reconstituted photos of the two men. 'Do you recognize either of them?'

She took them and examined them closely, then extracted a pair of spectacles from her shirt pocket and peered at them again. 'I remember this one,' she said, pointing at Max. 'He was a favourite of Jacques and Sylvie and I met him with them, but neither of the two names you mentioned rings a bell. And I don't recall ever seeing the other one. Which was the one you think was murdered?'

'Max, the one you recognized. Like Henri, he had a fake French identity, birth certificate, school records and reports – all simply made up at the Mairie.'

'Do you know what happened, how Max was killed?' she asked.

'He and Henri had been making money in the strawberry fields and planned to move on to work in the vineyards. They were camping *sauvage* near St Denis. They picked up a couple of girls and then disappeared. Max's body was found the next year after a storm uncovered his grave in the woods. He'd been hit over the head with a camping shovel.'

'This murder was in the summer of '89?' she asked. Bruno nodded. 'That was the summer before the Wall came down, when thousands of young Germans were getting out to the West through Hungary and Austria. Maybe Max and Henri realized the Democratic Republic was collapsing and fled to a new life in France.'

'Those faces in the Belleville Mairie you recognized from the Clara Zetkin orphanage, do you recall their names, anything else about them?' Bruno asked.

'No, we weren't encouraged to make enquiries. If any employment records or payslips from the registrations department still exist, I might be able to identify them by means of elimination but I'm pretty sure those files were destroyed.'

'Looking back, what do you think they were doing in Paris?'

'I assume they were planning to start new lives in France while continuing to serve the socialist revolution.' There was just a trace of irony in her voice. 'Perhaps they were used as underground organizers or spies, or as postboxes for other spies to communicate through.'

'Are you in touch with any other former employees of the Mairie who might be able to help us?'

'Not still in touch, but I know one or two who moved on to other Party strongholds in the Red Belt after they lost Belleville: one to Malakoff and the other one to Kremlin-Bicêtre.' She gave a half-smile and shook her head regretfully, as if recalling memories of happier or perhaps simpler times. She seemed suddenly aware of Balzac at her feet, gazing up at her sympathetically, and she bent down to stroke him. 'I won't give you names but I doubt they'll talk to you anyway. They'll probably retain more of the old political loyalties than I do.'

'Do you recall anything else that might be relevant?' Bruno asked, handing her his card when she shook her head. 'Well, if anything comes to mind, please let me know.'

'Is that it?' she asked. 'You aren't going to arrest me?'

'Why would I want to do that?' he asked, genuinely surprised by her question. 'You haven't committed any crime. You were a member of a legal party, working in a mairie controlled by that party after it won elections. You might have had suspicions that some of your comrades were conspiring to commit or assist espionage, but you only began to suspect when it was far too late to matter. You've been very helpful – and you keep an admirable garden. What's more, you like my dog and he seems to like you so he'd probably object if I tried to arrest you.'

She laughed aloud. 'That's a relief. I'd hate to go to jail for views I no longer hold.'

Before leaving he took down a brief statement from her, confirming that she believed she saw the murdered man at the Clara Zetkin orphanage in East Germany, where he was a pupil of Jacques and Sylvie Lefort.

After signing it, she asked, 'Do you think you'll be able to bring his killer to justice?'

'I hope so. But proving murder thirty years after the event is going to be difficult.'

20

Bruno put in his earphones, propped his mobile in the cradle on the dashboard and called Isabelle. He waited until he had the double green light that said their call was secure before setting off to drive from Carlux to Périgueux. He spent the first few minutes briefing Isabelle on the Clara Zetkin orphanage, on Jacques and Sylvie Lefort and on the new eyewitness placing the murdered Max in the former East Germany as a youth.

'The witness is – don't laugh – Rosa Luxemburg Delpèche, a disaffected old Communist who worked for the Mairie in Belleville,' he added. 'These East German orphans were being raised as native French speakers, equipped with French identities and then installed into France while their loyalties were to East Berlin.'

'So we have the Stasi connection, but one with nothing to do with the Rosenholz dossier,' Isabelle replied. 'That's particularly interesting because I also have news for you. Our old friend General Lannes was called to the Elysée yesterday evening to be told that they had just received a visit from the trendy and very political lawyer Maître Vautan. He arrived with a startling offer. He had a client who was prepared to give the Elysée a special version of the Rosenholz dossier relating to Stasi operations in France in return for immunity for any crimes committed on French soil.'

'What did Lannes say?'

'He said he would have to consult the Interior Minister and colleagues in the Department of Internal Security. The Elysée didn't like that. They want to keep this in-house for security reasons, even though we all know the Elysée staff are the most notorious leakers in Paris.'

'Obviously they agreed and he then briefed you.'

'Yes, along with the minister and two people we think we can trust at Internal Security. And now I'm briefing you. Do you think these Clara Zetkin orphans are part of the Rosenholz dossier or were they off the books, some special Stasi project that didn't get into the main files?'

'I don't know, but you said something about Maître Vautan suggesting his client had a special version of Rosenholz.'

'That's how Vautan described it. The problem is there's no indication of the crimes for which Vautan's client seeks immunity. It's a blank cheque. They could be signing up to forgive a paedophile serial killer and heaven help anyone in the loop if this ever gets out. Understandably, the Elysée wants some cover which is why they want to be able to say they consulted the security services.'

'I know this is quite a leap but something described as a special version of the Rosenholz dossier in return for immunity makes me wonder if Henri might be behind this, hoping to get away with murder. He must have some credible evidence from the orphanage. What about your German colleagues? Can you get them to launch their own probe into the Clara Zetkin orphanage and the Leforts? There must be some records: when they arrived in East Germany, under what conditions they were given asylum, or residence permits and what their status was.'

'I'll do that as soon as I've had a chance to brief Lannes. He needs to know about this orphanage. Then I'll ask DIS to look in their old files for this Lefort couple. When do you say they moved to East Germany?'

'Some time in the fifties, according to Rosa Luxemburg.'

'Right. Leave that with me. And what are you doing now?'

'Heading for Périgueux for a meeting with Prunier about whether it makes sense to arrest Henri Bazaine on the false identity charge.'

'The Elysée won't like that. If Henri has documentary evidence he might not be able to deliver it if he's sitting in a cell in Périgueux. But could such evidence be?' Isabelle demanded. 'How might he have got hold of the Rosenholz dossier? The whole thing was too bulky to smuggle out before the Wall came down. Maybe he got just the French section, but how would he have obtained it from some country orphanage far from Stasi HQ in East Berlin?'

'Maybe what Henri has is nothing to do with Rosenholz,' Bruno mused, thinking aloud. 'Maybe it's something different, like a register of the kids at the Clara Zetkin orphanage with their French names. Rosa, this woman from the Belleville Mairie, said the French couple were so devoted to the kids that they kept a scrapbook of them all growing up.'

'*Putain!*' Isabelle almost spat out the word. 'Is that possible? Keeping something like that must have broken every security rule in the Stasi's book.'

'Rosa said she saw it at the orphanage.'

'Hold on. I'm online, checking the timetable of the collapse of East Germany,' she said and went on to describe the process.

'May 2, 1989, Hungary started to dismantle the border fence with Austria. Some ten thousand fled from East Germany through Hungary in May and another twelve thousand in June. That's the number that got out and applied to West Germany for citizenship.'

'So, let's imagine it's May or June. Max and Henri are smart boys, they see the place is collapsing and there's a way out,' Bruno said. 'They get to Hungary and then to Austria but unlike the other East Germans, they already have their French ID cards, their French names and they're bilingual. They decide to come to France rather than West Germany where they'd probably be tainted as Stasi kids.'

'What if they stole the scrapbook and brought it with them as insurance?' Isabelle asked.

'There's only one scrapbook and Henri kills Max to get it. Does that make sense?'

'It's plausible as a working hypothesis,' Isabelle replied, cautiously. 'But if the Stasi knew Max and Henri had the scrapbook, they would have moved heaven and earth to track them down and get it back.'

'Only if the Stasi knew it was missing. What if Jacques and Sylvie never reported that it had gone? After all, they'd have been in trouble if they admitted to having kept the scrapbook in the first place.'

'I suppose you're right. Let me take this to Lannes. It's

certainly possible that this offer comes from Henri. I'll do some checking into this lawyer, Vautan.'

Bruno explained about Henri's own lawyer, the People's Pierre.

'I'll look into him, too. You'll be with J-J after this?'

'Yes, but wait – how much of all this can I share with J-J?'

'All of it,' she replied firmly. 'He's a professional. We can trust him.'

'Even if he's robbed of a murder conviction because the Elysée agrees to the deal and hushes up the murder?'

'Yes, even then,' she replied. 'It could be useful that J-J knows. It might help to persuade the Elysée that this might not be a sensible deal. The more people who know about it, the greater the chance of a leak. Any government found hushing up a murder would face a political storm. I should go. By the way, I emailed my Canadian contact at SCRS, their Service Canadien des Renseignements de Sécurité, about Loriot. We'll talk later. *Je t'embrasse.*'

The phone conversation had taken Bruno halfway to Périgueux and he saw he'd missed an incoming call from his contact at army records. He was making good time so he pulled off the road to return the call. Loriot, he learned, had served his twelve months in the army in 1987, mostly in a signals regiment based in Agen because he'd listed his civilian job as an apprentice electrician.

Once in Périgueux, Bruno had a few minutes to spare before his meeting, so he called in to see Virginie in the police lab. J-J had said her work on the skull was close to being finished. He was looking forward to seeing it, partly out of curiosity, but also to compare it with the composite photo of Max that he'd helped to assemble. However reassuring Rosa's decisive recognition of Max had been from the photo, Bruno suspected any able defence lawyer would be able to challenge its authenticity.

He parked in the cool underground garage at the police building and left Balzac in his van. He walked across the courtyard leading to the separate building where the lab had been installed. The entrance, office and storeroom were on the ground floor. In the basement were the lab, a small morgue and pathology room along with the shielded X-ray section.

As he trotted down the stairs he heard what sounded like a scream, and then a woman's voice shrieking at someone to stop, followed instantly by a grunted male curse, the sound of a slap and another cry for help. Bruno found the door locked. He stood back and slammed the sole of his boot as hard as he could against the door right beside the lock. It burst open to reveal the back of a gigantic man in police uniform with his hand up the skirt of a woman. The male figure began to turn at Bruno's charging entry, but too late. Bruno roared out a war cry as he kicked his boot hard up between the man's legs, then pivoted to strike the side of his knee and jerk him to one side. The man began to fall as his shattered knee collapsed.

As he fell, the woman shrieked again and slashed at the policeman's arm with what looked like a scalpel. She then raised it again to threaten Bruno, blood dripping from her nose, her eyes wide in rage and shock.

Bruno backed away, keeping his arms high and outstretched, open palms towards her.

'It's over, Virginie. It's okay. It's me, Bruno.'

Her white lab coat had been ripped apart from top to bottom revealing a torn bra and a small breast that was red from some rough grasp. She blinked as she recognized him, although she kept her scalpel at the ready.

'Are you okay?' he asked. When she nodded, he said, 'I have to look at your attacker, he's bleeding.'

He bent down to the cop who was curled up in a foetal position on the floor, blood soaking into his uniform and onto the floor from the arm Virginie had slashed. Bruno put one knee on the guy's back to keep him in place and used one of the plastic cuffs he always carried as a tourniquet to stop the bleeding from the man's arm. He pulled the tie from around the cop's neck to bind his ankles together.

'You bastard, I'll kill you for this,' the cop grunted, trying to turn over but held face-down by Bruno's weight.

It was the cop's left arm that was bleeding. But there was blood on the fingers of his right hand. Bruno glanced at Virginie and saw a smeared trail of blood stains on her thigh. *Putain*, what had the bastard done to her?

Bruno pulled a plastic evidence bag from his hip pocket, put it over the man's right hand. Then he called J-J.

'It's Bruno. I'm in the police lab downstairs where one of your cops has just tried to rape Virginie. He'll need medical attention since she slashed him in self-defence, and I'll be filing charges of sexual assault against him. We'll need a female cop and a doctor for Virginie.'

He turned to look at Virginie. She had somehow pulled the lab coat together with one hand. The scalpel lay at her feet.

She had the other hand to her face and was trembling, her shoulders heaving as she sobbed and hiccuped.

'Virginie,' he said. 'Are you okay? What did he do? Speak to me.'

He heard a muffled sob. Then she took a deep breath, looked at him and nodded.

'Can you tell me what happened?' he asked.

She answered in a gabble, the words and phrases running together. 'He keeps coming in to ask me out, day after day, and I keep saying no, I'm working, I'm busy. He won't stop. And today he just grabbed me, grabbed my breast really, really hard, thrust his hand up . . .'

'It's okay, Virginie, it's over. I'm here.' He was trying to make sense of the blood on the cop's hand and the smears on Virginie's thighs. He'd leave that to the policewoman J-J would be bringing.

'I need an ambulance,' said the cop, lying under Bruno's knee.

'You're under arrest,' Bruno said, and checked the man's arm. The bleeding had stopped and Bruno recognized the man's face, the one in the police canteen who had made that offensive joke about sheep-shaggers.

'Virginie, please, pass me your scalpel,' Bruno said. She simply stared at him until he added, 'I need to look at his wound, where you slashed him.'

She nodded, bent down to pick it up and handed it to him. Bruno cut away the sleeve of the cop's uniform and the shirt beneath to reveal a long, seeping cut running from the man's bicep down to his elbow. It didn't look too deep and the tourniquet was holding. He tightened the plastic cuff another notch and looked up to see Virginie staggering to the sink.

'Stop, Virginie. Please, don't wash anything away,' he said. 'We need the evidence to nail this bastard.'

'I'm going to be sick,' she said, and vomited into the sink.

As he spoke, he heard a clattering of feet coming down the stairs and J-J was the first in, a policewoman behind him and then a uniformed cop carrying a first aid kit. Finally, Commissioner Prunier himself came to stand, silent and glowering, at the door. J-J must have called him.

'We need medical attention, first for this young woman who's been assaulted, then for this cop whom I saw assault her,' Bruno said. 'I'm ready to give a statement. I should stress that I saw the cop with his hand far up this woman's skirt. There's blood on her thighs and on his right hand. That's why I covered it with an evidence bag. I believe the blood on his hand will be hers. I insist that this be checked at once. The cut on the cop's left arm was made by the victim in self-defence.'

'Right,' said Prunier, staring grimly at the scene. 'Commissaire Jalipeau, you're in charge.' He went on to give instructions for the immediate blood tests Bruno had asked for, as well as requesting a female medical examiner to look at Virginie. 'Nobody leaves this room until that's done,' he continued. 'Gardien Baldin is under arrest but also requires medical attention. I want statements to be taken from all three who were in this room when we arrived.'

He turned to the policewoman. 'You will accompany the victim at all times until further notice.' He turned again. 'Bruno, I'll take your statement myself. Come with me.' He led the way up the stairs and across the courtyard to the main building. They took the lift to his office on the top floor.

'That bastard Baldin is a menace,' said Prunier, once they were in the privacy of his office. 'But his dad was a *commandant* here so he gets away with a lot. He's also active in the union. Thanks to this sickening business, we might finally be able to get rid of him once and for all.'

'Let's do this right,' said Bruno. 'He ought to be dismissed, never to wear the uniform again. And he should be put on the sex offenders' list.' He pulled out his phone, checked that Prunier was happy for him to begin, and pressed the recording function.

'I'm recording this statement of my own free will,' he began. 'I arrived at the police lab at eleven thirty on this day, July tenth, to see the progress of the work of the young volunteer, Virginie, whose facial reconstruction skills I recommended to Commissaire Jalipeau.'

He went on to give a detailed account of what he had seen and done. He forwarded the sound file of his statement to Prunier's phone, who in turn forwarded it to his secretary sitting outside to be typed up.

'A couple of questions,' Prunier said, and turned on his own phone's record function. 'First, have you met Gardien Baldin before?'

'I know his face by sight from passing him in corridors and the canteen but didn't know his name until this incident.'

'What made you call at the lab at that moment?'

'I'd arrived early for an appointment with you and J-J, so I decided to use the time to see what progress Virginie had made on the facial reconstruction. I was the one who first proposed to J-J that we bring her here to work on Oscar's skull.'

'Last question: how much force did you use to restrain Gardien Baldin?'

'I used reasonable force since Baldin is a big man, nearly two metres tall and powerfully built. When I kicked down the door and saw him assaulting Virginie, I shouted at him to stop, kicked his groin to stop the sexual assault and then his knee to limit his movements. I then pulled him backwards, which probably prevented him being more badly slashed by Virginie's scalpel. He fell to the floor and I restrained him. I put a tourniquet on his left arm and called for help.'

'Right, that's it, thanks. We'll get all that typed up for you to sign. You'll have to appear at the disciplinary hearing against Baldin and at the trial. I'm suspending him from duty as of now.'

'Good,' said Bruno. 'And there have been some developments on the case with Henri Bazaine. It's all become a lot more complicated.' He explained the offer made by the lawyer to the Elysée, his own meeting with Rosa Luxemburg Delpèche and his discussion that morning with Isabelle. 'I suggest that before taking a decision on arresting Bazaine, you wait to hear from General Lannes, who seems to have taken over this inquiry at the request of the Elysée.'

'*Putain*, just how many French-speaking sleeper agents did the Stasi churn out from this orphanage?' Prunier asked.

'I don't know, but Rosa Luxemburg said she saw at least twenty kids and we have no idea how many were produced in previous years. Isabelle is contacting the German security people to see what they can find out. This Lefort couple had emigrated to East Germany in the fifties so they had thirty years to produce their fake French citizens.'

'And we never found any of them, never knew anything about this? It makes my head spin. I suppose I'd better wait to hear from General Lannes before arresting Bazaine. What would you do?'

Bruno shook his head. 'I don't like the idea of granting immunity to a murderer, if indeed that's what happened. But we may have no choice. If Henri really can give us information that identifies all the undercover agents the Stasi trained and sent us, it's probably worth doing the deal. Even though the Stasi is long dead, who knows if the Russians are still making use of these people?'

'You really think Henri Bazaine is behind this lawyer's offer to the Elysée?'

'I can't be sure but it looks likely,' Bruno said. 'That gives me an idea. We can check Henri's credit cards for train bookings and flight lists to see if he went up to Paris to see this fancy lawyer, Maître Vautan. If he drove, there should be a record on the autoroute tolls. Maybe he arranged it all through his own lawyer, the People's Pierre. Either way I think Maître Vautan would have wanted to see something that looked like proof before he went to the Elysée. I can't see Henri giving any lawyer the original scrapbook so he may have made a photocopy.'

Prunier scribbled a note. 'I'll get someone onto the travel records. What are the operative dates?'

'Henri couldn't have known we were looking for him until last Friday at the earliest, and the publicity about the Rosenholz dossier did not start until Sunday.'

'So if we can show he went to Paris since then, it looks pretty certain. We can arrest him and then search his place for the scrapbook.'

'It could be in a safe deposit box in a bank vault or hidden on his property. I don't think you have the manpower to dig up all those hectares of vines. And it might all be on microfilm, anyway. He was trained to be a spy, don't forget, so he'll know all these tricks. If I were him, I'd have buried the original somewhere very deep but kept a microfilm hidden close to hand. He could even have emailed some selected pages of microfilm to the lawyer in Paris while keeping the original in a safe place.'

'He'd have wanted to brief the lawyer in person, so let's see if he went to Paris.'

'It's worth trying,' Bruno said. 'But let's not expect to get a murder conviction. I doubt we'll ever be able to prove that Henri killed Max, unless he confesses.'

'Well, at least it wasn't a French citizen that he bumped off,' Prunier replied. 'That would really stick in my throat.'

21

From Prunier's office Bruno went to find J-J, without success, and then down to the car park to collect Balzac. He checked the lab to see if Virginie was still there. The place was empty but he was delighted to find the skull she'd been working on. It had been partly hidden by the screen of her laptop during the time he'd been in the lab. Now her laptop lid was closed and the eerily disembodied head of Max – there was no doubt who it was – stared out across the lab.

He was bald. But strewn beside him were three cheap wigs of fair hair, each of different lengths and shades of blondness. Bruno tried each one on the skull. None seemed quite to capture the curl and thickness Bruno recalled from the photo. But the shape of the face, the cast of the eyes, the prominent nose, narrow lips and thrusting jaw all seemed right.

Bruno let out a soft whistle of admiration. Even without those hours of scanning through the photographs in the St Denis archive, Max might have been identified from this reconstruction alone. Virginie had done an admirable job and it was outrageous that one of the Périgueux cops should have treated her so shamefully. He sent a text to her phone to say, 'This is brilliant. I'm full of admiration, Bruno.' He added a postscript reminding her of the invitation to spend the weekend in St Denis. Then he sent a text to Elisabeth Daynès in Paris, saying that Virginie's work on the skull had exceeded his highest hopes and when the case was complete, he'd give her a full report.

Balzac at his heels, he climbed the stairs to the courtyard and headed for the main reception area. The cop on duty told him that J-J was at the hospital with Gardien Baldin, while Virginie was with Commissaire Gouppilleau, the senior female officer at the station. He requested to be put through to her office. When Gouppilleau answered, Bruno identified himself and asked if Virginie would consent to see him. He was told to come right up.

The *commissaire* met him in the corridor and greeted him warmly with a firm handshake. 'Along with every other female cop in Périgueux I'd like to buy you a large drink,' she said. 'And that's a very handsome dog.' He couldn't help noticing that her police uniform had been extremely well cut and she looked more like a smart lawyer than a cop. 'With luck you might have lifted the curse of the big, bad Baldin, the most loathed man in the station. Come in, come in. Virginie has been telling me all about it.'

Bruno couldn't help but smile as he noticed the defiantly non-uniform red high-heels the *commissaire* was wearing. She saw he was staring at her shoes and smiled back at him.

'Even if I have to change into clodhoppers when I go out-doors, these help keep up my morale,' she said, steering him into her office.

'Hi, Bruno,' said Virginie from her place in a deep armchair.

She looked pale and fragile, wearing a policewoman's raincoat that was about four sizes too large for her. The blood on her face had been cleaned and a bandage had been taped over her nose. Her voice sounded as if she had a heavy cold. 'Thanks for turning up when you did.'

'I'm so sorry about this, Virginie, and just wish I'd arrived a minute or two earlier,' he said, as Balzac trotted up to Virginie and put out a paw. 'Don't worry. Balzac is just trying to say hello.'

'No, you arrived at the right time to stop matters going further,' said Gouppilleau. 'Arriving when you did was perfectly timed to nail a cop who's been a menace to every woman in this building, and heaven knows how many civilian women outside. How the devil did you get the better of that enormous brute?'

'I attacked him from the rear while he was otherwise engaged, probably trying to react to Virginie grabbing the scalpel,' Bruno said. 'She was doing a very impressive job of defending herself, shrieking the place down and she had all his attention. I could have come up behind him in a tank and he might not have noticed. I gave Prunier a statement and we'll need one from Virginie.'

'I already took her statement. Prunier sent me yours and they clearly agree,' Gouppilleau said. 'Gardien Baldin has been officially suspended and he'll be charged when he gets back from the hospital. I'll do that myself and I'll personally monitor the case from now on. I already know the female magistrate I want to take on this case, Annette, in the Procureur's office in Sarlat. I gather she knows you.'

'She's a demon rally driver,' he said. 'She once scared the

hell out of me when I had to act as her navigator.' He turned to Virginie, who was sitting forward and caressing Balzac's ears.

'Shouldn't you be at the hospital? I was worried about that blood I saw on your thighs and it looked like he really hurt your . . .' Bruno waved his hand in the direction of her breast.

'My breast is sore but the blood on my thighs was where he scratched me, trying to grope me and pull . . .' She paused, her eyes fixed on Balzac. 'That was when I grabbed the scalpel.'

'We had Virginie checked over by a doctor,' said Gouppilleau. 'She has a broken nose from where he slapped her but it's been reset by our police doctor. Thank heavens, Bruno, that you bagged that right hand of his. The scratch wasn't deep but that's the evidence of assault that will send him to jail.'

'It certainly should,' said Bruno, thinking it was never easy to win a case for sexual assault, and even less easy to convict a cop. 'I gather that Baldin has something of a reputation.'

'He does indeed, but he's also very active in the AlliancePN,' she went on, referring to the police trade union. 'So with all the other entirely justified complaints about all our cops having to do too much overtime and long shifts, he's been handled with kid gloves for far too long. I'm hoping that's now over. Prunier tells me that he's personally outraged by this.'

'That's good to hear.' Bruno turned to Virginie. 'I came to ask you if you'd like to come back to St Denis with me. You can stay with some friends of mine who have a lovely, welcoming house. She's our local doctor and he's a writer and journalist. I'm going to tell everybody what a brilliant job you've done on the skull. Our Mayor wants to take you to lunch and you can meet my horse who's just as handsome as my dog. You deserve a break after all the work you've put in, and I hate the thought of you going back to a lonely room in an empty student hostel.'

'Bruno is known to be a gifted chef,' Gouppilleau said, smiling as Bruno looked at her in surprise. 'Your colleague Juliette in Les Eyzies told me about your cooking,' she went on. 'You'd be surprised at the breadth of our intelligence network. In this job, we women have to stick together.'

'Bruno,' said Virginie. 'Did you mean it, the message you left on my phone, about my skull?'

'It's even better than I'd hoped,' he said. 'We put together a composite photo from various partial snapshots and you've got Max to perfection.'

'But I don't think I've got the hair right.'

'There's no reason why you should. You warned us about that, remember? Anyway, it looks like you're part of what's turned out to be a much bigger case. I can't go into details now because national security is involved but I think someday they'll be making TV shows about this case – and you could play yourself! I'm just so sorry that it involved this dreadful assault.'

'It was all over very fast once you turned up. And yes, I'd love to come down to St Denis and have a bit of a break. I've been working almost non-stop.'

'Your work has paid off, Virginie, believe me. Now, would you like me to take you back to the hostel and get a change of clothes?'

'I wish I got invitations like that,' said Gouppilleau. 'We have another mutual friend in Yveline, the gendarme *commandante*, and she says St Denis is the best posting she's ever had. She too says you're a good cook.'

'We like Yveline too,' said Bruno, wondering why he'd never before noticed that his women colleagues, whether gendarmes, Police Nationale or municipal, would naturally have their own networks and friendships. He had his own wide range of connections, male and female, from sports and hunting clubs to the regional archaeological society. He saw them as a real asset, not only in human, friendly terms but in the way people could share skills, tips and local knowledge.

'I'd really like to have a bit of a break and get away from Périgueux for a day or so,' Virginie said. 'But I wouldn't want to be in your way. I know you have work to do.'

'I thought you might like to see Elisabeth's exhibition at the museum in Les Eyzies, which led to your coming down here,' he said. 'Then you might like to meet a colleague of mine, the town policewoman and some other friends. I was on fire watch last night so I'll be spared that tonight and I'll have time to cook.'

'I'm a vegan,' Virginie said. 'I hope that won't be a problem.'

Bruno remembered the welcome gift of foie gras he'd given her and strove manfully to keep his expression unchanged. 'That means no butter, eggs or cheese, is that right?' he asked, trying to keep his voice neutral and wondering what she had done with the foie gras and cheese he'd given her. 'And no cooking with duck fat.'

Virginie nodded cheerfully and said, 'I don't mind watching other people eat meat and stuff. I used to eat it myself. And I don't do without butter. You can buy it made from soya milk, sunflower oil, salt and lemon juice. I even make my own vegan pastry. I could show you how to prepare it, if you like.'

Twenty minutes later, after a brief call to J-J who was still at the hospital with Baldin, and another to Gilles to say he'd be bringing Virginie, they arrived at the student hostel, where she packed a small bag and they set off for St Denis. Balzac was in the back of the van and the reconstituted skull of Max had been carefully packed in a hat box that was at Virginie's feet. Gilles and Fabiola now occupied a house that Bruno knew well. It had been Pamela's home when he'd first known her, before she and Miranda had taken over the riding school. Gilles came out from his study when he heard Bruno's van, shook hands with Virginie, and showed her to the spare room to leave her bag.

'What happened to her face?' Gilles asked when he and Bruno were alone. Bruno explained, briefly, and suggested Gilles not bring it up.

'OK, but what about dinner?' Gilles asked.

'I thought I'd cook, using your kitchen if that's all right. Virginie's a vegan so I thought it would be a challenge to make a meal from my vegetables, if you don't mind being guinea pigs.'

'No problem for me but Pamela's coming with the Baron, since you missed the Monday dinner,' Gilles eyes twinkled. 'Let's try an experiment. You prepare a vegan meal and see if the Baron notices. I doubt whether he's ever had one in his life.'

'Of course he'll notice. He loves his meat.'

'I bet you he doesn't – a bottle of wine on it.'

'Done,' said Bruno.

They had time for a cup of coffee with Gilles before Bruno drove Virginie to the museum in Les Eyzies, where Clothilde had promised to show her the exhibition of Elisabeth Daynès's skulls. Bruno put the hat box on Clothilde's desk and invited Virginie to open it.

'This is what I was hoping for when I first saw the exhibition,' he said as Virginie displayed the extraordinarily lifelike head she had made of Oscar's original skull.

'This is why I think your work is so good,' he added, pulling from his briefcase one of the photos of Max that Yves had put together from the various snapshots taken at the *félibrée* three decades earlier.

'Virginie refused ever to look at this photo, saying it would influence her work, but you can see the likeness is uncanny,' he told Clothilde. 'It's manifestly the same man.'

He used his phone to take a photo of Clothilde, Virginie and the skull and sent it off to Elisabeth in Paris. He sent her a copy of the composite photo of Max so that Elisabeth could see how close a likeness Virginie had achieved with the skull. Clothilde asked Virginie what had happened to her nose.

'Just an accident,' Virginie replied. 'It got broken but it's not serious and it doesn't hurt. The doctor at the police station gave me a painkiller.'

Clothilde glanced at Bruno with a raised eyebrow but tactfully left it at that. She praised Virginie's work and suggested she might like to look round the rest of the museum and visit the workrooms, usually off-limits to the public. Clothilde's colleagues were hoping to hear Virginie describe the reconstruction procedure over lunch and then take her to some other of the local sites. Bruno was just wondering whether he should explain to Clothilde what Virginie had been through, when she said eagerly, 'Yes, please. I'd really like to learn more about these prehistoric people.'

'We thought you might like to see the original Cro-Magnon

site where the first skeletons were found a hundred and fifty years ago, and then the Abri Pataud. Bruno has a *tendresse* for the young woman whose skull was found there,' Clothilde added.

'That sounds great,' Virginie said, while Bruno marvelled at the resilience of youth.

'I'll be back to pick you up around five,' Bruno said. He left Virginie at the museum and drove back to St Denis to tackle his emails and paperwork. He settled Balzac in his office and then briefed the Mayor and told him of Virginie's arrival, then checked on Albert's fire report. There had been a serious blaze that morning in the woods east of St Cyprien, starting in a section that had been clear cut a few months earlier, leaving a tangle of dry branches and twigs on the ground. It was the first time Albert had called in the water-dropping aircraft. Getting the blaze under control had required the fire engines of St Cyprien, St Denis and Sarlat, plus a hundred volunteers. Bruno opened his window and leaned out over the balcony, looking towards the east, wondering if he might see the smoke, but the warm winds from the south would be taking it north towards Montignac.

Why did everything have to happen at once? he wondered. The fires, J-J's obsession with Oscar, the attack on Virginie, Balzac's puppies, the Belleville Mairie, the Dresden orphanage and the mysterious offer of the Rosenholz material to the Elysée: they seemed to be rolling in on him like so many storm clouds. And what on earth did one cook for a vegan? He smiled at himself, knowing he could always relax by thinking of menus. He would make a cold summer soup to begin and *beignets de courgettes* which he could serve with *tapenade de tomates* instead of the usual *aïllou*. For the main course he could make the kabocha pumpkin dish that Ivan's new Japanese girlfriend had offered in Ivan's bistro. He'd seen the pumpkins on sale in the bio store. And *citrouilles rôtis a la sauge et aux noix* – roasted pumpkin with sage and walnuts – was a classic French dish, with shallots, parsnips and potatoes in the roasting pan alongside. He'd remove a portion for Virginie so that for the others he could add slices of *cabécou* goat cheese which would slump in the heat of the vegetables. He'd serve it with a salad of thinly sliced heirloom tomatoes of different colours from his garden, drizzled with oil; followed by *pêches au vin rouge*.

He had everything he needed in his garden except for the pumpkins and parsnips. He was about to make a quick trip to the local bio shop when the phone rang. It was Isabelle.

'Two bits of news. Despite General Lannes' objections, the Elysée wants to go ahead with the lawyer's deal; his client gets immunity in return for the Rosenholz material. And my colleagues in Canada have come up with some dynamite.'

Isabelle explained that her contact in Canadian security had sent a colleague based in Quebec City, accompanied by a uniformed policeman, to visit Loriot. They told him they were investigating a Canadian connection to Henri Bazaine at the request of the French police and asked him about the payments to Bazaine. Loriot became uncomfortable and said it was for consulting on different grape varieties and on techniques for mass marketing and box wines. Then they asked why had he paid Bazaine so often when immigration records showed that he'd only visited Canada once? What kind of consultancy was this? Loriot became even more uncomfortable and said he wanted a lawyer. Then they asked about the fake French ID that Loriot had used when he first came to Canada, noting that it could invalidate the Canadian citizenship he'd later acquired. When he remained silent, they played the trump card, asking if he'd ever heard from Jacques and Sylvie Lefort of the Dresden orphanage.

'At that point Loriot broke down,' Isabelle said. 'They arrested him for making false statements on his citizenship application, suggested several more charges that could be brought and now Loriot's lawyer is trying to reach a deal.'

'What kind of deal?' Bruno asked.

'He'll tell everything he knows if he can stay out of prison and be allowed to remain in Canada.'

'Does the Elysée know about this?'

'Not yet. I just briefed Lannes and he's going to let them know. He's hoping that they'll now reconsider the deal with Maître Vautan.'

'And in the meantime Henri Bazaine is allowed to remain free?' Bruno asked. 'Has J-J been informed of that?'

'I don't know but Lannes talked to Prunier. Is that not the chain of command you old military guys like to work with?'

Bruno smiled because he could hear the teasing in her voice and could imagine the mischievous grin on her face as she said this.

'In principle, maybe,' he said, chuckling. 'But in practice, we old military guys usually find it easier to work somewhat less formally, a bit like the way you and I try to keep each other informed.'

After ending the call he went to the bio shop and bought the pumpkins and parsnips and a big *tourte* of bread. On the way back he saw an unusual vehicle that looked like a furniture van that had been painted red, heading down the Rue de la République towards the fire station. He followed on foot, to see another strange engine drawn up on the forecourt. It looked like a giant off-road four-by-four with enormous wheels but it was obviously some kind of fire engine, with pump settings and coiled hoses stashed along the side. Ahmed, Albert's deputy, was standing talking to the driver of the huge van and Bruno asked him what it was.

'A water tender, carries about eight thousand litres,' Ahmed replied, before introducing Bruno to the driver who had come from Bordeaux.

'We really should have more tenders like this because there's never enough water when you're facing forest fires,' Ahmed went on. 'It's not like in town where you can connect your hose to a water main. And our power hoses pump out nearly a thousand litres a minute. With four hoses, we can empty a tender in two minutes.'

'Can't you stick your hoses in a river and draw it up that way?'

'If the river is close enough, we do. Anything over four hundred metres and we'll need extra pumps and we might run out of hoses. And rivers have silt and debris that can clog them. Quite a few houses around here have their own swimming pool, which is great because even a small pool can hold a hundred thousand litres. We've got drones identifying the pools near enough to the blaze to help. But if there are no pools, we're dependent on the aircraft dumping water.'

'But you pump water onto the flames. Just like you would with a house, don't you?' Bruno asked. He'd never thought much about the way firefighters had to work.

'We usually save our hoses for the hot spots, they're the main danger. A really bad one we have to try doing a knockdown to suppress it because they can suck in enough air to create their own small firestorm. Then they can move very fast, faster than a man can run.'

'What if you can't knock a hotspot down?'

'You get out fast and try to set a control line some distance ahead to stop it. That's what we mainly do on the ground, which is why bulldozers can be as useful as water when you're fighting wildfires. We try to set control lines to steer the fire into directions we want it to go, like towards a river that's wide enough to block the fire. We usually try back-burning, deliberately setting small fires ahead of the fire so it runs out of fuel.'

'Is there anything untrained people like me can do?'

'The main thing is to evacuate people in danger. We always need bulldozer drivers to help set control lines and people who are good with drones are really useful right now.'

'Do you have enough skilled people?'

Ahmed shrugged. 'You never have enough. But we have crews who've come in from as far north as Normandy. They're now fighting the fires in the Landes. Even with them and the aircraft, we're going to lose a lot of forest, that's for sure, and maybe some of the walnut plantations.'

'Are you on duty tonight?'

'Yes, while Albert tries to get some sleep. He's run ragged already. How about you? You're on again tomorrow night?'

Bruno nodded. 'What's the forecast on how long that south wind keeps up?'

'All week, at least. What are those blue things you're carrying?

'Japanese pumpkins, an experiment – I thought I'd roast them with shallots and potatoes with a few parsnips and get some slices of goat's cheese melting over the top . . .'

'Sounds interesting, let me know how it works out.'

'Will do. I hope it's a quiet night for you,' said Bruno.

22

Bruno collected Virginie from Les Eyzies and brought her back to visit the Mayor and show him her recreation of Max's head. He found him in an excellent mood. This usually meant that some event had gone entirely to his satisfaction.

'Just had the Defence Ministry on the line, one of the Minister's staff,' the Mayor said. 'As of tonight, the military will be taking part in fire-watch duties from their big transmission towers, not just ours but wherever there's a fire alert. A rare victory for common sense.'

Virginie thanked him for his support of the project that had brought her to the region, and opened the hat box to display the head she had crafted of Max. Bruno handed him a copy of the composite photo and the Mayor nodded appreciatively as he compared the two.

'I don't think I'd have believed it if I hadn't seen the result of your work with my own eyes. It's a remarkable achievement and your first solo effort, I believe. Presumably you will have to show this to your teacher in Paris, but after that and when the court case is complete, we'd be honoured to display your work here in St Denis.'

'Commissaire Jalipeau says he would like to have it for the

police museum,' Virginie replied. 'But now I've done the first one I'm sure I can make a replica for him very easily and I don't think he'd know the difference.'

Nor would we, thought Bruno to himself, as he led her downstairs to his van for the drive back to his home. And that means Virginie could have two contented customers, each with their own skull, and possibly even a third in Elisabeth's Paris showroom.

'What a lovely place and a terrific view,' she said, as Bruno parked in his driveway. She stepped out to admire his garden and watch Balzac trot off to see the geese and chickens. 'And you have so many vegetables growing here I'd have sworn you were another vegan.'

'No, I'm a happy omnivore but I do like growing and eating my own fruit and vegetables. We'll dine tonight with Gilles and Fabiola at the house where you left your bag.'

He went to the kitchen and brought out a wicker basket and let Virginie pick the courgettes, herbs and tomatoes he'd be preparing. He cut down onions, garlic and shallots from the braided strings that hung from beams in his kitchen. He added a carrot to the basket for his horse. Then he led her to the rear of his cottage and let her choose between the peaches, apricots and figs on his trees for their dessert. She took a selection of all three.

'Don't you entertain here?' she asked.

'Yes, often, but with a fire warning in place, the local fire chief has forbidden me from staying here overnight since it's so close to the woodland. As the local policeman I'm on his list of essential personnel, like the Mayor, doctors and pharmacists.

I'm staying at the Mayor's house until we get the all-clear. I'm very pleased that these fruit and vegetables we're taking away won't be going up in smoke.'

'What about your chickens?'

'If a fire looks like getting close, my job is to organize an evacuation for some neighbours who live out of sight but quite nearby, which means I'll have time to rescue the geese and chickens. I've already stored my essential documents and personal treasures in town. That reminds me, I need to bring up some wine from the cellar for our dinner tonight.'

'Is that why I'm staying at your friends' house, because of the danger of fire?'

'No, I thought it inappropriate to invite you to stay with me, and it means you'll make new friends. We're also dining there because Gilles wants to talk to you about your work on the skull. He mainly writes books these days but he was on *Libération* and then *Paris Match* for many years so he still does journalism. Now we'll call in at the stables so you can say hello to Hector, my horse. You may also meet another friend who's coming to dinner, Pamela. She runs the riding school, a cookery school and some gîtes for tourists.'

'I was raised in cities so I don't ride and I don't know much about horses.'

'Nor did I before coming here. I grew up in Bergerac and only learned about the country once I arrived in St Denis, over ten years ago,' he said. 'I didn't ride, didn't know much about dogs or chickens or even about gardening. You can learn all these things and every single one of them has enriched my life. I didn't know much about wine, either, but I've really enjoyed getting to know winemakers and beginning to understand a little of what they do.'

'My mum always used to say you should never stop learning because life never stops offering you lessons.'

'She sounds like a wise woman,' he said. 'Let's go and meet Hector, and Pamela, and two of Balzac's friends, sheepdogs called Beau and Bella.'

When they arrived at Pamela's place, she was in the court-yard of the stables with her horse, Primrose, already saddled. She greeted Virginie, saying, 'You must be the artist Bruno has been telling us about, or are you a sculptor?'

'I think I'm more a technician.'

'That's not what I hear about your work, and it's not what I saw at the museum of the creations your teacher made from skulls. I think what you do is extraordinary.' Pamela turned to Bruno. 'Do you want to take Hector out?'

'Virginie doesn't ride. And she just had a bit of an accident, broke her nose.'

'Poor thing. Miranda is about to start with the beginners, putting young girls onto a pony and walking them round the ring. Would you like to try that, Virginie?'

'Not today, but I'd like to watch while Bruno goes for his ride. May I meet Hector, please?'

Bruno led the way to Hector's stall, took the carrot from his pocket, broke it in half and gave half to Virginie and showed her how to hold out her hand and let Hector find his own way to the treat and not to worry; the horse wouldn't bite. He held out his own half-carrot first and told Virginie to watch from the side and see how delicately the horse took it.

'You'll feel his breath on your hand, very warm, and his amazingly soft lips and then without you noticing, it's gone and he's chewing away.'

Bruno put on his riding boots and cap as Virginie rather nervously held out her hand but then kept it immobile as Hector took his treat. He brought the saddle across, kneed Hector gently in the tummy as he tightened the girth and then fitted the bridle. He gave the rein to Virginie, suggesting she lead him out to the yard to join Pamela and Primrose. They showed Virginie the way to the rail from where she could watch the ponies walking sedately round the ring as Miranda stood in the centre, encouraging the little girls, some as young as six or seven.

Pamela let Primrose ease into a canter as they left the paddock by the lower path that led up a gentle slope to the church at St Chamassy. She was avoiding the woodlands, thought Bruno, perhaps nervous at the thought of fire. There wasn't much chance of a decent gallop on this track. It was the long, straight firebreaks between patches of forest that gave the best chance of the kind of run that Hector and his rider most appreciated. Still, with Virginie in tow he should not indulge himself; there were limits to how long one could watch small girls parading past, each on her placid pony. Within twenty minutes, they were back at the riding school, and as they rubbed down the horses Bruno explained his bet with Gilles.

'You!' she exclaimed, laughing. 'You're cooking vegan? Wonders will never cease. If this works, I might have a whole new task for you at the cookery school – we can call you the vegan master-chef of Périgord, if that's not a contradiction in terms.

How on earth can you cook, my dear Bruno, you of all people, without your beloved duck fat, without your cherished bouillon from wild boar, your cheese and your cream?'

'In the face of such a challenge, Pamela, I shall be inspired,' he replied, grandly. He made a flourish with his hand and bowed low in the manner of some Renaissance courtier, and Pamela playfully threw her brush at him. At this point Virginie appeared at the stable door.

'Am I interrupting something?' she asked, her voice hesitant but she was grinning.

'Not at all,' announced Pamela. 'It's an old Périgord custom to throw a brush at your cavalier after an enjoyable ride.' She paused as Virginie raised her eyebrows and then chuckled. 'Oh, dear,' Pamela added quickly. 'Please don't misunderstand me, I didn't mean to phrase it like that.' She giggled. Bruno laughed in turn and Balzac, not to be left out, jumped up. Virginie looked back and forth at them and then joined in the laughter.

'It's lovely to laugh like that even though it makes my nose hurt,' she said, and burst into giggles again.

'Now I have to cook,' said Bruno. He looked at Pamela, who was smiling at Virginie, thinking how fond he was of this generous, warm-hearted Scotswoman who'd made her home in the Périgord.

'And I'd better head for the shower,' said Pamela. 'Virginie, feel free to use the spare bathroom. Bruno, you should leave now if you're cooking at Fabiola's and I'll bring Virginie along in my car.'

With Balzac back in his favourite place on the passenger seat, Bruno drove the route he knew so well to Pamela's old house. After greeting his friends, he installed himself in the familiar kitchen with his basket of fruit and vegetables and the wines he'd brought. There was a bottle of Château Lestevenie white, which was certified vegan, which meant no egg whites had been used in the finings to clarify the wine. And then for the omnivores one of Château de Tiregand red and a bottle of Rosette from Château du Rooy, a slightly sweet white wine that was unique to the Bergerac and a perfect *apéro* for a summer evening. The white wines went in the fridge and the red wine he opened so it could breathe for a while before dinner.

First, he turned the oven on, set to a hundred and seventy degrees centigrade. He chopped the pumpkins into slices about an inch thick and put them into his biggest roasting pan with a small head of celery, equally sliced. He then mixed a cup of maple syrup into the same amount of olive oil, poured the mixture into the roasting pan and tossed the pumpkin and celery slices until they were all coated. He added salt and pepper and put the pan into the oven for twenty-five minutes. In that time, he made the soup, chopping four fat green peppers, peeling and then chopping two cucumbers, and tossing them all into a blender with two chopped onions. He added several cloves of garlic that he squeezed through a press, salt, pepper, olive oil, tarragon vinegar and two glasses of Bergerac Sec white wine. Once blended he put the soup into the freezer to chill.

Then Bruno washed the peaches, figs and apricots and put them into a bowl. Now he had just enough time to make the sauce for the pumpkins. He chopped a generous handful of fresh sage, put it into a bowl with a pound of walnut halves, added a pinch of sea salt and then poured in another splash of maple syrup and a tablespoon of olive oil and stirred them all together. He checked his timing. The twenty-five minutes were up. He took the roasting dish from the oven, poured the sage, walnut and maple syrup mixture over the pumpkin slices, tossed them again and put the dish to one side. When he served the chilled soup, he'd put it back into the oven. He then sliced the tomatoes he'd brought. He made a dressing with a little walnut oil and tarragon vinegar and tossed them with a couple of handfuls of shredded basil. He was washing his hands when Gilles appeared, handing him a glass of white wine and then loading a tray with plates and glasses to set the table in the courtyard.

'All in order?' Gilles asked. 'Will your vegan feast meet our mutual expectations? This is a bet I truly wish to lose.'

'Who knows?' Bruno replied, as they heard the unmistakable sound of Pamela's ancient Citroën *deux-chevaux*. 'I've never done this before.'

They went out to welcome their guests and Fabiola appeared looking enchanting in a sleeveless dress of light-blue silk belted with a white sash. Pamela was wearing a kaftan of red and gold that set off the colours in her chestnut hair. Virginie had changed into something that Bruno recognized from Pamela's wardrobe, an Indian-style garment of jodhpurs, tight on the calf, generously cut on the thighs, topped with an embroidered silk jacket. The bandage still covered her nose and tendrils of her pink hair splayed out from a white headband.

Bruno and Gilles raised their glasses in admiration and then the Baron's venerable Citroën DS, a car that dated from the fifties but still looked like something from the future, made its own grand entrance. The pneumatic suspension made the vehicle rock gently, like some prehistoric beast coming to rest, as the Baron braked it to a halt.

'This is a charming idea,' the Baron said, emerging to brandish a bottle of Veuve Clicquot champagne, which he proceeded to open. 'I'm honoured to be welcomed by three such glorious women.'

He was introduced to Virginie and avoiding her nose, kissed the air in the vicinity of her ears before embracing Pamela and Fabiola and greeting Gilles and Bruno. They were holding empty champagne flutes, ready to hand them to Fabiola, Virginie and Pamela once the Baron had filled the glasses.

'Not good news on the radio, a fire in the woods east of Belvès and another north of St Pompont. The *pompiers* are trying to prevent them joining up and becoming more serious,' the Baron said, drawing Bruno and Gilles aside and speaking in a low voice. 'With this wind we could be smelling the smoke before dinner is over. We might even have to move indoors from the terrace.'

Bruno knew the area, a thinly populated region with a lot of old woodland, stretching about twenty kilometres northwards to one of the most celebrated stretches of the River Dordogne, where it was flanked by the three castles of Milandes, Beynac and Castelnaud. Quietly he explained to the Baron and Gilles what he'd learned from Ahmed about the shortage of water tenders.

'We'd better eat soon, in case I'm called away,' he said, and asked Gilles to bring out the green gazpacho and start serving while Bruno went into the kitchen to put the pumpkins back into the oven. He sliced the fat *tourte* of bread and took it out to his friends on the terrace and sat down to enjoy the chilled soup.

To his surprise, Fabiola was holding Virginie's face. She had unpeeled the bandage and was looking carefully at her broken nose, still swollen and now marked by a wide purple bruise.

'How on earth did this accident happen?' she asked, glancing quickly at Bruno. 'I don't think you walked into a door. It looks to me as though somebody slapped you very hard.'

'It's all right,' said Virginie. 'Just a stupid cop. Bruno came along in time to stop anything worse happening.'

Merde, Bruno thought to himself. The story would doubtless emerge when Baldin was formally charged but he didn't want rumours to start spreading before that.

'You were doing very well on your own, Virginie,' he said. 'I think we'd better leave it there for now. The cop has been suspended, there's the usual internal police investigation under way and I'm told he'll be formally charged with assault. Now, we'd better eat before the next course is ruined. Red wine or white?' he asked, rising with a bottle in each hand, poised to pour.

Fabiola wasn't going to let it rest, though. Ignoring Bruno, she asked Virginie where she'd been treated. 'A police doctor. They didn't want me going to the emergency room at the hospital since the cop who attacked me had been taken there after I slashed him with a scalpel.'

'This sounds rather serious,' said Pamela. 'Are we to presume this was a sexual assault by a policeman?'

'I'm afraid it was,' said Bruno. 'But please do eat up. We have what could be a serious fire south of the Dordogne and I may get called away.'

He began to eat and the others followed suit, except for Fabiola.

'I'm very sorry that your visit here has been marred by this, Virginie,' said Fabiola. 'I thought you were working in the police lab in Périgueux. How come you were alone?'

'One of the staff was on maternity leave and the chief technician had been taken to hospital last week for an unexpected appendix operation,' Virginie replied. 'The third one was in court, testifying on forensic evidence. It was just bad luck that all three were absent.'

'Virginie's work has been a great success,' Bruno said, in another attempt to change the subject. 'She's helping us resolve a really fascinating thirty-year-old murder case.'

'A sexual assault in a police station, and the assaulting cop taken to hospital after being stabbed by a young woman with a scalpel,' said Gilles. 'You won't be able to keep that out of the press.'

'Nor should it be kept out of the press,' said Pamela. 'I've half a mind to call Phillipe Delaron. What about you, Gilles? What do you think?'

'I think we should listen to Virginie and Bruno and let the law take its course,' Gilles replied. 'This sounds to me as though it could be a messy case, a cop taken to hospital after being stabbed. The police union will get the cop a good lawyer. He might even try to get Virginie charged with assault.'

'Please, just stop,' said Bruno, rising to take his empty soup plate to the kitchen. 'And all of you be assured that there is irrefutable evidence that this cop was engaged in a sexual assault on Virginie. I won't go into details but this case is solid and the two top cops in Périgueux, male and female, are determined to throw the book at this bastard.'

He collected the rest of the soup bowls, except for Fabiola's who was still eating, and went into the kitchen to take the roast pumpkin dish from the oven, put the serving dish on a tray and take it out to his friends. To his relief, they were talking about the fire to the south, and sniffing at the wind to see if there was any trace of smoke on the steady breeze. Bruno put the dish onto the table and at once their noses caught the heady scent of sage, maple syrup and roast pumpkin. The conversation shifted at once to the food and the red wine, just as he'd hoped.

23

The call came for Bruno as they were enjoying their dessert of fresh peaches, asking him to report to the crossroads at the Siorac golf course, where the fire engines of St Denis, St Cyprien, Belvès and Le Buisson were assembling. Another team was gathering at Sarlat, he was told, and a third at Gourdon. Reinforcements were on the way from Cahors and Périgueux. *Mon Dieu*, he thought, this is a maximum effort. As he rose from the table, Fabiola's phone trilled out the opening chords of Noir Désir's '*Le Vent Nous Portera*'. She was being summoned as well.

Bruno had a sudden image of the powerful video that had accompanied the song, a mother and her child on a beach, the wind blowing away a sandcastle as the sky darkened and the mother searched in vain for her son as the wind drove her back. He shivered, hoping it was not an omen.

Dinner was over. Gilles decided to drive Fabiola to the clinic and then report with his car to the St Denis fire station. He and the Baron were both on the list of volunteers to help drive people being evacuated to the shelter at the St Denis *collège*. Pamela said she'd drive Virginie back to her place where she could stay the night, since Gilles and Fabiola would both be away from their home. She would also look after Balzac.

'Before we all go,' said Gilles, 'I have a question for the Baron. How did you enjoy the meal?'

'Very good, reminded me of a meal I enjoyed in the Algerian war,' he said, and then paused and his face widened into a smile. 'I'd almost forgotten how delicious a meal of simple vegetables could be.'

'I win,' said Bruno. 'Gilles bet me a bottle that you wouldn't notice.'

'But I didn't notice all through the meal,' the Baron said. 'It didn't cross my mind until Gilles asked the question in that rather pointed way which suggested that a private wager was at stake. And since I was given that clue, I'd call it a draw, except that we all won. It was a fine meal, Bruno. Off you go, and good luck.'

Bruno called the Mayor, who was already at the St Denis fire station. He immediately asked, 'What do you want me to do with your Land Rover? It'll be far more useful off road than your police van and I've made sure the petrol tank is full. Philippe Delaron is here, about to go to Siorac where I gather the control point will be.'

'Good idea. I'll come now for the Land Rover and I'd better change into uniform at the Mairie. Tell Philippe I'll see him at Siorac.'

The car park at the Siorac golf course was filled with police and fire vehicles, a command truck flying a tricolor beside a military signals van. A row of arc lights had already been lit against the gathering dusk. Philippe was waiting outside the command truck, talking urgently into his phone in such a way that told Bruno he was live on air with the local radio station. By now Bruno could smell the smoke. He reported to the command truck, saying he had a Land Rover available. He was given a large-scale map and a list of three remote dwellings near St Laurent-la-Vallée inhabited by two old couples and a disabled woman. They were to be taken to the Mairie at Coux and then he should report back. He checked the map he'd been given against his phone, identified the three remote cottages and set off.

His Land Rover took twenty minutes to get there, an endless line of cars coming the other way, their headlights dimmed by the smoke that was starting to thicken as the evacuation gathered pace. In St Laurent, he spotted a Gendarme truck with Yveline and Sergeant Jules directing traffic. He slowed, peeped his horn and waved. Yveline flagged him down and came across to his vehicle with a list. She put a tick beside the three addresses assigned to Bruno and told him to report back to her before heading for Coux.

'You won't have much time,' she said. 'The fire's getting close.'

He found the first house easily enough. After checking that they had their key documents with them along with a change of clothes, he installed the two old people into the bench seat alongside him. In the second house he found the disabled woman in a wheelchair with her young daughter, no more than eleven or twelve, Bruno thought. He lifted the woman from her wheelchair and laid her on one of the Land Rover's rear benches while the daughter folded the wheelchair. She went back for a suitcase and sat on it beside her mother. Bruno heaved the wheelchair onto his roof rack and secured it with bungee cords. The third house was harder to find. It was deep in the woods and by now the smell of smoke was strong and an ominous orange glow coloured the darkening sky to the south.

'There,' called the girl from the back. 'Off to the right behind us, I saw a light.'

Bruno reversed along the dirt track, saw a small unmarked turning to the right and a single light some fifty metres away in the trees. He drove down, thinking his police van could not have made it down this overgrown track. He turned the Land Rover for an easier departure, went to the front door of the house and knocked, noting the stench of a septic tank that had not been emptied for too long. No answer. The door was unlocked and he went in, almost gagging from the smell of rotting food and something else, something ominous. The main room was empty, and so was the kitchen, the sink overflowing with dirty plates. He called out the names of the couple who lived there but there was no reply.

He checked the bathroom at the back of the house by the kitchen, where the stench of the septic tank was even worse. Upstairs he found an old man asleep in a chair by a bed on which an old woman lay. He was holding her hand. Bruno at first thought she was dead but he checked her pulse. It was faint but she was alive. He woke the man, and led him, barely awake and unprotesting, down the stairs. He checked that the man had his wallet, found the woman's handbag, checked for her ID card and *carte vitale* and led the husband to his Land

Rover. He had to lift the disoriented and almost helpless old man into the back where he asked the young girl to keep an eye on him.

'Just shout if you need me,' he said, and went back upstairs. He was about to scoop up the woman and her bedclothes when he saw they were sodden with urine. He found blankets in a wardrobe, wrapped her in those instead and carried her downstairs. He put her onto the other bench in the back of the vehicle and used more bungee cords to hold her in place.

Back in St Laurent, he told Yveline of the condition of his last two passengers, adding that he didn't want to inflict this on the young girl for long. She had enough on her plate looking after her mother, let alone the two old people. Yveline nodded, saying the fire had started moving much faster than had been expected. Despite all the warnings on radio and TV, too many people had left their departure until the last minute. The roads were getting jammed. She sent him on his way, to join a slow-moving line of cars. When he finally reached the Mairie in Coux he found a line of waiting cars as volunteers tried to sort out who needed medical attention. Bruno was surprised at the number of elderly people there, some of them sitting on a low wall, others leaning on walking sticks, several in wheelchairs. He was impressed by their patience and stoicism, taken from their homes to an unknown place for the night.

He went in and saw the local Mayor's wife, whom he knew slightly, and explained about the old man and his probably dying wife. She checked the evacuation list and told him to take his passengers to the St Denis medical centre, where they had doctors and the facilities to deal with them. Bruno obeyed, although he thought there might be better uses for his Land Rover. He took the back way to St Denis, the hill road through Audrix, thinking the main road through Le Buisson might be blocked with traffic. It had taken him an hour to get from the old couple's house to St Denis, a journey that would normally take twenty minutes. And it took almost as long again to unload his passengers, ensure they were taken in and then drive back to Siorac.

There were lessons to be learned from this emergency. He'd have to file an after-action report suggesting that dedicated evacuation routes should be made in the future, with evacuating traffic allowed to use both lanes. Separate roads should be kept clear for police, fire and medical personnel. The planning should have been done already, except that nobody official had anticipated a fire such as this in the Dordogne. They should have done, Bruno thought, after the nine French *départements* in the south had been hit by fires during the same September week three years earlier, with thousands of people evacuated and the main north–south autoroute closed.

When he got back to the assembly point in the Siorac car park he saw Yveline's van again but there was no sign of her. He learned from Sergeant Jules that St Laurent had been abandoned and the *pompiers* were trying to establish a new control line to stop the fire along the D53 and D50 local roads at Veyrines. Bruno drew on his mental map of the region, thinking that the only line of resistance after Veyrines would be the River Dordogne itself.

'When we pulled out from St Laurent, there were fires on

the hills to each side of us, moving as fast we were. It was scary,' said Jules. 'Looks like you got your people out just in time.'

'Where's Yveline?'

'Down at the river bank. They've requisitioned refuse trucks and milk tankers and she's trying to get them filled with water and taken up to the fire engines for the hoses. They haven't got enough tenders since most of them were assigned to the fires in the Landes. The St Cyprien gendarmes are collecting those above-ground swimming pools, you know the ones, thick plastic sheeting in a cradle. There's a plan to move them to Veyrines and use the available tenders to fill them so the fire engines can recharge faster.'

'Sounds like a decent idea,' said Bruno. 'I'd better report in.'

Despite his uniform, Bruno waited in line for nearly twenty minutes outside the command centre before he could report. He was told to take back roads to Allas-les-Mines, and evacuate some more families between there and Milandes, but to use only the small road through the woods to Envaux. On no account was he to use the Allas bridge. The main road and bridge at Allas were reserved for the fire engines. It was at that moment that Bruno fully understood the problem of the bottlenecks at the few available river crossings. Along the twenty-kilometre stretch from St Cyprien to Castelnaud there was only that one narrow bridge at Allas.

A police vehicle drew up, blue light flashing, and Commissaire Prunier climbed out, pausing to greet Bruno as he entered the control centre.

'I have an idea – let's use the *gabarres*,' said Bruno, referring to the flat-bottom boats that in the past had taken barrels of good Bergerac wine down river to the port at Libourne. These days, they were pleasure boats that could take forty or fifty tourists on a river cruise.

'I'm on evacuation duty but can't use the Allas bridge because the fire engines need it,' Bruno went on. 'Given the traffic jams on other roads, that means dumping carloads of old and disabled people at Allas without being able to get them across the bridge. I suggest we call out the *gabarres* from Beynac and use them to evacuate people from the quay at Envaux. We can take them back across the river to Beynac where they'll be safe. *Mon Dieu*, they'd be out of danger just staying on the river.'

'That makes sense,' said Prunier, nodding. 'I'll call the Mayor of Beynac and get him to organize the *gabarres* and send them to Envaux. You start evacuating people to the quayside there.'

'Please make sure the control centre here knows that Envaux is to be the evacuation point,' said Bruno at the door. 'And that the Mayor of Envaux knows to keep that quayside open. If there are volunteers who can help elderly and disabled people get aboard the boats, even better.'

'Consider it done,' said Prunier. 'Now, get going.'

Bruno delivered his final load of evacuees to the quayside at Envaux just after two in the morning. Several lights were on and a group of people stood on the quay but there was no boat in sight. The local Mayor, whom Bruno had met when dropping off the first group, came to the Land Rover waving a mobile phone. As Bruno opened the door she said, 'I just spoke to them at Beynac. The *gabarre* is finally on the way.

The skipper was nervous about running aground if he sailed at night but finally agreed.'

'How many evacuees do you have now?' he asked.

'With the people in your vehicle, about thirty, all either old or disabled. After that we'll have to get our own people out. We've been told the bridge at Allas is off limits and the radio said the fire is moving fast towards Milandes. So here at Envaux we'll require a second boatload.'

'Do they have a reception group organized at Beynac?'

'Yes, I've been told they have doctors and social workers standing by and they've set up a basic medical centre in the castle.' She paused, then gave him a tired smile. 'It's really impressive how people are working together on this.'

'A pity we can't do it all the time.'

She nodded, still smiling, and he liked her at once. He could imagine the pressure she would be under, organizing the evacuation of her own village while trying to cope with the carloads of the elderly and disabled being brought to her quayside by Bruno and other volunteers. An attractive woman in her fifties with fine eyes, her hair was tied up loosely in a bun that somehow looked as if it had been done with care. This was a woman proud of herself, he reflected, elected by her neighbours and evidently efficient. She smiled at him again and to Bruno's pleasure the tiredness left her face. He had a sense of how she must have looked two, three decades earlier. He thought she looked even better now.

'We can offer you coffee, mineral water, wine, a cold beer or a cognac along with a *jambon-fromage*,' she said. 'I thought you might need food.'

He wasn't hungry but the idea of a baguette stuffed with ham and cheese was tempting since Bruno assumed he'd be working all night. 'Thank you, *madame*. I'd love a baguette and a *petit rouge*. Have you heard from the command post?'

'Yes, I was on the phone to them just before you came. They said you were bringing the last of the evacuees but they stressed that the wind is veering, now coming from the south-west. I'm to tell you that they are gathering the *pompiers* and volunteers at Castelnaud-la-Chapelle. They want to save the castle.' She paused and looked at him. 'Your face is filthy from smoke and I imagine you could use a bathroom. Come with me.'

She led him into a house whose door was open. Inside was a simple office, two desks and bookcases filled with files. She showed him to an anonymous bathroom, bare but sufficient. He assumed it was part of the Mairie. He washed his face, neck and hands and ran water over his head. When he emerged she was waiting with a baguette in a paper bag and a full bottle of red wine, already opened with the cork stuffed halfway in. He looked at the label and his eyes widened when he saw it was a Margaux from 2015.

'I've got the files and papers ready to put on board,' she said. 'I can't take the wine but I wouldn't want a bottle like that to go to waste. You should have it. Thank you for what you've done tonight. I heard it was you who had the idea to use the *gabarres*.'

'Somebody else would have thought of it. By the way, I'm Bruno,' he said. 'From St Denis.'

'I know,' she replied. 'I'm Marguerite.'

A boat horn sounded from the river. They went to the door and saw the *gabarre* approaching.

'Good luck at Castelnaud.' She turned and went to the quayside, giving instructions for the stretcher cases and wheelchairs to board first. Bruno took an appreciative mouthful of the wine, straight from the bottle, followed by a large bite of baguette. He chewed and swallowed and washed it down with another mouthful of wine. He replaced the cork, went back to the Land Rover to stash the food and bottle, and then began helping the evacuees to board.

'What did you see of the fire on the way here?' he asked the skipper after introducing himself. It had almost reached the southern bank of the river just before Milandes, he was told.

'What about the chateau?' he asked. Milandes was a place he liked and knew well, and he felt a twinge of concern for the fate of its collection of hunting hawks.

'The village and chateau looked okay, protected by its big car park. But from the island down to Milandes, it's woodland all the way back for twenty kilometres. The fire just raced through.'

'So I wouldn't be able to drive to Castelnaud on this side of the river?'

'Not a chance, we saw the fire jumping the road. You'll have to cross the river and take the north bank.'

That left Bruno no choice but to talk his way across the bridge at Allas. He waited on the quayside until told to untie the mooring rope, threw it back on board the *gabarre*, waved. Then he returned to the Land Rover and attached the magnetic flashing blue light to his roof. To his surprise, the bridge was clear and nobody was guarding it. The people of Envaux could have used it after all. That would be another item for his report.

Once over the river he turned east onto the narrow two-track road. It was usually packed with tourists throughout the summer, but now it was deserted but for the occasional ambulance, police car or fire truck. The glow of fire loomed terrifyingly bright across the river. The lovely castle of Milandes was a silhouette against the fire that had spread through the woods behind and the reflection of the flames flickered in the river. Bruno was stopped by a gendarme at the entrance to the village of Beynac, showed his police ID and said he was under Prunier's orders to get to Castelnaud.

From this vantage point, looking across one of the great bends in the river, he could see the farmland in the low-lying ground illuminated by the fires that covered the entire hill behind the crops. Those woods, he knew, ran all the way to the great medieval fortress of Castelnaud. There was something almost Biblical about the scene, the red glow of the sky seeping into the darkness of the smoke. The bright, shooting yellow bursts of flame seemed ready to set alight the dappled water of the river and dance in the ripples as each new flare signalled the incineration of yet another tree.

The gendarme handed Bruno back his ID card and waved him on. He drove beneath the huge cliff, now glowing red, on which perched the fortress of Beynac. It seemed to stand in defiance of the fires across the river, just as it had stood in defiance of enemies in siege after siege in the Middle Ages. The road here hugged the river until it escaped the town and continued north towards Sarlat. Bruno turned south, following the river bank to the bridge at Tournepique. Here it was the massive stone towers and walls of Castelnaud that were silhouetted against the flickering redness that loomed over the hill behind the fortress. Bruno felt a sudden lurch in his sense of time. It could be the Middle Ages once again, the embattled castle under siege.

24

Bruno was waved down just before the bridge and told to turn off the road and into a field, where scores of other civilian vehicles were already parked. He did so and walked across the bridge, checking his watch. It was twenty minutes before three. Dawn would break in less than three hours. He wondered if Castelnaud would still exist by then.

Police and fire trucks filled the town car park and the field where in normal times sightseers watched while enormous balloons were inflated to take a load of passengers soaring over the valley. A huge water tender was poised as close to the bank as it could get, giant hoses sucking up the river water. As soon as one left, heading for the far side of the hill where the *pompiers* were still trying to hold back the flames, a second took its place, thrusting its proboscis into the river like some beast at a waterhole. There was no sign of a third.

Dozens of men, presumably volunteers, were stretched out on the bank, resting or trying to sleep, while others were helping direct the fire trucks to the narrow road that led up the hill. Still more volunteers gathered around crates of bottled water that were disappearing as fast as they could be unloaded from a supermarket truck. Amid the bustle and shouting and sense of emergency, Bruno saw in the gloomy faces and lowered heads of many of the volunteers a mood of dejection, even of hopelessness. They had done their best but it hadn't been enough; the fire had won. He saw the same faltering morale in the expressions of the men standing in line at a mobile pizza truck that was providing free food.

Another fluttering tricolor marked the local command centre, this time with an *armée de l'air* communications truck parked alongside. Bruno wondered if the water-dropping aircraft operated at night. Presumably the pilots needed to sleep. Inside the command centre he found Commissaire Prunier, one phone to his ear, staring at the screen of another phone in his hand and telling someone the evacuations were complete.

'No lives have been lost so far. We managed to get the people out on *gabarres*, but the fire still isn't under control,' he was saying into his phone. 'What we'll need in future is a *gabarre* refitted to hold a fire engine that can suck up water and pump it out in fire hoses. Maybe a flat-bottomed barge would do. Perhaps you could put a team together when this emergency is over, Monsieur Le Prèfet, and run a cost and feasibility study. We'll speak tomorrow.'

Prunier closed that phone, nodded at Bruno and showed him the screen of the other one. It was obviously linked to a drone that was tracking the front line of the fire, heading for the fortress on the hill above them that dominated the village and the river crossing.

'Hi, Bruno, it looks like we're going to lose the Eco-museum, the walnut plantations and maybe everything this side of the bridge,' he said. 'The *pompiers* and volunteers are all exhausted and there are no more reinforcements. We've had to send a lot of men and equipment to Domme to protect the Frenchelon base. We're down to two water tenders and our one remaining mobile pumping truck was caught in the fire. It got out, but its tyres were burned so it's immobilized. I protested against losing the trucks and men to Domme but we had orders from the Elysée.'

As well as the famous walled bastide-fortress on the hilltop of Domme, the ridge also housed the main base of Frenchelon, the French intelligence electronic listening system that monitored the airwaves and the worldwide net, its name copied from the similar Anglo-American Echelon programme. Run by the Direction Technique of the DGSE, the French equivalent of the Central Intelligence Agency, the presence of the base was an open secret in the region.

'The wind is blowing sparks and cinders right across the containment line that was made a couple of hours ago. The volunteers spent half the night making it and then they had to run for it when the sparks blew right among them,' Prunier added, with a shrug of resignation. 'We're promised a dawn flight of aircraft dumping water and flame retardant but that may be just too little too late. The fire is moving too fast. The *pompiers* can't get any closer than the fortress car park and we haven't enough pumps so their hoses haven't got the range to send water over the top of that hill.'

'Have you visited the fortress?' Bruno asked. 'That war museum has three trebuchets, medieval catapults that were used to batter down castle walls. I saw them in action here, sending fifty kilo rocks soaring for more than two hundred metres. They might be able to pitch water over the top of that hill and at least buy us some time before the aircraft arrive.'

Prunier raised his eyebrows. 'Could you make one work?'

Bruno shook his head. 'I saw it done but you'd need local experts, the guys who built these modern copies. The Mayor would know who they are, or Monsieur Rossillon, the owner of the castle. It was his idea to have those trebuchets built and put into operation.'

'How would we get them to deliver water?'

'We'd need sacks, maybe those hundred-litre heavy-duty plastic sacks used for rubbish collection. We can use plastic ties to close the tops, put them to the sling on the end of the throwing arm and send in barrages of water that way. The bags would burst when they hit the ground.'

'Be realistic, Bruno. It may be an emergency but we still have to live with politics. The Prefect would have a fit and the Greens would go crazy if we used plastic bags. Plastic burns, and then there's the ground pollution problem.'

'Let's not tell him. It's usually better to apologize later than ask permission,' Bruno said, but then saw Prunier frown. He tried another tack. 'Maybe we can find some alternatives. Farmers use jute sacks and fishermen use waterproof ones to ship oysters and mussels in bulk. Get onto the main warehouses for the big supermarkets. They'll have some. You just spoke to the Prefect. Get him to wake up the supermarket managers and get their oyster bags shipped here – by helicopter, if necessary. If that doesn't work, tell them to ship every bag of ice in their freezers. We can pour the ice cubes into ordinary sacks and fire them.'

'Okay, let's try it,' said Prunier. 'I'd rather do something than just abandon this village and the castle.'

'I'll call the supermarket manager in St Denis. I know him well. Then I'll head up there to the bastion where the trebuchets are based with as many volunteers as I can round up and you get Rossillon and his team to join me. Tell him this could be the only chance we have to save his chateau.'

'He's here somewhere. He was one of the volunteers,' Prunier said, as Bruno called the home number for Simon, who managed the biggest supermarket in St Denis. A sleepy voice answered.

'Simon, it's Bruno. Wake up. We have an emergency. Those sacks at the supermarket in which the oysters are delivered. How many do you have in the warehouse? I remember once seeing a stack of dozens of them.'

'Bruno, off hand I just don't know. We send them all back at the end of every week so we'll have twenty or thirty, I suppose. Why do you ask?'

Bruno explained why he wanted Simon to drive to the supermarket, collect all the sacks and bring them as quickly as he could to Castelnaud. Simon should quote Prunier's authority and the police on the roads would be notified. As he ended the call he saw Prunier already speaking on his own phone.

'Monsieur Rossillon?' A pause. 'This is Prunier. Can you come to the control centre here at once, if you please.'

He turned to Bruno. 'You deal with him. I'll call the Prefect.'

'Wait,' said Bruno, explaining that the police on the roads should be notified that Simon from the St Denis supermarket was bringing a carload of sacks and should be allowed to cross the bridge. Prunier told an aide to take care of it and began calling the Prefect.

Usually a friendly, energetic man in his fifties, Rossillon was more than tired, almost swaying as he joined Bruno at the door of the control truck. Bruno introduced himself, explained his idea and saw the man's eyes brighten and his back straighten. But then his shoulders sagged.

'It's no good,' he said. 'They're pointing across the river, the wrong way.'

'There's a bulldozer here, the one they used to make the containment line,' Bruno said. 'Could that turn the trebuchets?'

'Maybe, yes, I think they could. And I've got some of those jute sacks. We use them for the armour.'

Bruno looked blank.

'When the medieval armour rusts, we put the pieces into the sacks with a lot of sand and roll them about to clean the metal. And they have more at the walnut orchard. We'll need string to close the bags but this might just work.'

Rosillon turned and shouted some names, and a group of men came up. As he explained the plan to them, Bruno found the bulldozer driver eating a slice of free pizza at the wheel of his enormous machine. Bruno described the task and the driver set off up the steep and curving road to the car park and the stretch of flat land where the trebuchets stood. By now Rossillon had gathered a score of men he seemed to know and sent most of them up the hill after the bulldozer in a couple of trucks. He sent another group to the walnut orchard and then followed his friends in a car, telling Bruno they all worked at the bars and restaurants that nestled around the castle entrance and had commercial freezers with plenty of ice.

Bruno found the Sarlat fire chief, explained this last, desperate bid to save the castle and village, and said they would need a water tender. The fire chief shook his head in disbelief and said it was ridiculous. Then he said it was impossible; he was about to evacuate the remaining trucks and firemen.

'We've got to be seen to try everything and it's the only chance we've got,' said Bruno. 'Our last throw.'

'*Putain*, you're right. We'll give it a shot.' The fire chief grinned. 'They'll never believe this when they see it on TV. It's worth a try – if only to keep the TV crews out of my hair.'

Ten minutes later, the two big trebuchets had been turned and were now pointing to the top of the hill, the red fire glow fiercely outlining the skyline. They stood ten metres high and the long throwing arms looked to Bruno even longer. Rossillon's team were hauling on the ratcheted wheels and pulleys that raised the huge counterweight and lowered the throwing arm.

'Sixteen hundred kilos of sand in that wood box,' said Rossillon. 'That's the counterweight. Now's the hard part. The throwing arm itself would only send it sixty, eighty metres. With the sling on the end we get the extra force, like the tail of a whip. But if we don't place the sling exactly right, it won't work.'

He helped his team fix the ropes with the big leather sling to the tail of the throwing arm. A small truck raced up to him, braked, and two men got out. They began hauling out sacks filled with ice-cubes, loosely closing the necks of the sacks with string. It took two men to carry each sack to the sling of the trebuchet.

'Stand back,' called Rossillon. He took a sledgehammer and approached the big machine.

'Wait, wait,' came a cry as a TV truck pulled up nearby and a cameraman jumped out, a colleague flipped a switch and the scene was bathed in arc light. A director shouted, 'Okay, we're filming, let her loose.'

Rossillon mouthed a curse at them and then with a powerful swing he knocked away the heavy bolt of wood that held the ratchet in place. The great weight plunged down and the long throwing arm swung over the massive oak pivot. The sling at the end of two metres of rope whipped over and the ice-filled sack soared into the air. Bruno saw it briefly silhouetted against the glow of the fire before it dropped down.

'*Mon Dieu*,' he said aloud in tones of disbelief. 'It worked.'

A cheer came up from the guys who'd already started hauling again on the ratchet and pulleys of the trebuchet that had just fired, even as Rossillon was supervising the loading of another sack into the second, slightly smaller one.

'I'm putting less ice in this one because I'm not sure of the range,' he said. Again, the throwing arm came down, and again the bag of ice was placed into the leather sling and Rossillon and his carpenter carefully straightened the ropes attaching it to the throwing arm. Rossillon handed the sledgehammer to Bruno, saying, 'This was your idea.'

Bruno knocked away the block of wood that had secured the ratchet and again the almost balletic swing of the throwing arm and the extra whiplash effect of the sling sent another sackload of ice over the brow of the hill and into the fire.

By this time, Prunier and the Sarlat fire chief and half the volunteers had joined them on the level ground that Rossillon called his *place d'armes* to watch the modern use of the medieval catapults, cheering as each one fired. By now they had the waterproof jute sacks filled with water from the tender. It took three men to wrestle it onto the sling and then Simon arrived in his car with his oyster sacks.

'I've got thirty-six sacks here,' Simon announced, throwing open the back of his car. 'And on the way I called my colleague at St Cyprien and he's bringing another load from his warehouse. And he's calling the hypermarket at Sarlat. They should have more.'

'That's great. We can forget the ice and just shoot water,' said Rossillon.

By this time the men had fallen into a routine. The sacks were placed empty in the sling of the trebuchet before they held each one upright to be filled by a hose from the tender. Then they loosely sealed the top with string, backed away and fired it off.

Bruno checked his watch. It was a quarter to four. Every three minutes, one sack of fifty litres and another of more like seventy litres of water, which meant seventy kilos of weight, was fired over the hill. If they could keep up the pace, that was thirty-six hundred litres each hour. Bruno told himself that maybe the glow of the fire was slackening just a little. But then he realized it wasn't the fire that was slackening but the lightening of the sky behind him to the east as the dawn began to break.

'I don't know if it's your mad idea or if we just got lucky,' said the fire chief. He had suddenly appeared at Bruno's side with a walkie-talkie. 'The fire engine in the car park has put down enough water to open a track halfway up the hill so any minute now the hoses will be putting down water onto the crest. We'll save this castle yet.'

The sacks that Simon had brought from the St Denis supermarket had all gone, along with most of those brought from St Cyprien. The sacks from the Sarlat *hypermarché* had not yet arrived.

'The aircraft have taken off and are on their way,' came a tinny but familiar voice coming from Prunier's mobile phone. 'Estimated time of arrival is twenty-seven minutes.'

'Alain, is that you?' Bruno said loudly, startling Prunier as he leaned his mouth close to the phone.

'Bruno, yes, it's me. Where are you?'

'Up at the castle with the catapults. I'll doubtless see you later.' He backed off, apologizing to Prunier and explaining that the air force communications man down below in the car park was his cousin.

There was time for six more shots from each of the two trebuchets before they ran out of sacks. And then they heard the first, faint growl of the aircraft coming up over the river from the west.

'They'll pass us, turn over Domme and come in from the east, with the sun behind them,' said the fire chief, facing the TV camera and speaking into the director's microphone. 'They'll drop just a little ahead of the leading edge of the fire, so the wind will help spread the water over the unburned wood and deny the fire the fresh fuel it needs to advance. Each of the aircraft will be dumping six thousand litres of water with fire retardant. After the big fires in Provence, we bought four more of these special firefighting planes.

'The aircraft are purpose-built Bombardier four-one-five models, originally designed in Canada as an amphibious aircraft that can operate from land or from water, and can scoop up water from lakes or reservoirs,' he added, as the camera swivelled upwards to get a shot of the three aircraft passing overhead.

Every eye followed them as they turned and came back, dropping lower and lower until they roared almost overhead, no more than a hundred metres above the brow of the hill. They banked to follow the line of flames and then one by one dumped a great red trail of water mixed with retardant. Was it the first rays of the rising sun that made them that colour, Bruno wondered, or was it the fire retardant? At that point the car from Sarlat arrived with its trunk full of sacks.

Three aircraft, each with six thousand litres, thought Bruno. And the trebuchets had thrown maybe five thousand litres in all, certainly less than a third of what the aircraft had delivered. But they had done wonders for the morale of the exhausted *pompiers* and volunteers, and Bruno had little doubt which of the firefighting methods would dominate the TV news reports later in the day. In the past week, the viewers had grown accustomed to film of the firefighting aircraft.

Prunier and the fire chief were looking at the mobile phone

that was connected to the small drone that lifted from the car park below and soared up, over the brow of the hill to film the effect of the water dumpers.

'Very impressive,' said Prunier, as Bruno came alongside to look down at the sight of the fire tamed. The creeping red edge he'd seen before on the images from the drone had gone, replaced by long dark stretches of doused trees with steam rising rather than smoke.

'We'll need another dump, just one more,' said the fire chief. 'In the meantime, the men from the Middle Ages may resume their bombardment.'

'I'm not sure we can do much more with this smaller one,' said Rossillon, from where he was scrambling with his carpenter over the structure that may have been smaller but still dwarfed them. 'The throwing arm seems to have sprung.'

'In a noble cause,' said Bruno solemnly. 'Fallen on the field of honour.'

They loaded the larger of the trebuchets with another sack of water but somehow Bruno could tell that Rossillon's heart wasn't in it. The sense of urgency, of their use as the last chance to save the castle, had gripped them and given exhausted men new strength. But now that the aircraft had arrived, that mood had dissipated. Every man could do the maths as well as Bruno. They might as well have pissed on the flames for all the good they had done. All that work, all that enthusiasm, for delivering just a few thousand litres, seemed pointless in retrospect.

'You men may be feeling that your work was in vain but believe me, it wasn't,' came the voice of the fire chief. He was addressing the volunteers and the trebuchet crews rather than the cameras, but Bruno guessed the man knew he was being filmed.

'I know fire and your medieval catapults made the crucial difference in that hour before dawn when the aircraft finally arrived. I was about to order an evacuation of this side of the river, abandoning this magnificent fortress and museum to the flames. But I saw the flames die a little with each sack you hurled at them. Well done, all of you. Monsieur Rossillon, you and your team have defended your castle in the great tradition of this mighty stronghold of Castelnaud. *Pompiers*, *policiers*, *militaires*, men and women and all the volunteers, my congratulations. This was the last battle of Castelnaud, and you have won.'

He raised his hand to the peak of his helmet and saluted them all as a great cheer roared up from two, perhaps three hundred throats.

'I always suspected he had political ambitions,' murmured Prunier in Bruno's ear. 'Now I'm sure of it.'

'Still, it was a pretty good speech, off the cuff and unrehearsed. He certainly knows how to inspire people,' Bruno said.

The fire chief strolled across to Rossillon who was checking the sling ropes of the trebuchet.

'With your permission, *monsieur*,' said the fire chief, taking the sledgehammer from Rossillon, who stepped back and gestured to the fireman to go ahead. The sledgehammer swung back once and then again, the fire chief making sure the camera was on him. Then he knocked away the beam holding the ratchet. The great arm swung over once more, the sling whipping its final thrust and one more oyster sack of water sailed off over the hill, spurred on by a new burst of cheers from the volunteers.

'And if this doesn't double the number of visitors to Castelnaud this year, I'll eat my old *képi*,' said Prunier.

But that didn't stop Prunier from taking his turn with the sledgehammer when Rossillon invited him to launch the next sack. Then each member of Rossillon's team, men and women alike, was granted a turn at firing the trebuchet before the aircraft returned for another dousing. This time it was judged complete. The great fire of Périgord was out.

25

Bruno was about to leave the *place d'armes* to take the curving track that led downhill when he saw a face he knew. The man was in the uniform of a *pompier* which was why it took him a moment to recognize him. It was Henri Bazaine.

'I thought you were a winemaker. I didn't know you were also a *pompier*,' he said. He didn't offer to shake hands and nor did Henri.

'I thought you were a cop. I didn't know you were also a firefighter,' Henri replied, deadpan. 'I've been a volunteer in the Bergerac brigade for twenty years and I've never known a night like this.'

A beat, as Bruno considered whether or not to speak out.

'Not even back at the Clara Zetkin orphanage?' he asked. 'I presume that's where you first learned about wine, making Riesling in the Elbe valley. And by the way, that asthma that kept you out of military service seems to have cleared up.'

Henri did not react. He just continued to look at Bruno with the same, studiedly neutral stare. Bruno wondered if General Lannes had been successful in dissuading the Elysée from accepting the lawyer's offer of a deal. After the dramas of the night, all that seemed a long time ago.

'Well, thanks for your work last night, you and all the other volunteers,' Bruno said.

'Thanks to you as well. Those catapults put new heart into everyone. Let's hope the politicians learn the lesson of climate change from this fire, before we have more nights like this,' Henri replied.

'I agree with you on that,' Bruno replied. 'But don't get your hopes up. Democracy is a wonderful thing, but politicians don't tend to win elections by telling people to stop using fossil fuels.'

'Or to stop flying and eating fast food,' Henri replied, with the glimmer of a smile. It did not reach his eyes. Bruno decided to forge on.

'What happened between you and Max?' he asked. 'Was it a fight over the Lefort scrapbook?'

'I don't know what you're talking about.' Henri's face was impassive once more.

'*Auf wiedersehen*,' said Bruno, as he turned aside and walked on down the hill, wondering whether it was worth telling Prunier of Henri's presence among the volunteers. Until he heard from Isabelle about the Elysée's decision, it would make little difference. It was now six in the morning, a new day. Perhaps he'd be able to have breakfast with Alain before getting some sleep.

At the bottom of the hill, where a long line of vehicles was waiting to cross the bridge, the parking area was in chaos as vehicles vied to leave. They needed a traffic cop, Bruno thought, wondering whether he should start sorting out the jam. As he pondered, a gendarme emerged from the crush, blew his whistle and began restoring a modicum of order. Then Bruno saw the fluttering tricolor that indicated the command truck and beyond it the blue of the air force truck. It had not moved. There was nobody in the driver's compartment so he hammered on the rear door. After a moment, it was opened by a sleepy-eyed stranger in air force blue.

'I'm looking for Alain,' he said. 'He's my cousin.'

'You're Bruno? He went looking for you. He said you were the guy who got those catapults going. So, *chapeau*, I doff my hat to you, but I'm knackered and I'm going back to sleep.' The door closed.

Bruno sat on the small step outside the truck door and closed his eyes, thinking how good a coffee would taste just now. And then he caught a strong whiff of the stuff. A young woman holding a tray filled with coffee cups was heading for the command truck.

'May I buy one?' he asked, reaching for some change.

'On the house. Our café would have burned down without you guys,' she said. 'Take two, you look like you need them. And we'll have some croissants in a few minutes.'

As she went into the command truck, Alain emerged from between two other trucks, saw the coffee and said, 'Is one of those for me?' Bruno handed over a cup and they hugged each other clumsily, with one arm.

'Was it really your idea, to use the catapults?'

'Not really, I just remembered they were up there and thought, hey, that would be worth a try. But you were here at Castelnaud the other day. You would have thought of it. That reminds me, how's the lovely Rosalie?'

'Fine when I saw her yesterday morning, before we got called up here.'

'You've chosen well there. All my friends enjoyed meeting you both, so you'll have a social life ready and waiting when you arrive. But tell me, is this work with the water-dropping aircraft a regular part of what you do?'

'Not at all,' Alain replied. 'There was an emergency call for our help yesterday and even though the aircraft are nominally part of the Service Civique, the flight crew are all ex-air force. They insisted on having our communications systems. They had some problems in Provence a couple of years ago when the cops and *pompiers* were trying to direct them. That's why we have a pilot in our truck as ground controller. I'm just running the electronics. But we haven't stopped. We were dropping water in the Landes yesterday and near Nérac before that.'

'Well, thanks for helping put our fire out. You should have called to say you'd arrived.'

'I had no idea where we were last night when we got here. We were just told to load up and get going so the aircraft could start dropping as soon as it was light.'

Bruno grinned. 'That sounds like the military I remember. But can't the planes operate in the dark?'

'They could but they have to fly quite low to get a concentrated drop and in hilly country like this in the dark, it's just too risky.'

Alain turned as his name was shouted from the truck and someone in air force uniform beckoned him to come back. 'Here we go again, off somewhere new.' He handed the coffee cup to Bruno.

'Give Rosalie my best regards.' They shook hands and as soon as Alain climbed into the back of the truck its engine started, and with a peep of the horn it headed for the bridge. Bruno watched it go and then went to the command truck to say he was signing off and going home for some sleep. He found Prunier there, being interviewed by Phillipe Delaron for *Sud Ouest*.

'This is the guy you should be talking to,' Prunier said to Phillipe. 'It was Bruno's idea to use the *gabarres* to evacuate people and he was also the one who told me we should try the catapults.'

'Is that right?' Phillipe asked, turning to Bruno.

'A lot of people were coming up with different ideas,' Bruno replied. 'In the military you learn to combine your arms, air power, infantry, armour and artillery. We had the fire trucks, the *pompiers* and volunteers as our infantry and we knew the air power would be coming once it was light. What we didn't have was artillery – and that was the gap the catapults could fill. When we realized just how fast the fire was moving we were desperate enough to try anything. The important thing now is to make sure we learn from this, to make proper plans and run exercises to get everybody accustomed to working together.'

'That's exactly what I told the fire chief,' Prunier said, turning back to Phillipe. 'We're forming a working group to draw up recommendations and I want Bruno to be on it.'

After taking some more photos, Phillipe went to interview Rossillon and Bruno asked Prunier, 'Any news from J-J about Henri Bazaine? I just ran into him; he's one of the volunteer *pompiers* from Bergerac.'

'Really? So he can't be all bad. No, I haven't heard from J-J since yesterday. And we found no trace of his taking a train or autoroute to Paris. Now I'm going home to get some sleep and drop off this filthy uniform at the dry cleaner. You should do the same. Do you know you smell of pee?'

'It's from one of the evacuees, a little old lady I had to carry who must've been incontinent. I've been smelling it all night.'

Bruno went home, fed his chickens, stripped off, climbed into the shower then turned off his phone and went to bed. He woke in the early afternoon, made coffee and had another shower before turning his phone back on. He had almost a dozen messages, two from the Mayor, three from the local radio station, two from J-J, one from Sabine, another from Rossillon and two from Isabelle. He called her first.

'I saw you on TV breakfast news with those medieval war machines,' she said. 'I don't think I ever saw you looking quite so filthy.'

'I stank even worse,' he said. 'Any news from the Elysée about Bazaine?'

'Yes, against our advice, they're going ahead with the deal. Bazaine gets immunity and in return the Elysée gets the Rosenholz stuff.' She then paused and the silence lengthened and then lengthened some more.

'Ah,' said Bruno, starting to understand. 'Once they have it, have the wonder boys in the Elysée promised to pass it on to you and our counter-espionage people?'

'Not that I know of.'

'You mean they're going to keep it?' Bruno said, in disbelief.

'Knowledge is power,' she replied. 'To be fair, they don't want a witch-hunt. I understand that and to an extent I sympathize with that point of view. But . . .' She paused again.

'But you're still a cop at heart,' said Bruno. 'And you don't want Bazaine getting away with murder.'

'Exactly,' she said. 'But I have an idea. What are you up to this weekend?'

'If you're thinking of coming here, we can take Balzac to visit his puppies.'

'I can't think of anything I'd rather do,' she said. 'Well, almost anything. But part of this trip might be official, depending on some meetings I have to arrange. I should be able to confirm sometime tomorrow.'

'Wonderful,' he said. Then he ignored the calls from the radio station and rang the Mayor.

'I just called to congratulate you,' the Mayor said. 'I think half the town saw the morning news on TV with you and the trebuchet.'

'Good for you. Everybody else is calling it a catapult.'

'And you seem to have a new fan in my esteemed colleague, the Madame Maire of Envaux. She said on TV that you were the one who arranged the *gabarres* to evacuate people.'

'Everybody is being very kind but the truth is we mishandled the situation,' Bruno said. 'We misjudged the speed of the fire. The evacuation routes weren't arranged in advance. Bridges that were supposed to be closed were left open and there was too little advance planning between the police, the *pompiers* and the air force. We need to do better next time because I think there'll be more wildfires like this.'

'I agree with you,' said the Mayor.' And not just here or in Australia or California where we see them on TV, but in more and more places as climate change speeds up. Did you see they even had them in Sweden a couple of years ago?'

'Exactly,' said Bruno. 'Prunier is planning to set up a working group in this *département* but you could use your Paris connections to make this a nationwide process. We need to do it.'

'We'll discuss this tomorrow when you come back in. I want you to take the rest of the day off. Get some sleep.'

Bruno ignored the remaining calls and since the Land Rover still smelled of urine, he washed down the rear benches and floor and drove with all the windows open to the riding school. Balzac, recognizing the sound of the engine, was running into the stable yard to greet him. His barking alerted Hector, who gave a welcoming neigh and then Pamela appeared at her kitchen door.

'Well done,' she said, coming to give him a warm hug, with Virginie following along behind. 'We saw you on TV and Virginie found a way to download it onto her laptop and emailed it to me, so I sent it to all our friends. Have you seen it yet?'

'No,' he said. 'And I don't think I need to. I was there. I'm told I looked filthy.'

'Everybody did, from the smoke.'

'*Bonjour*, Virginie,' he said, leaning forward to kiss her cheeks, and was slightly surprised when she wrapped her arms around him in a fierce hug.

'I'm in love with Balzac, he's wonderful,' she said. 'I learned how to saddle a pony and Pamela wants me to help with the little ones later today.'

'I feel the need for a ride on Hector,' said Bruno and looked at Pamela. 'Want to come?'

'I can't,' she replied, shaking her head. 'I have the big girls coming for riding lessons at four. Do you want to stay for dinner? Virginie is cooking us another vegetable feast.'

'Thanks, I'd love to but I have to see J-J about this case we've been working on,' he said. 'And I should go to the clinic and find out how some of the evacuees are doing. But first, I need a run with Hector.'

Virginie came into the stables as he was saddling his horse and said, 'I want to thank you for that kind message you sent to Madame Daynès about the head I made. She called me this morning to offer me a job at her studio, starting in September.'

'Congratulations, that's great news,' he said. 'You earned it. What will you do until then? Go back to Paris?'

'I have a week's more work at least in Périgueux, making the extra heads. After that, Pamela says I can stay here through the summer, learn to ride and help with the kids. She can't pay me but I'll be able to live here for free.'

'Good, she'll make a fine horsewoman of you. I'm glad you've enjoyed meeting my friends. I know they enjoyed meeting you.'

He walked Hector out, mounted and with a wave at Virginie, set off up the trail to the ridge, Balzac trotting at his heels. Hector seemed as eager for a good run as Bruno was. He cantered off the last shallow slope then began to gallop almost as soon as they were on level ground. They paused at the woods for Balzac to catch up and Bruno stared across at the familiar landscape that was still untouched by fire. He fervently hoped it stayed that way, and once Balzac joined them, Hector trotted through the trees to the long firebreak.

Balzac knew the place well and knew how fast the horse

would run so he stayed where he was, watching Hector canter at first and then move easily into a fast run, not quite a gallop. At the far end, Bruno slowed, turned and this time Hector went all out, as fast as Bruno could remember riding, an exhilaration so intense he heard himself whooping for joy until Hector slowed for the woods and Balzac barked in welcome at their return. Minutes later, the riding school came into view and Bruno could see Pamela's swimming pool was full of water, unsullied by ashes and empty of people. It looked very inviting indeed.

Bruno's phone vibrated. It was J-J and he thought he'd better take it.

'How's the TV star? And have you heard the news from Paris?'

'What news?' Bruno asked, thinking it better to be discreet about how far Isabelle had confided in him, with all that it implied for the closeness of their relations.

'The Elysée is letting Henri off the hook in return for those Stasi documents he's been sitting on. Prunier heard it from General Lannes, who didn't sound at all happy about it. I'd have thought you'd have heard.'

'I was up all night, firefighting. I've been catching up on sleep. So what do you do now?'

'I have a call in to Isabelle. She might have some ideas.'

'I wouldn't go up against the Elysée if I were you.'

'That's what Prunier said. And well done last night. We'll talk after I hear from Isabelle.'

Bruno unsaddled Hector in the stables, gave him a wizened apple from the barrel and rubbed him down while Balzac snuffled around their feet. Then he strolled up to the pool, stripped off to his undershorts and dived in, his momentum taking him underwater most of the length of the pool. He rose, swam three fast lengths and then floated, arms outstretched, his fingers fluttering, eyes closed, enjoying the heat of the sun on his face. He stayed like that until his head bumped gently against what he thought was the side of the pool at the shallow end, and he opened his eyes to see Balzac nudging him. He climbed out, patted Balzac and stood for a while looking up at the ridge, almost able to feel the water on his skin evaporate in the warmth. The breeze was still from the south and he sighed at the thought that there could be another heavy night.

'There you are,' came a voice. 'The medieval catapult man himself.'

It was Jack Crimson, grinning broadly, dressed in swimming shorts with a big towel around his neck. He dived in, making a massive splash that showered Bruno with water all over again, surfaced and blew like a grampus. 'I heard on the grapevine that this Rosenholz dossier business is nearly settled,' he said. 'About time, too.'

Bruno knew that Jack and General Lannes were old colleagues, and that although he was officially retired, Jack still worked as a consultant on strategic risks for some private clients. His access to old friends in British, French and American intelligence made him a usefully deniable go-between for them all. Isabelle had once described him to Bruno as a wise and trusted old owl.

'Glad to hear it,' said Bruno. 'I hope you'll say that to Jacqueline before she drops any more bombs on *Le Monde*'s op-ed pages.'

'On reflection, I'm rather glad she aired the issue the way

she did,' Jack replied. 'It focused a few minds, reminded people that they shouldn't believe everything they might read in the files of an enemy agency. Just think what damage could be done by leaking fake KGB files saying that this British statesman or that American politician had all along been in the pay of the Russians. Lies can get halfway around the world before truth gets its boots on.'

He ducked beneath the water and then began breast-stroking a stately circuit of the pool. Bruno's mobile vibrated, and once again it was Isabelle.

'Can you meet me with J-J at Bergerac airport tomorrow?' she asked. 'I'm on the morning flight from Paris, getting in just after nine.'

'Of course,' he replied. 'It will be good to see you. Can you stay long?'

'That rather depends on how things develop overnight,' she said. 'I can't explain now. Maybe tomorrow. By the way, we came across an interesting coincidence. If you have a copy of that law book by the People's Pierre, there's an acknowledgement to his dear friend and colleague, Maître Vautan.'

'Can you say what brings you down here, business or pleasure?'

'Somebody has to deliver to Henri Bazaine the presidential pardon that he demanded and I volunteered. But it may become more complicated. We'll know tomorrow. And make sure you come armed.'

26

It was a surprise the next morning to see Isabelle emerge first from the aircraft, wearing her uniform as a *commissaire* of police and carrying a briefcase emblazoned with the RF of la République Française. He had never seen her in official dress before. When they first met she had been a detective in plain clothes, working for J-J. Then she had been promoted to the staff of the Interior Minister, then to EuroJust in The Hague, the European Union's judicial coordination unit. In all of those jobs she wore civilian clothes, as she did with her most recent promotion to run France's coordination team with allies and EU partners on counter-terrorism. Bruno knew this had brought her a new rank, but to see her in uniform was a surprise. It must mean she was on a seriously official mission. He was glad that he'd decided to leave Balzac back at Pamela's riding school.

She was followed by a man in plain clothes carrying two overnight cases whom Bruno did not recognize. She introduced him as a diplomatic colleague without any further explanation, and then J-J embraced her in a bear hug, saying, 'The uniform becomes you, Isabelle. Still, however high your reach in rank, to me you'll always be my favourite young detective.'

She extricated herself from J-J's embrace, gave him a smacking kiss on the cheek and did the same for Bruno before leading the way to the waiting vehicles, saying to her companion, 'This old rascal is like a papa to me – he taught me everything I know about police work when I was based down here. And this is my old friend Bruno, chief of police of the Vézère valley, with whom I share a very special dog.'

'The catapult man,' said Isabelle's companion, in a French-Canadian accent. 'I recognize him from the TV news on the forest fire.'

'You see, Bruno? You're famous,' she said, as J-J's driver opened the door for her.

'We'll talk later,' Isabelle added quietly to Bruno. 'If you could go in the second car with the *mobiles*. We're heading to Henri's vineyard.'

The second car was a van almost filled with heavily armed *gendarmes mobiles*, the elite paramilitary unit who must have come in from Bordeaux. The *chef d'escadron* greeted Bruno with a salute and a handshake, then grinned and asked if he'd brought his catapult with him. The troops inside laughed, amiably enough, and made space for him in one of the three rows inside.

The commander climbed into the front passenger seat, turned to face his troops and said, 'This is Chef de Police Bruno Courrèges and if you haven't noticed it, you men, this guy wasn't always a cop. He's wearing the ribbon of a Croix de Guerre and they don't hand those out with the rations. I checked him out and he won it in Sarajevo for pulling wounded troops out of a burning armoured car when the Serbs were shelling the airport. You may also have seen him on TV yesterday, using a medieval war machine to put out a forest fire. We're glad to have you with us, sir.'

'Have you been briefed on the mission?' Bruno asked, to cover his embarrassment as they followed J-J's car down the N21 and then turned off to the right on the road to the main Bergerac vineyards.

'Standing by and providing a security escort, as required by the *commissaire*. That's all. Anything more you can tell me?'

Bruno shook his head. 'I know no more than you do. Beyond having powers to arrest someone, I'm not sure what I'm doing here.'

'Welcome to the mushroom club,' called out a gendarme from the back.

'Mushroom club?' asked Bruno. 'What's that?'

'Kept in the dark and fed on bullshit,' came the answering roar of half a dozen voices, speaking as one.

Bruno nodded, laughing. 'I see the job hasn't changed much.'

He wondered why Isabelle had called in the *mobiles*, usually only employed in hostage rescue or situations requiring a heavily armed response. If she was simply delivering to Henri his presidential pardon, Bruno saw no reason for their presence. He felt as frustrated as she evidently was that the Elysée was letting Henri off the hook in return for the scrapbook or dossier or whatever it was that he was using to buy his pardon. Bruno had wondered whether Henri might not simply be handed over to the German authorities to let them prosecute him for the murder of Max, a German citizen. But the proof of that was purely circumstantial, that Henri was there at the right time and place and with a motive. Certainty of conviction required more than that.

J-J's car stopped before they reached the Bazaine vineyard and the *mobiles*' van pulled in behind it. J-J stepped out and beckoned to Bruno to join him. He was shown into the back seat, squeezing in beside Isabelle and the diplomat.

'The *mobiles* have been briefed to come into the vineyard exactly five minutes after we go inside,' she said. 'It's just insurance, in case. But we don't want Henri seeing them before that and I think you deserve to be in at the kill, as it were.'

'In case of what?' Bruno asked.

'We'll see.'

They pulled into the vineyard. The door of the house opened as they climbed out of the car and Henri appeared on the threshold. He appeared to be alone.

'*Bonjour*, Monsieur Bazaine,' she began. 'We spoke yesterday evening and I have here the official document from the Elysée.'

'Please come inside,' he said, looking curiously at Bruno and J-J and the diplomat, as if uncertain what they were doing at this presentation. 'Why are these policemen here?'

'It's a courtesy since they have been involved in the case for which you are being granted immunity.'

Henri shrugged, gestured to them to enter but made no move to shake their hands as they passed him at the door. They were all steered into a large, rather old-fashioned and dark sitting room, in which the paintings on the wall were a motley brown colour with occasional lighter patches, as if generations of wood fires had darkened them and they'd never been cleaned. Some seemed to be gloomy landscapes, but Bruno thought he could make out a cow and a stream on the one closest to him. The windows were few and low and the furniture heavy, leather and deliberately formal. There were no flowers, no books or magazines on view, no television and no sign of anything electronic except for two lonely wall lamps. Above all, to Bruno's surprise, there were no other people present. Henri's wife and children were not to be part of this encounter.

'Thank you for receiving us, Monsieur Bazaine,' Isabelle said. 'As I told you by phone late yesterday, I have the honour to present to you the formal document of presidential pardon for any crimes or misdemeanours you may have committed on French soil.'

She placed her briefcase on a small side table, opened it and removed a scroll from which hung a ribbon of red, white and blue, which had been affixed with a seal of red wax. She handed the scroll to Henri. He unrolled it and read carefully through the text.

'That appears to be satisfactory,' he said. He pulled out a smartphone and punched in a number that had already been programmed into the device. 'Maître Vautan? This is Henri Bazaine. I have the document from the Elysée. Would you care to read out the version you drafted so we can be sure the texts agree?'

Henri listened on the phone and Bruno could make out the tinny sound of a voice reading aloud.

'That is identical to the phrasing on the document that has just been delivered to me,' said Henri. 'Please go ahead and surrender to the Elysée the item I entrusted to you.'

He closed the phone and turned to Isabelle with a triumphant smile, as if savouring this moment. 'That appears to conclude our business, *madame*.'

She nodded at him coldly, and said, 'It appears, *monsieur*, that your presidential pardon is allowing you to get away with the murder of Max Morilland, the man you grew up with at the orphanage near Dresden.'

'Murder?' Henri shrugged. 'It was a fair fight. Max was trying to make off with the scrapbook that my lawyer is now handing over to the authorities. I tried to stop him. He picked up the spade we'd used to dig the latrine. We fought over it and I won.'

'So, finally you admit that you killed him,' said J-J.

Henri shrugged again. 'It was him or me.'

The room fell silent. Then Isabelle said curtly, 'Commissaire Jalipeau, this was your case. Over to you.'

J-J moved forward with great speed for such a large man, and swiftly put a pair of old-fashioned metal handcuffs onto one of Henri's wrists but Henri jerked away too quickly for J-J to grab the other. Bruno moved in, grabbed Henri's free arm and pulled it up hard behind his back, using the leverage to force him down to his knees so that J-J could fix the cuffs onto the wrist. Then J-J picked Henri's phone from the floor where it had fallen and tossed it onto the couch.

'Monsieur Bazaine, I am placing you under arrest as the object of an extradition request received from the Dominion of Canada and formally authorized last night by the French Minister of Justice,' said Isabelle, taking another document from her briefcase. 'You are charged with blackmail, demanding money with threats from a Canadian citizen, Monsieur Loriot, and his company, Les Vins de la Nouvelle France, to the sum of two hundred and sixty thousand euros, together with another four hundred thousand French francs when that was the prevailing currency. You will now be surrendered to the custody of the Canadian legal attaché pending your transfer to the jurisdiction of the Canadian courts.'

'This is monstrous,' Henri said. 'Even without my presidential pardon, I'm a French citizen and cannot legally be extradited without a legal hearing. I demand to see my lawyer.'

'That's where you are mistaken,' Isabelle said, her voice flat. 'You're not a French citizen. You arrived in this country on false papers and have sought to disguise your true identity ever since. You are not a French citizen and never have been. Your claim to French nationality is void and you are thus not entitled to the legal rights that pertain to that status.'

With a roar of outrage Henri seemed to explode into action, rising to his feet and advancing as if he wanted to slam his forehead down onto Isabelle's face. Bruno was faster. He caught Henri's arm as he advanced, then swivelled to use the leverage to force him backward, where Henri tripped headlong over Bruno's outstretched leg. He landed with a massive thud as his back and shoulders hit the floor, but Bruno kept a tight grip on his arm to prevent Henri's head from slamming into the ground.

J-J put more cuffs, plastic this time, around Henri's ankles and with the sound of a roaring engine and the squeal of brakes, the *mobiles* van arrived in the courtyard. Isabelle was already at the door to let them in. Four stayed outside by their van, each facing a different direction, their weapons at the ready. Through the window Bruno saw one of them gesturing to Henri's son, who had appeared in the door of the *chai*, to go back inside. Two more gendarmes came into the living room and pointed their automatic rifles at the figure on the floor.

Isabelle turned to the Canadian legal attaché. 'Monsieur Delaurier, the prisoner is now yours. The military aircraft is waiting for you and the prisoner in the military zone of Mérignac airport, ready for the flight to Montreal. I am instructed to offer you all facilities for the transfer of your prisoner to the aircraft. And since the presidential pardon was obtained under false pretences, I hereby confiscate it.'

'What about his family?' Bruno asked. 'They should be informed. At least one of them is here. The son is in the *chai*.'

'J-J, perhaps you would inform young Monsieur Bazaine that his father is being legally extradited to Canada to face serious charges,' Isabelle said. She bent down to the floor and picked up the parchment scroll, replaced it in her briefcase, closed the locks, and turned to the *mobiles*.

'*Messieurs*, please secure the prisoner inside your van for the ride to Mérignac. And Chef de Police Courrèges, please accompany the *mobiles* and ensure the security of the prisoner on the way to the airport. We will see you at the entrance to the military zone.'

Once Henri had been placed inside the van and cuffed to the rings set into the floor of all such vehicles, she said quietly, 'And Bruno, you know we like justice to be seen to be done. J-J has made sure that you'll see some old friends at Mérignac.'

The trip took ninety minutes and was uneventful, the heavy-duty air conditioning inside the van compensating for the heat of the day outside. Bruno assumed the heavily armoured *mobiles* would be in danger of heat exhaustion without it. Henri lay on the floor, glaring at Bruno throughout the trip, even though

Bruno, recalling that he'd been a volunteer *pompier*, had placed a cushion under his head to spare him the bumps.

Although now best known as a civilian airport serving some five million passengers a year, Mérignac had also been a military airbase since 1917. Bruno was interested to see the military section, since he knew that in 1940 it was from this airfield that Charles de Gaulle flew to Britain to continue the fight for France against the Nazi occupation. As Base Aérienne 106 it is today home to Air Force Support Command, housing some three thousand civilian and military personnel, a parachute commando group and an air transport squadron. Bruno could see a French military Airbus 330 waiting on the apron as they stopped at the entrance gate to be checked by a guard and waved inside. Troops in camouflage gear with kitbags beside them waited in rows to board.

'We're able to use a routine flight taking French troops to northern Quebec for exercises with our Canadian allies,' said Isabelle, coming to the door of the van once the *mobiles* had descended and formed a loose cordon. Bruno undid the cuffs that attached Henri to the floor and helped him out. Isabelle saluted a waiting air force officer who escorted them all into the administration building and then into a waiting room where Sabine, in gendarme uniform, was waiting, arm in arm with Tante-Do. The older woman looked as if she had arrived directly from a session at her own beauty parlour, her make-up immaculate and her hair perfectly coiffed.

'*Merde*, not you again,' snapped Henri, with a sneering glance at Tante-Do and then rolling his eyes.

'Yes, me again, Henri,' she replied, her voice brittle. The

knuckles of her hand tightened as she gripped Sabine's hand. 'So perhaps you can admit you recognize me this time? Well, I may not be pleased to see you, but I am delighted to see justice done, however long after the event.'

Tante-Do raised her head defiantly and stared coldly at Henri and then repeated, 'Justice.'

The air force officer coughed, then signed a formal receipt for Henri and gave it to Isabelle. Two military policemen at once applied a separate set of handcuffs to Henri's wrists and a much looser set to his ankles. Each took one of his arms and frogmarched him outside to the waiting plane. All the soldiers on the apron turned to stare as he was bundled up the aircraft steps, followed by the Canadian diplomat.

Tante-Do burst into tears, tucked herself into Sabine's embrace, her shoulders heaving. Her voice was muffled but Bruno heard something that sounded as if she was telling Sabine that the young gendarme was the only family she had left. Sabine patted her on the back and murmured some words of comfort. Bruno watched them, affected by the words, thinking that Sabine had lost her mother and brother within the last year and her father was drifting out of reality. Perhaps it was true and Tante-Do was Sabine's family now. The thought struck Bruno that, thanks to Alain, he'd been reminded that he also had a family and the events of the last few days had brought them much closer than they had been before.

'That's that, J-J,' said Isabelle, putting her hand on the shoulder of the detective who had trained her in his craft and who was now staring almost sadly at the aircraft door through which Henri Bazaine had disappeared. 'My congratulations, my dear old friend,' she went on. 'You never gave up and now your cold case is finally closed. After thirty years you can at last take down that ghoulish photograph from your office door.'

'I suppose so, but I think I'd miss not seeing it every day,' said J-J. 'Somehow it doesn't yet feel that it's really over.' He stomped off to the cars outside without a backward glance, leaving Bruno and Isabelle alone. Some shouted orders from an officer at the plane steps got the troops lining up, ready to board.

'And what now?' Bruno asked her. 'You fly back to Paris?'

'No,' she said and gave him a look he knew too well and never grew tired of. 'I go to the ladies' room and change out of this uniform into something more comfortable. Then I was hoping you and I might collect Balzac and take him to meet his puppies. I really want to see them. After that, I have a few days off and you know how much I miss the Périgord.'

Acknowledgements

The idea for this novel began with a reminiscence from my good friend and neighbour, Raymond Bounichou, a retired officer of Gendarmes, about a case he was never able to solve. He still has the photograph of the skull of the unknown murder victim whom he dubbed 'Oscar'. Raymond tried for years to identify the body of the man who had been buried in a remote wood until unearthed by a dog. It remains a mystery that haunts Raymond to this day. As a last resort, he secured a magistrate's authorization to boil the head of the corpse, which at least allowed him to examine the skull and establish that the cause of death had been a blow from a camping tool.

The mystery of Oscar came to mind when I first saw an exhibition of the work of Elisabeth Daynès. She may now be best known for her reconstruction of the face of Tutankhamun from the skull of the ancient Egyptian ruler, which achieved worldwide renown when it appeared on the cover of *National Geographic* magazine. I was even more impressed by the way her reconstruction of the faces of prehistoric men, women and children from their skulls allows us to see not just the bones but uncannily real people. She has brought a new and highly personal dimension to the study of the long-distant past and her work has given me and many modern visitors to the Les Eyzies museum of prehistory a striking sense of personal connection to our remote forebears.

The Rosenholz dossier is real and its contents and its fate are much as described in this book. Its listing of the thousands of agents of the Stasi (the term comes from *Staatssicherheit*, or State Security) is a unique document of espionage and intelligence in the Cold War. Despite the efforts of the East German regime to destroy it and cover their tracks, the CIA obtained a copy and shared its contents with chosen allies, not including the French; the history of tension between US and French intelligence services is a matter of historical record. The *Le Monde* editorial cited in the text is an invention but its warning against taking as fact something found in the intelligence archives of a rival power is worth noting, as the Finnish security police learned to their cost.

The annual celebration of Occitan language and culture, the *félibrée*, or *felibrejada*, is a remarkable feature of Périgord life. These festivals emerged as a kind of resistance to the efforts of the Third Republic to eradicate Occitan and other local languages in schools and to make everyone speak French. As late as the 1860s, local authorities estimated that ninety per cent of the Périgord spoke the *langue d'oc* as their first tongue. Then it became state policy to ban the various *patois*, Breton and Provençal as well as Occitan. That period is known locally as the *Vergonha*, the shaming, in which local tongues were banned in class and offenders punished, often with clogs being hung all day around their necks. Since 1903 the festivals have been held in a different town or village in the Périgord each year. The songs, poetry and dances, and accompanying banquet (*taulada*) are intriguing and often magnificent in themselves; they also serve to remind us that the Périgord is not entirely France. It is older, with its roots stretching back far into prehistory, and with its own distinct mythology, language and culture.

To those of us who live in rural France, the volunteer firemen and women, the *pompiers*, are an essential and splendid part of life. They are the first responders not only for fires but also for medical and other emergencies. It is hard to conceive life in the Périgord without the skills, courage and public service of our neighbours who volunteer. I am grateful to the *pompiers* in my own village for their technical advice, and to Monsieur Kléber Rossillon and his team at the castle of Castelnaud while writing this book. Any mistakes are my own fault. I don't know if the *pompiers* have ever tried to fight fires with trebuchets but those at Castelnaud are very much worth seeing in action and I warmly recommend a visit to the whole fortress and its museum of the arts of war.

While researching this book I was delighted to learn that the trebuchet team at Castelnaud had already experimented with tossing bags of water. They also alerted me to a remarkable article on this medieval technology in *Scientific American*, the issue of July, 1995, which notes that some of biggest trebuchets of the Middle Ages could fire weights of a ton and more (1000 kilograms). A modern trebuchet built in England in the 1990s was able to fire a small car weighing 476 kilos (without its engine) a distance of eighty metres. The researches of the thirteenth-century mathematician Jordanus de Nemore on the use of pivoting counterweights to increase the range of these missiles had an important impact on the later work of Leonardo da Vinci and Galileo and the makers of mechanical clocks.

As always, much of what I write depends on my friends and neighbours in the Périgord, on their splendid cuisine and wines, on the stories and legends they love to recount, and on the landscape they and their ancestors have tended for millennia. My debt to them is very deep indeed, matched only by my gratitude to my family, always the first to read, edit and advise on my manuscripts.

Without the help of my wife, Julia, Bruno's cooking would too often end in disaster. All the recipes in this book come from the cookbooks we wrote together: *Brunos Kochbuch* and *Brunos Garten Kochbuch*, both published by Diogenes Verlag, my splendid German publishers. Julia and I are extremely proud that *Brunos Kochbuch* was named 'The World's Best French cookbook of the past twenty years' at the Frankfurt Book Fair in 2015, a prize awarded by Gourmand International. Without the work of our daughters, Kate and Fanny, Bruno's investigations would lead up blind alleys, be stuck up trees or sink without trace. Kate runs the brunochiefofpolice.com website and Fanny keeps track of all the characters, the books and incidents in which they appear and the meals they enjoyed. She also organized and ran the video readings and interviews that we made to stay in touch with readers and to entertain them when we and much of the world were all locked down under the threat of the Coronavirus. Thanks to Julia, Kate and Fanny, the world of Bruno is a family affair.

I owe more than I can say to the help and support of my literary agent, Caroline Wood, and to the skills of my editors,

Jane Wood in London, Jonathan Segal in New York and Anna von Planta in Zurich, and to the printers, copy editors, sales people, librarians and booksellers who bring these stories to the final, crucial link in the chain – you, the reader.

Martin Walker, Périgord, 2020.